T0372983

THE GRAPEVINE

THE GRAPEVINE

Kate Kemp

PHOENIX

First published in Great Britain in 2025 by Phoenix Books,
an imprint of The Orion Publishing Group Ltd
Carmelite House, 50 Victoria Embankment
London EC4Y 0DZ

An Hachette UK Company

The authorised representative in the EEA is Hachette Ireland,
8 Castlecourt Centre, Dublin 15, D15 XTP3, Ireland (email: info@hbgi.ie)

1 3 5 7 9 10 8 6 4 2

Copyright © Kate Kemp 2025
Map illustration by Tim Oliver

Grateful thanks to Bloodaxe Books for permission to reproduce lines from
'The Best Is Yet To Come' by Amy Key (*Isn't Forever*, 2018)

A CIP catalogue record for this book is
available from the British Library.

ISBN (Hardback) 978 1 3996 1897 7
ISBN (Export Trade Paperback) 978 1 3996 1898 4
ISBN (eBook) 978 1 3996 1900 4
ISBN (Audio) 978 1 3996 1901 1

Typeset by Input Data Services Ltd, Bridgwater, Somerset

Printed in Great Britain by Clays Ltd, Elcograf, S.p.A.

MIX
Paper | Supporting
responsible forestry
FSC www.fsc.org   FSC® C104740

www.orionbooks.co.uk
www.phoenix-books.co.uk

For Grace and Gary

Feelings often lack structural integrity –

we're all falling into each other.

Amy Key, 'The Best Is Yet To Come'

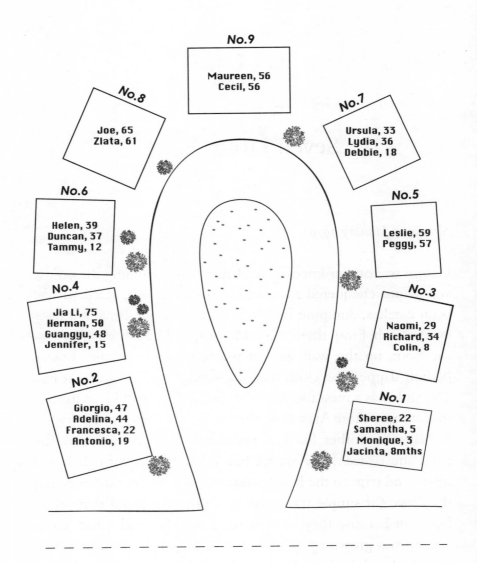

I

Seven Hours After

Sunday, 7 January 1979

Naomi was on her knees in the bathroom, scrubbing the yellow and white chequered tiles. In his rush to wash, Richard had been careless, dumping his clothes on the floor, leaving a dirty great blotch. From there, the odd smear and spatter spread across the floor, up the wall, against the tub, the lip of the shower. Naomi slapped the cloth into the sink, rinsed it, wrung it out. The sink was a mess too. And the grouting – would it stain? She shook some more Ajax from the tin.

Naomi's mother liked to say that a woman must play the hand she is dealt. She wasn't like other mums with their pot roasts, and trips to the beach, and docking pocket money rather than love for simple transgressions. She always said that wasn't her fault because they weren't the cards she held. Later, when Naomi was grown up, she said the same thing – a woman must play the hand she is dealt – but now it was an accusation instead of an excuse, said with half a lip lifted; smug, triumphant, implying that Naomi played her hand poorly. How galling to prove her right. *I had it coming*, thought Naomi. *My own damn fault for trying to change my hand.*

The towels, bathmat and toilet-seat cover were new, a matching set, yellow freckled with brown. She wasn't meant to be buying new things for the house, but when she'd shown Richard the picture in the Kmart catalogue, held the open page against the tiles so he could see how well they'd go together, presented it with a flourish of her arm and a wiggle of her hips, he'd laughed.

'Go on, you should have them,' he'd said. 'You funny little thing.' They would have to be chucked out now. No matter how many times she washed them, she'd never be able to look at those flecks of brown again without wondering.

As Naomi scrubbed and wiped and rinsed on repeat, she didn't rise from her knees because she didn't trust her legs to hold her. She bit hard on the inside of her cheek until she tasted blood. She wished she were a smoker.

There was blood on her watch strap near the clasp. It would have to go too. Quarter past three. Naomi was no stranger to the hours between midnight and dawn. They had become her recent companions, those hours that stretched time and distorted thought. Where problems grew personalities and anxiety waged war. Usually, the only accompaniment to her wakefulness was the house shifting its weight, stretching and easing itself. Now, though, she could hear Richard in the kitchen, also cleaning. She could tell that his movements were sure, efficient, unencumbered.

Sweat pooled between her breasts and trickled downwards. She was wearing the satin kimono that Richard had brought back for her from Takamatsu. He always knew what to get, what she'd love. He was good that way. The kimono stuck to her skin wherever it touched. Naomi drew it tighter, hugging it around herself as she sat back on her heels. She wished she could slide out of her skin and inhabit another – anyone else's would do. She wished she had a mum to look after her. Not her own; one who would talk to her in a soothing voice and make everything all right. She wished she weren't a mum herself.

A noise on the roof, possibly in the guttering – something scampering – startled her, and she looked towards the window, even though the blind was down and the curtains drawn. Birds? A possum? Maybe that wretched cat from across the road.

When she turned back, Richard was standing in the doorway.

'Stop crying,' he said. 'It's not fair.'

He didn't sound angry anymore. Just determined.

'Colin—' Her voice was hoarse.

So was his. 'He's gone back to sleep. Don't worry, he won't talk.' As if that was her biggest worry.

The strip lighting brought Richard's face into sharp relief. There was a trace of blood in the stubble under his chin, another in the curl of his ear. He'd have to shower again, shave.

Richard reached behind him and picked up a duffle bag. He held it gingerly, at a distance, his muscles working hard to maintain his posture. His face blanched.

'What's that?' said Naomi. 'It's not—?' She felt her centre of gravity slip.

'I'm *dealing* with it,' said Richard. 'I said I would. I'll cover some ground – the hills and the plaza. Then go back and check at the church again. And the creek. Stop worrying. And stop that whining noise. I'll be back before it's light. We'll go to church in the morning, all of us together, like everything's normal.'

Naomi turned her face to the wall. She closed her eyes. The cold of the tile against her cheek and counting her jagged breaths steadied her.

Colin hadn't gone back to sleep. When she opened her eyes, he was standing where Richard had been moments before, half the height of his dad. He was wearing his Road Runner undies, looking at the bathroom with wide, marsupial eyes.

'Mum,' he said.

3

'It's all right, darling.' *Darling* wasn't a word she normally used. It felt like talking with someone else's voice. Colin wouldn't look her in the eye. He stared at her knees, at the crossed indentations left by the tiles. 'Everything will be all right.'

But it wasn't all right. Nothing would ever be all right again. Not now that Antonio Marietti was dead.

Ants are social beings. They live in groups, which makes sense because on their own they are small and the world is big and full of danger. They work together because of evolution, for the survival of the group, nothing to do with liking each other or being nice.

The queen has all the babies (masses of them). The rest of the females do everything else: make the nest, get food, look after the littlies, detect danger and fight enemies. The males have two purposes: mating and dying.

The collective noun for ants is colony, which is pretty boring as far as collective nouns go, but that's not their fault.

Correction: there are other collective nouns. Army. Soviet. Swarm. State. Nest. Bike!

2

The Day After The Murder

Sunday, 7 January 1979

Tammy finished her latest entry, closed her journal, tucked it under her arm and slipped out the back door, unnoticed. A blanket of hot air and the smell of parched earth and gum trees steeped in heat came at her like a smack in the chops. It was a stinker of a summer — unusually so for Canberra — and there was nothing to do but flop about. It was boring as all heck. Real life, the juicy stuff, was off somewhere else, happening to other people, passing Tammy by. She had taken to wearing a scowl by default; she was that angry about the waste of it all. At twelve years old, she was running out of time for her life to get started.

It was Sunday morning, before church. The birdsong had dwindled from urgent dawn gossip to the occasional solitary and plaintive caw. But as Tammy ventured outside, they struck up a ruckus again. The sun, shamelessly naked, had resumed its position, and Tammy felt mocked by its sting, embarrassed under its glare. It was always there, always watching: *I see you. I see right through to the very bones of you.*

The back yard had decking — overbaked but not yet warped — a bricked barbecue area, then tiers of lawn and bark chip and plants, each level held back by railway sleepers, leading to the hills that rose behind Warrah Place. There was no fence between the back yard and the hills, just a tapering-off of shop-bought plants giving way to untamed scrub. One day, there would be another street behind hers and Tammy would be looking up at someone else's garden, their pool, their bedroom curtains. The city was gradually encroaching, chomping its way through the land, and Warrah Place was the gnashing teeth.

Tammy went over to the barbecue area, newly designated the Ant Behavioural Studies Centre. The barbecue was a home-made job, built by her dad, and the ants liked to congregate in the cracks between the bricks. Had she still lived on Warrah Place, and had she still been Tammy's friend, Narelle would have called her both Der-brain Boofhead and Brainormous Whiz-head for establishing a centre for ant studies, while failing to see the contradiction. But half a year ago, Narelle and her family had packed up their lives and moved back to their cows and flies and Driza-Bones in the country, because it turned out that making a new life for yourself in the city is not for everyone. Narelle might be gone – out of revenge's range – but she'd left behind her lousy opinions and a knot of dread in Tammy's guts.

On the last day of school, the middle of December, with the long summer holidays spread before her like a wasteland and only Christmas to break them up, Tammy had found her teacher, Miss Hoogendorf, emptying the classroom, and had asked her for a summer assignment.

'But it's the end of primary school for you,' Miss Hoogendorf said. 'You've finished. You won't be coming back here.'

So what? Tammy blinked. She couldn't be left for eight weeks with nothing to tide her over. 'A science one, please,' she said. Tammy liked science; a no-nonsense, exact subject.

Miss Hoogendorf shifted the pile of books she was carrying onto her hip. 'Listen,' she said. 'As a teacher, I shouldn't say this, but as a human being, Tammy, give it a rest, eh? It's the holidays. Live a little. See how it goes.'

Tammy tried to guess her meaning. Give what a rest? Being herself?

At the last parent–teacher meeting, Miss Hoogendorf had told Tammy's parents with a sickly, knowing smile that Tammy struggled with inference: reading between the lines. 'She's very ... literal.' Tammy said that things might be considerably better for all concerned if people just said what they meant as plain as they could without trying to trick people. Tammy's parents said they'd help her practise inference at home.

If Miss Hoogendorf were twelve years old and not a teacher, she would have been friends with Narelle Spencer and Simone Bunner, but not with her. Tammy could tell that sort of thing about a person. Miss Hoogendorf was young for a teacher. She chewed gum in the classroom, even though she wasn't meant to, smacking bubbles against her lips and snaking her tongue out to retrieve them. Sometimes she wore no bra and unsupportive tank tops, and Mrs White, the school secretary, said she couldn't understand – well, she *could*, actually – why the principal hadn't taken her to task over it. Miss Hoogendorf had had a thing with Mr Rickman, who taught Year Four and ran the sports department. But it didn't last long: Miss Hoogendorf was giggly and talked too fast one week, and was red-eyed and staring out the window the next.

On that last day of school, the book on the top of the pile balanced on Miss Hoogendorf's hip was *The Incredible World of Ant Kingdoms*. So that's the book that fell first when Miss Hoogendorf knocked into a desk, and that's the book that Tammy slid into her school bag when she helped pick up the rest. She set herself a summer assignment:

Using scientific experiments and the examination of texts, discover amazing facts about ant behaviour and society.

The Tupperware container was on the ground where Tammy had left it yesterday, its lid still ajar. She nudged it off with the toe of her sandal and crouched down to get a better look. Inside, there was a wedge of Christmas cake, its icing cracked and yellowing, and a cluster of dead ants. Tammy prodded the cake with her pen, then poked at the ants. She turned to a clean page of her journal and licked the tip of her pen.

Sunday, 7 January 1979.
6 Warrah Place, Canberra.
<u>*Christmas Cake Experiment*</u>
Findings: The ants are dead.
Hypothesis 1: They tried to lift the cake and, despite their phenomenal strength, it squashed them dead.
Hypothesis 2: They aren't really dead, just too full or sozzled on brandy and sleeping it off.
Hypothesis 3: Death via brodifacoum $(C_{31}H_{23}BrO_3)$.
Hypothesis 4:

Tammy couldn't think of a fourth hypothesis.

Suzi wandered over from one of her secret nowheres. One shoulder sat higher than the other, giving her a drunken walk. She had a torn ear and her eyes weren't positioned quite right on her face. She was one ugly cat.

Suzi nosed around the tub and Tammy shoved her away, securing the lid. 'Rack off out of it,' she said. She closed one eye and kept the other on Suzi. 'Father, forgive them, for they know not what they do.' It wasn't the right prayer for an ant funeral but she didn't know a better one. Suzi gave her a baleful, accusatory look.

Three years ago, Suzi had come down from the hills with a dead lizard in her mouth, nonchalant as you like, as if she already owned the place and owned Tammy too. Out of all the houses in all the suburbs in the whole of Canberra, Suzi chose Tammy's. Tammy thought about that a lot.

On that first day, Suzi ate the lizard on the back lawn, all of it except the guts, which she left on the doorstep.

'Lizard's gizzards,' said Tammy's dad as he stood over it, legs apart, fists on hips. He and Tammy had watched the whole grisly deed from the window in the family room.

'Lizard's gizzards,' said Tammy.

They said it over and over until the words got mashed up and they couldn't stop laughing.

It was Tammy's mum who had cleaned up the mess, scraping it off the doormat with a butter knife onto a piece of newspaper, pursing her lips and squinting to make sure she'd got every last bit.

Sometimes, even months later, Tammy's dad would look at her and mouth *lizard's gizzards* and they'd crack up all over again because Tammy was still a kid back then; easily amused and easily mollified.

Now there came the sound of stamping from next door: Joe dislodging dust from his boots.

Tammy liked Joe, even though he was sixty-five. She liked Suzi, even though she was only a cat. And she liked watching Antonio Marietti, who lived in Number Two, which everyone on Warrah Place called the Italian House.

A faded towel hung over the fence between Tammy's house and Joe's. Tammy draped it over the lid of the compost bin and climbed on top, keeping her bare legs clear of the plastic. It could burn like billy-o, that stuff. She rested her elbows and chin on the fence and looked into Joe's back yard.

Instead of just Joe whistling cheerily as he mixed concrete and hauled rocks, Tammy saw Joe and Zlata at the spot where their back yard met the hills, talking to three policemen. What was going on? Tammy couldn't hear anything. All three policemen held their caps in their hands. Joe scraped his heel in the dirt. All of them looked at the furrow he'd made as they continued talking. He scraped again. There'd be a trench there if he kept it up. Zlata put a hand on his arm and that stilled him. Tammy still couldn't hear what they were saying.

Tammy let out a tut of frustration and strained forwards over the fence. Eagle-eared Zlata looked up and saw her. She nudged Joe and nodded her head at Tammy and soon all of them, policemen included, were looking at her. They finished their chat. The policemen walked away, up the hill. Then Zlata went back inside and Joe came towards her. As usual, he wore no shirt. His skin had weathered and thickened. In the dip between his chest and shoulder was a puckered scar; a ten-cent coin that glistened. When Tammy had asked him about it once, he'd told her that's where cupid had shot him on the day he met Zlata. He could be a sap like that and get away with it because he was old.

This morning, Joe's walk was slow and ploddy. His face didn't fold into a smile that made his eyes disappear into creases. He didn't say: 'What's cooking, good-looking?' He rubbed his hands over his head, like he was trying to wipe away whatever was inside it, then put them on the fence between him and Tammy. One of his thumbnails was blackened.

'I wish you hadn't seen that,' he said. 'Is not good, Tammy, dear heart. Is not good.'

He stopped there. Tammy chewed her fingernails to hide her impatience.

Behind Joe, the screen door creaked open and slapped shut. Zlata again. She stood under the shade of the grapevine, keeping a watchful eye. Bunches of ripe and unripe grapes drooped from the vine. Although Zlata's features were distorted in the patchy light, Tammy could tell she was frowning.

Suzi sidled up next to the compost bin and got down to

the business of gnawing at her paws, pretending that she wasn't listening in.

'What?' whispered Tammy. 'What did the police want?'

'Antonio.' Joe whispered too, then clamped his mouth shut. He dragged a hand down his face, looked every which way, stalling. 'I can't hardly say – is very bad.'

Tammy aimed a huff upwards to blow her fringe off her forehead. The sun was lashing the back of her neck and her sandals were rubbing her sweaty feet. Even through the towel, the compost lid was beginning to burn beneath her.

'Antonio *what*?' said Tammy. 'You might as well tell me. I already know there's *something* going on.'

'His foot,' said Joe. 'They found his foot – *only* his foot – up in hills this morning.'

Had Joe gone mad? Was he getting his words confused? 'But I saw it on him yesterday. At the church working bee. Both feet, on his legs.' Tammy adjusted her own legs without letting her gaze slip from Joe.

'Is very bad,' said Joe again. 'And true. Police, they say so.' He shivered and swallowed hard.

Police! In the hills! A runaway foot! How thrilling.

Tammy looked into the distance, squinting. 'But why is it up *there*?' she said, as though Antonio had been careless.

Joe took her chin in his sandpaper hand and turned her head back to him. Her lips were squished into a goldfish pucker while he spoke urgently. 'No, Tammy, no, no, no, Tammy, no.' He shook his head, eyes pleading. 'I say too much. No snooping, Miss Snoopy. Is bad business. Trouble. You stay away.'

Tammy wrestled back her face. 'You don't need to worry about me. I'm perfectly equipped,' she said, because sometimes people, including Joe, needed reminding. She smiled to reassure him, but her mind was galloping, skimming over questions, not sure where to land. What might Suzi know? As much as

12

Suzi and Tammy belonged to each other, Suzi also belonged to the hills.

Joe's face was a warning. 'Keep head down, Tammy. Nose to yourself,' he said.

Tammy's hands were resting on top of the fence and Joe put his on top of them, holding on. Joe's hands shook more than usual.

'You OK, Joe?'

'I'm with you. I'm A–OK.' There it was: the smile that folded over his eyes.

A family of cockatoos started a squabble. A gecko scuttled across the fence, stopped instantly, not a breath of movement, then darted out of sight. Suzi sloped off. Tammy adjusted herself on the compost lid, found a bit of towel that wasn't yet hot. And the whole time, her heart thundered. At long last: something was happening.

Joe was looking glum again, so Tammy said, 'Hey. Maybe it's just any old foot that looks like Antonio's. A fake foot, even. Who's to say? Someone could have just put it there to have a laugh.' As she said it, she knew it to be impossible. Antonio's foot, like all of him, was wholly, gloriously his own. There could be no other like it.

The Mariettis had come to live in Warrah Place last winter, moving into the Italian House when Narelle moved out. It was called the Italian House because it was built by Italians who had lived in it before Narelle, and because Tammy's dad, who knew about buildings, said it would look right at home in Italy. It claimed its position at Number Two unabashedly, its tall, pale pillars standing majestic and proud. *Sneer if you dare.* Plenty did. Mostly, it was the audacity of the house having stairs inside that was objectionable – not like other houses that were forced to, being built on the side of the hill and therefore split-level, but on purpose; rooms stacked on top of each other just to show off. Even so, Tammy's dad thought it was about time the Italian House had Italians living in it.

'Fitting,' he said.

'We'll see,' was all Tammy's mum said. She thought they might be Catholics.

It was worse: according to the Warrah Place grapevine, they were posh. There were four of them: Mr and Mrs, a girl and a boy. Antonio was the youngest. He'd recently turned twenty-four, Tammy later found out, because finding things out was a particular interest of hers. Mr Marietti was in some senior position at the embassy. They had a new car, slick clothes, big hair-dos. They thought nothing of plane trips and everything of themselves. Except for Antonio. He was the only one who wasn't stuck-up. Tammy found that out too.

Tammy met Antonio on a cold day in July. She and her dad went to the milk bar on Carnegie Drive, a rare clandestine out-ing for a Blue Heaven milkshake for her and a Polly Waffle for her dad. The sky hung low, sodden with mist; the kind of damp that worked its way inside your clothes. She wore her new red poncho, which she loved, and her new desert boots, which she didn't, so she'd scuffed them up to make them look worn.

Antonio was leaning on the counter, buying a packet of smokes. Tammy had seen him before but not close up. While the shop man was fiddling with the cash register and Tammy's dad was dithering, changing his mind about what he wanted, Antonio grabbed some chewies from a stand; three packets, maybe four. He saw her staring at him, but she couldn't help herself; she had never seen a body hold itself so confidently before. He knew exactly what to do with his elbows and knees, unlike Tammy, who found hers to be too much there, too much in her way. And his hands – beautiful and exact – as he slipped the chewies into his pocket without paying. Tammy often felt her hands to be some sort of foreign, unsavoury things that she'd picked up by accident and couldn't fling off. He winked at Tammy, then turned to her dad.

'Mr Lanahan, gidday.' He'd learnt the lingo but not yet how to let it slide off the tongue. From someone else's mouth, it would have sounded embarrassing.

Tammy's dad put his hands on Tammy's shoulders and propelled her forwards, presenting her for display. 'This is Tamara,' he said. 'But we call her Tammy. Or Tam-bam. Or Tamalama-boom-bam.'

Tammy wanted to die.

But Antonio sang, 'Tamara, Tamara, don't say Tamara, I wanna see ya ta-day.' He winked again.

Tammy felt her face go as red as her poncho.

While her dad ordered the milkshake, Antonio closed in. He took a gold rectangular case from his pocket and held it up between his face and hers. His thumb moved up and down: *click zwish clunk, click zwish clunk.* It was a lighter, its flame tall and true.

'You like my Zippo, Tamara?' *Click zwish clunk.* 'You see the spark, no?' *Click zwish clunk.*

Yes, she saw the spark.

In the following weeks, Antonio became her favourite thing to watch. She noticed the way he leant on things: a car door, a fence, a rake or spade. She noticed how his hair flicked up at his ears. She noticed that he smelled of peanut butter and fire. She noticed that he often kept a pencil wedged behind his ear, which he sharpened with a knife, scooping the wood away from the lead in pretty patterns. Sometimes he put a cigarette behind his ear instead and there were times when he absent-mindedly put the pencil in his mouth or tried to write with a ciggie, which Tammy found hilarious every time. She discovered that the suit he sometimes wore belonged to his dead grandfather, although she never found out if it was the suit or the grandfather he was attached to. Most of all, she noticed the winks. He used them like seasoning, dishing them out all over the place. Everyone got them, even the oldies, but he had the knack of making each one count, and Tammy collected hers like seashells.

The winks made her feel powerful. Tammy didn't want to be like a boring queen ant having boring babies. And she didn't want to fetch food or build a nest. Tammy wanted to be a soldier, with oversized mandibles and a powerful sting. She wanted everyone to know she could dispense with enemies with one lunge.

Tammy went back to her dead ants and sat down in the mottled shade of a young jacaranda. Shade only gave the illusion of coolness. The whole city baked and sagged. Back in December, before summer had revealed its full wrath, Tammy had stared at the sky, daring it to do its worst, and the sky had stared back and won. She was tired now; tired of carrying summer's heft around on her back and in her lungs. Everyone was the same; sick of the heat and crabby with it too.

Tammy wondered what Antonio's foot looked like. Was it ripped off or hacked off or sliced off clean? What colour was it? She unclipped her pen and drew a line around her ankle. She imagined a saw cutting along the line. What did it mean to be missing a foot? With a harrowing feeling of horror that began in her chest and radiated outwards, it dawned on Tammy that Antonio might be, was likely to be, was very probably, dead.

Tammy felt queasy and let her head flop backwards. Light filtering through the leaves tripped over her, over the ground, and soon she wasn't sure if it was the light or the leaves or she herself that was moving. The upside-down hills pressed down on her from above. She imagined that she was lying on a creek bed, sucked under, losing her breath, water sashaying over her, over pebbles, over debris, while the sun got further and further away. She imagined meeting Antonio there, her hair threading through his. Time fell away. The city, the ground, the sky, the icky-sticky heat. Until it was just Tammy and Antonio and un-dulating water.

Suzi came and, standing over her, looked her dead in the eye as if telling her to get a grip.

'Thanks, Suze.' Tammy sat up. She rubbed at the line she'd drawn around her ankle, feeling her warm flesh beneath her fingers.

Finally, she thought of the question she should have asked Joe. 'Suzi, where is Antonio now?'

Suzi walked away, letting her tail brush under Tammy's chin.

Tammy shuffled closer to the barbecue and counted three bricks down from the top. At the fourth, she wedged her fingers around its sides and prised it out. She reached into the space left behind.

The metal was cool but soon warmed in her hand. Her thumb followed where his own had worn a shine.

Click zwish clunk, click zwish clunk, click zwish clunk.

Tammy had nicked it months ago. It was hard not to tell him, not to show him what a good job she'd done of taking and hiding it without him noticing. Had he missed it? Had he reached into his pocket and felt its loss? Tammy liked to think so. After all, he had taught her to steal. It was a symbol of their connection. And now, no one else could have it; only her.

Tammy went inside through the laundry door. She sat on the washing machine to reach the top shelf and took down the box of rat bait. She gave it a shake. Plenty left. Good. This time, she tucked it away in the corner of the shelf, propping up in front a container of shoe polish, the window cleaner and a bag of old clothes ripped into rags.

17

She stopped short of the kitchen, wavering, ears on alert. Would she tell her parents about Antonio? She took her time, coating herself with solemnity, readjusting her face, blanking her eyes. Would they notice?

'That's not how it works. You have to *want* to go.' Her mum's voice was muffled, her head in her hands maybe. She might be crying.

'Right then, I'll want to go,' said Tammy's dad. 'If that's what you want.' He was going to laugh, the idiot. He'd stuff it up if he laughed. 'I thought turning up was the idea. Being in the audience and sitting and standing at the right parts.'

'It's a congregation, not an audience. Which you know, don't you?' Yep, she was crying. 'Don't be a prick, Duncan. It's not nice.'

'Come on, Hells-bells. I'll go. I'll give it everything I've got – extra gusto.' In the quiet of the house, Tammy could hear the movement of cloth against cloth – he must be embracing her – a sniff; a kiss.

'And don't call me that.' She was cross, but there was also resignation, even the hint of a smile.

Tammy's mum appeared abruptly, nearly knocking into Tammy. They both recoiled. 'There you are. Where have you been? Never mind, it doesn't matter. Brush your hair, it's time to go.' She patted her own hair, smoothed down her blouse, slid her feet into her shoes, zipped up her handbag and didn't look at Tammy again.

On the spot, Tammy decided not to tell them. They didn't deserve to know. Instead, as they drove to church, Tammy hugged the knowledge to herself and tested its weight in her hands, savouring its gravity. Knowledge was treasure. Now she had to decide how to use it.

An ant's foot is called a tarsus. Even though it is already very small, it is divided into smaller segments, making it very flexible. It has two claws instead of toes, and a soft, sticky pad, and that's why ants are so good at climbing and clinging. An ant without feet is doomed to fall off things all over the place.

3

Tammy blinked in slow motion and clenched her back teeth to stifle another yawn. There was piety to be getting on with and a wayward foot to be thinking about, but the warmth of the sun was weighing down her eyelids.

Tammy sat on the end of the pew near the window. There was a close and cloying smell; a mixture of flowers, furniture polish and bodies, not altogether unpleasant. This side of the church was all window; floor-to-ceiling expanses of glass that made Tammy feel like a specimen in a jar. Who was doing the looking-in? God, perhaps. On the inside, grimy smears dotted the glass here and there at toddler height. On the outside, leaves and dirt and matted cobwebs gathered along the edges and in the corners as Tammy imagined snow might do in far-away lands. She watched a magpie poke its beak at the gravel in the car park. Her eyes closed. The image of a foot, looming large, came at her face, its toes wriggling, every toenail a winking eye. She lurched upright, peeled her thighs off the lacquered pew, one after the other. Then again. And again.

'Toilet,' whispered her mum, turning her head, but not her eyes, towards Tammy. It was more admonishment than question.

Tammy shook her head, no.

Sometimes Tammy hated her mum something fierce; hated her hesitancy, the way she cleared her throat even when she had nothing to say, the stupid laugh that came too late; hated the weight she carried on her hips and ankles, making her look like a bowling pin; hated her pointy nose and that she'd passed it on to Tammy. But most of all, she hated her one-track earnestness for whatever was her latest thing: yoga, decoupage, transactional analysis, macramé, calisthenics, religion and so on, one after the other, but none of them Tammy. Sometimes Tammy wondered what her mum's face looked like when Tammy was a baby; if her face turned towards Tammy and stayed there; if she smiled. When Tammy thought of her mum's face now, if she closed her eyes to picture it, it was always in profile, blurred, in the act of turning away.

On the other side of her mum, Tammy's dad leant forwards and gave Tammy a goofy grin. Tammy frowned at him. He'd cop an earful later if he wasn't careful. But her mum was busy nodding along to the beat of the sermon, mouthing the words as Pastor Martin spoke them, her fist thumping her thigh to punctuate the most important bits, willing him on to the finish. Tammy wished he'd hurry up. Pastor Martin had a nasal voice that got into your ears the way the smell of something rotten got up your nose.

They stood for the Creed. Tammy liked to look around to see if she could sift out those who meant it with their hearts from those who didn't. Her mum looked like she was on the final round of *Mastermind*, the clock running down. Her dad was examining his fingernails, his knuckles, his watch, unmoved that Jesus was crucified under Pontius Pilate, suffered death and was buried.

Tammy spotted Ursula across the aisle. Even though she was about Tammy's mum's age, lived on Warrah Place and was a regular at church, Tammy didn't know much about her. Ursula lived with her sister, and there was a niece too, just arrived. She was called Debbie, which was way cooler than Deborah or Deb. They kept to themselves. Maybe they were snobs.

Ursula's head was bowed and her eyes squeezed shut. Perhaps she enjoyed the weekly wringing-out of her soul as much as Tammy's mum did. But then Tammy began to feel that she was intruding on something private. Ursula looked like she was in pain, earnestly longing for one Lord, Jesus Christ, eternally begotten of the Father, to come again in glory to judge the living and the dead.

Ursula opened her eyes and turned her head to Tammy. There was a brief moment of bare-eyed staring at each other before they both jumped away.

Was that Cecil's braying voice, looking for the resurrection of the dead, and the life of the world to come, amen? Yes, there he was, three pews back. And his wife, Maureen. They lived on the other side of Joe, in the house that sat highest on Warrah Place, looking down on everyone else. Tammy had noticed that they'd skived off early from the working bee yesterday, leaving all the pack-up to others.

All this talk of being dead and buried, judgement and resurrection, and none of them had a clue about what had happened to Antonio right under their noses. When they got home, Tammy would sit her mum and dad down, telly off, no one talking except her. Once she'd delivered the news, parcelling it out in increments, they'd take her to each house on Warrah Place, saying: *Listen to what Tammy has to say. You're going to want to sit down for this.*

They sat for a hymn. On the pew in front of Tammy sat Colin, the boy from across the road, and his dad, Richard. No sign of his mum. Richard had a regimental haircut on top of a staid, no-nonsense neck. He had the look of someone wearing a uniform even when he wasn't. Tammy's mum once said that it was just as well Richard was in the navy and got to wear a uniform because he was born for it, and Peggy, who lived next door to him and whose veranda overlooked their back yard and partway inside their house if the light was right, said it didn't hurt the rest of them to have to look at him in it either.

On Richard's neck was a small mole slightly right of centre. It would be so easy to flick it with her finger. Tammy had the same feeling she got when she was on the escalator at the plaza and contemplated climbing over the edge and plummeting to the floor below. She didn't want to, and would never admit to having thought it, but knowing she could made her frightened she might.

As if he could feel her eyes on him, as if saving her from the temptation of flicking him, as if in prayer, Richard leant forwards, elbows on knees, and pressed his palms together.

Colin was sprawled out with his feet up on the pew. He picked at a scab on his knee and didn't look embarrassed when he saw that Tammy had caught him at it. Instead, he stared back at her, bold and steady. Tammy sighed. What more could you expect from an eight-year-old boy?

They sat there, Colin and his dad, calm as anything. No way could they know about Antonio. Imagine – Tammy sat up straighter at the thought – just imagine their faces when she told them. Colin would cack his pants.

Pastor Martin lowered his arms after the benediction, relaxed his shoulders and smiled. He swiped at hair that had fallen across his eyes, unfolded the bulletin and began to read the messages. They still wanted volunteers for teaching Sunday school, no experience necessary. There was a new flower roster. Also new: Bible study and fellowship on Thursday evenings at Helen Lanahan's house, all welcome. At this, Tammy's dad's eyebrows shot up and he glanced at Tammy's mum, who looked steadfastly ahead.

'And finally,' said Pastor Martin, 'a huge thank-you to Helen for organising yesterday's working bee. I think you'll all agree that the landscaping is coming along beautifully. Well done, Helen.' He paused and bowed in her direction. 'Thank you also to Duncan and Cecil for manning the sausage-sizzle afterwards [Tammy's dad waggled his head and raised an arm] along with many able helpers − thank you, ladies − to provide sustenance for all the hard workers. Speaking of which, we were delighted to see you there, Richard [another bow, this time in Richard's direction], an unexpected blessing. Just one more note on the working bee: a few tools have gone astray so please keep a look-out for them. See Helen for details. God bless you all!'

Outside, Tammy watched enviously as Colin and Richard got in their car and drove off, but not before Tammy's mum had nabbed Richard to ask after Naomi. 'Just feeling a bit crook today,' he said, and Tammy's mum nodded gravely. Ursula, too, scuttled away. Strange that her sister never came to church. How did that work in a family: one sister being a God-person and the other not? How old did you have to be before it was optional?

This was the bit Tammy liked least about church: hanging around limply while the grown-ups made small talk. She'd once asked her mum how she did it, where all the bright smiles and things to say came from, and her mum had laughed. 'Oh, no,' she'd said, 'I hate it. It doesn't come naturally at all. The whole time, I have to force it because it's really important to be polite.' Tammy knew that she should be thinking, *Wow, that's amazing she can do that.* But all she actually thought was, *What else is she pretending to be?*

People were clustered in small groups on the concrete be-tween the church and the hall. From the sky they must have looked like lazy ants not getting on with their jobs. Tammy's dad was talking to Cecil.

Cecil was a man who took up more space than his body was due.

'Still half-cut from last night,' he was saying. 'Work do down the club. Really laid it on.' He laughed in staccato, a surprising sound.

Maureen stood a little behind and to the side of her husband. She was slightly stooped, hinged at the hips. Her neck jutted forwards like a chook's, and her eyes behind her glasses did more than the normal amount of blinking.

There was no one Tammy's age to be with. The primary-school kids were still in Sunday school, their parents milling about outside, waiting. The high-school kids would be behind the manse, doing dares and talking about sex. Tammy occupied that perilous, hope-ridden land between primary school and high school, her on-the-cusp body awkward and her on-the-cusp emotions confusing. Neither felt under her control anymore.

Tammy chose a tree, one of her regulars, and began to climb. Her hands soon blackened where sap glued dirt and scrapings of bark to her skin. Wiping them on her dress did little to help. She climbed until she couldn't tell if she was gripping too tightly or not tightly enough.

Once her vision had caught up with the rest of her, she looked around below. There was her dad, sitting on a low wall in front of the hall, his legs splayed and swinging as he chatted and laughed. He ought to have a hat on. And there was her mum, moving from person to person, group to group, God's number-one cheerleader, a busy worker ant. In the opposite direction was the creek, almost dry these days. It was shielded by trees, but Tammy felt strangely comforted to know it was there. She had a good view of the new landscaping; virgin ground dug up, compartmentalised and rearranged according to the designs of the working bee committee. It looked like a kid's sandpit. A path of stepping stones, wending its way through, waited to be concreted over. Joe's work. Tammy's mum had managed to rope most of Warrah Place into helping yesterday. That was the last time Tammy had seen Antonio, making dusty footprints, now scuffed away, over there next to the trees that had got in the way of the plans, now chainsawed and laid out in rows. The remaining trees, Tammy's among them, loomed above.

Ursula's niece had been there too, at the end of the day. Tammy had watched from this very tree as Debbie had brought Antonio a sausage in bread. It had too much sauce on it. Antonio didn't like that much sauce. It wasn't Debbie's fault; she didn't really know him, not like Tammy did, otherwise she would have got it right.

Was that Antonio's last meal – a disappointing sausage?

Tammy felt dizzy, her head a Catherine wheel. She clung on and waited to be called to leave.

4

Ursula gripped the back of a chair she couldn't bring herself to sit on. She was still in her church clothes; hadn't even taken off her lace-ups or pantyhose though her feet and legs were swelling and itching in their casings.

They were in the dining room. On the table, at which Lydia and Debbie sat, were the remains of breakfast, the margarine softening, yesterday's *Canberra Courier*, a fresh pot of tea, made by Lydia to help with the shock, and three cups.

Ursula and Lydia had moved to Canberra five months ago from Sydney, wanting a fresh start where no one knew them. Debbie had moved in four weeks ago, also needing a fresh start following her spot of trouble. She'd be starting uni in February. On the whole, the arrangement was working out and there were no hiccups. Until now.

Lydia, a police officer, had taken the call from a colleague she was friendly with, while Ursula was at church. The shocks were twofold. The first was that Antonio Marietti was dead. Dear Antonio, who Ursula had such a soft spot for. Lydia had told Ursula what she knew in the kitchen while they waited for the kettle to boil.

'Keep mum about him being dead for now,' said Lydia. 'His

foot's been found, but without the rest of his body or forensics to confirm it, we can't officially say he's dead yet. We all know, though. You can tell by the colour of the foot and word has got round the station already. I'll eat my police cap if he's found alive.'

This was whispered to Ursula out of Debbie's earshot, on account of the second shock.

Debbie had been sleeping with Antonio. For a few weeks, they'd been sneaking around, starting up a romance that was a secret from everyone. By the sound of it, and by the devastation on Debbie's face, it seemed she'd been well on the way to being in love with him.

Ursula couldn't bear it. Debbie couldn't have her heart broken. Not again. Not after last time. It was enough to break Ursula's own heart.

'We're at the end of our tether, Ursie,' Ursula's brother, Merv, had said over the phone last November. 'Especially Glenda. Her nerves are shredded to bits.'

'I can't think there's no hope,' said Ursula, wanting to defend Debbie, the niece she hadn't seen since she was a little tacker.

'Of course you can't,' said Merv. 'You don't have kids. I don't mean that in a nasty way. Maybe that makes you what she needs.'

'What she needs?'

'We've tried everything. A year ago, when the shit hit the fan, we had no choice but to insist on separate living. I still don't think she understands that what she did reflects badly on all of us, the whole family, drags us down to her level. Maybe you'll get through to her.'

'Me?'

'She went about town slagging us off to anyone who'd listen. I'm a church elder, Ursie. I can't have that. How can I hand out Holy Communion on a Sunday when the whole congregation knows my kid is a hussy? Everyone knows what she is. What she did.'

'Merv, you know I live in Canberra now, don't you?' said Ursula. 'I can't just pop in for a chat.'

'I haven't told you the worst bit yet,' said Merv. 'She stole money from us to get to Sydney and have the thing done. Real kick in the teeth, that was. Our own money paid for it. On top of that, it would have been our grandkid, and she didn't spare a thought for our feelings on the matter.' Merv paused, and sorrow swept over Ursula. Poor Debbie. What an impossible position she was in. 'Yeah, course I know you're in Canberra. That's what makes it ideal. She's got these notions about going to uni.'

At last, Ursula understood why he'd called. 'You want her to live with me? Here? In Canberra?'

'Wouldn't ask if we weren't desperate.'

'Yes,' Ursula said immediately. 'Tell her I'd love to have her live with me.'

Ursula rarely felt certain about anything, but she was certain about this. She'd give Debbie the love that would have made such a difference to her.

'Don't you need to run it past your housemate first – what's her name? Linda? Lisa?'

'Lydia. And, no, Lydia will be fine with it.'

At the dining table, with the tea cooling in the pot, Debbie leant her elbows in toast crumbs and rested her chin on her hands. Her eyes were far away. So was her voice when she spoke. 'I'd just started to feel like I was coming good again, you know? Coming back to myself. He did that. He was what I needed.'

Ursula sat down, wondering if she was making things worse by hovering behind her chair. She immediately regretted it. Sitting felt like somehow accepting the news, acceding to defeat.

Only standing could she reject it. She'd do anything to take away Debbie's pain. For Debbie, and for Antonio. That wonderful boy with so much life in him and so much life ahead of him.

'How could we not have known about you and Antonio?' Ursula said, because it was easier than saying something about his death. 'With us all living under one roof?'

A brief moment of amusement passed over Debbie's face. 'Because you two are not the only ones who can sneak around with a secret. I learnt from the best.'

Lydia reached for Debbie's hand, even though Lydia wasn't much of a hand-holder. She gave it a few pats and put it back on the table. 'I know it's terrible news, and it will take a while to absorb it. But have a think. Anything you can tell us about Antonio? When was the last time you saw him?' she asked.

'Yesterday morning. No. Last night. No. Yes, yesterday morning.'

Lydia frowned.

'Early. I came home and he went to that church thing. The working bee. Actually, yes. I saw him there too, in the evening.' Debbie was babbling, her words and hands all over the place.

'Is there something you're not telling us?' said Ursula.

Debbie threw her arms out and turned on Ursula, her face contorted viciously. 'What do you want to know? What he was like in bed? He was a fucking animal. A machine. He could go all night long and then still keep going. You want to know how big—'

'Stop it,' said Ursula, reeling. 'Don't be vulgar.'

Their eyes met and they stared, horrified at what they'd said.

'I'm so sorry,' said Ursula. 'That was uncalled for.'

'I'm sorry too. I feel like I can't breathe. This heat is suffocating me. It's like a sauna in here.' Debbie looked around at the box of a room, at the flimsy curtains that didn't do anything to keep the sunlight at bay. 'I feel like a caged animal, and I just want to howl and scream and run wild and tear things to shreds with my teeth.' Her hands scrunched hair into her fists and Ursula became fearful she would rip wads of it out.

Then, as if a switch had been flicked, Debbie's shoulders and face slumped, and she shuddered. She pressed her thumbnail into a raised, red cut on her palm, making Ursula want to take Debbie's hand and smooth away her pain, which, in turn, made Ursula think about the potency and longevity of invisible wounds. How much pain could one girl bear?

Debbie noticed Ursula watching and hid her hands in her lap. Her lips skewed to the side as she fought off tears. 'I wasn't going to say, because it's embarrassing, but maybe it hadn't been going as well as I thought it was. As I wanted it to be. I thought, I mean, I know it was still new, we'd only been together a few weeks, and maybe he thought it was just a bit of fun and maybe I did too, at first, but then I thought it might really be something. You know?' She stared at the table. 'I'm such an idiot.'

Ursula gave a sympathetic peep.

'On Friday night, things got weird. It felt . . . off, and I thought he was just being a scumbag, you know, in the way that they do, going hot and cold, that sort of thing. And I stayed the night anyway and pretended it wasn't weird because I didn't want it to be, and' – she brought her hands to her face – 'oh, God. Do you think he knew? Do you think he knew something was going to happen to him?'

'I don't know,' said Lydia. 'But you'll have to tell the police everything you can remember.'

'Oh, Lyds, we can't,' said Ursula. 'What difference would it make? Debbie doesn't know anything useful. Let's just say we don't know anything and be done with it.'

Lydia smiled and gestured to herself. She was in her uniform, ready for work. 'Have you forgotten you live with a police officer?' She turned back to Debbie. 'Look at me. Here's what will happen. Officers will come to visit. Not me. Not my department. Probably from the Criminal Investigation Division. It's looking that way. And here's what you do. You tell them everything that happened. Everything you can think of. Believe you me, this is not a time to be acting cagey.'

'Lydia, please.' Ursula was aware that she sounded petulant; she would rather not but was unable to stop. 'Debbie hasn't done anything wrong.' Her glasses were sliding down her nose and she pushed them back up. 'Can't you keep us out of it?'

Lydia's face slackened. She leant back and folded her arms, and when she spoke again, the measured quiet of her voice held a hint of warning. 'I can't compromise my job. You know what it means to me. Don't ask me to.'

Debbie's voice cut through, putting a halt to the possibility for tension. 'I want to keep it a secret from the neighbours, though. About Antonio and me.'

'Of course, if that's what you want,' said Ursula.

'Why?' said Lydia.

'Because that's what Antonio wanted,' said Debbie.

'Why?' said Lydia again.

'I think it was because of his family. They're so far up their own arses. I reckon he knew they'd think I wasn't good enough for him. He wanted to avoid the hassle.'

'I hardly think—' began Ursula, indignant.

'Besides,' said Debbie, 'I couldn't handle it if the neighbours were all over me, sticking their noses in with false sympathy.'

'Fair enough,' said Lydia.

Ursula looked at Debbie's head, now nestled in the crook of her elbow on the table; the crumbs, a smeared knife on a plate, a drip of marmalade on the side of the jar, another on the table. It would attract the ants. Had they had breakfast together while she was at church? Had the atmosphere been light and breezy before they knew about Antonio? Carefree enough, certainly, not to wipe away spilled marmalade.

The window overlooked Warrah Place. Ursula could see four front doors from here and the driveway of the Italian House. She could have seen Debbie going back and forth if she'd been paying attention. How could she keep track of everything she had to pay attention to? Squinting into the late-morning glare was tiring. It pinched her face and made her glasses feel weighty and sticky on her nose. Oh, the extravagance of the sun! What a cheek to be so bold.

Debbie joined Ursula at the window. Neighbours were gathering in the middle of the street, lured by gossip, by scandal, by the delicious horror of a severed foot.

'That fucker,' said Debbie.

'Which one?' asked Lydia.

Ursula frowned.

'What should we do?' she said. 'Would it be worse if we went or if we didn't?'

'Don't look at me,' said Lydia. 'I'm going to work.'

Debbie was already off, picking her way down the hot driveway in bare feet. A police car pulled up outside the Italian House.

'Ursula,' said Lydia, drawing Ursula's attention away from the window.

'I'm scared,' said Ursula. 'I don't want people to know.'

'What do you want?'

Ursula faltered, then gave the same answer she always did: 'The impossible.'

Lydia sighed. 'Ursula,' she said again, this time in the reassuring way she sometimes had, the gentle tone that made the fear recede, at least for a while. 'It will be OK. We'll be OK.'

Lydia came to Ursula and gently took her glasses off. She pressed her forehead to Ursula's and they breathed in and out, in and out, in and out. They rolled their faces until their noses

33

touched, then lips, then chins, then lips again in a slow kiss.

'Debbie's going to be OK too,' said Lydia. 'It won't be like last year because she's got us now. We'll see her through.' She kissed Ursula again. 'Feel better?'

'I do.'

Lydia was right. She was always right. Debbie would be OK. They'd all be OK.

Lydia put Ursula's glasses back on her face, squeezed her shoulders, said, 'Oodles of love,' and left.

From the window, Ursula watched Debbie with the neighbours. Debbie had her arms folded in borrowed bravado and Ursula felt a desire to shield her. She also felt a stab of resentment towards Antonio's family. Why wasn't Debbie good enough for them? Ursula had no desire to share anything of herself, but why must Debbie hide her relationship and now her grief? It wasn't fair. Debbie was long overdue straightforward, uncomplicated happiness.

Ursula pressed her lips together and steeled herself. The least she could do was make sure Debbie didn't have to face anyone alone.

Ants are territorial. They don't like ants from other nests coming into their territory and taking food. If that happens, it means a full-on fight. Ant colonies have strength in numbers and that's what they use to gang up on anyone they don't like. They swarm together to do their bullying and attacking.

5

They drove through the streets of Canberra towards home with the windows cranked down, Tammy's hair whipping about her face. In the front, her dad put his hand on her mum's leg.

'Too hot.' Her mum twisted away. A moment later, she reached for his hand and put it back there.

They skirted the edge of the plaza and then public-service buildings; chequerboards of concrete and glass and pebble-flecked bollards, the perfect height for leapfrogging. Even on a Sunday, there would be important people doing important jobs in air-conditioned offices, because the economy wasn't going to fix itself, you know, and if Prime Minister Fraser didn't want to go the same way as Gough Whitlam and get chucked out by the queen, poor bastard, he'd need all the help he could get. Tammy's dad often used to pop into the office on Sundays, but these days God had to come first.

Further out they went, winding their way through bendy suburban streets with their freshly laid gutters, and still, Tammy nursed her secret. She was bursting to tell and dreading it too. She realised, suddenly, and with shock, that the person she most wanted to tell was Antonio. She felt a fresh wave of unexpected loss; a sensation of being dragged, her insides trailing behind.

They passed a lonely athletics track behind a chain-wire fence. A milk bar and bottle-o with their shutters down. The school, desolate and silent, closed for the holidays.

Out of her window, Tammy caught glimpses into other people's Sunday lives. Kids straddling bikes. Handlebar streamers. Older kids leaning on car bonnets. Long hair, short shorts, snug T-shirts, zinced noses. Dads firing up the barbie. Shirts on, shirts off, short shadows. Towels on the lawn. A dive-bomb splash in a pool (lucky ducks!). A boombox. Hopscotch. *Thwack* of ball on bat. Panting dogs; stretched-out cats. And overlapping all of it, the sticky smell of asphalt.

As they neared the playground on Carnegie Drive, Tammy looked into her lap. It was a known hang-out of the Year Nine kids. Rumour had it that on the first day of school last year, they had sniffed out the reject kids starting in Year Seven, held them down and drawn boobs and pubic hair on their uniforms in permanent marker.

Warrah Place was a right turn off Carnegie Drive, a sharp incline at first and then they were onto their little Petri-dish cul-de-sac. In the middle was a teardrop-shaped nature strip, around which nine houses hunkered and kept watch. They called it 'the island'. Every now and then, people came from their houses and converged there. It was the quickest and easiest way to get the rumour mill fired up.

From the car, Tammy and her parents craned their necks and saw Cecil and Maureen, Joe and Zlata, Ursula and Debbie, among others, surrounding two police officers. Peggy was crossing the road from her house with a cigarette hanging from her mouth, chin leading the way, elbows out and at the ready. Her husband, Leslie, loped along behind her. Tammy thought God had had a bit of a laugh when he put Peggy and Leslie together. He'd given Peggy all the noise and Leslie all the size. A tall, lumbering man, Leslie had a gentleness that turned what

37

might have been an intimidating bulk into a safe shelter. Tammy felt able to weather the storm of Peggy as long as Leslie was somewhere near.

'Jeez,' said Tammy's dad.

'No idea,' said her mum, although no one had asked.

There could only be one reason they'd gathered. Tammy had prepared for the perfect moment to reveal her news and now she'd have to rush it if she wanted to get in first. It was hardly ideal, but there was nothing for it. 'I have some information about that,' she said in her most important voice.

'Out with it, then,' said her mum. 'Quick.'

She told them about Antonio's foot as her dad floored his to get their little Datsun 180B up their steep driveway and into the carport. The telling lacked the proper dramatic edge, and they looked at each other, her mum and dad, not at Tammy, not even when her mum said, 'Are you sure you're not exaggerating?' and then, 'If there *is* some truth to it, fancy not saying something sooner!' They got out of the car, and went back down the driveway in long strides, already halfway down while Tammy was still slamming her car door.

Suzi was on the island, holding their place. The policeman doing the talking wore an ill-fitting uniform with sweat rings under his arms. He breathed noisily through his mouth between words. The top of his head came up to the shoulder of the other policeman standing next to him. His were sturdy shoulders, his collar crisp. His motionless, downturned mouth was much more in keeping with the seriousness of the situation. If anyone was going to find things out, it would be him, Tammy decided.

There was no room for Tammy to join the circle. On the outskirts, she strained to catch all the words but only managed to grab hold of a few at a time.

Searching now as we speak.

Yes, a positive identification.

Come to serious harm.

Missing, presumed dead.

Too soon to say.

Presumed dead. It had an air of finality and uncertainty to it at the same time. Tammy realised now that she hadn't really believed or expected it to be true.

Like Tammy, Mrs Lau was also shut out of the circle. Mrs Lau moved in a sluggish way, and not just because it was hot. It was like she had invisible weights tied to her shoulders and hips, dragging her down. Every bit of her looked tired, except for her eyes, which didn't miss a trick. Now, she hauled herself onto her tiptoes, looking for an opening, her shoes *slap-slap-slapping* the soles of her feet as she moved around the outside. As the tall policeman started talking, her efforts accelerated.

'Hold your horses, love,' he said. 'We'll get to you in a mo.'

But he didn't. Neither of them did. They told everyone they would visit each household in due course, then got in their car and drove away. Everyone watched them drive around the loop of the cul-de-sac.

'Right,' said Cecil. 'Probably best we get ourselves organised. You heard. They want any info we can come up with. I'm willing to coordinate and gather anything relevant to pass on. So, anyone got anything to say, come to me.'

'Oh get your hand off it, Cec,' said Peggy.

Sometimes the crunch and rumble of Peggy's voice, like a sack of rocks grating against each other, made Tammy forget to pay attention to what she actually said.

Cecil continued as though she hadn't spoken. 'Any thoughts so far?'

No one said anything. How was Tammy meant to find anything out if no one said anything?

'Who's looking after your kids?' Cecil asked Sheree.

'Yeah, I'd better get back,' said Sheree, staying put.

39

Sheree had three kids and no husband. She lived on the corner in Number One. Cecil held the view that Number One faced slightly more towards Carnegie Drive, so strictly speaking, Sheree and her scraggly kids didn't belong to Warrah Place, no matter what the post office said. Tammy's dad worked for the National Capital Development Commission. He said it was the beauty of a designed city, and a matter of pride, that there was a socioeconomic mix within suburbs, so that on Warrah Place, the big Italian House and Sheree's social-housing property could look at each other across the street. Tammy's mum said she wasn't so sure, that it might be better if there were more separation, you know, so everyone knew where they fitted. Then Tammy's dad said that maybe Tammy's mum didn't like being reminded that she grew up in houses much worse than Sheree's and sometimes no house at all, and there was no shame in that. And Tammy's mum said, *Piss off, Dunc, don't patronise me.* Tammy didn't know what to think, but she knew this: Cecil was up himself and Sheree's kids were grotbags.

'OK then,' said Cecil. 'I'll be the one to say it even if you lot won't. We're all thinking it. It was one of his own kind what did it. The dodgy sort – no offence, Joe.'

Tammy supposed Cecil said that because he lumped anyone who wasn't Australian together. Joe was from Yugoslavia, not Italy like the Mariettis.

'I mean,' Cecil went on, 'look at that house.'

They did, turning as one, all of them, as if they'd see something different this time.

'Clearly in with bad money, if you know what I mean,' continued Cecil.

'What, the Mafia?' Tammy's dad sounded shocked.

Cecil tapped the side of his nose.

Tammy made a mental note to ask her dad what a Mafia was. How quickly things had turned from sitting on a secret to

Antonio being presumed dead and Tammy knowing less than anyone else. Her brain had turned to soup and every time she scrambled after an idea, it outran her. Who could have done such a thing? And to Antonio of all people? None of it made sense.

Still shut out, still ignored, Mrs Lau sighed, turned and slapped her way back to her house. She leant into her driveway as she went up.

'How do you figure that? About bad money?' Peggy asked Cecil. 'Or is it just speculation?'

'I, for one, know for sure that Antonio Marietti was a thief,' said Cecil.

Maureen gasped. 'Oh, he never was. Surely not. Not that sweet boy.'

'Best keep quiet about what you don't know, eh?' Cecil said to his wife. In the heat, his face was red and blotchy, like an uncooked rissole.

'But we all liked him so much. *Everybody* liked him. I just can't believe he—'

'Leave it be, Maur.' Cecil spoke slowly, as if to a child about to get what-for.

Peggy sucked in a sharp breath. She licked her lips, her eyes flicking between Maureen and Cecil. Sometimes, when ant colonies get too big, they have to choose which ants are expendable, and sacrifice them. Tammy reckoned that Cecil would nominate Maureen to be sacrificed first. And she reckoned that Maureen might willingly agree to go.

Tammy wished Cecil would shut up. She didn't want everyone else to know Antonio was a thief.

'*Do* you know for sure, Cec?' said Tammy's dad, and Tammy was glad that at least *he* could be relied on to cast doubt and press for proper answers.

'Sure enough, since it was me he stole from. A solid-silver

mustard pot, matching spoon and all, passed down to me by my dad. Went missing one day after Antonio had been round to do a few jobs. Bet he hocked it quick smart for a pretty penny.'

Tammy hadn't known the pot was for mustard. She'd liked it for its pretty blue glass innards. She thought of it now, pushed down to the toe of a sock, the sock pushed to the back of her drawer. Hearing Cecil accuse Antonio of stealing it gave her a warm feeling deep inside, like she was connected to Antonio, like they were a team.

'That makes you the only one so far with a motive, then,' Peggy said to Cecil. She looked delighted.

Cecil hoicked up his trousers. 'Shut ya trap, Peg. It wasn't one of us. The way those lot carry on – no offence, Joe – bumping off someone like it's an everyday thing. One of them did it, for sure.'

'You can't mean his family,' said Tammy's dad. 'They've been back in Italy since before Christmas.'

'Speaking of,' said Cecil. 'Does anyone else think it's odd they kept buggering off back to Italy and leaving their boy here to fend for himself, especially at Christmas? It's not like he had anything to keep him here. No proper job. Bit of a drifter.'

'Oh, goodness, do you think someone's told them?' said Tammy's mum. Her voice wobbled and everyone looked anywhere except at each other's eyes, while Suzi wove an invisible web in between and around and through their legs. 'How old was he? Does anyone know?'

'Nineteen,' said Peggy, whose hobby was collecting other people's information. She was good at it but not as good as Tammy, because Tammy knew for a fact that Antonio was twenty-four. He'd told her so to her face. Nineteen – as if! 'Just nineteen.' Tammy thought Peggy was trying to sound sombre and almost got there.

'What did he actually do with himself when he wasn't doing

42

odd jobs around here for us lot?' said Cecil. 'Does anyone know?'

No one had an answer.

'Could have been them ones over there,' said Cecil, nodding at the Laus' front door, which had not long closed behind Mrs Lau.

'You might have a point there,' said Peggy, and Tammy stared at her. Everyone else did too. It wasn't like Peggy to agree with Cecil on anything. 'Well, they eat dogs or rats or some such things, don't they?'

'Do they really?' asked Maureen.

'Well, maybe not *them*,' said Peggy. 'But their people do. I saw a documentary on it. Did you see how she scarpered once the questions started?'

As one, they all looked at the Laus' house.

'They have those enormous knives.' Sheree was still looking at the Laus' house, her arms folded under her boobs. 'You know, for cutting through bones.'

'Cleavers,' said Cecil.

Maureen gasped. 'Well, I never knew that.'

'There's so much we don't know about them,' continued Cecil. 'That's the problem.'

'How about we cool it with the accusations.' It was the first time Debbie had spoken. She sounded angry. Ursula touched her shoulder and Debbie shrugged her off. Tammy moved to get a closer look at Debbie's face. Had she been crying?

'Who are you?' demanded Cecil.

Why did he say that? Cecil already knew who she was. They'd all been at the street party. Tammy had overheard Cecil talking with her dad about Debbie last week. 'One of those hairy-legs, you know, women's-libber types.' Cecil was laughing, eyes lit up. 'About to start uni. I asked what course she was doing and guess what she said — you'll never guess. Women's Studies. Women's Studies,' he said again, because he was hooting so hard the first

43

time. 'I told her she can come and ask me anything she wants to know, no need to go to uni for it! And she said – get this – she said, *It's precisely because of men like you that this course is necessary.* So I said to her: *If it's so necessary, I'd better sign up, especially if it's full of pretty little things like you.* She loved that, she did, bloody *loved* it.' There must have been something funny in what he'd said because Tammy's dad had laughed, although not as much as Cecil did.

Debbie continued to glare at Cecil and Cecil ignored her. The talking had dried up, but no one left. Arms hung limply. Feet shuffled. Peggy plugged her mouth with another cigarette, her cheeks hollowing as she sucked on it. Tammy noticed there was still a faint pen mark around her ankle. She licked her finger and rubbed at it. When she straightened, Peggy was looking at her with narrowed eyes.

'What I want to know is why the killer had to chop his foot off,' said Peggy to the group in a lowered voice.

It was the first time Tammy had heard someone say the word *killer* and she couldn't tell if the jolt that ran through her was fear or excitement.

'That's hardly the primary question,' said Cecil. 'The primary question has to be why someone killed him in the first place.'

'But the chopping off was hardly necessary, was it?' said Peggy. 'It didn't have to be so gruesome.'

Everyone got busier with thinking than talking then, until a child's wail came from across the road.

'Ah shit,' muttered Sheree. 'That's me off then.' Begrudgingly, she sloped away.

The front door of Number Three opened and Richard came out wearing his uniform and carrying a suitcase. He put the suitcase in the boot of his car and walked over to the island. Everyone stood up straighter.

'What do you make of it all?' Tammy's dad asked him.

Richard paused. 'I'd be very cautious about jumping to conclusions at this stage.'

At this, Peggy *hmmph*ed, folded her arms and glared pointedly at Cecil.

It must be nice to have others listen to you, not to have to say things really fast before someone butted in, Tammy thought. Richard always spoke quietly, with lots of pauses, during which people waited and leant in, ready to catch whatever he said next. The whole effect was curiously calming. Tammy had tried it out once at home. She stood very still next to the telly during *Are You Being Served?* and calmly announced that from now on she wished to be called Tamara, not Tammy. She wasn't sure if her mum noticed. Her dad did, though. He said, 'What are you doing, standing there like you've got a pole stuck up your bum?' Neither of them started calling her Tamara.

'Most of us saw Antonio at the working bee yesterday,' said Richard. 'Did anyone see him after that?'

No one said anything.

Tammy's mum had always had trouble coping with silence. 'We were some of the last to leave the working bee at about six-thirty, right, Duncan?' she said. 'Was he still there then? Yes, he was definitely there then. I remember saying goodbye to him. Oh dear Lord above, we left him there. And then . . .'

Richard looked at her kindly. 'You couldn't have known, Helen. No one could have known what would happen, whatever it is that's happened. We still don't know for sure. I spoke with the police earlier. Without a body, they can't be certain. I know it looks grim, but let's hope for the best.'

Helen turned to Joe. 'I'm sorry about your tools, especially after all the work you did. I take it you haven't found them yet?'

'No worries,' said Joe. 'They show up sometime.'

'Someone must have taken them in error,' said Richard. 'I bet you'll have them back by the end of the day.'

Tammy wished they'd get back to talking about Antonio.

'Did you see anything out on your jog this morning?' Tammy's dad asked Richard. 'Anything at all dodgy? Were the police already out on the hills?'

'No jog this morning. Slacking off, I'm afraid.'

'Quite right,' said Tammy's dad. 'Far too hot.'

'Will there be a funeral?' piped up Ursula, twisting the cross on her necklace. She spoke quickly, as though she'd been working up to saying something for a while.

'Don't let's get ahead of ourselves,' said Cecil. 'They don't even have a body yet. Well, not a whole one at any rate.' He laughed and Ursula shrank back.

'I'm sure there will be a funeral, Ursula, if indeed Antonio has died,' said Richard gently. 'But perhaps the police need to finish their investigations first.'

'Even so,' Cecil continued, 'is there much point? I mean, who would go, besides us lot? I doubt there'd be much of a showing, even if his family do come back for it. Bit embarrassing for them, I reckon. Now, my dad's do, when he went, huge, wasn't it, Maur? Church was packed, standing room only.' He rocked back and forth, jiggled loose coins in his pocket. 'Nah,' he said more quietly. 'I shouldn't think they'd bother with a proper do.'

Tammy kept her eyes on Debbie. She wondered if she was staring too much. The group started breaking up.

'Bugger me, it's hot,' said Cecil. He windmilled his arms, wafting a smell that could knock you down dead. 'I'm stewin' in me own juices here.'

Gross, Tammy thought at the exact same moment that Debbie said, 'Foul.'

Debbie wore cut-offs, a T-shirt with 'Make policy not coffee' written on it, and dangly earrings. She had layered hair with a flick, flushed cheeks and fire in her eyes. She had the look of someone ready to meet and knock for six whatever the world

– or Cecil – threw at her. Tammy's dress, patterned with red spots on a navy background, was neither long nor short. It had straps but not the spaghetti sort. In every respect it was boring, childish, mortifying.

Disappointingly, Debbie left without another word. Others drifted off too. No one had said anything remotely useful about Antonio, except everyone seemed suspicious of everyone else. People act differently when they get into a group. Tammy had been through enough at school to know that was true. You'd think – and hope – adults would grow out of it, though.

Richard went to leave but Tammy's mum had sidled up, blocking his way.

'We were thrilled to hear your news,' she said.

His face was blank at first and then he said, 'Yes. Thank you.'

'Poor Naomi. You're not to worry while you're away. I'll keep an eye out, check on her for you.'

'You're very kind.' He smiled, stepped sideways and was gone.

Tammy and Suzi stayed for a moment longer, turning their backs on their own house, the Laus' and the Italian House, squinting at Richard and Naomi's. What was this news that her mum was so thrilled to hear? And how did Tammy's mum know?

Tammy wished that clouds would roll in, that the sky would blacken. But it was just like any other day that summer. The sun bore down implacably, resolutely cheerful. Antonio deserved better.

Tammy deserved better too. It was just as she'd feared. The news had been all hers and they'd taken it from her with their grown-up hands and made it all theirs. Well, none of them knew how good she was at watching. Her scientific mind was good with details. She would find out what happened to Antonio in no time and have the upper hand again.

6

Guangyu Lau left the gathering on the island because walking away was the only option left. What would happen if she lifted the lid on her feelings and made herself heard? She wondered about that sometimes. About what would spill out, and the damage it could cause. She often spent night-time hours crafting words she would never speak.

Guangyu felt eyes boring holes in her back as she walked up her driveway. She retrieved her bag from her car, having forgotten it in her haste to hear why the police were on Warrah Place. Halfway home from work, Guangyu had noticed the police car on her tail, her alarm growing with every turn. She'd kept both hands on the wheel, eyes flitting between road and mirrors. By the time she'd turned into Warrah Place, still pursued by the police, she'd felt like she'd been winded by a horse kick.

Guangyu worked part-time, mornings only, as a veterinarian, and full-time as a container for her family's emotions. She'd put her name down for more shifts at the surgery, but none were forthcoming. Sundays were emergency clinics only, and that suited Guangyu just fine. Real-life emergencies were a reprieve from the imaginary ones that ran through her mind.

That morning she'd had a poodle with conjunctivitis and

anxious owners – an easy fix. Next, a pregnant white mouse – a surprise for the owners, who thought they'd bought only males from the pet shop. Then an out-of-towner passing through brought in a wallaby he'd hit on the Yass Road, cradling it on his lap, wrapped in his shirt, as he drove into Canberra. No hope for the poor thing, a young female. She looked at Guangyu thankfully, Guangyu thought, as she put her to sleep. The driver didn't look at her at all as he asked if he could keep it, and if it was OK to eat roadkill if it was still fresh and the blowies hadn't got to it.

Now at home, Guangyu drew open the curtains a sliver and turned off the lamps in the lounge room before sitting down on the couch. It was quiet. Jennifer would be in her room, her sanctuary. Guangyu hated not knowing what she was doing in there, not knowing what was going on in her daughter's mind, the direction her wandering thoughts took. Fifteen was a dangerous age.

It didn't matter where Herman was. He was absent even when he was present. He was probably unaware of the police presence or the gathering on the island, even though he knew what Guangyu had seen during the night. She doubted he would be able to pick out any of their neighbours in a line-up.

When they were still in Hong Kong, Herman had had boundless energy and talked at a rate of knots. Guangyu remembered the first time he'd come home from work and spoken of Australia. Soon it was every day. Herman's qualifications in economics were desirable, sought after, well compensated. He'd excitedly told Guangyu, Jennifer and Jia Li about houses with private gardens, enough bedrooms for one each – sometimes even a spare – every kitchen fitted with an oven. Australia: a vast, exotic land of plenty. They could go to Canberra, the capital city, the hub of economic reform and advancement. Herman had proudly showed them brochures espousing the recreational pursuits on offer: bushwalking, cycling, sailing, horse riding, paddling the rapids, meeting the local wildlife. Before they knew it, their dreams had morphed into plans.

Herman had retreated into himself soon after the move three years ago. Once garrulous and high-status, he was now lost and sluggish. He looked startled when spoken to, like a cornered hamster. Guangyu now had plenty of bedrooms and an oven in her kitchen, but she didn't know where her husband had gone.

She picked up Jia Li's notebook from the coffee table. In her mother-in-law's careful handwriting, she read:

> *national*
> *feminist*
> *affirmative action*
> *coriander*

Herman's mother had insisted on learning English when Herman and Guangyu got married. At first, Herman had been teaching her. She was slow and meticulous and slapped Herman's hands whenever he became the smallest bit exasperated with her. She had since moved on to cassette tapes and workbooks. Guangyu grudgingly admired Jia Li's progress, even though her motive, Guangyu was sure of it, was to deny Herman and Guangyu private conversations. Having grown up under colonial rule knowing her place, she was now determined to keep Guangyu in hers.

Jia Li supplemented her vocabulary by listening to ABC Radio, armed with a dictionary. Her lists of words were littered all over the house.

Guangyu flipped over the page.

> *lying bitch*
> *dole bludger*

divorce
wanka
marijuana
floozy
fuckwit

Jia Li appeared noiselessly. 'Why you close the light?'

'Hello, Ma.' Guangyu slid the notebook behind a cushion.

'And why you sitting your lazy bones down in middle of day?'

Jia Li carried her contempt in the cut of her mouth. Often, the merest curl of a lip would wither Guangyu, and so Guangyu carried out her small acts of rebellion – oversalting the soup or undercooking the rice, tidying away Jia Li's notebooks, untuning the radio during the night – in private, and in this way, she got by well enough.

Guangyu got up and turned the lamps back on.

'You tired,' said Jia Li. 'Too much worry. Bad for health.'

They sat side by side on the couch. Sometimes Jia Li's edges softened, and Guangyu wondered if the unspoken censure was all in her own mind, if there could be an easiness between them after all.

'I'm thinking of sending Jennifer away until school starts.'

Jia Li made a guttural sound that could have equally been approval or disapproval.

'How are your feet?' asked Guangyu. Jia Li suffered dreadfully with corns. Canberra winters had taken their toll.

'Bad.'

'The police were outside,' said Guangyu. 'On our street.'

Before she'd gone to work that morning, Guangyu had shaken Herman awake when she'd spotted policemen snaking a trail through the hills in their distinctive caps and blue shirts, some of them with search dogs. Jia Li had appeared as she always

51

did whenever the two of them were together. Guangyu had told Herman and Jia Li what she had seen during the night, of her sense that something wasn't right, but she couldn't put her finger on precisely what. They'd stared at her with non-committal eyes. Neither had anything to say. The burden was still hers.

'They said the next-door boy, Antonio, is missing, presumed dead. They're looking for a body.'

'Presumed dead,' repeated Jia Li, as if she wanted to put it on a list.

'The police said they'll come talk to us. I'll bake something for their visit.'

'Yes, this morning they come, when you were at your animal-doctor job. They tell me about the boy.'

'Why didn't you say so? Will they come back?'

'No need.'

'What did they say? What did *you* say? Did you tell them what I saw?'

'I say thank you very much and no thank you, we have nothing to say. And I tell them goodbye.' She made a shooing motion with her hand.

'But—'

'They call us Chinese!' Jia Li stood up. 'The policeman, he say, *You Chinese have good manners.* He is right about manners, but I wait until they send someone who call us Hongkongers, not Chinese.' She folded her arms to make it final. Jia Li didn't miss a chance to remind Guangyu that she was an outsider, born on the mainland and not Hong Kong. To remind Guangyu that she brought no useful connections to the marriage. That she was a wasted opportunity.

'But, Ma—'

'And now I say this to *you*: these people are not our people. Their business is not our business. Is *bad* business.' She jabbed her finger as she spoke, not unlike that odious man, Cecil. 'And I also say this: what you cooking for our lunch?'

Last night, Guangyu was outside in the inbetween time – too late to be night-time and too early to start the day. Around four o'clock. Night sweats had her up several times seeking out a drink, the outside air, space away from the sleeping lump of Herman's body.

The air was still; thick enough to chew on. Should she try for more sleep or give it up as a lost cause? For no reason that Guangyu could see, irritation swept over her, a hot flush in its wake. It crept up her neck, her heart on rapid-fire. She was cooking from the inside out. At forty-eight, menopause had come sooner than expected. She could live with the flushes these days; it was that hot anyway. But it was the anger – how it snared her in pernicious thoughts – that was the most difficult; always second-guessing whether it was justified or her own traitorous body playing tricks on her. She was losing her mind over it. Could it be that women all over the world were walking around masking that they were moments away from keeling over or blowing a gasket, pretending that nothing had changed? Did every woman accumulate rage over the years like compound interest? She had no one to ask.

Guangyu had found her first grey hair that week, nestled in close to her temple. A rite of passage, the turning of a page. She was grateful for that grey hair, a physical manifestation of hidden anguish. She hoped it would afford her more respect, although no amount of grey hair could ever invert her relationship with Jia Li.

The cat from next door appeared from beneath the oleanders and made a beeline for Guangyu. She headbutted Guangyu's leg gently. Guangyu smiled. Animals were the best tonic. She scratched behind the cat's ears and felt for the hard nub of scar tissue on one of them. She traced her fingers along the cat's ribs and down her front legs, finding the two bones that had broken and mended, crooked. She stroked under the cat's neck to palpate the thyroid gland.

'All good,' she said. The cat was a survivor. 'Clever cat.'

Guangyu rested her eyes on the middle distance; lone trees and tufts of shrubs were outlined in the insipid light. A figure moved into her field of vision, running. Richard. He was easy to recognise – such good posture; tall. He often ran in the hills, nothing unusual about that. But so early? It was not yet dawn. Possibly, he was wanting to get ahead of the morning heat, so perhaps not that strange after all. But then Guangyu saw that he was an unusual shape. He had a bag of some sort attached to his back. It hampered his stride and made him look awkward, although he moved swiftly. That was odd, wasn't it – to run with a bag so close to home? There were many ways these people were odd to Guangyu. How should she know what to make of it?

Richard stopped then and looked furtively around in all directions. Guangyu was glad she hadn't turned on a light. Instinct made her stand still and lower her eyes. She'd be happy to come across Richard during the daytime, happy to exchange a pleasant word, but at night, she did not want to be seen.

And what about that night, all those months ago, when the air was chilled instead of sultry, when she'd seen Richard and Helen in – what else could you call it? – a tryst. It was in the Lanahans' back yard, and Guangyu, having again taken refuge in her garden from night sweats, had had her thoughts interrupted by voices coming from over the fence, mere metres away. Guangyu remembered it vividly; she'd been so shocked by it. Hands on each other, urgent whispers, Helen distraught, Richard insistent. A wrenching apart.

And then. All those nights of noises from the Italian House

on the other side, carried from an open window through still nights, windy nights, cool nights and hot, rainy nights, moonlit nights, ink-black nights. Grunting, gasping, mewling, wailing noises. Only when Antonio was there alone, and the parents and sister were away.

Should Guangyu tell the police all of it? Some of it? How could she know what was relevant? And how could Guangyu ever speak of it without bringing shame on herself?

People should be more careful with their secrets, like Guangyu was. Yes, Jia Li was right. There was no need to talk to the police about any of this. And besides, once you started talking, where did you stop? Even though it was Richard who Guangyu had seen in the hills, it was his wife who made her uneasy. Every time Guangyu saw Naomi, she couldn't shake the feeling that everything about her was a big act. But what were the police supposed to do with that? No good could come from getting involved.

7

Twelve Years Before The Murder

1967

Naomi lived in a large house in a small town. It was just her and her mum; no dad on the scene, no siblings. The house had been left to them by dead grandparents, and although there was plenty of money for its upkeep, it had fallen into disrepair. They got into the habit of avoiding the worst rooms and there were no visitors to worry about, no playmates coming over after school or for sleepovers. It sat opposite the town war memorial and next to the public swimming pool. Naomi grew up to the soundtrack of other children having fun. Reasons why Naomi didn't go to the pool included: it was too soon after lunch; it was too close to tea; it was too hot and she'd burn to a crisp; it was too cold and she'd catch her death; the chlorine would turn her hair to straw; creepy men lurked around swimming pools; let's not advertise our wares by parading about in swimsuits like sloppy bitches on heat.

One of Naomi's mum's favourite refrains was, *Nobody likes a whinger*. She said it so often that Naomi stopped expressing opposition to any limitation or hoping for anything different.

It was a small life.

Naomi turned eighteen in 1967. She was in her final year of high school. For the most part, she believed herself content to live within the narrow confines of her mum's imagination and will. But then a teacher proposed a class excursion to the city. Sydney! The big smoke! That's when it started: the growing feeling of being on a precipice; of desires straining against their chains; of words that hadn't yet taken form catching in her throat. It was a feeling that came with an echo, a sense of something forgotten, kicked aside, papered over. Naomi felt a sudden need to have her wits about her. She was ready and, at the same time, totally unprepared.

Three weeks later, on a muggy evening, Naomi walked into a bar on George Street, Sydney, not far from Circular Quay. She had washed her face and wore a flattering dress borrowed from one of the other girls. Her hair was tucked behind her ears. She was dazzled by the glitz. Her eyes flittered all about, not knowing where to land. And then, they locked on a man's. He smiled, and his smile anchored her.

It could so easily have never happened. What were the chances of her being in Sydney at all, or that her group did a walking tour of the gardens and construction site of the new Opera House, or that the Marble Bar was nearby and had only just started allowing women in for two hours per night?

Richard bought her a drink. It was sweet and punchy.

'I want to know everything about you,' he said, sipping his beer.

Naomi was at a loss. 'I've never had much to say for myself.'

'Maybe you've never had someone to listen.'

Naomi held her hands in her lap after looking for pockets her dress didn't have.

'What's your favourite colour?' he asked.

'Depends. It changes all the time.'

'What does it depend on?'

'That changes too.'

She giggled and Richard's smile broadened. Naomi liked the shape his hand made when he held his beer glass.

'What are your hobbies?'

Naomi frowned, giving it some thought. 'I don't think I have any.'

'Well, what do you like doing with your time?'

'What time would that be, then?'

'A-ha. Very funny,' said Richard. 'Clever girl.'

Was she? What did he mean? Naomi had simply meant that she'd never felt time was something that belonged to her. Her mum was the family timekeeper, always.

'Counting breaths,' she said. 'That's what I do.'

Richard's gaze was intense. One of his long legs stretched out straight from his chair, towards her. Naomi looked around the bar, storing mental images that she could think over later. It was fancy, every bit of it covered in marble, gold, carvings, oil paintings, stained glass, columns and arches. Even the ceiling was intricately decorated. The opulence was too much to take in, so Naomi focused on facial expressions, postures, movement, and how it made the spaces between people change. She was aware that Richard was still looking at her.

'I'll buy you another drink if you want, but if you're not used to it, perhaps you'd better not,' he said.

Naomi shrugged. 'You choose.'

He bought her a lemonade and had his next question ready.

'What's your favourite food?'

'Oh, that's an easy one,' she said immediately. 'Mettwurst and cheese and jam on toast. But the toast has to be cold before anything goes on it, so it doesn't go soggy; you want it crisp like a cracker. And the cheese has to be Kraft – you know, the one in silver paper. And the best jam is apricot.'

'And how often do you eat this concoction?'

'Every day.'

Richard was looking at her like she was his favourite dessert. Naomi was pretty sure she heard what he said next, but she wanted to be absolutely sure, and she wanted to hear it again.

'What?' she said, cupping her ear.

Richard leant in close.

'You're exquisite,' he said.

The next day, Naomi went back to her home town, back to school, back to her mum. It was a rapid romance, carried out covertly over correspondence. The postmistress was complicit, having taken pity on Naomi after being on the receiving end of a tongue-lashing from Naomi's mum for delivering post damp from a rain shower. She kept Richard's letters to Naomi held back at the post office for Naomi to collect after school, greeting her with a pantomime grin and a double thumbs-up on the days when there was one.

Those letters had an extraordinary effect on Naomi. They tightened the seams of her, giving her definition. She had always felt too loosely constructed, made of flimsy stuff, liable to fall apart with the slice of a quick-unpick, a pin pulled out, a tug of thread. But now – *now* – she had shape, she had form, she had the sense of a future, of territory she could step into. There was a man – a good-looking one – who wanted her.

They got engaged during a phone call made from the payphone outside the swimming pool on Naomi's last day of school.

'I know what I want,' said Richard.

There was no need to ask Naomi what she wanted. It was plain as day.

'When you know, you know,' said Richard. 'No point hanging about.'

They had the wedding reception in the town hall. They could have afforded a reception in the club in the city half an hour down the road, but Naomi's mum said there was no point since the marriage wouldn't last. Richard had been charming. He'd called her *Mum* from the first time he'd met her and he made her laugh – an impossible feat. He took everything in his stride. Nothing fazed him. He reeked of city sophistication but was still accommodating, personable, interested in other people.

'He'll tire of you once he's had his fun,' Naomi's mum told her. 'That's not his fault. Any man would. Your looks will fade sooner rather than later, take it from me. Richard's a man who will need more from a wife than you can give him. Take that from me too.'

But Naomi belonged to Richard now. She didn't have to take anything from her mum anymore.

Ants live in cracks and gaps and inside walls and up in roofs. This is very clever because it means they can be close to where people keep sugary things to eat and still be difficult to find. When ants die, their body casings are left behind, which could give away the whole colony, but mostly, humans sweep them up like they're bits of dust or rubbish, without noticing they are dead body parts.

8

The Day After The Murder

They'd had their Sunday lunch: roast lamb – 'Too hot for gravy,' said Tammy's mum, 'we'll do without' – cooked in the new whizz-bang wall oven that had a timer on it and could turn itself on while they were at church.

'Are you sure it won't burn the house down while we're out?' Tammy's mum had asked the first time.

'Better while we're out than in,' said Tammy's dad, and then: 'Yes, I'm sure.'

Tammy's mum cleaned that oven more than anything else, constantly reaching for the cloth, giving the oven lingering, loving strokes, turning away, then coming back for a few more dabs. Tammy wanted to make fun of her, to join forces with her dad like they always did, but it was no use; he was just as pleased with the oven because at last he could afford to buy her something nice. A colour telly would have been nicer, but no one had asked for Tammy's opinion.

They ate quickly, half expecting a knock on the door from the police making their enquiries, wanting to be prepared and not mid-mouthful when it came.

62

'Get your shoes on, Tammy,' said her mum as soon as they'd finished. 'We're going over the road to do a check on Naomi since she didn't make it to church again. We can watch out for the police from there if we have to.'

Tammy thought it a good plan. Naomi hadn't been seen since the news had taken hold of Warrah Place. She might have something useful to say.

Two police cars sat outside the Italian House but there was no sign of any officers. Blue-and-white tape now stretched across the front of the property, casting an ominous sense of danger over the whole street.

'Mum, does that mean they found something inside?' asked Tammy.

Her mum pointed her nose in the direction of the house like a ferret, as if she could sniff out any news. She didn't answer Tammy.

Sunlight glinted off the windows. There was no chance of seeing inside. No chance of seeing if anyone was looking out. Antonio was missing and the rest of the family were away so there shouldn't be anyone there. With a shiver, Tammy turned her back on the house.

An expanse of lawn, dry and cracked, lay between the road and the front door of Number Three. There was a scattering of trees, set up like a frozen game of What's the Time, Mr Wolf? with the front door as the wolf. Two young gums stood well back, playing it safe. A bank of lilly pillies watched from the sidelines.

Tammy's mum knocked on the wolf's back. 'Yoo-hoo, Naomi?'

No answer.

'Naomi?' she called again, more softly this time, when surely it should have been louder.

Still nothing. She opened the door and stuck her head inside.

'Naomi? It's just me – Helen.'

It felt wrong to walk inside, but what else was Tammy to do since it was her own mother leading the way? There was a time when Tammy's mum and Maureen would walk into each other's homes – back before Tammy's mum started using a shop-lady voice to talk to Maureen – the bounce of the screen door and an elongated and cheery *hello* sufficient. This didn't feel like that.

Inside, it smelled like a caravan that had been shut up and left in the sun. Tammy blinked away the residue of outside light from her eyes. The curtains and blinds were drawn, the only light coming from the sliding door leading from the dining area to the back yard, cracks of brightness seeping in around the edges of the windows.

Tammy's mum kept up a light chatter, a litany of nothing-much-to-say. *Just popped over . . . awfully hot still . . . have you heard . . .?*

She stopped when they came across Colin scrunched up on the floor outside his parents' bedroom door. He said nothing, just peered at them from behind his knees. Tammy's mum moved closer, arm extended, as if approaching a wounded animal that might bite. She put her hand on his head, a touch that was somewhere between a benediction and a pat.

'It's all right now.' Giving a short knock on the bedroom door, she pushed it open and went in. 'Oh, dear Lord above.'

Tammy got onto her tiptoes, trying to see past her mum's shoulder. Not long ago, her mum was an *Oh, Lord* sayer, until she decided that adding a *dear* and *above* changed it from blasphemy to prayer. She had a knack for changing the meaning of things when she wanted to. It was something Tammy wished she could get the hang of.

Tammy had never seen inside the big bedroom before. The door had always been closed and now she could see why: it was another world in there.

All of the furniture was white. Glossy white. There was a kidney-shaped dressing table, three mirrors on top, folded out. Glamour in triplicate. Some of its drawers were open, spilling their contents. On its surface were bottles, pots, brushes, puffs, lids on and lids off. It held the lure of a magic box.

On the wall was a painting with an elaborate gold frame. In it, three girls, older than Tammy but not by all that much, were on a beach, naked and wading in the shallows, froth and spray gathering around their ankles. One of them had turned to the others and was beckoning them, her smile private and sly, like they were all up to something that Tammy wouldn't understand. Below the painting was a vast headboard covered in white velvet. The whole room was carpeted in clouds.

Tammy's mum crept closer to the bed, and now, at last, Tammy caught sight of Naomi. She was curled, caved in on herself, like her middle part was missing. She lifted her head. Her eyes were wild and her face doughy. On one side, her hair was glued down. A string of saliva hung from her mouth and she wiped it away with the heel of her hand.

'Antonio,' she moaned.

'So you have heard, then,' said Tammy's mum. 'Yes, of course. Richard knew. You must have spoken about it. Terrible, isn't it?'

'Oh, God. Richard.'

'Don't you worry about Richard being away. He's already asked me to help. It's all agreed. Anything you need, I'm here.' She was straightening the covers as she spoke. 'Come on, let's sit you up. We don't know if the police have found the body yet.' Her voice was like a lullaby, soft and soothing. 'Antonio, I mean. Calling him "the body" is so impersonal, don't you think? Anyway, we don't know anything for sure yet. I'll let you know as soon as I find out. I just can't get over the foot being cut off. I mean, what kind of whack job does that? It's so bizarre.'

'Stop,' said Naomi. 'I can't bear it.'

'Me either. It doesn't bear thinking about. Can you imagine the depravity of someone, to do something like that?'

'I think I'm going to be sick.'

Tammy's mum bustled Tammy back out of the room and shut the door on her.

Colin was still being weird, hugging his knees and staring at the floor. *Pathetic*, thought Tammy. Him and Naomi both. Everyone was upset about Antonio, Tammy more than anyone. Why did Colin and Naomi need to draw attention to themselves by making such a big song and dance about it? Tammy decided to leave Colin be and have a stickybeak around while there was no one to stop her.

There wasn't much to see in the kitchen. The benches were wiped clean. A folded dishcloth hung over the tap. There wasn't even a toaster or kettle out. Nothing. Who lived like that? On the breakfast bar there was a wooden bowl of overripe apricots. There was something rank, lewd even, about them: their on-the-turn smell and the careless way in which they'd been forgotten. A neat trail of ants ran from the skirting board, up the breakfast bar and into the bowl. Clever things. One ant caught Tammy's attention. It was going in the opposite direction, against the flow, not moving in formation towards the apricots, but tumbling over the others, pressing on regardless. Debbie. That ant was Debbie, choosing her own direction, not letting anyone bar her path. Tammy watched until it disappeared into a crack in the skirting board.

She moved on and stood on the threshold of the lounge room. She knew from the few times she'd been sent here to play with Colin – never mind the age difference or that girls mature much faster than boys – that children weren't allowed in there. Its entrance was open; a broad arch without a door, never closed off by more than a rule.

Tammy slipped off her sandals and lined them up neatly on

the tiles. She lifted each foot in turn to inspect them. Grimy. She considered putting the sandals back on, but the tiles were cooling her hot feet, and she wanted to feel the soft blue carpet under her bare toes. She went in.

Inside, it was darker, and again, Tammy had to wait for her eyes to adjust. As she did, she became aware of the ticking of a carriage clock that seemed to grow louder and more insistent, a sound that belonged to this room only. The clock sat in the middle of the mantelpiece, flanked by two enormous vases filled with peacock feathers. There were heavy curtains, much bigger than the windows themselves, hanging to the floor where they puddled. They matched the couches; all were the same blue material. A chandelier hung low, and Tammy was scared of standing directly underneath it.

Turning back the way she'd come in, Tammy saw an enormous picture on the wall next to the entrance, and her innards jolted, almost toppling her. Three sets of eyes were watching. Her toes clung to the carpet as she swayed, breathed, righted herself.

It was a framed family portrait, almost life-sized; one done properly in a studio with a mottled background (blue, of course), not just a snap taken by a relative. Tammy stared greedily at the people in the picture in a way you weren't allowed to in real life.

In the photo, Richard smiled broadly, welcoming you in. Tammy could tell that Naomi's gaze had moved from Richard to the camera a mere moment before the click. Hers was an open-mouthed smile, unable to hide the mirth in her eyes at the funny thing Richard had probably just said. Colin, a toddler, was in his father's arms. His mother's hand rested on a pudgy thigh. In contrast to his parents' faces, Colin stared blandly at the camera, seemingly unaware that he was enough for them, that they were enough for each other, and how extraordinary that was.

67

Tammy decided, all at once, that she didn't want to be in the lounge room anymore. All that blue. It was too much. Before she left, she knelt down next to a coffee-table leg and ran her thumbnail along it, working at it until a tiny sliver splintered off, then a bigger piece, and then a bigger piece yet. There. She'd left her mark.

She held the splinters of wood in her palm. They weren't much. The peacock feathers on the mantelpiece seemed to be nodding to her, daring her. She selected one from the back, bending, twisting and yanking, while the ticking of the clock became a ticking-off – *tsk, tsk, tsk* – until she had plucked out an eye. Much better. She put it in her pocket along with the splinters, glad of her achievement, glad to be getting the heck out of there.

She felt lighter as she moved through the dining area, even though the air was close and clammy and those apricots were stinking the place out with their sickly sweetness. She could hear her mum's muffled voice coming from the bedroom.

There was a washing basket on the table, in the middle, surrounded by placemats, like a plate of food waiting to be dished up. Tammy pulled it closer. The clothes inside were damp, had been washed by the smell of them, although there was definitely something fusty about them too. How long had they been left, waiting for someone to hang them up? Quite a while; some of it was already dry, the creases baked in. Tammy's fingers rifled through. Towels. Colin's pyjamas and grungy undies. Something satiny, slippery and floral – exotic. Richard's clothes: shorts, socks, pants, a surfie T-shirt with rolling waves and stains across the front. It must be for painting.

At the bottom of the basket, Tammy's fingers closed over something hard. She pulled out a small booklet with a green cover. *REPUBBLICA ITALIANA. PASSAPORTO*, Tammy read, mouthing the syllables heavily. It opened easily to a page

68

with a tiny grainy photo of Antonio, instantly recognisable and yet, disappointingly, looking not much at all like the Antonio she knew. 'What can I do to help?' she whispered to him. Tammy was still staring at the photo, trying to find Antonio in there, when a scrabbling sound startled her. She dropped the passport into the washing basket and let loose a small shriek.

A pair of eyes, seemingly disembodied and peering through the sliding door, were fixed on her. They blinked. This was no picture on a wall.

Tammy's first thought was that Antonio's spirit had come for a visitation; her next that the Holy Ghost had come to condemn her for what she'd done in the lounge room. Then she saw that it was only Sheree, her face bracketed by cupped hands and her nose pressed against the fly screen. The sound she'd heard was one of Sheree's kids trying to pull open the screen door.

Sheree waved at Tammy. 'Open the door, there's a love.'

Tammy shoved the washing basket under the table and opened the door. In they came, Mama Duck and her three grotty-faced ducklings behind her. First came Samantha, aged five, in a terry-towelling playsuit that was too small for her. She looked at Tammy disdainfully as she flounced past. Next came the baby, Jacinta, the grubbiest of them all, wearing only a sagging nappy and dragging half of the outside in with her, mostly in her hair. And then Monique, aged three, riding a tricycle with rusted handlebars and faded red bucket tray over the lip of the doorstep and into the house.

'Thanks, kiddo,' said Sheree, chucking Tammy under the chin.

Sheree made straight for Naomi's bedroom and went in without knocking. Samantha made straight for a cupboard in the kitchen and opened it without asking. She took out a packet of biscuits and put one in her mouth before giving one to each of her sisters. Surprisingly, she also held one out to Tammy, but she held it in her fingers instead of offering the packet. Tammy shook her head, even though they were chocolate chip, then immediately regretted it, but it was too late to backtrack.

Meanwhile in Naomi's bedroom, Tammy's mum and Sheree were engaged in a scuffle of words about something, loudly enough for everyone to hear their hands-on-hips voices. Tammy went back to where Colin was still sitting, so still that he must have a numb bum by now. Then her mum came out and knelt beside Colin and asked him what he wanted to do.

'Lunch,' he said. 'I want some lunch. Please.'

'That settles it, then,' said Tammy's mum, looking triumphantly over her shoulder at Sheree. 'Off you come with me, poppet. Mum's feeling a bit crook and needs a little lie-down. I'll fix you up something to eat, you poor thing.'

Tammy went to retrieve her sandals and, on the way, stubbed her toe on the tricycle. In the bucket tray was a toy Smurfette. It fitted perfectly into Tammy's palm, disappearing as she closed her fist over it, so she took it as revenge for her toe.

Outside, the police cars were gone from the Italian House. Instead, there was a news van there. A reporter holding a microphone and a man holding a camera both beckoned to Tammy's mum.

'Not now,' she called, shielding her face from the camera. 'Can't you see I've got *children* with me?'

Colin stuck close to Helen, using her to hide behind, trying to match her pace with his little legs.

Tammy didn't pay as much attention to the news people as she might because she was busy doing maths in her head. She was kicking herself for not taking the passport, but she didn't need it to remember what she'd seen. Under the photo of Antonio was a date: 25 May 1959. That made Antonio nineteen, not twenty-four. She did the maths again and got the same answer. Antonio had lied to Tammy. It hit her like a kick in the guts.

9

Two Weeks Before The Murder

Saturday, 23 December 1978

When Richard pulled into the driveway mid-afternoon, he was pleased to find Antonio in the front yard but not pleased to see that he was watering the plants. It was far too early in the day, the sun still too high. Everything would scorch.

Richard eased the car door shut, not wanting to draw Naomi from the house just yet. He took off his sunglasses and looped them through the top of his shirt.

Antonio yanked on the hose and flicked it like a whip to dislodge a kink. He moved to the side of the house. He was pretending not to have seen Richard, which Richard found amusing. *Fair enough*, he thought. He might have done the same when he was a kid and the boss turned up while he was working.

Antonio was considered an affable chap, if somewhat reserved with Richard. He was popular on the street and liked a chat. No one had a bad word to say, and Leslie personally vouched for the kid. These were important considerations for Richard. He could only have someone trustworthy around the house, around his family. Antonio was also directionless and lacked purpose, and that irked Richard. He couldn't understand it. How could you be nineteen and still have no idea what you wanted to do with your life, no drive, no ambition? He must be a disappointment to his parents, but Richard blamed the parents as much as Antonio. How a kid turned out was a reflection on the way they'd been brought up, on the parents themselves. It was up to the parents to provide a steady guide and firm hand. Too many parents dodged their responsibility.

'Hey there,' said Richard, approaching.

Antonio grunted in response and gave another tug on the hose.

'I wanted to have a quick chat before I go in, man to man,' said Richard, adding, 'No, nothing about your work. All's fine there,' when Antonio looked alarmed.

His work was not entirely fine. Richard suspected he was a slacker. It seemed to take him an awfully long time to get the simplest tasks done. But then, Richard was a practical, can-do kind of man. He was used to feeling let down by others who weren't. Besides, doing odd jobs around the house was secondary to why Richard really wanted him there. He needed an ally, a partner, another pair of eyes around the place when Richard couldn't be there.

'I don't suppose Naomi says an awful lot to you,' said Richard, 'but I reckon you've probably noticed . . .' He broke off, trying to decide how to put it. 'Over the years, she's been susceptible to different kinds of moods.'

Richard paused to see if Antonio was following him, but Antonio was studiously blank, giving nothing away.

'Moods where she turns inwards and ruminates on things. And her behaviour can become unpredictable. I can't help feeling of late that we might be heading for a crisis point.' Richard paused and stretched his arms to release tension. His whole body hummed with energy, ready for action. It had gone well

72

beyond hoping things would right themselves, and now he was just waiting for the moment to intervene. Intervening was the easy part. Richard was a doer. It was the waiting he hated. 'It's difficult to keep track when I have to be away. That's why I wanted to talk to you.'

Antonio turned off the tap at the wall. He made a right angle of his arm and began winding the hose in loops around his hand and elbow.

'She's a good mum on the whole,' Richard went on. 'Don't get me wrong about that. It's just that sometimes she can get distracted. Preoccupied. And with Colin, well, he still needs a mum who's on the ball, who remembers he's there. He—'

Richard's train of thought was interrupted by female voices coming from the street and Antonio flattening himself against the lilly pillies to get himself out of view.

It was the policewoman, Lydia, in uniform, and a girl walking down Warrah Place towards Carnegie Drive. Richard stepped in beside Antonio and crouched down, too tall to be hidden by the lilly pillies, and stifled a laugh. He felt like a schoolboy hiding out behind the bike shed.

'So that'd be the niece, then,' said Richard in a hushed voice once they'd passed.

Antonio averted his eyes.

'I see how it is.' Richard chuckled. 'Got in over your head already, have you, mate? That's fast work. Been there myself, many a time, in the good old days.' Richard stood to watch their retreating backs. 'She's pretty.'

Antonio hung the coiled hose over the tap. 'Your boy's fine,' he said. 'You don't need to worry.'

Only after Antonio had left and Richard had gone inside did he wonder if Antonio might have been hiding from Lydia rather than the niece, and specifically, if it was the policewoman he wanted to avoid. That afternoon, Antonio had been sullen and unforthcoming, which Richard had put down to Antonio's age and being intimidated by him. But what if there was more to it? What if the kid had landed himself in trouble with the police?

Contrary to what you might think, the queen ant doesn't control the other ants. She doesn't get to be the boss. Her job is just to have babies. But it's a good idea to keep her alive because after she dies, the rest of the colony can only live for another few months. Some queen ants, if they don't get stepped on, can live for up to thirty years. The queen has two sets of wings, which she sheds once the ants make a new nest for new babies. Maybe that's to make sure she doesn't jack it all in and fly away.

IO

The Day After The Murder

Sunday, 7 January 1979

'What do you want in your sandwich, Colin? Is cold lamb OK?' Tammy's mum called from the kitchen area, buttering the bread.

Colin and Tammy watched from the family-room table. Colin looked to Tammy, but how was she meant to know what he wanted? She shrugged.

'Yes, please,' said Colin.

'Cucumber?'

Colin leant towards Tammy. 'Does she mean in the sandwich?'

'Yeah,' said Tammy. 'Lamb and cucumber.'

'Together? At the same time?'

'Yes.'

'In the same sandwich?'

'What's the matter with you?'

Colin looked down and spoke out of the corner of his mouth. 'I've never had more than one thing in a sandwich. On toast, yes, but not in a sandwich.'

'Really?'

'Is it good? Should I do it?'

76

Tammy's mum was leaning against the wall, arms folded, having come to see what was taking so long.

'Depends on what you like,' said Tammy.

'Wow,' said Colin. 'It's like a sandwich stew.'

'What? No,' said Tammy. 'It's nothing like a stew. It's just a sandwich.'

'Casserole,' said Tammy's mum. 'A sandwich casserole. Not stew. Stews are for peasants, and we are not peasants.' Her shoulders were shaking. When was the last time Tammy had seen her laugh? And when had she started saying casserole instead of stew? It was still the same old scrag end cooked in the same old Crock-Pot.

'No way. No peasants here, no siree,' said Colin. Did he even know what peasants were? 'OK, I'll have a sandwich casserole, please.' He was laughing too.

'You're both loony tunes,' said Tammy. Their laughter rankled. It was strange, jarring, after a morning of tight emotions.

'Oi,' yelled Tammy's dad. He had his head in a cupboard in the kitchen. 'Who left the lid off the Christmas cake? The ants have got in the tin.'

'Are they dead?' called Tammy.

'No, they bloody are not.'

'One sandwich casserole, coming right up!' said Tammy's mum.

Colin was still perky after his sandwich. Clearly, all he needed was feeding and a laugh to break him out of that morose business at his house earlier.

Tammy's dad was in a mood of his own. He'd dragged a chair up close to the telly in the lounge room and was watching the cricket in his shorts and singlet. He'd twisted his legs into a knot with needing a wee but couldn't go because he was convinced a wicket would fall if he left the room. So far, Australia had lost two matches in the Ashes and won one. Tammy's dad had lots of opinions about cricket. About Kerry Packer disrespecting the game by pinching the best players for his World Series. About the players who took off for more money – *Shame on you, Greg Chappell* – and degraded the integrity of the game. He'd tell anyone who'd listen that it was a bloody travesty, was what it was. He felt it as a personal betrayal and Tammy felt sorry for him, mainly for making a mug of himself over a game that was mostly standing around on the grass waiting for a catch or sitting in the stands waiting for a bat.

'Do you think we should have the cricket off?' said Tammy's mum, who had no interest in cricket. 'Out of respect for Antonio?' She was on the couch with her Good News Bible open, jotting down notes for next week's sermon, but keeping one eye on the window in case the police came. She'd suggested Tammy's dad might like to smarten up, and he'd said he wasn't putting on more clobber in this weather, cops or no, not on his flamin' day off.

'It's a distraction, Hells,' he said. 'I'll go out of my mind if I keep thinking about what some sick bastard did to Antonio. Feel free to respect him in another room if you feel the need.'

Tammy and Colin moved listlessly from room to room, unable to settle at anything. It was too hot to do anything outside, so they ended up in Tammy's bedroom. There were two beds: Tammy's and a spare. The idea had been that Tammy could have friends stay for sleepovers, but that hadn't worked out. Between the beds was a new desk, all ready for high-school homework. It was made of pine and smelt important. Tammy lay sprawled on the blue eiderdown on her bed, and Colin perched on the edge of the red eiderdown on the spare bed. He was fidgety in the usual way of little boys, legs jerking and feet jiggling on the floor.

When Colin's finger started to tap his knee, an image came to

Tammy's mind of Antonio tapping a cigarette from its packet. A week ago, maybe two. Tammy had been on the island with a cup of water and a magnifying glass, trying to see if ants could swim. When she had seen him emerge from his house, she'd skipped over to him and they'd met under the big tree near the Laus' driveway. Antonio wasn't a stay-at-home person; it was easy to come across him on his way to or from somewhere. Tammy had pointedly ignored Peggy, who'd been watching from her front garden with her arms folded. Antonio had caught the cigarette in his lips and tapped another loose. He'd offered it to Tammy and laughed when she'd balked, not knowing what to do. He'd lit his smoke with a match, striking it towards himself. Tammy had been taught it was only safe to strike a match away from yourself. Had he been looking for his Zippo? Would she dare to ask him about it? Nothing obvious – she could maybe say that she missed seeing it and wondered. Antonio, with the hand that held his smoke, had tucked Tammy's hair behind her ear. She'd jumped. Smoke had got in her eye and she'd blinked furiously. Antonio had laughed again. 'Run along, Tamara. Go play.'

Tammy couldn't believe she had to babysit Colin when she needed privacy to think about Antonio and come up with a plan. Perhaps Colin might have his uses, though. She picked up her journal and flipped to the back. She wrote *Warrah Warriors Watching* and underlined it, then considered it, pleased with the alliteration, but crossing out the *s*. Just one warrior; she was on her own.

'What do you think your dad would say about Sheree walking into your house like she owned the joint? And what would he say about her kids eating your biscuits?' she asked.

'I don't think he'd mind about the biscuits,' said Colin. 'He's not a big biscuit person.'

Interesting, thought Tammy, making a note. So Richard *would* mind about Sheree. She didn't blame him. Tammy decided to try again.

'Can you think of any good reason why Antonio's passport would be at your house?'

Colin considered the question for a while. 'Yes,' he said. 'I'm guessing it's because he left it there.'

Tammy remembered that Antonio worked at Colin's house and decided that Colin's answer was acceptable – *just* – but not helpful. Her two other questions were more important and more urgent, but they weren't ones she could ask Colin: why had Antonio lied to her about his age? And if he'd lied about that, what else might he have lied about?

'I don't suppose you have any more awe-inspiring details to share about Antonio or what happened to him?' It was worth a shot.

'I didn't see anything, and I have not a word to say about it,' Colin said.

'Well, yes. Obviously. I wouldn't expect you to have seen anything. But have you heard anyone talking about it?'

He didn't seem to care.

'Did you see the news van outside before?' said Tammy. 'Do you think they're going to put us in the newspaper?' Maybe she'd be allowed to get a decent haircut if there was a chance of getting her picture in the paper.

Colin got up and opened a wardrobe door. 'Can I've a look in here?'

'Seems you already are.' Tammy closed her journal.

'Whoa.' He opened the other door. 'Is – is this all yours? All of it?'

'Sort of.'

Tammy's wardrobe was jam-packed full of clothes, rows of hangers smashed together, shelves stuffed. An in-your-face array of colour and excess. Tammy's mum was wild for a bargain, buying clothes in sizes bigger than Tammy whenever the sales came along. Those clothes waited, biding their time, for Tammy to grow into them. Her mum also kept all the clothes Tammy had grown out of, just in case. Those clothes also waited, biding their time, for the almost-babies that never came.

Colin stood in front of the wardrobe, gaze roving, eyes on fast-forward. He still hadn't changed out of his church clothes.

'Do you remember Narelle who lived in the Italian House before the Mariettis?' said Tammy. 'Well, she was my best friend. She was the same age as me so we could have proper grown-up conversations, you know?'

Colin didn't say anything. He reached out. His fingertips trailed over the clothes, skimming quickly over some, lingering over others. He seemed captivated by a blue velvet cape, running his fingers this way and that over it, back and forth, but when he moved on to a frock made of some gauzy, floaty material that shimmered when he moved his fingers beneath it, he gasped.

'What do you call this stuff?' he asked.

'No idea. How come you're here anyway?' said Tammy. She hoped it wouldn't be a regular thing. She had experiments to conduct, chemicals to titrate, plans to devise, things to find out. She didn't have time to entertain a little kid.

'It's Mum. She's sick as a dog.'

'What's wrong with her?'

Colin cocked his head. 'She's taken to her bed because she's in the family way. That's how your mum said it.'

It sounded like the sort of thing her mum would say. At first, Tammy was confused, wondering how Naomi, so petite and neatly arranged, could be in anyone's way. And then, of course, she understood. Thank goodness she hadn't said anything out loud to embarrass herself.

'Can I?' asked Colin, pulling out a plain yellow dress with orange piping. It was one Tammy had outgrown years ago.

'If you want,' said Tammy. Viewing him upside down, because she was now lying on her back, her legs scissoring against the wall, she noticed that his clothes were grubby. And she remembered that there weren't any of Colin's shorts and T-shirts in the washing basket at his house. 'Hasn't your mum washed your clothes?'

'Should she have?'

'You don't know much, do you?'

Colin started taking clothes out of the wardrobe, holding them up against his front, putting some on the spare bed, putting some back. Tammy's legs stilled and she twisted around to watch more carefully. Colin wasn't just rummaging through clothing; he was setting free the ghosts of the almost-babies.

Tammy sat up, eager now.

'Yeah, go on,' she said. 'Put on anything you want.'

Colin had returned to his first choice: the yellow and orange frock. He cleared his throat and looked pointedly at Tammy.

'What?' she said.

Colin sighed. 'Turn around, please.'

'Oh, right.' Tammy turned and sat cross-legged on her bed facing the wall. 'But you're only a kid.'

'Nevertheless.'

The *nevertheless* bothered Tammy. What was a boy like Colin doing with a word like that? It was a word Tammy would have liked for herself, and she didn't want to share it with him. Tammy added Colin's *nevertheless* to the list of things that weren't what they should be that day.

Joe trembling.

That wild look in Naomi's eyes when she lifted her head from the bed.

Sheree.

And Antonio. His passport. His lie. His foot.

Colin looked at himself in the mirror. The dress hung from his shoulders, his stupid knees and stick legs poking out beneath. He smoothed down his fringe with his palm. Suzi came in to have a look and rubbed herself against his legs. Colin looked pleased with himself.

'You know,' he said, 'I bet Narelle is missing you too.'

'What would you know about it?' said Tammy, because being mean was easier than the truth. Unable to bear herself, she got up and walked out.

The dining room overlooked the lounge room below; a wooden rail between them. Tammy had a spot she liked, wedged into the corner of the rail, where, crouched low, she had a view of the front door and a partial view of the lounge room. It was an excellent listening spot with access to the lounge room, entrance area and, if the door was left open, the family room as well.

Tammy watched her mum idly flick through her Bible, and thought again of the almost-babies. She wanted to think kindly of them, tried her absolute hardest, but jealousy is a tricksy bugger — it creeps its way into you like the tendrils of a vine, taking hold. How was it fair that her mum put all her attention on the kids that never were, and not on the kid she had?

11

Helen had a page of notes on the Parable of the Sower. She had many thoughts about rocky ground and soil laden with thorns. She looked up when Duncan turned down the volume on the telly. There was a break in play for tea. Duncan sat on the couch and narrowed his attention on her. He did that sort of thing: it was part of his set-up for a conversation, no matter if she wanted one or not. She put her notebook down between them, kept the Bible on her lap and decided to get in first.

'Why do you think the police are saying *presumed dead*? If they can't say for certain, why say it at all?' Helen cut off Duncan's reply, saying, 'It's upsetting. What I'm worried about is that no one seems to have seen him since the working bee. We don't even know if he came home afterwards.'

Duncan waited this time.

'It was my idea. I arranged everything and got everyone involved, including Antonio. What if I'm associated with a death, if he even is dead, just because I was trying to do a good thing? It was meant to bring everyone together! Community spirit and all that. Richard didn't seem to think they were connected, did he? The way he was so certain Joe's tools would turn up.'

'Shit, Joe's tools,' said Duncan, as if he'd just joined the dots. 'I reckon it will raise alarm bells if they stay missing. That's the last thing the poor bloke needs.'

Duncan allowed a pause to pass before changing tack. 'It's a good thing you're doing, Hells-bells. For Naomi. Looking after the boy.'

So that's what he wanted to talk about.

'Not so proud now, is she?' said Helen. It was difficult to admit, even to Duncan, how much she craved a friendship with Naomi. Looking after Colin gave her an in. Duncan was still looking at her, so she went on. 'Besides, I couldn't leave him with that woman. Sheree. Did I tell you she was there, poking her nose in? It was so strange, the way she waltzed in there, wanting to take Colin with her. She can barely look after the ones she's got. You should've seen the state of them. Practically feral.'

'All I'm saying is, watch yourself. Be careful.' He touched her hair. 'Please, love, take care.'

'You needn't worry. I'm not even jealous of her. I'm not.'

The ad for roller doors came on the telly. 'Don't you think we should get one?' said Helen, gesturing at the screen. It wasn't the first time she'd asked. The ad came on so often and they looked so snazzy with their remote control. But Duncan said from a structural-engineering point of view there was no way in hell it would work on their carport, never mind the additional physics point of view of stopping on a steep incline to work the controller. Helen still thought there was a good chance of changing Duncan's mind. He liked her to be happy.

But Duncan continued to look at her, not the telly, with a quizzical expression, and Helen had the familiar feeling that Duncan noticed more than he let on, had more thoughts than he put words to. She hoped he had the good sense to keep a lid on them.

'OK,' she said. 'I'll say this only once and only to you, mind. It's just that I don't get why Naomi gets to be pregnant again

85

when she's never even said she wants another one. And what's more, I don't get why Sheree gets to fall pregnant at the drop of a hat. I mean, never married, and three different deadshit dads—'

'Hey. I'm a deadshit dad. And we weren't married when you got preggers with Tammy.' Duncan grinned and ran his finger down Helen's nose. She had a strong urge to wipe his touch away.

'That's different. *We're* different.'

He eyed the Bible in her lap. 'And getting more different by the day.'

'What's that supposed to mea—'

'Oop.' He sprung up. 'Commentary's back on.'

Duncan adjusted the volume and settled in his chair. Helen breathed easy. But he wasn't done yet. Again, he turned the volume down, and leant over the back of the chair, his elbow hooked, as if he were reversing a car.

'Listen, I've been thinking . . .' He stopped; didn't seem to know how to go on. 'This thing with Antonio . . . Not just that . . . But that too, because there's going to be a lot going on around here. I mean, the media's already turned up like they're at a carnival and everyone's on edge and the whole thing is going to be stressful, right, and it's hard not to be thinking about it non-stop. Even with all of that, it's more that generally . . .'

'Duncan. Spit it out.'

'I reckon you should go back to work.' He combed his fingers through his beard and winced.

'What?'

'If you want to.'

'Why?'

'Don't say no yet. Not until you've properly thought about it.'

'Do we need the money?'

'It's not the money. We've never had it so good.'

'It's because of the church, isn't it? You resent it.'

'Nah, it's not that at all.'

He sighed heavily, as well he might. What did he expect her to say?

'I just thought it could be a good thing. You know, make you feel useful again. No,' he rushed to add. 'No, I didn't mean useful.' He raised his hand in surrender. 'I mean a sense of pur- pose – yeah, more that sort of thing.'

Helen thought about Parliament House, soon to be defunct if they ever got on with building the new one. She thought about the windowless typing pool room tucked well away from the chambers, with its exposed breeze blocks, ceiling peeling away where nesting possums had pissed on it. If you had to stay late, you could hear the possums scurrying, scrabbling, growling. She thought about the smell of carbon paper, the clack of keys, the snap of handbag clasps, red lipstick, perfume and no air to be had, overhead lights, gossip, rumour, innuendo, inflection. Long, long days of wanting the outdoors so badly it made her skin prickle with the yearning.

'But Tammy,' said Helen.

'She's older now, she can do more for herself. We could make it work.'

'Make it work how exactly? You're flat out with work just to stay in the game. It's not like you're about to pick up any slack. And unemployment's so high. The jobs just aren't there.'

'If you don't want to work, you could go back to study. Do a course or something.'

'I trained on an Olivetti. They'd be obsolete by now.' Duncan opened his mouth, as though about to interject. 'As are typing pools, what with those fancy photocopiers they have now.'

'There's always a need for office girls.'

'I'm hardly a girl.'

'You're missing my point.'

Oh, she got his point all right. It was plain as day. He was asking her to give up on having another baby. Only he was too gutless to come out and say it.

The last time Helen had been pregnant was in the winter, about the time the Mariettis moved in. She had new boots. Second-hand from an op shop, because old habits and all that, but new to her. Black. Knee-high. Lace-ups; seventeen hooks each side. Bit of a rigmarole to do up, but worth it. A higher heel than she was used to, and a half-size too big, but better that than too small. And only a few scuff marks. Helen coloured them in with black texta and that did the trick; practically as good as new.

Duncan had met the Italians the day before and said they were fine, nothing to worry about. Peggy said they were *très chic* but uppity with it too, and they could do with pulling their heads in. That made Helen nervous, especially with them being foreign. She didn't know how to be around sophisticated people. She didn't like how they made her feel. But surely in this instance, with them being new, on the back foot, worried about fitting in, they would be grateful for the hand of friendship. Right?

She might not have gone had she not read the article in *Cosmo* about locus of control and taken the quiz. It turned out that Helen scored highly for an external locus of control.

There was a family joke, started by Scott, her eldest brother, and all in good fun, that Helen single-handedly kept the pop-psychology industry afloat with all the self-help books she read. *Wanky woo-woo bullshit*, her dad called it, waving his hands around Helen's head as if he were casting a spell, and everyone would laugh, and he would beam and thump her shoulder – no harm done. Helen would laugh too, because if she didn't, they'd say, *Look at her, cracking the sads*, and say it was proof that none of her books had worked.

This locus-of-control business was different. It really spoke to her. She had all the classic features of someone who believed that things happened *to* her rather than *because of* her actions; that she was at the mercy of external forces, not her own abilities and choices. She'd moved on from transactional analysis – that *I'm OK – You're OK* stuff. It was exciting at first, really seemed like the answer, but eventually, she had to accept that it lacked the depth she needed, was too limited in its scope to address the ailment at the heart of her psyche.

Well, all that was about to change. She was going to decide her own destiny, to claw back control and bring it where it belonged: to her. *You and me, little bean, we're taking charge.* She might as well start by meeting the new neighbours.

Helen finished lacing her boots. 'Come on, little bean, let's go,' she said, hands on her belly.

Eight weeks along, she reckoned. This time it would be OK. This time she had God on her side; God, who wasn't stingy with his power, who said anything you ask for in my name I will give you; the ultimate, benevolent – *this time, please, God, fingers crossed* – baby-giving force. No, not fingers crossed: that was her external locus of control talking. She was in charge, no crossed fingers needed.

Nothing to it, she told herself as she approached their front door. All you have to do is tell them your name and welcome them to Warrah Place. Just natural, home-grown friendliness.

On the gravel next to their front door, a young *Grevillea juniperina* 'Molonglo' had plonked itself, self-seeded while the house was otherwise occupied with the comings and goings of old and new owners. Cheeky little mite. She crouched low to get a better look at the waxy spider-leg flowers. She hoped the Italians would let it stay but doubted they would; the prickly leaves put people off and not everyone liked yellow.

Mr Marietti opened the door, smiled, said to call him Giorgio. Then there was a pause – was it long enough to be awkward? – before he invited her in.

Giorgio's hair was slicked back in perfect comb-furrows, curling up at the nape of his neck. His teeth were ridiculously straight, and the full set were on display when he smiled. As he ushered Helen in, her hand brushed against his jumper. She'd never felt anything so soft. She'd heard of cashmere; maybe this was it. His slacks were for making an impression, though it was Saturday. Who wore tailored slacks on a Saturday?

He took her into a front room overlooking Warrah Place. It had been a family room in its previous life; a hotch-potch of multicoloured bean bags and children's toys covering the floor. Now, even in its disorganised state, it had transformed. The dark-wood furniture was upholstered in sophisticated beige, which made the boring old quarry tiles look beautiful, more orange than brown, more modern than dowdy.

The boy Duncan had mentioned – Antonio – sat on an up-turned box, hunched in front of a large, colour television, tuning the channels. He waved and called, 'Ciao,' but didn't divert his attention from his task, except to slurp from a mug, then put it down on an over-laden sideboard that had been left skew-whiff in the middle of the room, repurposed as a dumping ground.

Helen didn't know if she should sit. She wasn't invited to. There was a couch, but it had an open suitcase on it, clothes spilling out. The few chairs that were unoccupied had their backs to the wall, as if they were at a bush dance in a town hall, hopeful and ignored.

Why hadn't she thought to bring anything? She tried to tell herself it was because she and her baby were enough. It wasn't her fault they didn't know that.

'My wife would adore to meet you,' said Mr Marietti – Giorgio. (Was that a cough or a scoff from Antonio?) 'Alas, she is sleeping. I know, I know – who sleeps when it is lunchtime? But at least when she is sleeping, she is not complaining, no?'

'Oh, is it lunchtime?' said Helen, who had been eating

90

whenever she felt like it since she was now eating for two. 'Have I come at the wrong time?'

'As you can see,' he gestured to the room, 'we are in disarray. We live in boxes.' He must mean *out of* boxes. He wasn't so perfect after all, then. 'My wife, she is hoping that if she does not unpack, she will wake up in Rome, and Canberra will have never happened. In the meantime, we have to go scavenging in boxes when we want a plate or a cup. What can I say? We live like savages.'

A young woman, startlingly beautiful, came into the room abruptly, looking hopeful, then crestfallen when she saw Helen.

'Hello,' said Helen, stepping forward. 'I'm welcome.'

Shit.

'I mean—'

'My daughter, Francesca,' said Giorgio.

'My shoes?' said Francesca.

Helen looked at her boots. The light was better in here, streaming through tall north-facing windows onto the tiles. Her hasty, crude black texta markings were clearly visible. 'No, my shoes,' she said, looking up and noticing that Antonio was also looking at her boots. He turned back to the telly, but not before she saw his smirk.

'You are not the courier,' said Francesca. It didn't sound like a question, so Helen didn't answer it. Francesca broke into rapid Italian, clearly displeased.

'She is missing her shoes. Such drama, no?' Giorgio sighed. 'She thought you were the airline courier, bringing her shoes.'

'How could they lose a pair of shoes?' asked Helen.

'Not a pair. A suitcase. An enormous suitcase of shoes.' Giorgio spread his arms wide. 'Anyone would think her life depended upon a suitcase of shoes,' he said, raising his voice at the last, and Francesca sent him a death stare. Giorgio shook his head and said to Helen, 'You women and your need for shoes.'

He looked at Helen's boots, then at her face, regarding her anew. She felt under scrutiny, as if he were trying to understand something about her.

Giorgio and Francesca argued loudly in Italian. Hostility looks the same on faces, foreign or not. Antonio made a comment, also in Italian, and Francesca turned on him. Their argument became more heated and Francesca boffed the back of his head. Antonio laughed, enraging her further.

Helen didn't know what to do. Could she slip out? Should she? Was it not rudeness in their culture to ignore a guest like this? Why on earth had she come? Would they be different if Duncan were here? She was certain the answer to that was yes. People always responded differently – warmly – to Duncan.

Helen rubbed her upper chest in a circular motion with her fist, a self-soothing tactic she'd developed as a child and never grown out of. She visualised a protective shield enveloping her and her baby. Her head filled with white noise. She couldn't think. She felt claustrophobic, enclosed, suffocating. Voices became muffled, and receded. The air thinned; she couldn't get enough of it. Her mouth dried up. She tried to stand straighter but felt something slip inside her. Her boots were too tight. Her cardigan scratched at her. Something pulled at her elbow.

It was Giorgio. He was beside her now. She tried to look at him but her vision clouded and the floor tipped, coming at her. In that moment, time expanded, and she was a kid again, lying in the back of the Buick, all three kids packed in like luggage, trying to get to sleep. She could smell the grog and fags and tuna sandwiches that clung to her dad and his clothes, and that worked its way through the whole car. Giorgio was pushing her. Why was he pushing her?

She put one hand on her belly, on her baby, *Oh my baby*, and the other flailed about uselessly. Time stretched further, and

Helen considered with wonder that in this moment, it was her left hand that reverted to being dominant and knew to protect her baby, that all those school years of having it strapped behind her back to train her right hand to hold a pen could not undo her left hand knowing what job to do. Her right hand still sought purchase. She needed something to hold onto. Just as she understood that Giorgio was steering her towards a chair, her searching hand connected, and it was only as he leapt back that she realised it had landed on his crotch. There was the sound of a bark, harsh and barbed: Antonio laughing. Helen sank into the chair and her head sank between her knees.

As her awareness gradually returned, the first thing she noticed was how unyielding the wooden arms of the chair felt as she gripped them. She raised her head and saw that Francesca had left the room, and Giorgio and Antonio were staring at her.

Outside, it was drizzling. She hadn't brought a coat. The drizzle turned to rain as Helen made her way home. Fat drops landed on her as she passed under the Melaleuca tree in the Laus' front yard. The railway-sleeper steps next to the driveway turned slippery in the wet, so she took her time.

She was soaked through by the time she got to her house. Relieved to be finally home, safe, Helen took the inside stairs two at a time, and on the last, turned her ankle in her boot. Her ridiculous, too big, too high, coloured-in boots. She wept as she unlaced them, intoning, *We're OK, little bean, we're OK, little bean,* like a prayer.

Why, when she had done nothing wrong that she could put her finger on, was she the one left feeling ashamed? Not one of those Mariettis had a skerrick of shame about how they had behaved, no compunction whatsoever about the power they had over her feelings.

That night, Helen took two hot-water bottles to bed. In the dead of night, while Duncan breathed heavily, she clutched the blankets to her chin and felt a coming-away, a departure. She knew before she checked for blood. It took eight days for the miscarriage to be complete. She got sepsis and had to take a course of antibiotics that gave her thrush.

Helen blamed the Italians for all of it.

Duncan leapt from his chair and hollered. A wicket, then. No, not a wicket. Australia was batting. A half-century for Allan Border.

'I wonder what the family will do,' said Helen. 'If they'll come back.'

'Who?' said Duncan.

'The Mariettis.'

Helen couldn't understand why they'd bothered to move to Australia at all, since they constantly flitted back and forth between Canberra and Rome, and Giorgio was the only one who had a job here. She suspected it was mostly to show they could afford all those plane tickets. Only Antonio had seemed to make an effort to settle, to stay behind whenever the rest of the family tagged along on Giorgio's work trips.

'They're coming back this week,' said Duncan. 'Not sure what day yet. Depends on flights.'

'How do you know that?' And why hadn't he told her before?

'Phoned 'em. While you were over the road. Thought I should. I spoke with Giorgio.'

'How much was that? International call, not just long distance. And during the day too?'

'Can't say cost was my major consideration. Jeez, Helen, their boy's missing and come to grief.'

'Of course,' said Helen. What was Duncan doing with their phone number in Italy? 'How are they?'

'How do you think?' Duncan hung onto the back of his neck with both hands, contemplating the impossible. 'Actually, he sounded more angry than anything else. I'm so glad I didn't have to break the news to him. They'd already had a call from the police. You know, it was interesting. The police asked him about Antonio's state of mind. Not sure what they might have been implying by that. Anyway, Giorgio said Antonio had phoned him yesterday before the working bee, morning our time, about midnight in Rome. Giorgio put him off because he was tired. Antonio said he had something to tell them and would phone again after the working bee.'

'What was it?'

'Well, that's the thing,' said Duncan. 'They don't know. Now it looks like they never will. He didn't phone back. Giorgio says he knows in his heart Antonio is dead.'

'I refuse to believe it,' said Helen. 'Plenty of people live perfectly adequate lives with a missing limb.'

'I don't think you're considering—'

'Richard said we should hope for the best and I agree with him. The alternative is too awful to think about. Presumed dead is not the same as *dead* dead.'

A few minutes later, Duncan said, 'Oh, I nearly forgot. Giorgio also said the police told him how they know it was Antonio's foot. Joe identified it. It was the foot with the birthmark on it.'

'That's so strange,' said Helen.

'Not really. It was such a big birthmark. Any one of us would have recognised it.'

'No, I mean it's strange Joe kept quiet about it earlier on the island. Don't you think that's strange? That we were all talking about it and he didn't even mention that he'd seen the foot and identified it?'

'I wouldn't read too much into it. Joe's not keen on crowds at the best of times.'

Regardless, Helen thought it wasn't fair for some people on Warrah Place to withhold information from others. Everyone was shaken. Everyone was scared. Everyone had to cope with not knowing what was going to happen next. 'I wish I knew what Antonio wanted to tell his parents,' she said. 'It's really going to bug me now.'

'Whatever it was, Giorgio said Antonio sounded happy. He was that cut up about it when he told me. Listening to him, the injustice of losing his boy and the pain of it, made me think. I'm so lucky to have you and Tam.' Duncan moved closer, put his hand on Helen's shoulder and looked searchingly into her face. 'We're good, us three, aren't we? Maybe we're all we—'

Fortunately, there was a knock on the door.

Some beetles get into ants' nests through nefarious means — that means trickery. They feed by sucking the juice out of young ants when they are still larvae and can't defend themselves.

12

Tammy's legs were seizing up, stuck in her crouching spot, but it was nothing she couldn't handle. An accomplished watcher had to put up with these things and it had paid off. Now she knew that Antonio had something important to tell his dad. And that Joe had seen Antonio's foot with his own eyes. The knock on the door prevented her from returning to her journal to mull things over. It was a knock that meant business, the kind that didn't want to wait.

Peggy blustered in, waving a newspaper.

'Newspaper!' she said, unnecessarily. She huffed and wheezed, out of puff from the short trip across the island and up the drive-way. 'Yesterday's!' She thrust an open page in front of Tammy's mum and dad. 'There!'

Three heads huddled over the paper. Their hunched backs looked like beetles.

'Grassfires,' said Tammy's dad. 'No wonder in this heat. Bit of a worry, though.'

'Homicide,' said Tammy's mum. Her hand went to her throat. 'Heavens to Betsy!'

'No, not that,' said Peggy, folding down the paper and tutting.

'That was just a bank robber shot by police. There. The pigs. Wild ones!'

'Wild pigs?' said Tammy's mum. 'In Canberra?'

Peggy folded her arms smugly while Tammy's dad peered more closely at the paper, then straightened.

'But we're not anywhere near where the pigs were seen,' he said. 'And the ranger got rid of them. We all saw Antonio alive after that.'

'So?' said Peggy. 'The pigs have done heaps of damage. That must mean there's loads of them. All over the place.' This appeared to thrill her. 'You know how big they can get, right?'

'Surely you don't think a pig . . . *ate* him?' Tammy's mum winced as she spoke and Peggy gave a noncommittal gesture to let the possibility stand.

'I dunno,' said Tammy's dad. 'Sounds a bit far-fetched. I reckon the police will find the rest of Antonio's body any minute now. Not sure it does us much good to speculate in the meantime.'

'Richard said we shouldn't jump to conclusions,' said Tammy's mum.

'Anyway Peggy,' continued Tammy's dad, 'outside earlier, it sounded like you were accusing Cecil.'

'Like I said, one wild pig or another.' This seemed to tickle Peggy, and she started cackling, which soon turned into coughing.

'Are the news people still outside?' asked Tammy's mum. 'I don't like them being here. It's not respectful.'

'They won't hang around long,' said Tammy's dad. 'It'll be news for a day, then they'll move on.'

When she'd recovered from her coughing fit, Peggy said, 'Didn't see anyone. By the way, don't tell Cecil about the pigs. I want to see his face when he realises he's the last to know.' She fanned her face with the folded newspaper. 'Cor, it's hot in here. This room really does catch the sun, doesn't it? Who shall I go to next? I haven't seen Naomi today.'

'I wouldn't,' said Tammy's mum.

'Why's that then?'

'Not sure she's up for a visit. Bit under the weather, you know, bad dose of morning sickness.'

'That so? Well, she won't mind me. I'll just go for a little look-see.' Peggy had moved closer to Tammy's spot, and now she turned, craning her neck to fix Tammy in her sights. 'I see you, missy.' She was close enough for Tammy to see her lipstick bleeding, her drawn-on eyebrows, and the look that pinned Tammy to the spot. 'Skulking about in your own house. Well! Watch out for pigs! Hooroo.'

Tammy decided there and then to discount Peggy's wild pig theory, not least because, if proved true, Peggy would get the credit for it.

When she went back to her room, she found Colin fast asleep on the spare bed in a different frock: floral with a lace collar and ruffled hem. He was surrounded by a mismatch of fabrics and colours and patterns. His head was haloed by a soft quilted dressing gown in the palest blue, made even paler by multiple washes. Were it not for the sneakers on his feet, he would have looked like the angel that goes on top of the Christmas tree.

Imagine if anyone from school saw her hanging out with Colin looking like that. He was a pitiful stand-in for a friend her own age, not that she had any candidates clamouring for that spot. Simone Bunner had seen to that. Tammy felt humiliated by getting sprung spying by Peggy. In a particularly unfair twist, it summoned memories of all the humiliations she'd suffered last year, lurching from one to the next like a marionette on tight strings. It had all kicked off during the last summer holidays, before Antonio arrived, before Narelle turned against her.

On a lazy day that was otherwise unremarkable, Tammy went over to Narelle's house. They'd been best friends long enough for Narelle to be woven into Tammy's sense of self. Privately, they called themselves the Warrah Warriors; invincible to the nth degree. Others called them the dynamic duo; two peas in a pod; double trouble. It was impossible to think of one without the other.

Tammy had new jeans. She was eleven and was growing hips. *Womanly*, Peggy had whispered to Tammy's mum, loudly enough for Tammy to hear. The word scared the crappers out of Tammy.

She climbed over the fence into the Laus' back yard, kept low and close to the cover of oleanders, then over the next fence into Narelle's back yard. The Italian House didn't look so foreboding from the back.

'Hi-le-gi Na-le-ga re-le-gelle. I-le-git's me-le-ge,' Tammy called in their shared language that fooled no one but bound them to each other. She heard movement from inside the room. There was a small tear the size of a child's finger in the screen on Narelle's window. In a well-practised manoeuvre, Tammy flicked the inside latch and the screen swung free.

Curiously, there was no one there. She climbed through. But the hairs on the back of Tammy's neck stood to attention. She didn't like pranks and it wasn't like Narelle to pull one—

A giggle came from under the bed, followed by shushing. It wasn't Narelle's giggle, which Tammy knew inside out. The source of the giggle slithered out on her belly and stood up, followed by Narelle, who smoothed down her T-shirt and looked at the floor.

'This is Simone Bunner and she's just moved to Canberra and her mum works with my mum and she's got a sister starting Year Nine and Simone's going to be in our year at school isn't that great?' said Narelle all in one breath.

'I'm Tammy Lanahan,' said Tammy. Should she shake hands? She got hers halfway to Simone before she changed her mind and wiped it on her jeans instead.

Simone looked at Tammy and chewed gum with her mouth

open. Tammy knew she was being assessed and not coming up to scratch.

'I know who you are, Tammy Lanahan.'

'Simone brought nail varnish.' Narelle laughed nervously.

'Cool,' said Tammy.

Tammy didn't know anything about nail varnish. Her mum didn't wear it. It was exotic; something for other people.

'Shame,' said Simone. 'There's only enough for the two of us.' She stood shoulder to shoulder with Narelle.

Five bottles of varnish sat on Narelle's desk, different shapes and brands, in shades of brown and pink and red.

'Besides,' continued Simone, picking up one of Tammy's hands and inspecting it. 'I hardly think you'd want to draw attention to chewed fingernails. My mum says it's a filthy habit. What do you think, Tammy?'

Tammy's skin burned where Simone was touching it, but she didn't dare move. She stood there stupidly, unable to think of a thing to say. She looked at Narelle, but she didn't say anything either.

'Oh my *godfather*,' Simone eventually said in exasperation, dropping Tammy's hand like it was lava. 'And Narelle said you were *clever*. I'll make it easy for you, shall I? It's time for you to go now. Ta-ta. Off you pop.' She shooed Tammy towards the window with a flick of her wrist.

Tammy turned, with shame-slapped cheeks, and climbed back out of the window to a reverberating cacophony of silence. On the way, the hem of her jeans, her lovely new flares, caught on the latch, and she had to reach back in, trying desperately to free it, trying desperately not to tear it, trying desperately not to fall while hopping on one leg, and trying desperately not to cry.

'Leave her,' Simone told Narelle. 'She's just putting it on because she doesn't want to go. Pathetic, really.'

From then on, things got steadily worse.

★

There were four weeks left until school started. Narelle was gone from Warrah Place, gone from school and gone from Canberra. Simone was not. There wasn't enough time for Tammy to grow a new personality and fix everything Simone hated about her. But what if she cracked the case of what happened to Antonio and his foot? That would set her up in prime position and Tammy knew exactly what would happen then: Tammy would be in and Simone would be out.

Tammy opened her desk drawer next to Colin's sleeping face and got out Smurfette. How inspired to take it in the first place!

Outside, there was a slick of oil where the news van had been, a swirl of rainbow metallic colours in it. A swell of hot, dry breeze made the police tape flap and crackle, and then the gust died down and the tape hung limply. After the noise and cluster of people on the island earlier, it was deathly quiet, the street deserted, but Tammy still felt watched. She kept her head down and walked purposefully, as though she were doing what she was meant to.

In Sheree's back yard, there were bits of broken plastic in primary colours scattered all over the place. There was a half-deflated space hopper, its lopsided smile a creepy grimace. A bucket filled with dirt. A red lilo. A pile of dog turds, bleached white. They didn't even have a dog. And there, face down on the grass, a doll, naked, her bum shiny and poking up in the air, her arms ripped off.

Tammy knocked on the screen door before she could chicken out.

'Come in,' called Sheree.

Tammy found Sheree on her hands and knees in the kitchen wiping up baked beans from the floor. She groaned as she got to her feet.

'These bloody kids are going to be the death of me,' she said. 'Now. What can I do you for?'

Tammy presented Smurfette on an extended hand. 'This ended up at our house. I don't know how. Must have been Colin.'

'Ta, love. Can't say we missed it. We've got so much crap around here.'

'Maybe your kids should look after their stuff better,' said Tammy.

'You're telling me!'

Tammy was about to launch into questioning Sheree about where she was last night, say, between the end of the working bee and dawn, when she saw something on the floor that made her stop in her tracks, mouth hanging open. How had she not spotted them when she came in? It must be because there was so much stuff lying around.

'What are you doing with those?' she said. It was a pair of shoes, like thongs, but stylish, with thick, dark tanned leather straps. They were Antonio's, as familiar to Tammy as if they were her own. He'd been wearing them all summer.

Sheree laughed in an embarrassed way. She went to pick them up and then thought better of it.

'Oh, those,' she said, standing in front of them. 'You know how it is. Everyone takes their shoes off when it's hot. They can end up anywhere.'

Even Sheree must have known it was an unsatisfactory – and suspicious – answer, because she nudged Tammy out of the door.

'How long have they been here?' said Tammy.

'Best get on home, pet,' said Sheree. 'Your mum'll start to worry.'

'Did *he* leave them here or someone else?'

'Bye now.'

A buzz of excitement rose in Tammy as Sheree closed the door on her. She'd caught Sheree red-handed with Antonio's shoes. She wasn't sure what it meant yet, but Sheree's guilty face told her it was sure as heck worth finding out.

The Canberra Courier

Monday, 8 January 1979

Severed Foot Leads To Murder Investigation

A severed foot was discovered by bushwalkers on the outskirts of Canberra early yesterday morning. Police have revealed that the foot belonged to Mr Antonio Marietti, 19, of Warrah Place.

A positive identification was made by Mr Marietti's neighbour, Mr Josip Pavlović, by way of a distinctive birthmark on the foot in the shape of a number eight. Mr Pavlović declined to comment or explain why he was in the vicinity at the time Mr Marietti's foot was discovered.

Mr Marietti was last sighted on the evening of Saturday, 6 January, at a church event and did not return to his home afterwards as expected. Until today, the police had declared that Mr Marietti was missing, presumed dead, but we can now report that an active murder investigation has been opened.

'Without a body, it's always a delicate decision about when to open a murder investigation,' Detective Sergeant Mark Leagrove told reporters. 'But our forensics team were quick off the mark in establishing that the foot was severed post mortem. We know that Mr Marietti is deceased, and the evidence we have so far points to murder.'

Several entrances to the hills have been cordoned off and the public have been asked to keep away while the police conduct searches for a body. 'I know there will be public interest in what has occurred, but we are asking the public to stay away. It is imperative that we recover

Mr Marietti's body quickly. We don't want our work to be hampered by potential crime scenes being interfered with, even unintentionally.'

Another of Mr Marietti's neighbours, Miss Sheree Williams, told reporters, 'The police said not to worry but how can we not? I've got kids. I never really knew Antonio, not more than to say "hi" to in passing, but everyone seemed to like him. Who could do this to him?' Struggling with her emotions, she added, 'I just can't believe it. What's this place coming to?'

ACT Police are appealing to members of the public with information to come forward.

13

Five Months Before The Murder

Sunday, 6 August 1978

Duncan crouched low by a rhododendron bush on the edge of his property and felt the ground. There had been a heavy frost and the earth was hard, but not frozen. This spot would do.

Mist clung to the surrounding hills, making them seem larger than they were. It was early and the weak sun would dissolve the mist later, but for now, Duncan felt the dampness close in on him and was glad.

It had been four weeks since Helen's last miscarriage. Blaming the Mariettis for it made a change from blaming herself, and Duncan was ashamed to admit he would rather they be blamed than him, but Helen's bitterness was hard to take, wherever it was directed. Not that he could say so. His job was to support Helen no matter what, and he was good at it. But who would have thought that biting your tongue, nodding your head, gentle murmurs of agreement, would require so much effort? He was tired.

This here was just for Duncan. Something he needed for himself. He leant the shovel against the bush and took the booties from his coat pocket. Knitted in white wool, laced with shiny satin ribbons. Tiny. Dainty. Unnecessary. Duncan brought them to his face and smelt them. He kissed the toe of each one.

A memento from each miscarriage was dotted around the garden and Duncan knew each spot by heart. In the early days, he would think each time was the last, that there would be a baby when they tried again. Now, he was already casting his mind around for other suitable spots. It felt like a betrayal; of Helen and of the babies – his children – he had stopped believing in. He just didn't think he could handle it anymore: the hope. His heart couldn't take the hope.

Duncan laid the booties on a hanky on the ground to keep them clean and began to dig. The shovel clanked and scraped against small stones. It bit into compacted earth. It was hard going and Duncan had to put his back into it.

The figure emerging from the mist was upon him before Duncan noticed him approaching.

'Jesus.' Duncan straightened and clutched at his chest. 'Where did you come from?'

'Sorry,' said Antonio. 'I called out, but I don't think you heard.' He told Duncan he'd been out walking in the hills.

'On your own?'

Antonio avoided eye contact. 'I'm used to it.'

Duncan followed Antonio's gaze to the booties on the ground. 'It's symbolic,' he said. 'For the loss. Poor little mite.' He felt himself choking on sadness. 'A miscarriage,' he added, in case there was any confusion.

'Is your wife joining you?'

Duncan shook his head. 'She doesn't know. She has enough on her plate.' He started to dig again. Antonio stood to one side with his hands in his pockets. 'You don't have to stay for this,' Duncan said over his shoulder.

'I don't mind,' said Antonio. 'If you don't mind.'

Duncan was surprised to find that not only did he not mind,

but he was glad of the company. Having a witness to his grief intensified it, but in a way that felt right and proper. His shoulders heaved with the pain. He stabbed blindly at the ground with the shovel, his face streaked with tears, until Antonio's hand on his own stilled him, stilled the shovel.

Antonio took over the digging while Duncan collected himself.

'You're a good lad,' said Duncan. He hadn't expected that having someone here would make him feel that his loss mattered too.

'Not really,' said Antonio, facing away.

Duncan wrapped the booties in the hanky and placed them in the hole, and, together, he and Antonio scooped earth over them with their hands, smoothing it over and brushing away any larger stones.

'Thank you,' said Duncan, but Antonio was already on his way home. He hunched over a cigarette to light it as he walked.

The next day, Duncan returned to the rhododendron bush for a visit. A small cross, symmetrical and straight, whittled from pine, its join secured with twine, had been pushed into the mound of earth.

14

Two Days After The Murder

Monday, 8 January 1979

A fly was trapped in the room. Incessant buzzing. And now another one. Twice the frenzy. Butting heads against the window, each other, the inside of Naomi's skull.

The flip of minutes on the clock radio.

Her own throat swallowing.

Other sounds: a car door, its engine, tyres on the road; the postie's motorbike: stop, start, surge, stop; birds: gentle cooing, angry remonstrations, a kookaburra in fits; Sheree yelling at her kids; a knock on the door, two knocks, more.

What day was it?

Why couldn't she sleep?

It must be daytime. Cracks of light from behind the curtain hurt. Naomi pushed a finger onto one puffy eyelid. It hurt more. She pushed harder, traced the arc of pain along her eyebrow.

Something smelt off.

There was a cup of tea on her bedside table. And a gingernut. Must have been Sheree. The tea was pale, a film on the surface. Naomi stuffed the biscuit into her mouth.

Had Sheree put Colin to bed? When?

She supposed Colin was with Helen now. She supposed he was all right. She supposed she ought to be grateful. *Helen*, though. Sanctimonious cow.

Helen didn't know how good she had it. A husband who cared about what she wanted. A husband who *only* cared about what she wanted. What Naomi wouldn't give . . . If Naomi had that, she wouldn't have had to lie. A tower of lies too high to stay standing.

She was fragmenting, parts of her becoming untethered. Disintegrating. She observed it all dispassionately. If she was going to fall apart, she might as well go the whole hog.

You've always veered towards histrionics. Her mum's voice. Untrue and unfair. Naomi never gave voice to the vast majority of what she felt. She didn't want to think about her mum.

Naomi rolled over. It only mildly alarmed her when she understood that the foul smell was coming from her. Her nightie was stiff, crusted under her armpits and down her front.

If Richard were here, he would lead her, maybe carry her, to the bathroom and wash her. It was something he'd done before; she had a memory of it. But Richard wasn't here.

Naomi slithered out of bed and onto the floor. Her bones were mush.

Her nightie had ridden up. Naomi held onto her thighs, raked her nails down them in raised red lines. She pulled her skin taut, white, then let it go.

The carpet was 100 per cent polyester, 50 per cent off. Not cream or off-white, but white-white. Pure white. A ridiculous buy for a couple with a child. She'd been flushed with love. Giddy playing house. She remembered Richard rolling his eyes when she said she wanted it. So, there was another memory. If she could find more, she might be able to patchwork herself together again.

Still the flies buzzed.

The wardrobe door was open. Naomi looked in the mirror, but not at her own eyes. She fixed on a spot over her shoulder, an echo of a face already fading from view.

'I hate you,' she said. 'I hate you, I hate you, I hate you.'

It was true. By the end, she hated him. But only after he hated her first. And only because she loved him so much.

The roiling returned, her stomach writhing and bucking.

Oh God.

She'd hated Antonio at the beginning too. The first thing she noticed about him was his hair. He had a marcel wave that she hoped was accidental but thought was probably not. That should have been her first warning sign: what business was it of hers to have hopes about his hair?

Leslie from next door brought him over one cold and wet Monday towards the end of July. Colin was at school. There had been high winds the night before and a deluge of rain, bloated drops that pelted down and made a racket on the roof. The lawn was covered with leaf litter and fallen branches. The gutters were clogged. Richard had arranged for Leslie, a landscape gardener, to do odd jobs for Naomi whenever he was away. But now Leslie wanted to share the load. Or so he said. More like, his kind heart wanted to give a leg-up to the Italian kid just arrived on Warrah Place; get him started on a bit of work.

'You don't mind, do you?' said Leslie. 'Better than an old duffer like me.' He waved to Peggy who was pretending not to watch from their back deck next door.

Naomi did mind. The kid had a churlish, superior look about him.

Antonio wore a black turtleneck under an old-fashioned suit that was too big for him. He carried himself loosely and leant heavily on one hip in a cocky slouch. He took a pencil that was tucked behind his ear and flicked it back and forth between his fingers casually. It might have been an impatient or nervous gesture; it was impossible to tell. His fingers were long, thin and delicate, almost feminine. Nothing like Richard's. When he returned the pencil to his ear and lifted his hands to light a cigarette, Naomi noticed his slim wrists, tanned by another sun.

Leslie was explaining the sorts of jobs he did. 'Just ask Naomi. She'll tell you what needs doing.'

'The instructions come from her?' said Antonio, and Naomi had no idea if he was seeking clarity or being disparaging. Her hackles raised.

Leslie chuckled. 'Richard likes her to be well looked after.'

Would it kill either of them to acknowledge that she was standing right there? 'My husband is away a lot,' she said. God, why did she feel the need to explain herself? Richard would know what to say, how to handle this hothead. But Richard was away for three months this time and wouldn't be back until October. She'd have to work out how to handle Antonio on her own.

'Why would he keep leaving you?' said Antonio, like it was her fault; something she had coming to her.

'It's his job.'

'It's his job to leave you?' he said with half a smile. 'Some job.'

Naomi felt herself being toyed with and there was nothing she could do to prevent it. He looked her over lazily, all over, his expression inscrutable. Had she looked away sooner, she might have missed it: the flicker of uncertainty in his eyes; a chink in his façade.

He turned away from Naomi and gave Leslie a grin, hooking his arm up and over Leslie's big shoulder. 'Thursday,' he said. 'I'll come Thursday. Fix that.' He pointed to the fence that had nothing wrong with it.

'But the guttering,' said Naomi.

He was already walking away.

She hated him for his insolence. She hated him for making her feel old for caring about insolence. She hated his stupid hair, his stupid suit, his stupid long, impossible eyelashes, his stupid honeyed voice. More than anything else, though, it was that look of uncertainty, a moment of indecision, that her mind kept returning to. It spoke of something else beneath the surface. That what you see is not all that you get.

Later, much later, Naomi would wonder if she knew then. Knew that she stood on a brink; that a path lay before her, and her toe was already hovering over the line.

15

Guangyu had finished work and was driving home at lunchtime as usual. Today's *Canberra Courier* lay on the passenger seat, opened to the grainy picture of Antonio. The police still hadn't visited the Lau household again, at least not when she was at home and not that Jia Li had told her. As Guangyu ate her breakfast that morning, she could see police searchers still dotted over the hills. Maybe they'd been at it all night. Had they found a body yet? The newspaper said what Guangyu had felt must be true from the start: Antonio had been murdered. But seeing it in print hadn't helped her decide if she should talk to the police after all.

It was a twenty-six-minute drive from work to home, but if Guangyu drove slowly, she could eke it out to thirty, maybe more if the lights were in her favour. Those were precious moments of solitude. The city had not come to a standstill as it should have. The continuation of normal routines was as disturbing as the dismembered foot itself. What other atrocities might be allowed to happen if there was no great drama over this one?

Guangyu yawned despite her worries. Last night, her wakefulness had been interspersed with dreams about finding Jennifer's severed foot in the strangest places: in her bed, in the soup pot, in the shower – wherever her dream-self turned, there it was. She couldn't shake the image, even during daylight hours. Maybe she should book Jennifer a ticket to go to China for the rest of the summer. She could tell Jennifer it would do her good to connect with her grandmother, her heritage. Things weren't right on Warrah Place, and Guangyu's instinct to protect her daughter, fierce at any time, had never been stronger. At the same time, she didn't think she could bear to be apart from Jennifer, to have to wonder at such a distance if she was all right. Guangyu felt all at sea.

Squinting into the glare, she almost missed seeing Ursula on the footpath ahead, weighed down by a string bag that knocked against her leg as she walked, throwing her off balance. She had no hat. Everything about her drooped. Foolish to be out at this time of day. It was pushing forty degrees. Guangyu tussled with indecision. No. She wouldn't stop. It was Ursula's choice to be out and Guangyu's to be alone. She didn't need the aggravation. But then she saw an echo of Jennifer in Ursula's posture, and her heart cracked open. The lowered head with the tucked-in chin. The stilted gait: every step an apology, an attempt to blend into the background.

Guangyu pulled over.

'Do you need my help, Mrs Lau?' said Ursula, clearly and slowly, peering through the window.

Guangyu regretted stopping. 'Get in.' She nodded at the door and tossed the paper into the back.

'Ah. You're offering me a lift.' Ursula put her bag in the back-seat and herself in the front next to Guangyu, while Guangyu tapped the steering wheel and checked her mirrors. 'This is very kind of you. I think I made a mistake, walking during the height of the day. I normally get a bus from work, you see, but, well, I thought a bit of a walk might do me good. Clear my head. That was the idea. I can see it was stupid now. Stupid . . .' she said again, trailing off. Ursula's fingers fussed with her skirt, her handbag, her hair, the cross on her necklace. She pushed her spectacles up the bridge of her nose. Perpetual motion. 'It's difficult because I find that when I'm inside, I'm longing to be out, and once I'm outside, I immediately want to seek refuge inside. It's ridiculous, always wanting what I haven't got. Which do you prefer, outside or in? No, don't answer that. It's a stupid question.' Ursula flounced in her seat, frustrated with herself.

Guangyu didn't know what to say. Such theatrics. She indicated and pulled away from the kerb. The traffic was light, pedestrians scarce. Sensible people weren't out on hot streets at this time of day.

Ursula waved a hand towards the newspaper on the backseat. 'I read that too. At work this morning. Everyone was talking about it. I didn't dare say it was our street.' To Guangyu's ear *our street* implied an intimacy, a sense of community, that she didn't feel. 'Murder is such an ominous word, isn't it? I suppose it has to be for such a dreadful thing. I hope we can have a funeral soon. It feels too awful not to be able to say goodbye. Deb— well, all of us need that, I think. We're all in limbo until we know his body's been found and we can have a funeral. I keep feeling scared I'll come across it. His body. That's terrible, isn't it? To feel frightened of finding it when everyone wants it found?'

'I wouldn't mind finding it,' said Guangyu, 'if it meant this awful business was over. I'm more frightened of a killer than a dead body.'

'Gosh, yes, you're right. That's so frightening I've blocked myself from thinking about it. You're very brave. I'm not. I wish I was, but everything scares me. Would you believe even the police scare me?' Ursula immediately pressed her lips together, like she regretted saying so much. Perhaps she realised how ridiculous it sounded to be afraid of the police when she lived with Lydia. But Guangyu didn't point this out or press her further. She didn't want to be backed into disclosing her own reason for being frightened of the police.

'I work part-time at the library,' Ursula went on, rescuing them both with her prattle. 'I'd like more hours, but, well, so would everyone else.' Guangyu didn't know that about Ursula. She was about to tell Ursula about her work as a vet, about wanting more hours too, but Ursula carried on: 'You have a teenage daughter, don't you?' Yes, she did, but Guangyu didn't get a chance to say so. 'They're such an enormous worry, don't you think?' Again, Ursula didn't pause. 'I fret about my niece, Debbie. Her parents — my brother and his wife — have given up on her because she went off the rails a bit. They say she's a bad egg, but I can't think that's right. No one's a lost cause, and Debbie's a lovely girl — she just needs to find her way again. Can you give me some tips? For dealing with teenage girls?'

This time Ursula waited for an answer, but Guangyu didn't have one. 'I haven't a clue,' she said. 'I wish I did.'

Ursula nodded to the backseat again. 'I brought Debbie a stack of books from the library. Classics. *Tess of the d'Urbervilles*, *Anna Karenina*, *Great Expectations*, et cetera. The sort of thing that helps give perspective on one's life. Besides, you can't go wrong with the classics for general self-improvement.'

They passed a bus shelter, concrete and orange plastic, and a concertina bus, serpentine, also orange, a gaudy approximation of the rich ochre of this vast land. Guangyu was tempted to turf out Ursula at the bus stop and continue on her way in peace. But Ursula seemed to have run out of things to say, thank goodness, so on they went.

As they drove, Guangyu wondered if Ursula saw Canberra in the same way she did. A city of embassies, wide roads, an artificial lake, swathes of greenery, squat houses, sleek modern churches for the streamlined forgiveness of sins. Buildings in the brutalist style loomed large, each a standalone piece, so unlike

Hong Kong with its collage of rectangles, its clamour of straight lines and corners, its high-rises and mountains closing in. Water as reprieve. Seasonal cherry blossom to soften. In Canberra, space was swollen, with room for the eye to roam. Smells seeped leisurely from a distance. Guangyu sometimes felt cast adrift in the expanse. There was also something odd about living in a designed city among people who hadn't called this land home for generations on end. It made their lives, their stories, at once more precarious and more urgent without centuries of the land telling them who they were. It had been a long time since a place had known Guangyu as its own.

'It's very . . . big here,' said Guangyu. She wasn't making sense. She didn't know what she wanted to say.

'Is your country not big too?' said Ursula.

Irritation flooded Guangyu in a hot flush. Ursula's spectacles were dirty – how could she see through those greasy smears? It irked Guangyu to have to look at them.

They had stopped at the lights and a car behind them honked. Guangyu jumped, noticed the traffic moving around them and hurriedly put the car into first. Someone gave her the finger as he drove past and Ursula tutted.

'Poor Antonio,' Ursula began again. 'It sharpens the mind, don't you think, this business of murder? No, that's not it. More that it does away with superfluous things, petty things. So you're left with the things that matter.'

Ursula wasn't finished. 'I grew up in the country. I keep thinking back to when I was a kid on the farm, and how free I felt. And how long it's been since I felt free. Riding my bike down by the creek, bumping over tree roots, clanking my teeth. Legs outstretched when I'd got a bit of speed up. Or swimming in the dam. My body feeling at ease in swimmers. Oh, goodness me. I can remember it now, aeons ago, not feeling self-conscious about my body. We had a rope swing tied to a tree. Legs tucked, knees to nose, dive bombs. Yabbie nips. Sludge on the dam bed. We flicked it from our toes at each other and up our own backs. Dried off against the water tank, hot corrugated iron on our skin. Climbed onto the back of the ute when we stayed out too long and Dad came to get us after milking time.' Her tone was light yet reverent, full of gladness, like she was reciting a list of treasures, but turned pensive when she said, 'I hope Antonio had a happy life, short as it was. I keep thinking about growing up and all the choices we have to make and the costs they incur. I hope Antonio stayed free from all that.'

It was a curious thing, thought Guangyu, how people sometimes felt safer saying things to an outsider, to someone who didn't mean anything to them. It wasn't the first time it had happened since Guangyu moved to Australia; people either shared too much or nothing at all.

They went on in silence while Guangyu sifted her many thoughts into some sort of order. Unexpectedly, Ursula's elastic personal boundaries had the effect of loosening rather than tightening Guangyu's.

'When I was little,' she began, 'I was with my grandmother in our village and we were standing outside our neighbour's house, my hand in hers. My grandmother is very forthright. Always has a lot to say.' Where was she going with this? Ah, yes. 'And this neighbour gave me a pin. I can picture it exactly. A small enamel pin of a swallow in flight. I don't remember why she gave it to me, maybe no reason at all, but it was very special to me and I was overcome with feeling important. I held my thank-you ready, waiting to give it, knowing my place and that I mustn't interrupt. But before I could say it, my grandmother scolded me and yanked hard on my arm and apologised for my rudeness because I hadn't said thank you.' Guangyu's throat thickened. 'I think that's the first time I remember not feeling free like you described.'

'Goodness me,' said Ursula, and Guangyu was grateful for

it because it felt entirely the correct thing to say, and because Guangyu wanted to stop talking about it now.

'That village,' said Ursula. 'Is that where you're from?'

'I don't know where I'm from,' said Guangyu. 'Crazy, huh?' There was a complicated intersection and Guangyu had to concentrate, get in the right lane. 'It depends who you ask. My husband would say I am a Hongkonger, one hundred per cent. To his mother, I will never be Hongkonger enough. My mother would say I am still a Guangdong Province village girl. To my grandmother, I might as well be Martian. I'm sorry. I'm not explaining well.'

'You're explaining perfectly,' said Ursula. 'And what would *you* say?'

Guangyu laughed. 'I don't know.' The laugh dried up abruptly and she felt close to tears. Bloody hormones. And as soon as she thought that, another flush was upon her. A pang of longing for the landscape of her childhood was matched by a pang of guilt for turning her back on it in an attempt to belong in Hong Kong, and to what end? She gripped the steering wheel more tightly. 'In this country, they say look ahead, get with it, the future's where it's at. They say new beginnings are for sale and everyone's buying.'

'Golly,' said Ursula. 'Are *you* buying?'

Guangyu sighed.

'My husband,' she said, 'he says the Australian way of life is ours for the taking. He got that off the radio. Expanding new horizons. New multiple-culture society and new friends. *Pfft*. Three years, and his only new friend is his camera, bloody *click-click* here, bloody *click-click* there.' Guangyu ought not to talk about Herman like this, but she was too hot to care and was discovering that telling the truth was like tugging on a string that kept unravelling. 'He's not expanding anything. He's tucked up tight as a sausage. And my daughter, Jennifer—'

121

'Yes, tell me about Jennifer. She's a good girl, yes? Quiet.'

'Maybe quiet to you. At home she is Little Miss Chat-back.' Guangyu hunched closer to the steering wheel, paused at a T-junction; she'd momentarily forgotten the way home. She took a right turn. 'I worry for her. She says she sticks out too much, that there's nowhere to hide. But why should a girl of fifteen want to hide? She should be living life! But people look and she doesn't like the looking. Sometimes they say things.'

'She wants to hide?'

'Tries to.'

They stopped at a red light behind a panel van. Guangyu liked a stop-start journey. It wasn't so bad to have company, not so bad to have extra time with Ursula. She wiped sweat from her face with her hand. 'But I feel the opposite,' she said. It suddenly seemed vital to say that she wasn't the same, vital that she be understood. 'I feel hidden. Invisible. And I'm tired of it. It's not what I want. Even when people look at me, they see something else, something they've decided I am. It's not me they see.'

Said out loud, it sounded absurd, an indulgence. But in private it made sense: Guangyu felt lousy with invisibility. For the whole of her marriage, she had tried to forget she was Chinese and be a Hongkonger instead. Was she now doing the same thing in Australia? Had trying to fit in made her turn her back on who she was? Guangyu wished the lights would change so she could concentrate on driving. The van in front was dirty. Someone ought to clean it.

'I'm sorry,' she said, embarrassed. 'I don't know why I said that. I shouldn't—'

'Stop. Yes. I mean, yes, you should have, because . . .' Ursula twisted in her seat to face Guangyu again. 'Because yes. *Yes.* That's it. What you said. That's it *exactly.*'

Guangyu looked at Ursula cautiously. Ursula leant her head

back against her headrest, her hands held limply in her lap. She was crying silently, allowing her tears to fall without wiping them away.

The traffic began to move. They would be home soon. Having said too much, Guangyu now fell silent.

When Ursula spoke again, it was with wonder: 'I thought nobody knew. I thought nobody else knew what it is – what it costs – to live in the world and not be seen.'

Then she laughed, a singular peal of delight that startled Guangyu. But Guangyu smiled, because Ursula hadn't thought she was talking nonsense. And then she brought her hand to her mouth and chuckled, because for the first time in a long time, she felt a little less alone. Ursula, of all people!

At first, they laughed haltingly; shy, sly glances setting one another off. The laughing surprised Guangyu, and it was the surprise of it, how it was unexpected, unlooked for, that made her laugh all the more, her shoulders getting involved too. Then they laughed uproariously, open-mouthed, until eventually all that remained was hiccups.

'I can't remember when I last laughed so much,' said Ursula.

Guangyu looked at Ursula's legs and her hands resting, relaxed, in her lap, and had an urge to touch her. A human touch would be nice. She hadn't known she'd missed it. Heat rose and she knew her face had reddened. Her breath came faster.

Ursula was watching her. A look of confusion passed over her face.

'I didn't expect this to happen,' mumbled Guangyu. 'You and me. It's nice.'

The confusion on Ursula's face deepened and developed into alarm.

'No,' said Guangyu quickly. 'Don't worry. I'm not being fresh. I didn't mean that. I don't want sex with you.' She didn't reach out a hand to reassure Ursula. She kept her hands to herself.

Ursula gasped. 'You know?' She shrank away, backing into the car door. 'Me and Lydia?'

Guangyu gave a curt nod.

'*How* do you know?'

'When you're on the outside, you see things. Sometimes it's a good view from there.' Guangyu sighed. 'It's the way you look at her. I used to look at Herman that way. At first, I thought maybe I was reading it wrong, that it was a cultural difference. But I've been here a while now and I don't think so. I think love looks like love, wherever you're from.'

'Is this a trick?' said Ursula. She was steely, guarded. 'Is that why you picked me up? To threaten me? Is it blackmail?' She clutched at the cross on her necklace.

All loveliness was undone in a moment.

'No,' said Guangyu. 'None of that.'

They turned into Warrah Place.

'Here, I think,' said Ursula, nodding for Guangyu to stop behind a news van and police car.

Guangyu understood. They'd already had enough drama on the street. As they passed the Italian House, they saw a cameraman and reporter talking to a policeman at the front door. Guangyu pulled into the kerb, out of view of the Italian House. There was nobody else around apart from two girls wearing matching terry-towelling dresses in Tammy's front garden. No, not two girls. It was Tammy and that unfortunate boy, Colin. And the cat. The two children were hunched over a book that Tammy was writing in.

Ursula made no move to get out of the car. 'Have I overreacted?' she said. 'I get scared very easily.'

Guangyu wanted to say as little as possible. 'I'm not wanting to hurt you.'

'Does everyone know?' said Ursula.

Guangyu shrugged. 'I don't know. Most of them are stupid. That's in your favour.'

Ursula snorted and Guangyu snuck a glance at her.

'And you won't tell?'

'Haven't so far.' As if she had anyone to tell.

Silence extended between them and filled the car, and still, Ursula made no move to get out. Guangyu made no move at all, fearful of Ursula's reaction, fearful of being misunderstood.

'It feels strange to call you Mrs Lau,' said Ursula. 'May I know your name? Or is that the wrong thing to say?'

'Gwen,' said Guangyu. It's what they called her at work. It was good enough, she supposed; easy. 'Call me Gwen.'

'Well, thank you for the lift, Gwen. I won't forget it. And, well . . .'

'Do you not drive?'

'I never learnt. I know, it's unheard of for a farm kid not to drive. It's just that I gave it a go and I was no good at it. And there was always one of the older kids around who wanted to. Now I'm too old. And I'm scared to try.'

'Huh,' said Guangyu. 'I'll teach you.' It was an impulsive offer, not thought through before it was made. Not like Guangyu at all.

'I'd be terrible at learning.'

'No matter. I am very good at teaching.'

Ursula grinned like a birthday girl at her own party. She opened the door but didn't get out. 'Wait. You said, "Call me Gwen." Is Gwen actually your name?'

'Close enough.'

'Can't I have your real name? Please?'

Guangyu hesitated. Ursula had no idea what she was asking, of course she didn't, but the effect – the dread, the burden, the indecision – was the same, regardless.

'Guangyu.'

'Gwarn You,' said Ursula. 'Is that it?'

'Almost. Pretty good, actually.'

'Don't give up on me,' said Ursula earnestly. 'I'll get better.'

Sometimes ants need to find a new nest. This could be because their old nest falls apart or is too small or they've eaten all the food or the neighbours turn nasty. Maybe it's because they're sick to death of everything being the same. Whatever the reason, when they need a new home, they send out scouts. The scouts have a long list of requirements. The scouts get to decide on a good spot for a new nest without having to get permission from the queen first.

16

Three Days After The Murder

Tuesday, 9 January 1979

It was Tuesday: two days since Antonio's foot was found and still no progress on the search for a body. It felt like they'd been searching for weeks rather than days. The heat had a way of doing that: making time sluggish as well as people. You could spend all day flaked out doing nothing, and still feel knackered at the end of it. Just ruminating could really take it out of you.

At breakfast, Tammy's dad said the police were going to take down the cordon to the hills and widen the search area.

'Does that mean we can go in the hills now?' asked Tammy.

'Absolutely not,' said her mum.

Tammy's dad said that Antonio's parents had come back late the night before and were spitting mad, like it was everyone on Warrah Place's fault he was dead.

'It's easy to turn the blame outwards rather than take a painful look inwards,' said Tammy's mum.

'Hells–bells, they've lost their boy,' said Tammy's dad, like everyone didn't already know that.

The Mariettis packed up a few things from the house and left again, whether to a hotel or all the way back to Italy, no one knew.

They didn't even stay one night in that house, leaving so quickly they forgot to turn the lights off. It was typical of Tammy's bad luck to be in bed and miss it all. Her only consolation was that nearly everyone else had missed it too. Cecil came over during breakfast to see what he could find out. He said it wasn't fair he didn't get a first-hand look at them. He reckoned it was the least he and the rest of the street deserved after copping the Mariettis' share of media attention and police questioning as well as their own. 'It's like being under a bloody microscope,' he said. Then he took Tammy's share of toast and she had to make some more.

Tammy might not have seen the Mariettis, but she did see the police knocking on Sheree's door yesterday, and she heard Sheree's voice louder than normal when she opened the door (and that was saying something), like she was trying to make up for being nervous, like she had something to hide.

Tammy had also seen Ursula and Mrs Lau in a car together yesterday, which might not have been that interesting in itself, but they'd stopped the car and then taken ages to get out. And *that* was decidedly weird. If they were friends who had plenty to chat about while sitting in a hot car going nowhere, they'd been keeping it secret. And all secrets were big business as far as Tammy was concerned.

Peggy turned up shortly after Cecil, seemingly to gloat over seeing the Mariettis. 'It's just like you, Cecil,' she said, 'to want to poke your nose into the family's grief to see if it's up to scratch.'

They both left after that since there wasn't any more gossip to squeeze out of anyone. Tammy wrote down everything they said.

Colin was the next to arrive, looking for breakfast.

'Jeez,' said Tammy's dad, giving Colin's hair an affectionate tussle, 'it's like Grand Central Station in here.'

Colin was becoming a sticky fixture. Tammy's mum called it *doing our bit*, but since it was Tammy he hung around like a bad smell, she was doing more bits than anyone else and thought it only reasonable that she should have a say about it. But no.

Tammy and Colin went to the Ant Behavioural Studies Centre. Tammy leant her back against the brick concealing Antonio's Zippo, but the truth was, it had lost its appeal now that Antonio wasn't alive enough to miss it. It was getting harder to remember all the details of what Antonio looked like, how his voice sounded, how he moved.

Colin found the hideout of click beetles and Tammy only found crummy old earwigs. She would have found the beetles eventually, and more quickly too if she didn't have to put up with Colin yabbering on.

'Why are we doing this part?' Colin held the lid with the beetles and earwigs on it while Tammy tried to dab their backs with a dot of Liquid Paper. He was being a sook about the beetles just because he'd found them. No one really cares about beetles. It was meant to be nail varnish instead of Liquid Paper, but she didn't have any. She bet Debbie had some. She'd been thinking about Debbie, wondering if you could catch being cool by being near someone cool, kind of like osmosis.

'Hold it still,' said Tammy. 'It was in a book.'

'Yeah, but why?'

'Look,' said Tammy. The little buggers wouldn't stay still. 'If you can't get on board with the scientific method, you can go home.'

That shut him up.

They let the creatures loose on top of the ants' nest – Tammy had to flick some of them off the lid with her finger – and waited, Tammy's pen poised over her journal.

Colin wriggled his toes. They hung over the edge of the sandals he was wearing. He'd chosen them because Tammy said their colour was pewter, not silver, and he thought that was ace. He needed to learn how to sit in a dress so he didn't show

130

his grungy undies, but Tammy wasn't about to teach him. She wasn't his sister or his babysitter or his mum or anyone to do with him at all.

The first thing Colin did when he turned up that morning was dive into Tammy's wardrobe and pick out a short halter-neck dress. Tammy put on jeans so she wouldn't be the same. She'd allowed him to talk her into wearing matching dresses yesterday and then got annoyed because that's how someone can burrow their way in before you realise it. She was annoyed again now, but this time it was because she was hot in her heavy jeans and Colin had pockets of air-flow.

'What are we looking for?' said Colin.

'Don't you know anything? We're not looking for something in particular. We just record our observations.'

War. Tammy was looking for war. Carnage. Maybe the beetles would eat some ants. Or the ants might send out a swarm raid. She'd like to see a swarm raid.

Nothing doing. Some of the beetles wandered off. Some were playing dead, or were dead. The ants took no notice.

'Our experiments are too limited in scope,' said Tammy. 'We have to branch out. Investigate new habitats, like we're scouts. We'll start with Number Seven.'

'We can't go to someone else's house,' said Colin. Tammy raised her eyebrows and clicked her tongue. 'That's different. Your mum invited me. We're not invited to Number Seven.'

'Look. You're either committed to scientific rigour or you're not. If not, you might as well go home.'

'I'm committed.'

'More's the pity.' Tammy gave a long, woe-is-me sigh. 'Come on, then.'

They crept up the driveway of Number Seven. Suzi came with them as far as the driveway, but no further. She was either standing guard for them or sending a warning that this was a fool's mission. It was getting harder to tell with Suzi these days.

Colin stopped to point out a row of ants in the seam of the concrete halfway up, and Tammy, feeling exposed, steered him off the driveway and onto a steep bank dotted with spiky shrubs and a ground cover of bark chips. There weren't any police cars or news people on the street yet, but that didn't make things better. They could arrive sneakily and start watching you before you even knew they were there.

'Now what?' said Colin.

'Look for ants.'

'What about you?'

'I'm looking out.'

'What for?'

'Stop asking questions.'

Colin looked sullen and grumbled about the bark chips being rough on his bum but started poking around regardless. Tammy fixed Sheree's house in her sights but there was nothing going on there, so after a sweeping glance over Warrah Place, she turned to watch the nearest window of Number Seven. She was about to tell Colin to move on, sneak around the back, when she saw the shape of Debbie move past. Her stomach flip-flopped but she didn't allow her face to flicker. She crouched low as if ready to start a running race, still watching the window. Sure enough, Debbie appeared again, and then again. She was pacing. Animated. Talking, but not to anyone else, just herself. Tammy knew when she was watching someone who thinks they are alone. You just get a certain kind of feeling. She stood to get a better look and that's when Debbie looked at Tammy. First, just her face turned, and then her whole body, and Tammy rubbed her nose and looked past the house, into the distance. She went for a lost-in-thought pose, then a startled one when Debbie knocked on the window and called out, 'Oi, you ratbags!'

Colin's little legs scrabbled at the bark, trying to make a run for it, but he kept sliding down. Tammy was exhilarated at being caught, exhilarated at Debbie's body turning towards her like a searchlight, and even more exhilarated when Debbie opened the front door.

'Oi,' Debbie said again, and Tammy hauled Colin up to the door. 'What do you think you're doing?'

'Ants,' said Colin, just as Tammy said, 'We're here to help.'

'What with?' said Debbie.

If Tammy took two steps forward, she could rest her chin on Debbie's folded arms. 'What are you doing at the moment?' she said.

Debbie put her hands on her hips. 'Painting placards.'

'That then,' said Tammy.

It could go either way: invited in or out on her ear. At last, Debbie smiled and made way for them to come inside. 'I like your chutzpah,' she said.

It didn't matter what that meant, and Tammy certainly wasn't going to ask. Whatever it was, Tammy had it and Debbie liked it. That was enough.

The house smelt strange. Not cooking smells. Not cigarettes. Not quite perfume either. It was unfamiliar, otherworldly. Going inside felt like choosing to step across a threshold, like making a decision. Tammy did so gladly, her wits about her and firing on all cylinders. *Look and learn, Tammy.* She'd never been inside this house before, not even before Debbie arrived.

Debbie took them into the dining room. Tammy and Colin went straight to the source of the smell, more intense now, on a telephone table in the corner.

'Incense,' said Debbie, her arms folded, apparently amused at their interest.

'Like frankincense,' said Colin. 'Brought to the baby Jesus by the wise men.'

'No. It's nag champa. But, yeah, something like that,' said Debbie.

Debbie wore a loose white blouse with embroidery all over the front and a cord lacing up the opening. She also wore a long batik skirt and an anklet that jingled when she walked, but it was the criss-cross, sagging cord on Debbie's top that Tammy couldn't tear her eyes away from. It looked half undone rather than half done up. Tammy's breasts, such as they were – two fried eggs on a plank of wood, sometimes painful and itchy – were a mortification. Tammy hunched her shoulders forwards, concaving her chest, to hide them under her T-shirt.

'I thought you said you were here to help,' said Debbie. 'Let's get to it.'

The table was covered with construction paper and wooden sticks and masking tape and pots of paint and brushes balanced over jars of water. Debbie hadn't put newspaper down. There was paint on the table, paint on Debbie and paint on the carpet. If Debbie was going to get in trouble for the mess, she didn't seem to care. Wow.

Some signs were already painted and leaning against the wall:

2 4 6 8 GAY IS JUST AS GOOD AS STRAIGHT

ABORIGINAL LAND RIGHTS. NOW!

BOYCOTT FRENCH CHEESE. STOP NUCLEAR TESTING IN THE PACIFIC

Others had been outlined in pencil and were waiting to be painted. Two of them were facing Tammy:

EQUAL PAY FOR WOMEN

Debbie had made a start on 'STOP URANIUM MINING'.

'I like how you're doing the shape of a stop sign around "STOP". That's very inventive,' said Tammy.

'It's pretty standard actually,' said Debbie.

'Oh.'

'Here's one for you.' Debbie pushed 'MY BODY MY CHOICE' in front of Colin. 'The sooner you learn the better. Hang on, can you paint inside the lines?'

'No,' said Colin. 'Not a bit.'

'Maybe do some free drawing instead, yeah?' She gave him a fresh sheet of paper and pulled a bunch of textas and a bunch of pencils, each held together with a rubber band, from a backpack on the floor. 'Express yourself however you see fit.' She touched his shoulder where the tail-end of the halter-neck's ribbon draped over it. 'I mean it. You're on to something important, something profound, freeing yourself from gender stereotypes. See if you can find expression through your art. Don't hold back.'

'What should I do?' said Tammy. 'I could do some decorations around the edge?' She picked up 'YA BUNCH OF MONGRELS', turned it the right way up, read it and held her nerve.

Debbie took it back from her. 'How about you do your own. Pick something that matters to you. An injustice that needs to be put right. What do you need to say about it? Get your voice heard.'

Tammy got the gist. This was great. She was right about Debbie. Tammy could really do with having Debbie in her life, especially now Antonio was gone. She picked up a paintbrush and got started, clawing her hand around the brush to hide her disgusting nails.

'I s'pose you want to talk about Antonio,' said Debbie. 'Like everyone else.'

Yes! thought Tammy. They were basically kindred spirits already.

But Colin piped up with a very firm 'No', and Debbie said, 'Thank God for that. Don't see why we should have to be in the doldrums all the time. Moving on, what's with the sneaking about? You want to watch it. I don't like sneaks. It's bad enough with that camera crew prowling round like a pack of rabid dingoes.'

'Oh, it's OK,' said Colin. 'We're not sneaks. We're scientists.'

Debbie gave Tammy an enquiring look. Tammy sent one back, using her eyebrows to say, *See what I have to put up with? He's nothing to do with me.* It was a shame Debbie didn't want to talk about Antonio. She was clever and likely to have useful observations and contributions to make. Tammy could do with all the help she could get.

'Even scientists should knock on the front door like normal people. Not spy through windows.' Debbie dipped her brush in the red paint pot.

That was an invitation, wasn't it? As good as saying, *Turn up whenever you want.* Soon it would be the most normal thing in the world to hang out together, just two normal people (Tammy and Debbie, not Colin) hanging out. And they would marvel, chuckle while sharing knowing looks, that there was ever a time when they didn't know each other.

'Actually,' said Tammy, 'I'm the scientist. I've been investigating the properties of poison. And its potential efficacy for dealing with enemies.'

Debbie looked up sharply from her placard.

'Scientifically speaking, of course,' said Tammy. 'Anyway, yes, let's not talk about Antonio. It's all anyone's doing. So boring. Let's talk about the working bee instead. I wonder if you saw anything there out of the ordinary.'

'Nope,' said Debbie, pouring red and blue paints onto a plate and mixing them to make purple.

'Right,' said Tammy, not expecting a dead end so soon. 'Me too. Well then, I wonder if you've had much to do with Sheree? Have you met her yet? Because I've been wondering if there's something a bit off about her.'

'You do a lot of wondering,' said Debbie.

That wasn't a no. It was the kind of answer someone gave if they had hot information and didn't want to talk about it in front of a little kid like Colin.

Tammy decided to be less direct. 'I think your aunties are very interesting. They must feel very lucky to have you come and live with them.' Tammy paused to dip her brush in paint and let the compliment do its work. 'Does Ursula happen to have any special friendships that you know of?' She stopped herself from adding, *Like Mrs Lau, for instance?*

'What I know is that you shouldn't pry,' said Debbie, her voice stern. 'Especially about Ursula and Lydia. Leave them alone.'

It was a slap-down and it stung.

'I like your selection of textas,' said Colin after a while, and Tammy could almost like him for filling the silence. 'None run out. This is even better than watching telly.' He added under his breath, 'And ants.'

'I don't watch telly,' said Debbie. 'It's ... so mainstream. Designed to rot your brain so you'll comply. Nah, I'm more interested in counterculture. Not being a sheep. Making a difference. *Being* the difference, yeah?'

'Yeah,' said Tammy.

'Oh,' said Colin.

'I guess telly's OK for kids and old fogies,' said Debbie.

'Phew,' said Colin.

'I like your hair,' said Tammy before Colin could tell Debbie how much telly they'd been watching.

137

'Ta,' said Debbie.

'It really complements your features,' said Tammy. 'It's the flick. The flick works really well.'

Tammy had never been to a hairdresser. Her mum had read an article in *Women's Weekly* about cutting your child's hair with sticky tape. The instructions said to comb the fringe, then attach a line of sticky tape. The idea was that the sticky tape gave you a straight line to cut along and the hair would come away easily with the tape, no mess made. Except that the kitchen-drawer scissors were blunt and both they and the sticky tape pulled at Tammy's hair. And the fringe would spring up afterwards, leaving a great expanse of embarrassment between her hair and her eyebrows, and Tammy would cry. And her mum would call her an ungrateful wretch and say never again would she cut Tammy's hair. And that would be a lie, a big fat unfortunate lie.

'I really mean it,' said Tammy. 'It flows so beautifully around your face.'

Debbie's eyes sparkled and she half smiled.

'We're the same, you and me.' Tammy flicked her finger back and forth between Debbie and herself.

'Oh?' said Debbie.

'Cos you're starting uni and I'm starting high school. We're both in transitional phases. The same,' she said again for good measure.

'Jesus,' said Debbie. 'You're going into high school? I thought you were much younger than that.'

Tammy bristled and squirmed on her chair.

'Bugger me.' Debbie blew air sideways between her teeth. 'They're going to eat you alive.'

Tammy put all earnestness, all of the truth, into her voice when she said, 'Is that something you can help with?'

Debbie broke off a laugh abruptly, before it had even got

going. She considered Tammy carefully, like a puzzle, a project. 'Yeah, maybe I can help with that,' she said.

Tammy didn't want to be the first to break eye contact.

'Maybe you could start with less talking out loud about poison and enemies,' said Debbie. 'And other people's business.' Then she said, 'Here. Show us what you've done.'

All of Debbie's edges had softened; there was a stillness and gentleness there. No way would Debbie lie to her or trick her, not like Antonio had.

Tammy held up her sign and turned it the right way up.

SIMONE BUNNER SUCKS DOGS' DICKS

She'd run out of room and the final three letters were more squashed than she'd like, but she was pleased that she'd positioned the apostrophe correctly. Not everyone would get that right. Simone Bunner wouldn't, for one.

Debbie took one look and laughed. It came out of her like an explosion.

'I've extrapolated it from some graffiti I saw,' said Tammy. She reckoned it was the sort of thing Debbie meant when she was talking about counterculture. She thought it was spot on, actually, the real deal, no joke.

Debbie started wheezing. 'Fucking fantastic,' she said. 'Although ...' She got herself under control and frowned. 'We're meant to be sticking it to the patriarchy, not doing their work for them.'

Tammy put her sign face down and leant her elbows on it. The paint was still wet and would be smearing on the table. She didn't know what she'd done wrong, only that she had and now everything was wrong.

The silence thickened.

Tammy watched Debbie's fingers reach for a texta. Debbie

kept her nails short — who wanted long, flashy nails anyway? — but they were a lovely, elegant shape, and her fingers moved beautifully through the air, like a mermaid swimming, like a ballerina dancing, like a feather caught by the wind. Tammy slithered her own hands under the table. From now on, every time she caught herself biting her nails, she'd slap herself across the face, hard. Two slaps for biting the skin around her nails. Three slaps for drawing blood.

'Do you know what I love?' said Tammy. 'I love it when you're so comfortable with someone that you can sit in silence and it doesn't get strange.'

'Uh-huh,' said Debbie. She drew a butterfly on the corner of Colin's picture of a dog or elephant or potato or whatever. 'This OK with you?' she asked him and he nodded.

'Like now, for instance,' said Tammy. 'This isn't weird or awkward at all.'

'That's so pretty,' said Colin. 'You're really good at drawing. Can you draw me a picture to colour in?'

'Sure thing. What do you want?' Debbie grinned at Colin, leant in close to him. They shared a look.

Colin was nothing but a weasel, weaselling in where he wasn't wanted. Laying low, acting all innocent and naive and then pouncing when Tammy was down. After all the putting up with him she'd done. Traitor.

'A family,' said Colin.

Boring.

'Really?' said Debbie. 'All righty then.'

She *was* good at drawing. Really good. She had drawn a mum and a dad and was starting on a kid when she flung her arms up in the air and cried out and scrunched up the paper. 'Debbie, you *wanker*,' she said. 'Let this be a lesson to you two. How easily the tyranny of the heterosexual nuclear family and its implications for state control can sink its teeth into you. How hard it is to dismantle the patriarchy when it invades every aspect of our lives and consciousness, when sex dualism determines all cultural systems, when men keep us enslaved to our biological functions. It's all so *fricking* exhausting. Still, we fight. We fight. We fight. You gotta be on guard all … the … time, because bloody men will rip your power away from you. Just like that.' She snapped her fingers furiously, then picked up the drawing, unscrunched it and tore it to pieces. 'Let's start again. My God, what would Germaine say?'

'Is Germaine your friend?' said Colin.

'My best friend,' said Debbie, and a rod of jealousy shot through Tammy. 'Got me through, well, a terrible time.' Her mouth grim, she started to draw a woman. 'I even met her once,' said Debbie. 'At a book signing. Germaine Greer. I've got two copies of *The Female Eunuch*, one for everyday use, and one – the one she signed – kept for best.'

Debbie drew five women, an assortment of children in different sizes and a dog. Two of the women were holding hands. She coloured in a child's face and arms with a brown pencil.

'Who are they?' said Colin.

'A family,' said Debbie. 'Like you asked.'

Colin stared at the picture for a long time. 'Is it still a family without a dad?'

Debbie scoffed. 'Course. Hang on.' She pulled it back towards herself and drew a cat. 'For Tammy.' She winked at Tammy. 'You like cats, yeah?'

'Yeah,' said Tammy. And all was right and beautiful with the world again. Just like that. She snapped her fingers under the table.

'Haven't seen your dad around for a bit,' Debbie said to Colin. 'What's the story there?'

'He goes away to work,' said Colin. 'To keep us safe. He's a navy man.'

'Safe from what?'

'Dunno,' said Colin.

'And is he a good bloke, your dad?'

'Mum says he's our hero. So that's good.'

'You don't mind?' said Debbie. 'Him being away?'

'My job is being the man of the house while he's gone,' said Colin, which wasn't a proper answer to Debbie's question, Tammy thought.

Debbie must have thought so too because she gave up on Colin after that. Tammy was glad because she was feeling left out, and what was the point anyway? Everyone knew Richard was a good bloke. She'd once heard her mum and Maureen agree that it was a great shame there weren't more men of integrity like him around these days. One of a kind, they said, like they were sad about it.

With her placard finished and in disgrace, Tammy's attention wandered. She watched curlicues of incense smoke rise from the stick. Then she nearly fell off her chair. Next to the incense on the telephone table was a stub of pencil. But not just any pencil. It had been sharpened with a knife in distinctive patterns, like flower petals. It was a pencil that Antonio wore behind his ear. What was Debbie doing with it?

Before she'd considered what to say, Tammy leapt from her chair and grabbed the pencil. 'What are you doing with this?' It sounded like an accusation. She lowered her voice and tried again, going for a casual tone. 'Where did you get this?'

Debbie brushed her hand through her hair. 'Oh, I don't know,' she said, as if it were beneath her interest. 'Oh, wait. Yes, I do. Ursula brought it home from work. She said she found it in the library. I'd better give it back to her.' Debbie took the pencil from Tammy and dropped it into her backpack.

Jeepers creepers, thought Tammy. That was two strikes against Ursula. First, her secret car-talk with Mrs Lau, and now this. And this was a big one. What was she doing with Antonio's pencil? And why had she lied to Debbie about where she got it from?

Until she could write it down and think things through, she wouldn't say anything more. It was clear Debbie didn't know there was something shady about her auntie, and Tammy didn't yet have enough information to present to her. For now, she had to act normal.

Debbie told them she'd had a year off between high school and uni. She wasn't a mature-age student exactly, but she certainly had more life experience than other first years. She wasn't there just for the fun, you know; she had a contribution to make.

'What did you do?' Tammy asked in her best normal voice. 'On your year off?'

'Pulled schooners at an RSL Club.'

'Was it good?' said Tammy, wondering if she might do it too.

'No, it was ratshit. Working in a dingy club in a hole of a town, pulling beers for men who mistakenly thought their appeal matched their appetites. Hey, that's not a bad line.' She pulled an exercise book out of her bag. 'I could use that. I'm writing this essay on the patriarchy, getting a head start on uni. It's about how women feel ashamed because of the things men do to them, how they carry what doesn't belong to them. I'm calling it . . . Custodians of Shame.'

'Wow,' said Colin.

'Cool,' said Tammy.

'I want to get it published one day,' said Debbie. 'That's the dream. Then, one night, I'll be home alone, because I reckon I'll get my own place soon, and the phone will ring, and it'll be Germaine, and she'll say it really struck a chord, like it articulates something that no one has said before, but when you read it, you instantly recognise it as truth. She'll say it's hard-hitting, a game-changer, none of the usual derivative bullshit. And then after that, sometimes, late at night, Germaine will phone me up and say, *I hope you don't mind. I just want to pick your brains about something.'*

'Far out, Brussels sprout,' said Colin.

'We gotta hold onto our dreams, right, kid?' said Debbie.

Colin went quiet and still. Debbie touched him gently and asked if he was OK.

'Don't mind him,' said Tammy. 'He zones out sometimes. Quite a lot actually. Not very bright, I don't think.' The last, she said in a stage whisper, with exaggerated mouth movements.

'Debbie?' said Colin, his voice small. 'Am I the patriarchy?'

Debbie cocked her head. So did Tammy. She wanted Debbie to say yes.

'Nah. Not you, numb-nuts.' Debbie made a goofy face, then turned serious. 'But keep it that way, yeah? Watch yourself.'

'I will,' said Colin. 'I promise.' After a while he said, 'Debbie?' again. 'What should we do about the patriarchy?'

Debbie grinned. 'We take it down.'

'Can we really do that?' said Colin.

'Too bloody right we can. And the time to do it is now. That's what's great for our generation, we can dare to do things. Not like the generation above us, all stiff and stifled. They can't tell us what to do anymore. They've lost the right. We can push boundaries. Smash boundaries. We can change the world!'

It was a rallying cry. A call to arms. Tammy felt more alive, more involved, more necessary than she ever had before. Like beatification, like atonement, like communion, like baptism, all without having to go to church. The Holy Sacrament of Debbie. Tammy was in. A 100-per-cent convert.

17

Three Weeks Before The Murder

Saturday, 16 December 1978

Debbie was done up to the nines for dancing. A mini and platform shoes. Gold glitter dusted on her cheekbones. A dab of
patchouli oil behind each ear. She'd gone in heavy with kohl in
a cat's-eye stolen from the sixties, because why should the goths
and vamps and punks have all the fun? And if she was doing
it for herself and not to conform to some fucked-up beauty
standard, then that was all right, right? She had her bus fare and
an extra tab, in case the first one didn't kick in, tucked into her
bra so she didn't have to carry anything.

Debbie had arrived in Canberra five days ago, shrugging off
her home town. She was ready, more than ready, to make the
city hers, and she was starting with a gig at the ANU Refectory.

Doc Neeson held the microphone out. To her, just to her.
Don't let the bastards grind you down. Don't let the bastards
grind you at all – that was her problem in the first place. A guy
next to her wore a shark's tooth on leather around his neck,
and Debbie bared her teeth, all of them. She had sharks' teeth,
gnashing teeth to rip and maim, and the guy flung his head
about and sweat flew from his hair, and his sweat was her sweat,

and she flung her head about too and grinned at him like a loon, the Brewster brothers doing their thing on stage, weaving the rhythm on two guitars, the beat threading its way through her broken tissue, repairing her damaged womb, torn by the doctor's hook. The beat, the beat, the beat. Her feet thumped the floor. I'm here, I'm here, I'm here. Her fist punched the air. I will not succumb.

Wet hair slapped her back and her face.

The guy elbowed his way in front of her. A strobe light turned his hair red.

Eyes shut.

Edgar's red hair. Red beard. His smile. That crooked tooth. His hair, his beard, his smile.

Eyes open.

She scraped her fingers down her own face to check it was there.

Eyes shut.

Red hair. Red beard. That smile. Stubby fingers she'd thought boyishly endearing for a man his age. Run-of-the-mill Y-fronts, the sort a mother or wife washes and folds. Freckles on his back. Turning away and putting on his pants.

'Edgar?' she asked.

'Excuse me.'

Someone was tapping her shoulder. It felt like a hammer. A face came up close. Too close. Whoa. A voice in her ear, a jackhammer in her brain. 'Can you please get off?'

She was standing on a feather boa. The girl shouting in her ear tugged on the other end. The girl had bad eyes. Bad intentions.

She stumbled to the loos, other bodies sweeping her along. She stopped and kissed the wall to thank it for holding her up, for being her support, for being there when she needed a friend.

When she came out, the lights were on, and the inside of her head turned neon. The roadies were packing up, the Refectory emptying. The feather boa hung from the ceiling and Debbie tugged on it until it came loose. She wrapped it around her neck.

Outside, Christmas lights had turned the city to a fairy paradise. Debbie didn't want to get a bus home yet. She headed in the direction of City Hill, drawn by the tall skinny trees that swayed to the music in her head. They nodded and waved and welcomed her among their number. Soon, she felt drawn by roads and cars and buildings, so she made her way down Constitution Avenue. Cars welcomed her with toots, but they were too fast for her and made her dizzy, so she got off the road. She decided on Commonwealth Park next because it was near the water and water was life.

There was a kerfuffle ahead. A swarm of men. It was like cymbals clashing in her head. Bodies moved discordantly, out of sync and with sharp edges. Someone was on the ground, surrounded by kicking legs and punching fists. *Fucken dago*, they spat. Peals of laughter. Piggy grunts.

The figure on the ground was a familiar shape. A fist ploughed into his eye and his head snapped back. He curled up like a dead beetle.

The fist was attached to a redhead. Sunburnt shoulders and neck. Debbie came at a gallop, releasing a warrior cry. She got right up in there among them, wielding her elbows and fists and snarling. 'Piss off, ya scumbags.' She lost her shoes on the way.

They backed off, probably more from the shock of her than the threat of her.

'Crazy bitch!' It was the redhead yelling as he retreated.

The man on the ground was mewling, whimpering. She looked closer at him. The fray had cleared her head. He was from her street. The Italian. About her age. She bent over him to look closer. He wasn't crying after all but laughing. She saw recognition register on his face too.

147

'Hey, I know you.'

She'd hardly say that. Yes, she'd clocked him and knew that he'd clocked her, but she'd avoided him because she wasn't in the market for meeting men, especially ones who oozed masculinity like they thought it was worth bottling. She was done with men.

'My damsel in shining armour,' he said, on one knee while clutching his side. His nose dripped blood.

'Antonio,' he said, pointing to himself.

'I know.'

'You're Debbie.'

'I know.'

He laughed again and gingerly straightened up, testing his body as he did, stretching this bit then that, to see if it was still in working order. He walked over to her shoes and picked them up, saying, 'Least I can do after you saved me,' and carried on walking until he got to a busy road. Debbie followed. She'd lost track of which direction they were facing.

Antonio sat on the grassy verge with his feet on the kerb and his head between his knees. At least his nose had stopped bleeding. His face was a mess. Dirt from the ground had mixed in with the blood. Debbie plonked herself down next to him and felt she might never get up again. Adrenaline leeched from her body, leaving her depleted, forlorn. She looked at Antonio.

'Show me your eyes,' she said. He'd taken a belter. It might need seeing to.

'Show me *your* eyes,' he said.

'Huh,' they both said when they saw.

'Good trip?' he said.

'Mm-hm.'

'Coming down yet?' he asked.

'Hoo, yeah,' she said. And then: 'Nope.' She swung her head from side to side like a pendulum. 'Nope. Nope, nope, nope.'

'I have my car,' he said.

'Is it dark inside?' She didn't think she could face the harsh lights of a bus. She was covered in goosebumps.

When they got to his car, Antonio opened the door for her and it creaked loudly. He was still holding her shoes. When they got in, she became aware of her dress riding up and also that he wasn't gawping. She noticed that the feather boa around her neck wasn't a feather boa at all, but a straggly bit of tinsel.

'My dad only bought me this second-hand pile of junk.' He sounded genuinely aggrieved.

'Boo-fucking-hoo. Poor baby rich boy.'

Debbie's dad had kicked her out of home on her last day of school.

Antonio pulled out the choke and pumped the pedal.

'You're going to flood it,' said Debbie.

'I know what I'm doing.'

The car started. He revved it and grinned.

They passed a deflated Santa on a roof.

'What were you doing in the city?' said Debbie.

'Playing the pinballs.'

He was just a boy, playing pinball machines. She'd been wary of him when she'd seen him around Warrah Place, the way she was with all men. But look at him – he was just a beat-up boy.

'What'd you do to them to piss them off? Don't tell me. It was nothing, wasn't it? They were racist pricks, right? Jesus Christ. Mongrels.'

He drove to Red Hill Lookout. Debbie didn't mind. In fact, it felt like exactly the right thing to do; the right place to be.

Antonio parked the car and they walked up the path. The Carousel Restaurant had closed for the night and was dark except for a soft glow from overnight lights left on.

God, wouldn't she like a drink of water. She must have said so out loud because Antonio led her to a tap outside the public toilets. He cupped his hands under the tap while she drank from them. There was no reason she couldn't have cupped her own hands, but that's what he did, and she drank and drank and it was lovely. Antonio splashed water on his face and dabbed it with his T-shirt, revealing a skinny body. Not at all like Edgar with his soft roundness.

Antonio tried to vault over a fence, but his painful ribs put a halt to that. He awkwardly swung his body over, laughing and groaning. Then Debbie managed to get over in her dress, and they sat among the rocks and dirt and tufts of spinifex.

The view was indistinct, two-dimensional shapes in the distance. Street lights lit up Anzac Parade like a runway, watched over by the dark presence of Mount Ainslie.

Antonio lit a cigarette, drawing on it deeply before handing it to her, and then lit another for himself. He leant back on one elbow, his legs stretched out and ankles crossed. Debbie didn't much like smoking but was starting to get the hang of it. She'd be properly into it by the time uni started, she reckoned.

Antonio slapped at his ankles.

'Little bastards,' he said.

'You must have sweet blood.'

'Mosquitoes don't bite you?'

'Nah. Bad blood,' said Debbie. The ground was hard and stony, the grasses scratchy, but she felt entirely comfortable.

'I heard you had an in-between year,' said Antonio. 'Between school and university. Very European of you.'

Where did he hear about that? What else had he heard?

'What did you do?' he said, chiding, mocking. 'Go find yourself? Take a spiritual quest? Lose a year taking drugs?'

'Fuck you.' He thought she was lazy, indulgent, an airhead. She'd heard it all before.

His body changed. She couldn't have said how exactly, just that there was a different energy to him, an energy that was solely focused on her. He nudged her with his shoulder. 'Seriously. Why the year off?'

'I was busy,' said Debbie. Why not just say it? She had nothing to be ashamed of. 'Busy being pregnant.'

He leant away to get a better look at her. 'You had a baby?' He peered behind her as though she were hiding a baby, and this time she nudged him with her shoulder.

'I had an abortion.' She took a breath and spoke the rest in a rush: 'I used my pocket money to get a Greyhound bus to Sydney and booked into a shonky hostel in Kings Cross. I had to convince two doctors I'd kill myself if they made me have the kid so they'd write down I was unfit to mother.'

'*Oddio*,' said Antonio, and although she had no idea what that meant, it didn't matter, because what he did next was pull her to him, his arm clamped around her, pressing her to his sore side, the side that he had been holding because it was bruised and bothered him when he moved and breathed. He cradled her head in his hand. It was what her mum and dad hadn't done. It was what Edgar hadn't done. No one had until now.

He waited a long time, until her body had stopped shuddering, before he asked, 'Do you want to tell me?'

Antonio took one end of the tinsel still wrapped around her neck and wound it around his neck too, while Debbie decided where to start.

Debbie had written copious love letters, outpourings of her heart, her writing getting smaller towards the end of each page to cram in all the love she had to give, and then spilling over onto the next. She slipped them into books. A furtive handover in the classroom. She wanted love letters in return, but Edgar never wrote any.

Edgar said they were meant to be together. Said they were made for each other. Said he'd never felt this way for anyone else. The promise was implicitly there, wasn't it? Afterwards, she raked over every conversation in her mind. An implicit promise, yes? Was she going mad?

Antonio leant away to look at her full-on. He must have got a crick in his neck, what with how long he was turned to her and looking.

'Are you judging me?' she asked. With someone else, it would have felt awkward, the way he was studying her, but Debbie's usual alarm bells weren't ringing.

'Never.'

Antonio didn't say anything else, but he did murmur encouraging sounds. He was on her side. She wasn't mad.

The showdown had come on Speech Night. Her last day of high school. Edgar told her to stop. Stop talking to him. Stop writing to him. Stop walking past his house. Debbie said she would tell everyone. He said no one would believe her; would see it for what it was: a silly schoolgirl crush turned nasty and vindictive. She knew he was right. She had no proof. Even the baby in her belly was no proof.

Antonio pressed her closer to him again, although it must have pained him. He shuffled a smoke from the packet, pulled it out with his lips and lit it with one hand. They shared it, passing it back and forth between them.

'Your parents,' said Antonio. 'Were they unhappy about the baby?'

'That's the understatement of the century.'

Debbie passed the smoke back to Antonio and he gestured for her to finish it. He lit another one. 'I think our parents are so busy being disappointed in us, they don't even think if we are disappointed in them,' he said.

'Oh my God, right, yeah?' said Debbie.

They started to play Who's the Biggest Fuck-up.

'I won't go to Mass with them,' said Antonio.

'Snap,' said Debbie. 'Heathens on the fast track to eternal

damnation. Equal points. I'm doing Women's Studies at uni.'

'I'm not going to uni at all.'

'Why not?'

Antonio shrugged. 'I was tired of trying to please them. So I stopped. It makes life easier. Happier.'

'Fair enough. Good on ya.' Debbie felt a lightness that was new and not chemically induced. She'd released something that had been weighing her down. 'You know what I'm going to say next, and you know you can't beat it. Getting up the duff by your teacher while you're still at school.'

'Edgar was your teacher?'

'Geography.'

'Wow.'

'Go on, beat that,' said Debbie, chuckling. She felt free. 'Unless you've knocked up some girl and done a runner, I win.' There was something else to say, something serious. 'What I can never say to them – to all the people who have judged me and laid their shit on me – is what a fool I feel I've been. Because they said it first.'

Debbie fiddled with blades of long grass, picking and shredding them. Maybe if she could get enough, she could plait them and make crowns for her and Antonio. She got to work on it. Antonio yawned and laid back on the ground.

'Tell me a story,' said Antonio. 'A lullaby.' He closed his eyes.

'I snuck into his house once,' said Debbie. 'Through the laundry door. It was around the time our baby would have been due. Did I tell you his wife had just had a baby when he got me pregnant? I found that out later. Did I tell you he had a wife? Anyway, I got into his house, through the laundry door and into the kitchen. Just walked in, calm as anything. I thought maybe I'd say something to his wife. Or maybe just let her get a look at me. So, I got to the kitchen and I was thinking, *What next?* But the baby was crying in another room, proper full-on howling, and I walked down the hall and then I heard its mum crying too. His wife. She was crying and pleading with it to go to sleep. I'd never heard anything so pathetic. Imagine pleading with a baby. Anyway, I went back to the kitchen, turned the gas in the oven on, left the oven door open and went out through the laundry again.'

Antonio sat up. Not so asleep, then. 'Did you? Did you do that?'

'What do you think?'

'I think I don't know you well enough to know if you're joking. But I think I know you well enough to know that's the way you like it.'

Bingo.

Dawn crept up on them and took them unawares. In a nearby tree, white corellas lined a branch like pegs on a Hills Hoist. Birdsong rose and dipped all around them.

'It's pretty,' said Antonio, looking around at the pops of violet brought by the first light. 'All the purple flowers.'

'Don't be sucked in by a pretty face,' said Debbie. 'It's a thug. A killer. It's called Paterson's curse.' Farmers hated the stuff. 'Causes liver failure in cows and horses.'

Three kangaroos, two adults and a joey, appeared. Or maybe they'd been there all along, eavesdropping. Antonio gasped when he saw them and reached for Debbie's hand. His excitement was contagious; so childlike. Real cute. Debbie had seen many kangaroos before, but not this close, not so inquisitive. She squeezed Antonio's hand.

'*Maestoso*,' said Antonio, full of awe.

The largest kangaroo was a big fella, a brute of a thing. Debbie didn't tell Antonio that kangaroos knew how to box, that they wouldn't stand a chance if it came to that.

Moments passed in stillness and silence, humans and kangaroos regarding each other. Debbie and Antonio held their faces close together, feeling and hearing each other's breath. When at last the kangaroos bounded away, Debbie felt that an exchange had occurred. She felt both enriched and bereft. One look at Antonio told her he felt the same.

Dawn had broken and the light was nothing special. They were used to the view and the sun was starting to burn. Antonio had taken his shoes off at some point during the night. One foot had a splodge of a birthmark on it, like spilled paint. His toes sprouted dark hairs. Debbie felt grotty in last night's clothes. Lazy Sunday traffic was picking up, and dog walkers and joggers were invading the space that had belonged only to them during the night. The magic was gone.

Antonio said he was hungry. Debbie wanted to brush her teeth. She said it felt like the poo fairy had visited and shat in her mouth. Antonio laughed and patted her head where it rested on his shoulder.

They left behind a tidy pile of cigarette butts and a coil of tinsel.

They hadn't even kissed. There was no hint of him trying it on. It was pure and peaceful; the perfect antidote.

18

Five Months Before The Murder

August 1978

Peggy told Naomi that Antonio was charming. Maureen agreed. 'An irrepressible flirt,' she said. 'So funny.' Naomi couldn't see it. With her, he was curt. He turned up whenever he wanted. He refused cups of tea. He left without saying goodbye. What was so wrong with her that he could barely bring himself to be civil?

After a week of the fence listing drunkenly, it was clear that whatever Antonio had done to it hadn't held. Naomi watched him use two hands to hold the fence in place and then realise he lacked a third to finish the job.

He saw her watching and coughed. 'Would you be willing to help?'

Holding the strut, Naomi noticed how he planted his feet and balanced his weight, leaning over her. He was much slower than Richard and lacked Richard's brawn, but there was something graceful and elegant about Antonio's body and how it moved. It affected her, had a pull on her. He took the pencil from behind his ear and put it between his teeth, his lips gently resting on it.

It was obvious he had no idea what he was doing.

Naomi's lips twitched. He noticed and leant his forehead against the fence in defeat. He spat the pencil into his hand.

'You're on to me,' he said, and now he smiled ruefully. 'Are you going to give me the sack?'

'Of course not.' Naomi laughed openly now, and Antonio shook his head, rolled his eyes at himself and laughed too.

'Now what?' he said.

'I reckon we bang some nails in and hope for the best.'

As they knelt on the wet lawn, side by side, their arms aching from holding the fence, they heard Peggy's voice on the other side, so close they both jumped.

'Who's the prettiest boy on the planet?'

'Mr Solomon. Mr Solomon. Mr Solomon,' came a squawked reply.

Antonio looked at Naomi in astonishment and Naomi cracked up silently. She shuffled closer to Antonio and whispered, 'It's her pet bird. She puts it out in its cage to get some sun. You wouldn't believe the stuff she says to it.'

'Who does Peggy love most in the world?' came Peggy's voice again.

'Mr Solomon. Mr Solomon. Mr Solomon.'

'And?'

'Right back atcha.' Mr Solomon wolf-whistled.

'What a good boy,' said Peggy. 'Stay right there. I'm going to get you a cuttlefish.'

As they heard Peggy slide open her back door, Antonio, in a fair approximation of Mr Solomon's voice, called out, 'Peggy stinks. Old battleaxe.'

'What?' Peggy was back in a trice. 'What did you say?'

Mr Solomon said, 'Battleaxe,' in the same tone Antonio had used.

Naomi and Antonio let go of the fence, hands over their

mouths to stifle their laughter. Naomi clasped Antonio's shoulder.

'Leslie?' called Peggy, her voice moving to the other side of the deck.

'Do "cranky old crank",' whispered Naomi, thrilling at the feel of Antonio's ear on her lips.

'Cranky old crank,' squawked Antonio.

'*Leslie*,' called Peggy, more urgently.

While Peggy remonstrated with Leslie about what he'd been teaching Mr Solomon, and if not teaching per se, what he'd been saying that Mr Solomon had overheard, Naomi and Antonio sat with their backs to the fence, shoulder to shoulder, and waited for their silent fits of laughter to subside.

'Poor Leslie,' said Antonio once Peggy's and Leslie's voices had receded inside. 'I think I landed him in it.'

Naomi started laughing again. 'I've never done anything like that before.'

Antonio looked at her in surprise. 'Never? You never messed around with your friends at school, making jokes on people?'

'I didn't really have friends.'

'I don't think I can believe that.'

'My mum scared them away, I guess.'

Antonio looked at her like she was the most fascinating thing in the world. 'You really never messed around when you were a teenager? What did you do to be rebellious?'

'I didn't. I wasn't allowed. I missed out on all that.'

'It's never too late,' said Antonio, his expression suggestive, then turning more serious, more intense.

'Don't be ridiculous,' said Naomi. Then, all at once and inexplicably, she felt she was about to cry. 'Excuse me,' she said, going to stand up.

But Antonio's hand grabbed hers and held her back. 'Don't,' he said. 'Don't go.' He wouldn't release her from his gaze, nor her hand from his. 'What have I done? I didn't mean to upset you.'

'It's not your fault,' she said. 'You struck a nerve, that's all. And now I feel very foolish.' She pressed her forehead to his shoulder. She couldn't bear it if he saw her face.

For some time, he sat rock still. Neither spoke.

Then he gently steered her face upwards so he could see her and she could see him.

He touched his face to hers. The lightest feathery touch. Cheeks, noses, foreheads, fingertips, barely brushing, continual motion. She brought her hand to the curls at his neck.

Naomi felt his lips smile against her cheek and then his breath as he chuckled.

'What's funny?' she asked.

'Not funny,' he said. 'Lovely. It's like kissing without lips.'

At the word *kissing*, Naomi was brought back to reality with a thud. What was she doing?

'We mustn't,' she said. 'I'm m—'

He stood swiftly. In an instant, he'd withdrawn, cool as a cucumber. 'Then don't.'

'What?' said Naomi, her body already wanting to snake its way back to his. 'Wait.'

But he'd already pocketed his smokes and lighter. The pencil went behind his ear. He put on his jacket in one fluid motion and left.

A week passed without Antonio returning, during which all Naomi wanted to do was rewind time to before she said, *We mustn't*. Was it the fun they'd had with Peggy and Mr Solomon she wanted to return to? Or having someone touch a vulnerable feeling and neither of them running? Or was it the kiss that so nearly was?

It was all of that. She wanted all of that and more.

When he finally came back, he stood before her with what seemed to be all the courage he could find. He kept his back against the front door that Naomi had closed behind him and didn't venture further into the house, as if he wanted to be able to make a quick getaway.

'I've come to apologise,' he said formally. 'For what I did. For leaving so abruptly.'

'Why did you?' she asked. 'I didn't want you to.'

'I know,' he said, looking pained and abashed. 'I have no excuse. I am *idiota*. To be so forward—'

'No, I meant leave. I didn't want you to leave.'

He raised his eyebrows, started to speak, stopped, then started again. 'Then why did you say we shouldn't do it?'

'I don't know.' Naomi laughed in a self-deprecating way. 'Maybe because I thought it was expected; that it's what I should say. Because I didn't know what else to say.' She forced herself to stay put and keep her voice steady. 'Maybe because I couldn't think straight with you so close to me.'

Antonio took her hand and placed it on his chest, making an offering of his hammering heart.

When they kissed, Antonio was tentative and gentle. He waited for her to deepen the kiss and set the pace, answering in kind. It was a delicate and attuned call and response, desire accelerating the more they spent it. Kissing Richard had never been like this. He would never relinquish control, never yield to her.

'Are you ready for this?' said Antonio. 'For me?'

An absurd thought came to her: *Look at me, Mum! What are you going to do about it? There's not a thing you can do to stop me.*

'I'm ready.'

They stayed awake all night, talking and kissing. They left it as late as they could before Colin woke up for Antonio to leave. He didn't slink out and make a dash across the island for home, but sauntered casually, smoking, taking his time, like he was aware Naomi was watching his every step from her bedroom window. He returned as soon as Colin was at school. They compared notes about how gritty their eyes felt. They laughed about their sore, cracked lips and Naomi's pash rash.

On the weekend, they made a cubby hole out of blankets and chairs in the family room with Colin. Then Naomi took Colin to Sheree's and asked if she could have him for the day – she wouldn't normally ask, only she had so much to do that Colin would be bored out of his brain and she'd happily return the favour sometime.

Naomi and Antonio spent the rest of the day snuggling in the cubby.

Sneaking around like weak-at-the-knees teenagers went on for days. Naomi felt her desire come at her like a charging bull and couldn't understand why Antonio didn't take things further. Then she remembered that he *was* a teenager and that she – no matter how she felt – was not. She mustered some pluck, took him by the hand and led him to bed.

Later, with her head in the crook of his shoulder, she said, 'Promise me something.'

'Anything.'

'I'm serious.'

'So am I.' He'd been tracing her fingers with his own and now gave her hand a squeeze. 'Can I smoke in here?'

'You can do anything you want.'

He lit a cigarette. 'In that case, I'll make a list.' They adjusted their position so he could sit up. 'What did you want me to promise?'

'No hiding anything from each other. No trying to guess what the other one feels or thinks or wants.' Naomi propped herself up to get a better look at him. 'No games. Only honesty.'

'Oh God, yes,' said Antonio. 'What a relief. It was a nightmare trying to hide from you how I feel. And I'm terrible at it.'

19

Four Days After The Murder

Wednesday, 10 January 1979

Naomi got out of bed while the rest of Warrah Place slept.

She put on a simple shift dress, no buttons or zip to tax her. Her skin was dirty, her mouth and lips were dry, her hair was flat and greasy. She didn't care.

She got in her car and drove towards the plaza, Antonio's passport on her lap. She rode the clutch, but it didn't matter because the car wasn't real, the road wasn't real, this sparse city and its people now cartoonish. Nothing was real anymore.

A roller door on a shop front clattered open as if a new day were possible. Even at this hour, people walked on footpaths, got out of cars, waited for buses, looked at their watches, yawned. She passed a construction site, where workers had turned up early, thinking they could get a head start on the heat. Garbos whistled merrily and called obscenities to each other in jocular tones. The sight of them made her go faster, wondering how much of their rounds they'd done, how much more to go.

Perhaps Colin would wake up and find himself alone and wonder where she was. But she couldn't think about Colin now. Antonio filled every inch of her mind. His name permeated the air and she breathed it in: *Antonio, Antonio, Antonio*.

The plaza car park was empty.

Naomi parked haphazardly, paying no heed to the white lines. The first bin she came to was full and stinking. She tentatively plucked items from the top first, then reached in deeper, not caring what her hands touched. She spilled the contents onto the ground, a pile forming at her feet, chip wrappings, tissues and serviettes, food in various stages of decomposition. Soiled nappies. A clothes hanger. A shoe. Aluminium cans. Cigarette butts. Sodden receipts and bus tickets.

She abandoned her search and moved on to another, and then another. How many were there?

Think, Naomi. She tried to put herself in Richard's shoes. She was certain he said he'd been to the plaza, smug about how clever he'd been to send the police in any direction but his. But where at the plaza would he choose?

She found a bank of industrial bins out of the way behind the shops, exhaust fans whirring above them.

The police had only found Antonio's foot. Naomi couldn't bear knowing that Antonio's beautiful body lay somewhere as belittling as a plaza bin; broken, in pieces, not afforded the dignity of a burial. It was intolerable.

Naomi opened the lids, reeling at the smell. She bent deeply to scoop out armfuls of rubbish, getting more and more desperate as the pile grew bigger and time ran out. She hadn't thought through what she would do if she found him, only that she must.

And then the truck came into sight and she ran to hide from the mess she'd made. Before she did, though, she took Antonio's passport from her pocket, kissed it one last time and dropped it into the nearest bin. It hurt her to do it, but the risk of it being found in her home was too great. As distraught as she was, self-preservation still kicked in. She had to protect herself, and Richard.

164

In her car, Naomi closed her eyes and sat in the smell of other people's rubbish and her own failure. *I'm sorry, my love.*

The car park had filled up. People were locking their cars, doing their shopping, coming back and driving away. The day was getting hotter, but Naomi kept the windows wound up. Her dress was damp, her limbs heavy, her breaths shallow.

It was too early to feel the baby's movements, but a welcome trick of the mind made her certain the flutters she felt were her baby beckoning her. It was a sign; confirmation that what began as a hope had turned to certainty. A gift. She hadn't recovered Antonio's body, but she had a piece of him growing inside her. A secret piece, hers alone.

Eventually, Naomi started the car and drove away without going into the shops. There was nothing she needed except Antonio. She laid a protective hand on her belly and closed her lips around his name.

20

The camera crew parked outside the Italian House blocked the road, forcing Lydia to drive up the wrong side of the cul-de-sac, doing nothing to dampen her fiery mood. Most of the time she loved being a police officer, but not today. She went past Naomi getting out of her car and making a beeline for her front door. Normally, Naomi walked with a short-legged, girlish skip, presumably to keep up with Richard's long-legged stride. Now, she walked woodenly. Pregnancy slows you down, Lydia supposed.

Lydia didn't stop to say hello to Naomi or even wave. She stormed into her house and then the bedroom, yanking off her bow tie, undoing the buttons on her jacket and the zip on her skirt; the skirt with one measly kick pleat. She flung off her shoes, followed by her clothes and cap. In her bra and half-slip, she threw her police-issued handbag at the rest of her uniform on the floor.

'Good shift?'

Debbie was leaning against the door frame, arms folded, struggling to contain her mirth. Lydia had forgotten that she might be home.

Tension now released, Lydia's body sagged.

It was small for a master bedroom. The bed dominated. There

was one chair, laden with Lydia's clothes. The en suite was more of a cupboard.

Debbie came into the room and sat on the bed. 'What happened?'

'Doesn't matter,' said Lydia.

'Tell that to your clothes,' said Debbie, nodding at the tangle of Lydia's uniform and kit on the floor.

Lydia sat on the bed too. She raked her hand through her hair, as was her habit. It fell back immediately into place, curtaining her eyes. She always put off getting it cut longer than she should. On anyone else, it might have given off a sense of mystery, of something concealed. But Lydia was a plain speaker, always had been. What you saw was what you got. She had a strong jaw that gave her an air of authority. It was handy for her job.

'I got that close today. That close.' Lydia held up her thumb and forefinger, a sliver of air between them. 'I walked around a corner and right into the middle of a drugs deal. A big haul. They ran, of course, and then . . . It was a total balls-up, arse about face. I can't run in those.' She gestured scathingly at the court shoes. 'They come off as soon as you get going. And the skirt's too tight. Can't get a proper stride. By the time I've opened the handbag to get the handcuffs out, it's too late. The blokes get all the right clobber and we don't.'

'That's totally fucked up.' Debbie stood up, indignant. 'You can't stand for that. Seriously.'

Lydia wasn't sure she should be telling Debbie any of this. She was liable to turn up at the station with a bloody placard. It felt good to get it off her chest, though. 'General Duties is all right, I s'pose, but what I wouldn't give for a crack at Criminal Investigations.'

'You want to do more hardcore stuff? Murders and that?' Debbie's voice was small. The puff had gone out of her.

Damn, thought Lydia, she'd put her great big galumphing

167

foot in it. Debbie might put on a tough show, but the Antonio business was far from over. Lydia felt embarrassed on behalf of the Force, and some responsibility too, that neither a body nor a suspect had been found yet. And now she'd have to have a try at the touchy-feely stuff with Debbie.

'Listen.' She put her hand on Debbie's shoulder, uncomfortably aware that she was still in her bra and slip. Some conversations required more clothes. 'I know—'

Debbie stood up again and spun on her heel, bright and breezy, and Lydia's hand fell away. It was impossible to keep up with the mood changes in this girl.

'I wish I was a lesbian,' said Debbie. 'Do you think it's too late to try?'

'I'm not sure there are any rules,' said Lydia. 'But I don't think wishing is gonna cut it, sadly.'

'Did you always know?'

'Yep.'

'And did you always know about Ursula?'

'Oh yeah.' Lydia went to the chair piled high with discarded clothes and found her daggy, home-only shorts, the elastic in the waist on its way out. She put them on before removing her slip. Then on went a tank top, also daggy, also only for slobbing around in at home. 'The first time I went into the library – not usually my scene, you know? – was to get my kid brother out of the house because he was driving everyone round the bend with his noise. I had this brainwave that I'd take him to the library because you have to be quiet in a library and maybe he'd shut up for a sec. Anyway, that's the first time I saw Ursula.'

'And?'

'And that was it. I was a goner. She wore a green blouse with a bow at the neck and a beige skirt and her shoes—'

'Lace-ups, right?'

'Lace-ups,' Lydia confirmed. 'But when she reached high to

put books onto shelves, her heels popped out of the shoes and then she'd have to wiggle them back in. She always tilted her head to read the title on the spine instead of tilting the book. I could have watched her all day.'

'That's kind of sweet,' said Debbie. 'Do you believe in all that stuff about soulmates? One person for everyone? I wouldn't have thought you were the type.'

'Didn't used to be. And maybe it's not that way for everyone. All I know is, I got lucky.'

Debbie looked lost in thought.

'You're going to hate me for saying this,' said Lydia. No young person liked being told they were young. 'You're young. I know you were keen on this Antonio fella. But you've got stacks of time to find someone to love. It'll happen.'

'Haven't you even told anyone you work with that you're a lesbian?' Debbie said, bypassing these last comments. Fair enough, Lydia supposed. 'Don't you have friends there? Don't you hate denying who you really are?'

Lydia couldn't stop the heat rising to her face. She winced.

'Wait,' said Debbie. 'They *do* know. You've told them.'

'Not in so many words. It's just . . .' Lydia wafted her hands around her body airily, around her face. 'I never actually said at work that Ursula is my sister. I can't carry a lie that well. Also, Ursula can pass as straight, easily. Me, not so much. Sometimes I try to give the impression, but my heart's not in it.'

'Does Ursula know they know?'

'No. And—'

'I get it.' Debbie made a zipping motion over her mouth. 'Not a word. Our little secret.'

Lydia felt a surge of dread. She and Ursula didn't keep secrets from each other. It was something that defined their relationship: no barriers of that nature. But now, she'd somehow got herself into a situation where she was colluding with Debbie against Ursula. She wanted to retract it. It was entirely wrong; a risk she'd never intended, never wanted, to take.

Neither of them heard a knock or the front door open so were startled when a deep voice called out, 'Yoo-hoo.'

They came out of the bedroom to find Cecil ushering Maureen, Leslie and Peggy through the front door and into the dining room.

'What—' began Lydia, alarmed.

'Good. You're home,' said Cecil. He elbowed Maureen out of his way and stood in front of the window.

Lydia looked to Debbie for an explanation, but she looked just as bemused as Lydia felt. She searched her mind for a good excuse to ask them to leave.

The door clattered open again and in came Tammy and Colin. 'Look, your little shadows are back,' Lydia said as an aside to Debbie. Tammy and Colin had taken to following Debbie around like besotted puppies.

Then Sheree came in with her three kids in tow.

'Who asked you to come?' said Cecil.

'I did,' said Leslie. 'You said it was important.'

'Get over yourself, Cec,' said Peggy.

'Nice to see you too, Cecil,' said Sheree.

Peggy was counting heads. Lydia still hadn't been able to work Peggy out. She was abrasive but Lydia preferred straight-talking to games and innuendo. Leslie she liked a lot. Heart of gold, that one.

'Did anyone tell Joe and Zlata to come?' said Peggy.

'Thought it best not to,' said Cecil.

'Why?' said Peggy.

'Never you mind.'

'What's going on?' said Lydia, her desire to find out overriding her desire to get rid of them.

'Good question,' said Cecil. 'That's what we want to know.'

They'd all crammed into the small room, taking up all the space around the dining table. How would Lydia explain to Ursula that she'd let them all pile in? Leslie had his arms tucked in tight, trying and failing to make himself smaller. Cecil peered from the window down the street to where the cluster of media crew were gathered.

'Thought it best we meet here,' said Cecil. 'Away from prying eyes.' He let go of the curtain, and when Peggy took up his position he told her to move away. 'They might see you, and we don't want to attract attention.'

Lydia looked at her watch. Ursula should be home by now. Thank goodness she wasn't. She'd freak out if she saw all these people in her home. To maintain their secret, they avoided socialising in general, and having people in their home in particular. Sometimes it was only a small thing that could give you away and Ursula didn't want to chance it.

Debbie leant against the door frame, her arms folded, one ankle crossed over the other. She looked amused.

'Right then,' said Cecil, looking at Lydia. 'So?'

'So what?'

'We want an update,' said Peggy.

Expectant faces all turned to Lydia. Even the kids were quiet. For a moment, Lydia basked in the authority afforded her, forgetting that she was wearing threadbare shorts with an unreliable waist. She imagined that she were lead detective, dispenser of information and reassurance.

'Right. OK, then.' She had a voice, a tone, for work, and she used it now. 'A thorough investigation is under way and sometimes that takes more time than we'd like,' she said.

'Like following leads?' said Peggy. 'How many leads have you got? And why hasn't anyone told us what precautions we should be taking with a murderer on the loose?'

'Yeah,' said Sheree. 'How much danger are the rest of us in?'

'How do we know we don't have a serial killer on our hands?' said Cecil, glaring at Lydia for maximum impact.

'As I was saying,' said Lydia, 'there is a process to follow and the officers on the investigation will be meticulous in pursuing evidence and—'

'Blah, blah, blah,' said Cecil, waving his arm about. 'We want details.'

'Well, I can't really say—' said Lydia.

'Can't say or won't say?' Peggy said, her body leaning forwards accusingly.

'Look, I'm not on the team investigating. I have different duties. It's not like all the information gets passed around. There are procedures—'

'So you said,' said Cecil. 'Do you really expect us to believe you can't find anything out? Look, if there's someone on the street who's under suspicion, I want to know about it. I've got a right to know about it.' His voice was getting louder.

'You mean, you want a heads-up if *you're* under suspicion,' said Peggy.

There was a flash of anger directed at Peggy, and Lydia wondered, not for the first time, what went on behind closed doors in Cecil's house. She looked at Maureen, her posture curved in on itself, and decided to find a moment sometime to have a quiet word.

'What did you mean about not telling Joe and Zlata to come?' Peggy asked Cecil.

Cecil stretched his arms out even though there wasn't room. It was getting hotter, the air thicker, with so many bodies sardined in. 'Hasn't anyone else put two and two together?' he said. 'Joe's missing tools, tools that could be used to murder a person and chop off a foot? And then being the one to identify said foot?'

'Surely that points to his innocence?' said Leslie. 'He'd hardly help the police by identifying the foot if he was involved.'

'Or,' said Cecil with emphasis, 'it makes him look more guilty. Because he just happened to be on the scene.'

Leaving this to wend its way through the group, and as if just remembering that his wife was next to him, he asked Maureen, 'Where's Helen? I told you to get her.'

'I tried,' said Maureen. 'She wasn't in. I got those two instead.' She nodded at Tammy and Colin.

Tammy looked up from a notebook she'd been writing in, as if she were taking minutes of their meeting, and chewed on the end of her pen.

'You two,' said Cecil to Tammy and Colin. 'Just keep your heads down.' He did a double take at Colin. 'What are you wearing, boy? You look like a bloody sissy.' To the group, he said, 'We need Helen to keep an eye on the Laus, since she's next door. You know, report back on anything iffy. Since the police are bloody useless' – he shot daggers at Lydia – 'we have to cast our suspicions wide. Not rule anything out. You'll tell Helen, Maur. Think you can handle that?'

'Hey—' said Debbie.

But Cecil warded her off with his hands up. 'Now, before you get going on me, it's not about their colour. Not a racist thing.' He jabbed the air with a finger. 'I've got nothing against them as a race. I've even got nothing against them lot specifically. Seem nice enough on the surface. It's only—'

'Only what?' said Debbie.

'Only they haven't made much of an effort. To join in.'

'Join in how? What do you expect?'

Cecil huffed. 'Well. First thing, I've never seen one of them show some appreciation. You'd think they'd show some bloody appreciation.'

'What exactly are they meant to appreciate, Cecil?' Debbie spoke through her teeth, saying his name carefully.

'Being here. Everything. All of it.' He flung his arm towards

173

the window as if to encompass Warrah Place, Canberra, the whole of Australia.

'Besides,' said Cecil, momentum building, 'and I say this out of kindness, I can't think why they'd want to come to Warrah Place. Surely they'd be happier going someplace they fitted in. Like wherever that last batch of boat people settled, know what I'm saying?'

'But, Cec, the boat people are from Vietnam,' said Sheree.

'So?'

'So the Laus are Chinese.' Sheree spoke like she was talking to one of her kids.

Cecil shrugged. 'Same diff.'

'Oh my God,' said Debbie.

With his attention still on Sheree, Cecil said, 'Can't you tidy your yard up a bit? There's a camera crew right opposite your house.'

'If it means that much to you, sure.' Sheree's tone was even, her face inscrutable, but it was clear to Lydia she was taking the piss. Lydia decided that she liked Sheree.

'Come to think of it,' Cecil went on, 'how do we know the murderer isn't one of your fellas still sniffing around? There was trouble with one of them a while back, wasn't there?'

Sheree remained silent, but there was nothing inscrutable about the look of contempt she sent Cecil.

'You remember, don't you?' Cecil appealed to Peggy and Leslie. 'It was before your time,' he said to Lydia, 'but you would have had your hands full with that one. Actually, make a note of that, would you? Something to tell your superiors to take a look at.' Lydia kept her hands on her hips. She noticed Tammy scribbling in her book again. 'Anyone know when Richard's back? We could do with another sensible head around here. It's a shame Naomi's out of action too.' He sighed dramatically and Sheree copied him, exaggerating his posture and making Debbie laugh.

Surprisingly, Tammy piped up. 'Does anyone think it's strange that Antonio's foot didn't have a shoe on it?'

'No, I don't,' Sheree said immediately.

'I do,' said Tammy. 'I think there's something fishy about missing shoes. We should definitely focus on that.'

'I want to know why the parents were in and out like a flash, just grabbed some things and left,' said Peggy, while a convoluted set of looks were exchanged between Tammy and Sheree that Lydia couldn't make sense of.

'That's a very good point,' said Cecil.

'Whose parents?' said Maureen.

'Whose do you think?' said Peggy, exasperated. '*Antonio's.*' Lydia wondered if there was anyone who escaped Peggy's hostility.

'It's bloody typical,' said Cecil. 'Ashamed to show their faces, leaving us to mop up their mess.'

'Bit harsh,' Leslie said under his breath.

'I don't think so,' said Cecil. 'Bit suss more like it, sneaking back in the dead of night, then disappearing again, not being willing to face the rest of us. They come over here, get murdered, and leave us to deal with the fallout. It's not an ideal situation.'

'Look, let's wind things up,' said Lydia. 'I know everyone's concerned. The hot weather is having an effect on all of us, making us more on edge and frustrated. It's hard to stay level-headed when—'

'You can't fob us off like that.' Cecil cut across her and she felt the remnants of her authority dribble away.

One of Sheree's kids grabbed hold of Lydia's leg with sticky fingers. Cecil was at the window again, jabbing a thumb at the news van. 'And no one's to talk to those lot. Best not. Can't trust 'em. They'll paint us in a bad light. You hear?' He glared at Sheree. 'They're a pack of mongrels. No one say a word to them.'

At last, Cecil ran out of steam. They all traipsed out, leaving Lydia and Debbie in a room filled with silence and a sense of escalating unrest. It made Lydia nervous. They needed a breakthrough in the case. She'd seen what could happen when a group lost confidence in the police. It only took one or two hotheads to get them riled.

21

While the unauthorised gathering was taking place in her dining room, Ursula was sitting on a pew in the middle of the church, not too upfront, not skulking at the back. There was something about being there on a weekday that felt like wagging school to watch *Days of Our Lives*, or drinking wine at lunchtime, or being on holiday and forgetting what day it is.

Yesterday, Ursula had taken her first driving lesson with Guangyu. The driving had been hopeless, but the burgeoning friendship was not. There was a moment – it was such a silly little thing – when Ursula mentioned that she didn't much like pop music but had to listen to it all the time now they had a teenager in the house. And Guangyu innocently asked if it felt different for Lydia, having Debbie there, since she was Ursula's niece and not Lydia's. Guangyu couldn't have known how the question would rock Ursula, not because of the question itself, but because with Guangyu, Ursula didn't have to scramble to keep her mask intact. She could face Guangyu's question freely and truthfully. It made her wonder: could there *ever* be a chance of living with Lydia in the open?

'Greetings.' It was Pastor Martin, approaching from the rear of the church. He sat beside Ursula, keeping a respectable distance, but not enough to leave her alone with her thoughts.

'I'm just . . . that is to say, I wanted to . . .' she began, not sure how to explain her presence.

He raised both hands to stop her. 'No need. Hardly surprising after the dreadful events of the weekend. I've been coming in frequently myself, seeking solace.'

Dreadful events? Of course. He meant Antonio. Strange how something so momentous and monstrous could vacate her mind for even a moment.

'We're all very shaken,' said Ursula. 'He once did me a great kindness.'

It was the week before Christmas. Ursula was lugging shopping bags up Warrah Place after work. She'd picked up a few extra bits: the ingredients for her grandmother's stollen recipe. She was hoping the reminder, the connection with family, would do Debbie some good. She'd also bought a pair of fluffy gloves for Lydia – not for now, of course, but Lydia had a January birthday, so she never got wintery things. Canberra winters were cold and it could be something to look forward to, Ursula reasoned. For Debbie, she had bought a trinket box made from wicker and small seashells.

Before she heard his footsteps, the Italian boy, Antonio, had fallen into step with her and was reaching for one of her bags. 'Let me,' he said. 'No, really,' he added when she tried to protest.

He looked into the bag and raised his eyebrows at the gloves. Yes, of course, they were a daft idea. Ursula would return them and get something else. He lifted out the trinket box and rotated it to inspect it.

'For my niece,' said Ursula. Why did she feel the need to explain?

'Nice,' said Antonio. 'She'll love it.' How would he know?

'Have you got something for me?' He peered into the bag. 'No? Oh, now I am sad.' He pouted.

As they neared the end of the cul-de-sac, Ursula looked anxiously at Peggy's house. It didn't escape Antonio's notice.

'Are you worried about the gossip? About you and me?' he said. He looked gleeful, mischievous. Ursula couldn't tell if he was being conspiratorial or making fun of her. Probably the latter.

'You're ludicrous,' she said.

'I know. It's a problem.' He winked.

'She intimidates me,' said Ursula in a moment of candour, looking again towards Peggy's house. 'She dresses so well. And I always feel wrong-footed, the way she's so sure of everything she thinks.'

Antonio looked thoughtful and Ursula felt foolish. 'I have a Christmas present for you,' he said, like it was an announcement. 'Are you ready for it?' What was this nonsense? 'It's a secret.' He leant in close and whispered, 'Peggy's secret.'

Ursula couldn't help herself. She leant in too.

'Her secret is that she's a bitter old woman and she can't stand it. A cranky old crank. She's jealous of you. For being younger than her. And she only has her pet bird to talk to. And Leslie, who she treats like a pile of rubbish. And also, she never leaves the street. Never goes anywhere else. Because she's scared. She's lonely and scared and you have nothing to worry about.'

They had reached the foot of Ursula's driveway.

'There,' said Antonio, handing over her shopping. 'Happy Christmas.'

'Leditschke.' Pastor Martin said her name like he was savouring it, drawing her back to the present, where she was in a church and Antonio was dead. 'A good, strong Lutheran name. Am I right in assuming you descend from one of our original forefathers?'

179

'My great-great-grandparents,' she confirmed. 'It was just my great-great-grandfather who arrived in the end,' said Ursula, 'with five children under the age of twelve. His wife died in childbirth on the boat, the child too, not far out from port. After such a long journey from Silesia.'

'Our pioneers were heroic, steadfast in their faith under such trials,' said Pastor Martin. 'My lot came a decade after yours. It was tough, but their way was greatly aided by those who'd established the community before them and welcomed them.'

'Actually,' said Ursula, 'I came here to pray for someone. I wonder if you could help?'

'Help with prayer? That's my number-one job.' He said it like he was making a joke.

'Help with doctrine.'

'I'm no great scholar, but try me.'

'I have a friend and she has a nephew,' Ursula began, wading in, wondering if she was about to go under. But she had to know. Antonio's death was a reminder of how quickly life could be taken away. 'And the nephew, well, he thinks he might be inclined towards . . . that is, he thinks he might have . . . homo-sexual tendencies.' Ursula was blushing furiously.

'Ah, I see,' said Pastor Martin. 'You are right to pray. I mean, prayer is always the answer, but in cases like these, it's often the only answer.'

'What do you mean?'

'Tell me more about the young man. Does he have faith?'

'Most certainly, yes.'

'And he seeks guidance on living within God's ways?'

'Yes. And he seeks . . . understanding. He wants to know if he can find acceptance in the church.'

'Oh, no question about that. He would find complete accept-ance as a child of God.'

Ursula's heart raced. She knew that her flushed face was close to betraying her. 'That's a relief to hear,' she said. 'My friend has been so worried. So worried about her nephew.'

'He is very blessed to have her – and you – in his corner. The poor chap will need all the help and prayer he can get. Abstinence is not an easy path.'

'Abstinence? But I thought you said . . .'

'Maybe I'm not being clear. The homosexual, er, propensity, is not considered a problem; the scripture has nothing to say on that aspect. After all, there is no evidence to suggest that people can help it. And no evidence that treatment methods are effective in correcting the defect, unfortunately. But the *expression* of the propensity, the, er, homosexual behaviours if you like, it's those that must be denied.'

As if something leaden and lifeless had settled on Ursula's chest, she struggled to take a full breath. 'And if he doesn't abstain?'

'He would always be welcomed at church. But if he doesn't repent of his sin and seek to live in accordance with the confession of faith, the sacrament would have to be withheld.'

'I see,' said Ursula. A life without Holy Communion – the gift of having her relationship with God put right and cleansed anew – would be like having her heart ripped from her body.

'Shall we pray together?' said Pastor Martin.

Ursula felt compelled to run, her muscles tightening in readiness, but she couldn't. She must keep her mask in place. She bowed her head and hoped she wouldn't cry.

She was saved by a small cough. It was Helen, standing at the back of the church, looking impatient.

Pastor Martin looked at his watch. 'Goodness,' he said. 'Sorry, Helen. I lost track.' To Ursula he said, 'Stay as long as you like. The Spirit will guide you. I have to go now. The newer members of our flock must be nurtured.'

★

'What's the matter?' said Lydia, when Ursula got home.

'Nothing,' said Ursula.

'You've missed the fun and games,' said Debbie. She looked more cheerful than she had in a while, and that was something to be glad of, at least.

'What happened?' asked Ursula.

'Nothing,' said Lydia. 'Nothing important.'

Ursula was about to question them further, but there was a strong, formal knock on the door.

It was a police officer, one from that first day on the island, named Mark. Lydia rated him, said he knew his stuff. He'd already been to ask them questions and they told him everything. Lydia made sure of that. Why was he back again? Debbie let him in, whatever cheerfulness she'd had evaporating in an instant.

'Go on in,' said Lydia, pointing to the dining room. Her voice was strange; it contained a squeak not normally there.

Ursula took note of Mark's fresh and starched uniform. She took note of Lydia's scungy clothes and watched Lydia shrink into herself. But Ursula needed Lydia to be strong and in charge for both of them now. Since talking to Pastor Martin, Ursula felt the need to cling to her secret more tightly than ever. What a fool she'd been to allow herself to be lured into hope. She tugged on Lydia's arm and pulled her into the kitchen.

'What does he want?' whispered Ursula.

'I suspect we won't know that until we go in there and find out.' Lydia put calming hands on Ursula's shoulders. 'Look, we have to think of Debbie. Think of all she's been through. The sooner the investigation is over, the sooner she can deal with it, so let's be as helpful as we can. Right? Wouldn't hurt my standing either if I can be of use.'

'Lyds, I'm scared.'

'I know.'

Did she, though? Even if Ursula were to tell Lydia, word

for word, what Pastor Martin had said, Lydia still wouldn't understand, not fully, because only Ursula was a Christian. Only Ursula had to choose between her church and her love.

'You go in first,' said Ursula. 'I need a moment to settle.'

Ursula paced several laps around the kitchen before going into the dining room. She sat as far away from Lydia as possible lest she lose her mind and reach out to touch her.

'. . . in the vicinity of Woden Plaza.' Mark was speaking in a formal tone. 'Now we're not looking for a body so much as further remains.'

'What?' said Ursula.

'They've found more chopped-off pieces of Antonio,' said Debbie. She spat the words out and got up, took a few paces and circled back. She was so agitated she didn't know what to do with herself. 'Although apparently he isn't Antonio anymore. Now he's just *dismembered remains*.'

'What?' said Ursula again, her voice higher and louder.

Debbie's face had paled, save for red blotches appearing on her cheeks and neck. She sat again. 'I'm confused,' she said, although she sounded more disgusted and angry than confused. 'The foot was bad enough. But now this? What possible reason would someone have for doing that to his body?'

'That's a question we're still looking for an answer to.'

Ursula felt a rush of guilt over how preoccupied she'd been with herself. Poor Antonio. This must feel worse for Debbie than it did for Ursula, having to listen to horrific details about someone she'd had feelings for. Surely she should be spared?

Ursula placed a hand on Debbie's arm. She had to reach across the table to do it. 'How about you go make a pot of tea?'

'No, thanks,' said Debbie. She sat back and surveyed Mark, as though Antonio's death were his fault.

'We're widening the search area again,' Mark said to Lydia. 'We haven't established a link between the two locations, the hills and the plaza, and we're yet to recover a weapon or weapons.' He rubbed his eyes and Ursula wondered if he was having sleepless nights. 'Pity the poor garbos who made the discovery at the plaza. Three to four days in this heat. You can imagine.'

'Are we thinking there might be multiple people involved?' asked Lydia. 'Given the expansive area under consideration?'

'A distinct possibility. Can't rule it out. It's an unusual one, that's for sure,' said Mark. 'Listen, we could really use your eyes and ears around the place.' He leant in closer to Lydia and steepled his hands under his chin. 'You've got good cop's intuition.'

Lydia's face remained grim, but Ursula knew she was beaming on the inside. 'The neighbours are getting antsy,' she told Mark. 'Accusations flying around all over the place, but nothing beyond airing old grievances as far as I can see. I don't think anyone would take matters into their own hands at this stage, but you should be aware of possible racial tensions.'

'What she means is that Cecil Dodds is a racist pig,' said Debbie.

'Has Cecil been on about the Laus again?' said Ursula. 'That man!' She was incensed. 'For what it's worth, I know that Guangyu Lau couldn't have been involved. She was at work on the evening in question. An overnight emergency surgery. She's an excellent vet, you know.'

'Good to know,' said Mark. 'Thanks.' He made a note in his small notebook, which immediately made Ursula frightened that she'd jumped the gun. Why had she spoken without thinking it through first? 'Can anyone tell me about the Kreegers at Number Three? I've not had an answer to any of my knocks on the door.'

'Oh, there's nothing to worry about there either,' said Ursula, glad to move on from Guangyu and ignoring the quizzical look on Lydia's face. 'Richard is away. He's in the navy. Can be away for weeks, even months, at a time, but everyone prefers it when he's home. And Naomi has been unwell, I gather. So much so that Helen over the road has been looking after her boy. Helen can tell you anything else you need to know.'

Ursula had done a good job, she thought. Anyone would think that she was well liked and well connected in the community, not a closed-off guardian of a secret and teller of lies about her friend.

22

Five Days After The Murder

Thursday, 11 January 1979

Helen and Duncan leant into the bends as they went up Black Mountain at speed. It was early morning, but not early enough for Duncan, who wanted to be one of the first onto the build site.

Helen's shoulder slammed into the door. 'Hardly necessary,' she said.

'I'm busting my balls here.' Duncan clenched his teeth and the steering wheel.

'That's not my fault.'

'Didn't say it was.'

Not out loud, anyway.

'Although . . .' said Duncan, 'the hold-up this morning didn't help. I don't think I could have been any clearer last night that it had to be an early start.'

'I know.'

'I wouldn't say it if it didn't matter.'

'I know.'

'And I'm happy for you to have the car.'

'Gee, thanks.'

'I can get a lift back to the office with Jim.'

'Great.'

It was Thursday. Bible study day. Helen needed the car to go to the manse so she could go through the readings and teachings with Pastor Martin. There was a lot to get done and she could do without Duncan being narky.

Helen looked up at the tower as they neared the top of the mountain. It was close to completion now. The construction had been going on since '72 and it wasn't easy to maintain the enthusiasm expected of an engineer's wife for seven years. What material difference would a telecommunications tower make to her life anyway?

'Don't you think it should have a bit more ... I don't know ... design?' said Helen.

Duncan stared at her, took his eyes off the road for too long.

'I just meant—'

'Helen, we have designed the heck out of this thing. We've been nominated for an Institute of Concrete award.' He leant forward to look up through the windscreen, squinting against the sun. He sighed. 'I know what you mean. But the whole department is so squeezed. There's no one left with any vision. We're all too busy trying not to get the sack.'

Helen felt a jolt of alarm. 'Are you worried now? You said you were safe.'

'I'm safe. As much as I can be.' He patted her thigh like he was placating a dog. 'Really.'

Helen knew all about it; the wives talked, even if Duncan glossed over it for her benefit. But it wasn't something that touched her. So what if Duncan wanted to give her false re-assurance? As long as he promised he would keep his job, she would hold him to it.

Closer now, the vast rings on the tower looked like a rudimentary UFO.

'I suppose it will do its job. Telecommunications and all that,' said Helen. She'd heard talk that by the time it was complete, the technology would already be obsolete. She considered it a kindness that she didn't mention it to Duncan.

'The restaurant might be good,' said Duncan.

Helen supposed a revolving restaurant was terribly modern. But she wasn't good with heights, was prone to seasickness and still wasn't au fait with the rules of posh eateries. She still wasn't entirely sure what au fait meant, for that matter, or if she might embarrass herself by using it incorrectly – for example, while in a restaurant that spun her around until she was dizzy. On the whole, she wasn't keen.

'Shit,' said Duncan, pulling up sharply and yanking on the handbrake. 'Barry's already here. And he's got the green clipboard. Shit. *Shit*.'

'Is the green clipboard bad?'

But Duncan had already grabbed his hard hat and was striding over to a cluster of men in short shirt sleeves and serious frowns. There was a wet patch in the centre of his back. Then he stopped and returned to the car. Helen was in the middle of sliding into the driver's seat, arching to get her backside over the gear stick. The vinyl of the seat was warm and tacky from Duncan's body. He stuck his head in through the window.

'I'm worried about Tammy,' he said. 'I think we need to talk about her.'

'What's the matter with her?'

'I don't know exactly. Don't you think she's . . .'

'What? A spoilt brat? Getting too big for her boots?'

'I was going to say unhappy.'

'Tammy's fine.'

'Have you noticed she's always writing in that journal?' said Duncan. 'What's she so preoccupied with?'

'It's a phase. All girls get preoccupied. It's normal. I think I know a little more about young girls than you do. They're meant to be moody. Besides, aren't you in a hurry? Or did I have time for breakfast after all?'

'Oi, Lanno,' called one of Duncan's workmates. 'Shift your arse.' And that settled it; Duncan took off at a trot.

Helen wound her way down the mountain, through dry sclerophyll forest. She was enveloped by brittle gums, scribbly gums, red stringybarks. She leant her face towards the open window to be more among them, to greet them, to breathe them in, to pay respect. She was going too fast to get a good look at the undergrowth, but truly, it was the giddy heights, majestic trunks and homely smell of the gums that she was a sucker for. They reminded her of the only times she was truly happy growing up.

As a child, Helen was unusually prone to languor. She would sit in stillness, eerily so, examining the veins of a leaf, or swirls of colour in bird droppings, or the points of intersection in a cobweb. She'd prise open a gumnut with her teeth, stroke the powdery scales of a bogong moth or the striations on a sheared rock face. She considered her own body as no more and no less than an arrangement of cells that allowed her to get about. But then, she would shift out of stillness, and pins and needles would come, and she would resent the intrusion, resent the reminder of her physical form and its insistence and limitations.

So, Duncan was worried about Tammy. It was just like him to deposit his worry on her and then go to work.

Helen was still regularly struck by the shock of Tammy. When Tammy was placed in Helen's arms moments after her birth, Helen didn't recognise her. She didn't know what she'd been expecting, only that it wasn't Tammy. This baby was a stranger, entirely her own being, separate from Helen, and certainly not an extension of Helen – is that what she'd expected? Hoped for? She looked nothing like the one photo Helen had of herself as a baby with her thick mat of black hair. Helen had looked at Tammy and thought, *Oh*. There was wonder. An unexpected thrill at seeing someone entirely unknown. But there was loss there too, a drop of disappointment.

When Helen got home, the news van was gone from outside the Italian House. Good. Helen hoped they wouldn't be back. What with the heat and the police asking probing questions, and the media intrusion, and everyone watching everyone, and resenting being watched, it was like living in a pressure cooker. Helen hoped the Bible study would calm fraught nerves and bring people together in mutual support.

Tammy and Colin were on the front lawn in matching playsuits, doing handstands. Suzi stood to one side like an umpire. Helen remembered buying the playsuits in Target. She'd bought the same floral print in orange, yellow, green and pink, all different sizes. Colin was wearing the yellow, Tammy the green. She couldn't keep ignoring it – Colin and the clothes – now that it was obvious it wasn't a one-off. It would reflect on her, of course, Colin being under her care for the time being. Helen was surprised that Naomi hadn't asked for him back. She seemed perfectly happy to let him skip across the road each day early in the morning. And he stayed until Tammy went to bed and Helen told him it was time he went on over to get some sleep too. The longer it went on, the more likely it was that Naomi would feel grateful or indebted. Is that what Helen wanted? She wasn't sure. It would just be nice if Naomi defrosted enough to realise that they would make excellent friends.

The kids came clamouring towards her as she got out of the car, asking for icy poles. She shooed them away and headed over the road to deal with the clothes situation while it was fresh in her mind and before it really got out of hand.

Helen let herself in without bothering to knock and walked

through the kitchen with purpose. The door was always unlocked now to allow for Colin's comings and goings. It was a wonder Naomi felt safe in an unlocked house with a murderer still at large.

From the bathroom came the sound of the shower running. Helen didn't bother to quiet her footsteps or slow her movements. Looking after their boy made her an extension of him, and she therefore had every right to be there. Besides, she'd be gone before Naomi had finished her shower.

It smelled rank in Colin's bedroom. From a chest of drawers, Helen collected undies, shorts and T-shirts. Bold colours, prints and stripes. Helen would like to have a baby boy. Maybe she could be a good mum to a boy. There was a pile of bedding on the bed. Thinking she would neaten it up, Helen pulled back the quilt to reveal a heap of clothes, a hotchpotch of winter things. And under that, a yellow stain spread in a wavy pattern. That would explain the smell, then. She pulled the quilt back up.

On her way out, she paused by the lounge room. She'd always liked this room. So stylish. But now it was dark and stuffy. Helen went in and opened the curtains and windows. That was better. The house was getting whiffy, and she didn't know when Richard would be coming home. The least she could do was air the place out for him.

Now there was light streaming in, Helen noticed that the coffee table was covered with photo albums, not neatly stacked, but strewn about haphazardly, most of them open. She put down Colin's clothes and picked one up. The first page was given to a title, *Our Honeymoon* in fancy script, surrounded by waxing and waning moons. Pregnancy must have made Naomi sentimental. Most of the snaps were of Naomi, on the beach. Helen flicked through them quickly. There were a few of Naomi and Richard together. Taken by some passer-by perhaps. What had they made of the happy couple? Then Helen came across one of Richard on his own.

He was on a balcony, the ocean behind him. A line of shade cut through his face. It wasn't the best picture of him, but it was real. He was relaxed, happy. His hair was longer than it was now. She peeled back the sticky film, took the photo and smoothed the film back into place. It wasn't stealing if they still had the negatives and could get another print made.

Voices sailed through the open window: Peggy and Leslie on their back veranda. Helen moved closer to the window when she heard her name.

'Bit early to be getting ready for Helen's do, isn't it?' said Leslie.

Peggy didn't answer. Then, 'Have you seen my opal earrings?'

'Can you really do yoga in that get-up?'

'It's not yoga anymore.'

Helen could tell each time Peggy sucked on a cigarette, even though she was well practised at talking through deep inhales.

'Back to macramé, then? Robotics?' It sounded like Leslie was smiling.

'Macrobiotics.'

'That's the one.'

'Nope,' said Peggy. 'She's changed it again. It's . . . Bible study.'

'Oh, Pegs, I'm sorry.' Leslie sounded truly devastated for Peggy and Helen felt the betrayal all the more because she would never have expected it from him.

'I suppose it was only a matter of time,' said Peggy, and then there was unintelligible mumbling. Perhaps she had faced away or was lighting another cigarette. Helen strained to hear.

'She's a joke.' Peggy's voice was as clear as a bell now. 'It's the girl I feel most sorry for. And then Duncan, although he has to bear some responsibility. What was he thinking, marrying her?'

There was a pause, during which Helen wished she could tear herself away. It was like purposely prodding a wound.

Leslie spoke next. 'Joe's wound up something rotten about that boy.'

'Is he now? That's interesting.'

'Poor Tony. I can't stop thinking about him.'

'Why do you do that?' said Peggy, turning her ire on Leslie. 'Call him Tony as if you knew him better than you did? It doesn't make you seem interesting, in case you didn't know. It's crass and makes you look a fool.'

There was another pause, during which Leslie absorbed the blows of Peggy's words. Why did he put up with it? Why didn't he retaliate? Peggy could do with a taste of her own medicine.

'If there's anything off about us, people will suspect,' said Peggy, and Helen supposed she was still talking about Leslie looking foolish.

'Suspect what?'

'Us!'

'Of what?' said Leslie. 'Murdering the poor boy?'

'I don't know. Maybe.'

'Come on now. No one is suspecting anyone of anything.'

'You old dolt. Of course they are. I am too.'

'Not the Laus still?'

'You never know,' said Peggy. 'And Cecil's got a real mean streak. I don't think we know the half of what he's capable of. And why are two sisters living together and not mixing? I mean, have you ever been asked into their house? We practically had to force our way in yesterday. Even Helen – there's something shonky there. She has a past, I reckon.'

'I reckon we've all got one of those,' said Leslie.

Helen shifted her weight, waiting to hear exactly what Peggy thought was so shonky about her.

'The question is,' said Peggy, 'which of them are wondering

about us?' There was a pause and then she went on. 'You know, Bible study's not a women-only thing, I don't think. You could come too.'

'Steady on. There's no need for that.' Leslie's voice took on a tender note. 'You don't *have* to go, my dove.'

'You know I do.'

'If they want to talk about you, they'll find some way to do it, whether you're there on Thursdays or not.'

There was a long silence.

Then a door banged.

Helen had a horrible taste in her mouth. She brought both fists to her chest and pressed hard, leaving white knuckle marks that turned red.

As Helen stumbled back through the kitchen, she realised that the shower had stopped running. She'd forgotten all about Naomi. In her haste, she brushed against the fridge and magnets clattered to the floor.

A door opened.

'Hello?' called Naomi from the bathroom. Her voice was insipid, stretched thin. 'Is anyone there? Sheree? Colin? Hello?'

Helen kept moving, without answering Naomi, without picking up the magnets, slipping the photo of Richard in between the folds of Colin's clothes. She closed the front door behind her.

As she crossed the island, the Laus' car pulled into their drive-way. Mrs Lau and Jennifer got out. Jennifer looked down, looked away, looked anywhere but at Helen. But Mrs Lau took off her sunglasses and fixed Helen in her gaze, her face steely, immobile. Helen had been meaning to go over and see if they were OK, what with them living next door to a murdered boy. She had planned to sympathise with them about the dreadfulness of it all. She could go over now; it was a good opportunity, probably the best she'd get. But Helen had a lot to do. Bible study to prepare for. Tammy and Colin would still be wanting icy poles. And she wasn't good with teenage girls. They, and their judgements, made her nervous.

Helen gave a wave – a jaunty wave for goodness' sake – and hurried home.

The Canberra Courier

Thursday, 11 January 1979

Human Remains Found At Shopping Centre As Police Baffled By Murder Case

The gruesome murder of Antonio Marietti, 19, of Warrah Place, continues to baffle ACT Police. Canberra's garbage collectors made a grim discovery yesterday, one that the police had failed to make despite searching for four days. Human remains assumed to belong to Mr Marietti were found in a bin outside Woden Plaza.

Yesterday, Detective Sergeant Mark Leagrove, who heads the investigation, gave a statement to reporters.

'We're working flat out around the clock,' he said. 'There's no need for the public to be unduly alarmed. That said, we appeal to anyone with information to come forward, no matter how minor.'

Asked if the entirety of the body of the deceased had now been recovered, he replied, 'Not as yet, no.' Asked if any suspects had been identified, he replied, 'Not as yet, no.' Answers that will not inspire confidence in the worried public.

Warrah Place resident and spokesman for the local community Cecil Dodds had this to say: 'No one's got a scooby what's going on. What I can tell you is that the impact on the community is huge. Our womenfolk haven't slept a wink.

'Look, we're an affluent area of the city. We welcome all sorts, but this sort of thing shouldn't happen here. We need the police to sort it out. We've even got a police officer living on the street. Fat lot of good she's done us.'

He added, 'I'm all for multiculturalism. But you have to ask yourself, at what point has it gone too far? Where do you draw the line? At murder?'

The investigation continues.

196

Ants have amazing defence systems. One type can flatten its head to block the entrance to the nest like a door and all the other ants have to knock on it with their antennae to be let in. Some ants will just let their legs fall off if they get caught. Some ants will explode with a yellow goo that kills both them and their enemies. If a colony is big enough, it doesn't matter if some ants die. They won't even get noticed because there are plenty of other ants that can take over their jobs no problem.

23

Tammy was still chewing when her mum started clearing the plates. Chop and veg for tea. Lumpy, gluey mash; a sorry state of affairs stuck to the roof of her mouth.

Helen bustled Colin out the door. 'Off you pop now, pet. See you tomorrow.' He dragged his feet as he left.

Tammy had particular responsibilities on Thursday nights. She had to blow dust off the dried-flower arrangement in the lounge room, wait for it to settle, then polish the coffee table. One of the walls was exposed bricks. It attracted cobwebs that Tammy was meant to deal with. When Thursday nights used to be yoga, Tammy had to push the furniture to the edges of the room. Tonight, she helped her dad bring in extra chairs. The dining chairs looked prim and gangly and ashamed of themselves next to the couch.

Tammy's mum came in and rearranged the chairs, handed Tammy a feather duster and said, 'A good going-over, yeah?'

Tammy's next job required careful timing. She had to put a record on to play early enough so it was playing when people arrived, but not so early that it had finished before her mum could say, 'Oh, Tammy, *do* turn that off,' as if they were people who played records so often that they'd forgotten not to on that occasion. Tammy knew all that without being told, because covering up the truth of who you are was in her blood.

She had a measly three records to choose from: *Songs from Joseph and the Amazing Technicolor Dreamcoat*, *The Magic Flute of James Galway* and Cleo Laine's *Gonna Get Through*. The Cleo Laine was a present from Tammy's dad to her mum for her last birthday. Sometimes her dad would put it on and drink wine and say, 'Come on, Hells-bells,' and he'd sing along to 'Just the Way You Are', and sometimes Tammy's mum would sing along too, and they would call the record 'Cleo' like she was a friend who popped in from time to time, and sometimes all this would happen after Tammy's bedtime when she wasn't meant to see any of it. Not lately, though. Nothing like that had happened for a while.

Tammy had Cleo out of the sleeve and on the turntable when she called out, 'Mum, is it time for Cleo yet?'

'Not Cleo,' called her mum. 'James Galway. Did you hear me, Tammy? James Galway.'

Maureen arrived first with lamingtons. Peggy was hot on her heels with so much hair piled up on her head it was a wonder the maggies hadn't set up a nest in there. Her plate of chocolate bikkies looked so good it made Tammy's nose itch.

By the time Ursula arrived, the room was filling up, each body a heat-bomb. The coffee table was also filling up and Tammy mentally ranked the plates in order of deliciousness. There weren't going to be enough chairs. James Galway was getting drowned out by chatter. It seemed everyone wanted to come to *the Murder Street*, especially since they'd been in the newspaper again today. Peggy and Maureen were standing separately by the window. Mrs Whatsername, the church organist, tried to target them with a dose of fellowship, but Peggy blew smoke at her, so she backed off.

199

Ursula stood awkwardly by the door while Helen closed it behind her. Ursula looked dismally at the laden coffee table and Helen looked at Ursula's empty hands.

'This'll be good,' said Peggy as an aside to Maureen.

'I'm so sorry,' said Ursula with her saggy face. 'I didn't know. No one said— Or maybe someone said? At any rate, I should have known. All my fault. I'm sorry.'

'It doesn't matter. Not at all,' said Tammy's mum, but her eyebrows said otherwise.

Peggy smirked, and Tammy did too, because she knew what it was to be on the receiving end of those eyebrows, and she knew that Ursula had been concealing information about Antonio's pencil which she shouldn't have had in the first place, and so deserved whatever Tammy's mum dished out.

Ursula peered into the room tentatively, looking like she didn't know how or where to place herself. She was clunky, out of step and out of tune. The sense of familiarity made Tammy despise Ursula all the more. How did a person grow that old and not grow out of it?

Tammy turned her attention to Peggy and how she held her cigarette aloft, tracking it back and forth to her mouth, and remembering how Antonio sometimes held his cigarette pinched between his thumb and finger, flicking it with his middle finger. That's how Tammy would smoke, for sure. Like Antonio. Like she meant it. She wondered how Debbie would hold a cigarette.

Maureen picked up Peggy's plate of biscuits. Tammy saw a big cobweb hanging on the wall like bunting. She hadn't bothered with the dusting.

Ursula came and stood perilously close to Peggy's cigarette hand.

'Quick,' said Maureen, fanning herself with her free hand. 'Dig in before they all turn to puddles.'

Tammy took one quickly. Ursula also reached for a bikkie, seemed to remember she hadn't brought a plate, looked nervously for Tammy's mum, and retreated again.

'Oh, for goodness' sake,' snapped Peggy.

When Sheree arrived, everyone turned to look. She had tripped over the step on her way in and laughed as she righted herself. When Sheree laughed, she laughed loudly from her belly, with abandon, the fillings in her teeth on display.

'Thanks so much for having me, Helen,' she said. 'Can't tell you how nice it is to get away for a grown-up night out. I brought these.' She handed a plate of party pies to Helen and waved a bottle of wine in the air.

Tammy's mum sniffed as she read the label on the bottle.

'Not quite the sort of night out you're after, I don't think, but thank you anyway. Why don't we put this here' – she put the bottle next to the door – 'and you can collect it on your way out.'

Sheree looked around, eager to make a start on the room. She saw Tammy, Maureen, Peggy and Ursula by the window and gave a wave that shook her whole body.

'And don't worry about the money for the sitter. It's my pleasure,' said Tammy's mum in a voice that carried.

Sheree turned back. 'Oh Jesus, you're paying her? Debbie never said nothing. I thought she was just being nice, offering like that. Well, thanks, Helen. You're a real gem, you are.'

They both came to the window. The sun had set. Bugs clamoured at the fly screen. Pastor Martin was late.

Tammy's mum frowned at the plate in Maureen's hands. 'They were meant to be for after.' She tried to take it, but Maureen wouldn't let go.

Sheree took a Tim Tam. 'Oop, slippery bugger.' She ate it in two bites and licked her fingers.

'What's the topic for tonight?' said Peggy. 'Reincarnation?

Tarot? Have you told your preacher friend that's what you used to be into, because it wasn't that long ago—'

'I thought, since we've suffered a bereavement, it would be a good opportunity for us to come together in prayer,' said Tammy's mum.

'Is Guangyu Lau coming?' asked Ursula, in a way that was both hopeful and shifty.

'I'm not expecting the Laus, no,' said Tammy's mum, breaking off the filthy look she was giving Peggy.

Ursula sighed. 'That's a shame.'

Peggy saw a chance to poke. 'Did you even ask them?'

'Actually, no,' said Tammy's mum. 'I thought it would be insensitive.'

'What?' said Sheree.

Peggy laughed.

'I just thought,' said Tammy's mum, 'it's likely they have their own religion. Something Eastern, perhaps—'

'Like the great God of Tarot?' said Peggy.

'And I didn't want to offend them with an invitation and make them feel awkward about having to explain.' Tammy's mum looked pointedly at Peggy. 'It's just plain good manners.'

Tammy grabbed another bikkie and took a bite before her mum could stop her.

'Go and turn off the record, Tammy,' ordered her mum. But Tammy didn't move. It would finish soon anyway. And then her mum would have to go and rescue it from the needle.

'Right,' said Peggy. 'It's just us, then, since Naomi's a no-show again. I take it everyone's read the newspaper?'

'Has anyone else had another visit?' asked Ursula. 'From the police? About the body parts they found?'

All eyes turned to Ursula. She reddened, reached for the cross on a chain around her neck. It seemed important to her, the way she touched it so much. Tammy wanted it. To add to her

202

collection. To get Ursula back for the pencil. Now *there* was a challenge.

'When did they come?' asked Peggy.

'Yesterday.'

'You've known since yesterday, while the rest of us had to wait to read it in the paper today?' Peggy was spitting chips. 'Where exactly was it found?'

'In a bag. In a bin,' said Ursula. 'I thought everyone knew.'

'Where? In a bag or a bin? Or in a bag in a bin? Which is it?' said Peggy.

'It was a plastic shopping bag. He – the policeman – said that to Lydia, not to me. I don't know what bin. I don't know if he said or not.'

'And you didn't ask? Imagine having a sister in the police and still not knowing what to ask.'

'I suppose I thought—'

'You said body parts. Was it a part or parts? What parts? The paper only said remains.'

'I don't know. He didn't say. I don't remember if he said.' Ursula was visibly upset, twisting her hands, touching her chest, grabbing at the cross. 'Have none of you had another visit?'

'Imagine not asking what body parts.' Peggy wouldn't let it go. She smoked furiously, her eyes still fixed on Ursula. 'I think you know more than you're letting on. I think you've got inside information and you're keeping it to yourself. And I think that makes you look dodgy as all hell.'

Beside Tammy, Ursula quaked and was silent. Her hands pressed her cross to her chest. Tammy thought she looked dodgy as all hell too. It was satisfying to have someone else think so, even if it was Peggy. Tammy was busy storing up all her observations to put in her journal later. So far, she had a double page for Ursula, another for Sheree, and another titled *Other Goings On*. It looked like she'd have to expand Ursula's section.

Eventually, Peggy released Ursula from her glare and rounded on Maureen. 'And where does Cecil get off, talking to the newspaper like that, like he was representing us? Spokesman for the street, my arse. Some nerve! Makes him look like he's got something to hide too, putting his side across first like that. I've a good mind to talk to them myself.'

Maureen ignored Peggy entirely. 'What does everyone think of the new plastic bags?' she said. 'I like them. Sturdier than paper ones, don't you think? I wish all the supermarkets would use them.'

'Pretty nifty pigs that can put bits of body in a bag, eh, Peggy?' said Sheree. 'There goes your wild-pig theory. And, Maureen, I think plastic is grouse. Great stuff. The way of the future.'

'Why do you think the newspaper didn't report what body parts they found?' said Peggy. 'Do you think the police are purposefully hiding that information? From some of us, at least.' She tilted her nose up at Ursula.

'Why does it matter what parts they found?' said Tammy's mum. 'It's too gruesome to think about.'

'I just want to know,' said Peggy.

'But why? What difference could it make to you?' said Tammy's mum. 'I don't think a morbid fascination with the details is edifying.'

A fug of smoke from Peggy's cigarette hung above them. Heat pressed down. Tammy was surrounded by women's perfume and faces in make-up layered with a sheen of sweat. She probably wasn't the only one being unedified by thinking about the gory pieces of a dead and chopped-up body. She wanted to go to the plaza and have a look around, see if she could find anything the police had missed, but how could she do that with no way to get there on her own and with Colin hanging off her all the time?

'Does anyone else think it's weird that Naomi can't manage

204

to show her face at all?' said Peggy. 'She hasn't contributed one iota.'

'I miss Naomi,' said Maureen. 'Such a pretty face. Lovely girl.'

'Ha!' said Sheree. 'Naomi's not all she's cracked up to be.'

Peggy was on her in a trice. 'What do you mean by that?'

'Nothing,' said Sheree. 'Forget it. I'm not about to bitch about someone behind their back.'

But Peggy had taken hold of Sheree's arm and was steering her away from the others. Tammy heard her say, 'Let's have a chat, just you and me . . .' Tammy was about to follow, because if Sheree was going to say something about Naomi, it was probably untrue and a dead giveaway about Sheree trying to avoid attention, and therefore something Tammy should know about. But Maureen held the plate of biscuits under her nose and said, 'Let's see if we can stuff a whole Mint Slice in our mouths without looking like toads. You go first.'

That's when the front door opened again and Pastor Martin called out, 'Greetings!' before kicking over Sheree's bottle of wine.

'Oh, good,' Peggy's voice rang out. 'Now we can start the séance.'

Tammy's mum's mouth went paper-cut thin.

24

Nine Days After The Murder

Monday, 15 January 1979

A policeman arrived mid-afternoon. Naomi observed the shape of him through the screen door, silhouetted by the sun. He was tall, like Richard, though heavier set. It probably wasn't a good idea to keep ignoring his knocks or the instructions to phone him that he left in the letterbox, brought in by Sheree with silent judgement.

At least she was dressed.

He invited himself in.

Naomi went through her usual spiel, explaining why her husband wasn't home: that he was in the navy and therefore spent stretches of time away from home; that, yes, she supposed the allure of travel wore off after a while; that, yes, she missed him but knew his work was important; that, yes, haha, he always got a warm welcome on his return.

Throughout her marriage, Naomi had accepted and enjoyed the second-hand respect afforded her via Richard and his job.

As she spoke of Richard, the policeman became less formal. He said his name was Mark. They stood in the kitchen, next to the breakfast bar – the breakfast bar where Antonio had pinned her on one desperate afternoon, where she had pushed back into him and wound her legs around him.

'Now,' said the policeman. 'I'd like to ask you some questions about the disappearance of Mr Antonio Marietti.' He flipped open a notebook.

Is that what they were calling it? A disappearance? It sounded like a magic trick. Maybe he was trying to spare her.

Naomi felt light-headed. She held onto the bar, leant against it, placed her fingers where Antonio's had been.

'You're looking a bit peaky there.' He put his hands behind his back and lifted his chin, presenting his chest. 'Any reason you might be feeling anxious about this chat?'

'Forgive me,' she said, rubbing her forehead and then her eyes. 'It's the morning sickness. I can't keep anything down. It makes me a bit woozy.'

His gaze flicked to her belly and snagged on her breasts on its way up. He blushed.

'Say no more. You poor thing. More like all day and night sickness, right?'

He steered her to the lounge room, deposited her on a chair, and pulled another closer to sit opposite her, still wearing his shoes and leaving dusty prints on the carpet. He looked around – for what?

'You got any family nearby?' he said. 'A mum to come and help?'

'No,' said Naomi. 'She's not . . . here to help.'

'Look. Here's what I'll do.' He wrote something down on his notebook, tore off the page, folded it in half and handed it to her. 'That's my number at home.' He registered Naomi's surprise and went on quickly. 'Give my wife a call. Her name's Shirl. She had it bad. With all three of ours, and worse each time. Crook as a dog, fainting, blood pressure through the roof, the . . . you know' – here, he waved vaguely at his crotch, and no, Naomi didn't know – 'you name it, the works. Keep trying if she doesn't answer. Lord knows what she does with her days. Consider it my thanks to your husband for his service.'

He talked more about his wife and his kids and Naomi listened half-heartedly, the details passing her by, nodding and murmuring here and there, waiting for him to get to the point.

She was ready when he did.

'He did some work around the house for me. Odd jobs. Mainly outdoor stuff. Chopping wood – we had some branches come down from an old gum out the back. What's that? Yes, it is a yellow box as a matter of fact. They can be a menace, yes, but in this case, I think it was a storm that brought it down rather than a limb drop. You're right, I suppose this is the sort of weather to watch out for. No, thanks for offering, but don't bother yourself. Although, you're welcome to go have a look if you want to, of course. Anyway, Mr Marietti – Anto—' She swallowed hard. It wasn't easy to give away his name. But she tried again. 'Everyone called him Antonio – fixed the fence, did a bit of pruning, that sort of thing. Didn't have much to say for himself. But then, why would he have much to say to me? We weren't contemporaries. Is that the right word? I mean, he must have had friends his own age, younger than me. I wouldn't know about that. I'll be thirty this year. He did the work. I paid him. That was the extent of it.'

She had ended up prattling, afraid of pauses. The policeman – Mark – jotted down a few notes. Naomi couldn't see what he had written.

'It was while Richard was away. Just to help out, you see. General upkeep. I think I already said that, yes.'

Other words, unbidden, rose to her throat: *What would you say if I told you everything that happened? Would you say that it was my fault? That I wanted too much and now I've had to pay the price. Antonio, my Antonio, has paid the price too, but I'm the one who*

208

somehow has to go on without him. Richard is all I have left. And I can't tell you any of this because that would leave me all alone, and I'm more scared of being alone than anything else. Even Richard.

Naomi swallowed the words down and they settled in her gut, a dead weight.

Naomi was used to carrying unspoken words. Throughout her marriage to Richard, she had held onto a secret, tucked deep inside her, shrouded in shame, and that secret was that she didn't want children. Not now, not ever, and there was no chance of changing her mind. The instinct, intact in all other women as far as Naomi could see, was, in her, entirely lacking. A failing of nature. It was impossible to manufacture any enthusiasm for the idea of motherhood, not after knowing first-hand the damage a bad mother could do.

In the early days, Richard wasn't in any hurry, and Naomi's secret stayed safely shut away. They went together to the doctor to get the pill. And then, very quickly and without warning, Richard *was* in a hurry. He wanted a houseful of little Kreegers, the more the better. They went together to the doctor to stop the pill and ask how long they could expect to wait.

Naomi had to shop around before she could find a sympathetic doctor on her own. The first refused to prescribe the pill without the consent of her husband. The second got increasingly sweaty and short of breath as he quizzed her on her sexual history and activities. The third, Dr Fraser, a woman with the energy of a kelpie, foisted a starter pack and prescription on her without wanting to know her marital status or even her name. 'God,' she said. 'I wish I could give these out as freebies to every woman in Australia. Tell your friends to come.' Naomi wasn't sure she had friends. She supposed making friends was something you were meant to learn young. She stopped short of asking the doctor to be her friend.

She hid the pills in a pin cushion secured shut with a nappy pin of all things, tucked into a sewing box she never used. Her movements to open and fasten the pin cushion each day were furtive, even when Richard wasn't in the house.

Richard was getting frustrated. It had been fourteen months of trying, and nothing. He was used to getting what he wanted, so where was his baby? He didn't believe in tempting fate, only being prepared, so he brought home a steady stream of baby clothes, nappies (and, yes, nappy pins), blankets, a rattle, a crib – all sorts of baby paraphernalia.

It was inevitable, Naomi supposed, that she would stuff up. Richard booked a week away on the coast, a change of scenery. A chance to de-stress and recharge their batteries. Free time to really put their minds to the task at hand. Naomi considered multiple hiding places for her pills: her purse; the camera case; her jeans pocket; a tampon box; taped to the inside cover of a romance novel. She carefully weighed the risks of each place. In the end, she forgot to bring them at all. One bloody week. A fortnight after they got home, everything started to taste off, metallic. She wanted to sleep all the time. By the end of the following week she was chucking her guts up.

Naomi never blamed Colin. It wasn't his fault she'd been stupid. Not his fault that there was something wrong with her; that she was unwomanly and unmotherly and unworthy. She would try to make it up to him; find ways to compensate for her failings. But she wouldn't make the same mistake again.

Except she did. This time, Naomi's mistake was simply getting carried away and forgetting to take the pills even though she had them close at hand. Her mum's voice echoed in her head: *Stupid, sloppy bitch.*

Naomi saw the policeman – Mark, he insisted – to the door. The sun had dipped low enough to be obscured by the Lanahans' house over the road, the hills behind a featureless outline of themselves. Long shadows stretched over the island towards Naomi, like reaching fingers.

She stood there long after he'd gone, eyes locked with Mrs Lau, who stood on her balcony. It wasn't the first time the two women had watched each other. She gave Naomi the heebie-jeebies. It was very forward of her to stare like that. There was no way of telling if there was benevolence there or something sinister. Was it a mistake to tell the policeman that she and Antonio were nothing more than a loose, ad-hoc, odd-job arrangement? Would Mrs Lau say otherwise? Had she ever seen Naomi at Antonio's house? Naomi had forgotten to factor her in as a threat.

Naomi shivered. She wrapped her arms around herself and counted her breaths. In her hand, the policeman's home phone number was getting damp and crumpled. Her mind traced over the last words he spoke before he left: *We'll have to come back and do a search of the property, as it's the closest thing Mr Marietti had to a workplace. I'm sorry it'll be an inconvenience.*

25

Eleven Days After The Murder

Wednesday, 17 January 1979

Guangyu watched Jennifer fry slices of Spam to eat just before tea. It bothered Guangyu. There was perfectly good fish ball soup in the pot on the stove next to the frypan that she could have if she was determined to ruin her appetite.

'All I'm saying is that you have all this time in the holidays,' said Guangyu. 'There are plenty of books you could be reading.'

'No, thanks,' said Jennifer. 'Not for me.'

'How do you know you won't like them if you don't try? I've heard *Tess of the d'Urbervilles* is very good. Good for girls nearing womanhood.'

'Save me.' Jennifer flipped over the Spam with a spatula. 'I'm not you, Ma. Chances are, if you like it, I won't.'

Guangyu tried another tack. 'You could try a new sport?'

She was met with silence. Jia Li looked up from her notepad. She was sitting next to the radio, her ear pressed close to the speaker. Herman sat in an easy chair, sifting through sleeves of photographs, oblivious to all around him, impervious and impenetrable. He had neither help nor comfort to offer Guangyu.

'You could make friends with Tammy,' suggested Guangyu,

not knowing when to give up. 'She's right next door and going to the high school this year. She's not that much younger than you.' Guangyu was well aware that three years felt a *lot* younger to a fifteen-year-old.

'I know what I could do,' said Jennifer, reaching for a plate, and Guangyu's heart swelled with hope. 'I could mind my own bloody business and make my own bloody decisions about how I spend my holidays.'

'Poor Jennifer,' said Jia Li. 'You give her such hard time. Always on her back.'

Jennifer sat down next to Jia Li with her plate of Spam and a fork. They shared a look that blatantly excluded Guangyu, and nudged shoulders.

'When I was your age ...' began Guangyu, not knowing where she was taking this.

'Let me guess,' said Jennifer around a mouthful. 'When you were my age, was it the Japanese chasing you or dropping bombs on you? Or was it the communists trying to kill you? Or recruit you?'

Guangyu shushed Jennifer at the mention of communists. All these years later, she couldn't stop herself from looking over her shoulder. When neighbour betrayed neighbour and families informed on their own, words were weapons, and Guangyu couldn't shake the habit of handling certain words with care. Especially now, with tensions running high on Warrah Place, the way neighbours watched each other and assessed each other, the way they worried about being watched and assessed. Guangyu wasn't oblivious to the suspicions she and her family were under. She was certain Jennifer felt it too. It was impossible to miss the side-eyes and backward glances. Silence accompanied by charged eyes was as loud as an accusation. She knew full well about the gatherings at Helen's house on Thursday evenings and not once had she been invited.

'At least the communists didn't try to make you play softball and wear knickerbockers or force you to be friends with pip-squeaks,' mumbled Jennifer, breaking into Guangyu's thoughts.

'I would never have spoken—' began Guangyu.

'To your ma like that,' interrupted Jennifer. 'Yeah, I know.' She took her empty plate into the kitchen.

Jia Li beckoned Guangyu closer. 'You too soft on her,' she said quietly but not gently. 'That's why she no respect you.'

Guangyu sat down next to Herman, hoping that proximity would help her feel less alone. The nervous feeling in her chest was physically painful and there was no relief. She longed for a night of uninterrupted sleep. If she had more sleep, maybe then she would handle things with Jennifer better.

Beside her, Herman's head emerged from his photography box. He placed his hand on Guangyu's arm and applied pressure. She was too tired to feign interest in his photos now.

The pressure on her arm increased. 'Look,' he said.

He dropped a photo in her lap. Guangyu looked at Herman and then at the photo. She held it close to her face and then at a distance.

She gasped. 'It's pornographic.'

Jennifer was back from the kitchen in a flash. 'Let me see.'

'Hush your mouth,' said Guangyu, her thoughts running at double-speed.

'Fine,' grumbled Jennifer. 'I'll never speak again.' She huffed off to her bedroom.

Jia Li padded over in her slippers and leant in to look.

In the foreground of the photo was a close-up of a branch of the jacaranda tree in the back yard in full glorious purple bloom. The photo had been taken in the springtime. In the background, over the fence in the garden of the Italian House, were two fig-ures, shown from their waists up, both naked. They were blurry about the edges and they were embracing so it wasn't easy to

214

tell which arms belonged to which body. Even so, there was no mistaking, once you spotted the head of thick wavy hair, the delicate girlish neck, that the two figures were Antonio Marietti and Naomi Kreeger.

'You know what this means?' Guangyu said to Herman. 'It doesn't prove anything exactly, but if I show it to the police, they would know there was shady business going on. Something worth looking into. It wouldn't just be me being a crazy lady.' Then again, Guangyu didn't say, if she started talking to the police, would they ask questions about more than a dead boy?

Close up, Herman's face looked old. His chin had weakened and he was getting jowly. His mouth, perhaps through lack of use, drooped downwards at the edges.

'You think I should show this to the police?' Guangyu asked. 'You decide.'

'Why did you give it to me? You don't think it's too risky? What if the police start coming over more? What if they start looking into . . .' Guangyu's eyes and head flicked towards Jia Li.

Herman's cheek twitched but his gaze didn't waver. Maybe he had been paying attention after all.

'There was a killing. An immigrant, not like us, but like us?' He was searching Guangyu's face for answers she didn't have. 'Young, like Jennifer.' He swallowed, hard. Herman was scared, Guangyu realised. 'You decide,' he said again.

Then he glanced nervously at his ma.

Jennifer had been grumbling to Guangyu about being kept awake by Mrs Cheung's moans coming through their thin, papery apartment wall. Jia Li was grumbling about being kept awake by Jennifer tossing and turning all night. Guangyu wished they would both hold their tongues and hold onto hope that they would soon be in Australia.

They were ready to leave Hong Kong but there was a

stumbling block, and it was a big one: Jia Li. She had no birth certificate, no documentation, no identification papers, and without those, her application to emigrate had stalled. Herman went to meeting after meeting with officials, trying to acquire the necessary papers, only to be sent to another office, until he was going in circles and chasing his own tail. Guangyu feared their dreams would come to nothing.

Mrs Cheung was another stumbling block. What would she do without them? For months, the Laus had been caring for their elderly neighbour. It was the moaning that alerted them to her predicament. They found her fading away, bedbound with an ulcerated leg, in an airless room. The doctor had said it was only a matter of time but wouldn't be drawn on how much time.

One evening, when Mrs Cheung could only manage a simple broth with pork fat and her eyes had begun to dull, Herman sat at the cabinet in her bedroom, sorting out her correspondence, making a growing pile of papers to be discarded. Guangyu fed Mrs Cheung patiently from a spoon and wiped her chin gently. She sensed Herman's body freeze and looked up to find him staring at her, his eyes wide, his mouth agape. She looked at the paper in his hand and he turned it around to face her. A birth certificate, dated 28 November 1892. Close enough. It would do.

The plan formed, gained weight and was agreed on wordlessly, all within a matter of seconds. As Herman folded the paper with shaking hands, Mrs Cheung became aware of the shift in atmosphere in the room. She turned her head towards Herman. Guangyu placed her palm to Mrs Cheung's face and calmly tilted her head back towards her. She smiled warmly and offered her another spoonful of broth.

Mrs Cheung died that night.

Jia Li had her travel documents within a week. The secret

bound Guangyu, Herman and Jia Li. No one could ever know what they had done.

The photograph of Antonio and Naomi lay on the flat of Guangyu's palm, both feather-light and heavy with import. It was a boon and a dilemma. She had something tangible. Not proof exactly, but it was a lead. It was more than her word alone. But Jia Li was the dilemma – could they keep their secret if the police started poking around? – and she stood in front of Guangyu now, leaning down to look at the photograph.

'Not our business,' said Jia Li. Like a shot, she plucked the photograph from Guangyu's hand. She ripped it in half, then quarters, then eighths, while Guangyu closed her fist on empty air.

Slave-maker ants are so busy and so specialised that they don't have to do any other jobs. They go rampaging through other nests, using brute force to kill ants and steal their babies (pupae or larvae). Some slave-makers are more crafty. They spray chemicals that trick ants of another colony into fighting each other. Or they spray a chemical that will make ants so spaced out they forget to fight when the slave-makers come to carry off the babies.

It is unusual for slave-makers to completely destroy a colony. They leave them beaten but able to recover, so they can come back and have another go the next year.

26

Thirteen Days After The Murder

Friday, 19 January 1979

Colin had been dropping hints about not wanting to go home all day. 'Mum's in a flap,' he said. 'The police have been looking through everything.'

'They only had to cos Antonio worked there,' said Tammy. 'Nothing to get your knickers in a twist over.'

'They've made a mess. She doesn't like mess. Even watching ants is better than Mum and the mess.'

Tammy wasn't sure where she was going with her ant project. She had facts but no conclusions. Same with Antonio's murder. She had lots of observations and suspicions but no conclusions. And the pressure was building. With thirteen days gone since Antonio had been murdered and eighteen days left until school started, desperation was creeping in.

It was Friday afternoon and Tammy's dad was let off work early for a change.

Tammy and Colin wore matching Holly Hobbie nighties, selected by Colin and grudgingly agreed to by Tammy. The clothes Tammy's mum had brought home for Colin remained in a pile on Tammy's desk, untouched. The nighties had floaty sleeves and flounces at the hems. Their skin was on high alert with static electricity. Colin had chosen one too big for him. It skimmed the floor as he walked and he kept rolling his shoulders to stop it slipping off. He looked like a starlet.

'Right, chaps,' said Tammy's dad. 'It's just us tonight. Mum's at a prayer retreat for the weekend.' He said the words *prayer retreat* carefully, like he was holding them with oven mitts.

'What's a prayer retreat?' said Colin.

Tammy's dad frowned. 'Not sure exactly.'

'What will she be doing?' said Tammy.

'Dunno,' said her dad. 'Praying, I suppose.'

'Can't she do that here?' said Colin.

'All excellent questions,' said Tammy's dad. 'Maybe they get better results if they go somewhere special to pray. Extra points. I'm not sure of the rules, to be honest.'

'That makes sense, I suppose,' said Colin, but Tammy wasn't at all sure the explanation was theologically sound.

'I've got a question about souls,' said Colin. 'Our souls are in our bodies while we're alive, right?'

'Don't see why not,' said Duncan.

'What happens if we die and our body is in pieces?' said Colin in a matter-of-fact voice, as if everyone didn't know he was talking about Antonio. 'Can pieces of our soul find each other again? And what happens if they can't? Can our souls still get into heaven?'

'You're losing me, mate,' said Duncan. 'But I don't think it's anything you need to fret about.'

Colin didn't look satisfied, so Tammy said, 'I reckon the soul stays together no matter what happens to the body. Like, the soul lives in the body but doesn't need the body.'

'Yeah, that's the ticket,' said Duncan. 'Well done, Tam.'

'Theoretically, at least,' said Tammy. 'I don't think there's any scientific evidence.'

After a while, Tammy's dad stopped looking at her and turned to Colin. 'Do you live here now?'

'Pretty much.'

'Nights too?'

Colin shrugged. 'Not so much.'

'Scoot over the road and ask your mum if you can stay here tonight.'

Colin's face lit up. He gathered up the hem of his nightie and was off like greased lightning before Tammy's dad could change his mind.

'So, Tamalam Lanahan,' said Tammy's dad as soon as Colin had gone. 'What's with Colin and the frocks?'

'Dunno.'

'Has he got no clothes of his own?'

'Yeah, he does.'

'So why is he wearing your stuff?'

'He just likes it, that's all.'

'Hmm.' Her dad stretched, then rubbed the back of his neck with both hands. 'Do you think we should be worried about it?'

'You mean cos of Mum?'

'Nah, not Mum.' He moved on quickly, like a stone skimming water. 'I was thinking about Colin's dad. What if he comes home and sees . . . I mean, if he thinks we've turned his boy into . . .'

'Into what?'

'Not sure exactly. So, you don't think we should worry? No? That's good. Great. Nothing to worry about. OK then, we won't worry.'

Tammy's mum had left a shepherd's pie in the oven to be heated up, its mash topping forked in even furrows. Tammy's dad looked at the knobs on the oven, turned a few, peered through the glass door with one eye shut and then the other, asked if anyone knew how to work the bloody thing, and finally declared it too hot to put the oven on anyway.

They ate Fruit Loops while watching *Young Talent Time*, each of them adding more Fruit Loops or milk to their bowls at will, a continuous topping-up. Everyone was in a good mood; whimsical verging on reckless: Tammy's dad because he'd got off work early and had had a few beers, Colin because of the sleepover and Tammy, despite herself, because her dad was in charge, because of the Fruit Loops, because of Holly Hobbie, because for just this moment, it felt like a giant pause button had been pushed.

Once, while Tammy's dad was passing the milk to her, their eyes met — a silent agreement that there was no need to tell Mum about any of this.

Afterwards, there was no *time for a bath now* and no *go brush your teeth*. They just got tired and went to bed, Colin in the spare bed in Tammy's room because the spare room was chock-a-block full of yoga mats and macramé yarn and a loom and a yoghurt-making machine and a meditation gong and other stuff long forgotten. And a pram and a cot and a basinet under it all.

But it was no good. Tammy's teeth felt furry, and although she tried to avoid touching them with her tongue, she eventually gave up and got out of bed to brush them.

On her way back from the bathroom, she heard voices coming from the lounge room, and snuck into her watching spot near the wooden rail.

It was the policeman from that day on the island, the tall one.

'What do you know of your neighbour, Mr Pavlović?'

'Who, Joe?' said Tammy's dad. 'Great bloke. Salt-of-the-earth type. Makes his own plonk. Shocking stuff.'

'Hm. Seemed a jumpy type to me. What do you know of his background?'

'Not much. Came over from Yugoslavia some time ago, but

222

I don't know when exactly. I gather he was over there during the war, poor bloke. They had a hard time of it, that area, didn't they? But Joe's not one to talk about it. Never complains about anything. He's a cheery sort, generally.'

'It was Mr Pavlović who identified Mr Marietti's foot for us.'

'Anyone could have done that,' said Duncan. 'Antonio wore these sort of Italian thong things. We all knew about the birthmark.'

'We've been given some information, by one of your neighbours, that Mr Pavlović is missing some tools.' He didn't say so, but Tammy would bet anything it was Cecil, the rotter.

'That's right. Ever since the church working bee.'

The policeman referred to his notebook and Tammy wished she had hers to hand. 'A pick. Spade. Axe. Chainsaw. A body doesn't dismember itself. You knew about the missing implements and didn't think it would be of interest to us?'

'Well, now that you put it like that, I can see your point.'

'The thing is, Mr Lanahan, our forensic team have analysed the remains we've been able to recover. The striations on the bone fragments match the blades of a chainsaw.'

'Look, Joe's a good egg, I'm sure of it.' Tammy was sure of it too. The tools going missing was a coincidence, a waste of time. Some ratbag nicked them or put them somewhere by mistake. She was proud of her dad for standing up for Joe. 'Listen,' her dad went on in a hushed voice, 'what can you tell me about the remains that have been found and how much is still out there? Only, the mind can run away with things it doesn't know.'

'There's been nothing further since the plaza discovery.'

'And the . . . bits . . . found there?'

'It's a bit grisly. I'll spare you the details.'

Tammy's dad glanced around him, up towards the dining area, past Tammy. Tammy froze. 'I can handle it.'

'It wasn't easy to tell initially, what with it being summer . . .'

He trailed off. Perhaps he would have liked to spare himself the details. 'At any rate, the remains are . . . mixed – I mean, various . . . items. A forearm. A hand. A portion of leg.' Tammy could hear air whistling in and out through her dad's nose. 'All bundled up in butcher's paper.'

Tammy's dad put both hands on his head and bent at the waist. 'Oh boy,' he said after a shaky breath. As he straightened, he said, 'Butcher's paper? I heard it was a plastic bag.'

'Did you?' the policeman spoke sharply. 'There was a plastic bag as well as butcher's paper. Where did you hear about it?'

'My wife told me. Bit of gossip from the Bible club, I think.'

Tammy's legs were aching, seizing up from crouching and staying still. *A forearm. A hand. A portion of leg.* Tammy mentally repeated the items, so she could write them down later.

'It's a bit of a relief, though, truth to tell,' said Tammy's dad.

'How so, Mr Lanahan?'

'That it was down the plaza, I mean. With the foot found in our hills, it all felt too close to home, know what I mean? But maybe it was just some random – dreadful but random – event. Random killer for a random reason. Random that the foot ended up here.' He broke off and the policeman waited, letting the silence expand. Tammy's dad rubbed the back of his neck like he always did when he was nervous. 'You know, it's a shame Richard missed his jog that morning. Might have seen something. Or maybe it's lucky for him he didn't go. He's a fit bloke, could hold his own, but still, who'd want to come across a nutcase in the hills?'

The policeman looked at his notebook. 'Mr Kreeger from Number Three? He normally jogs in the hills?'

'When he's at home, yes. Very conscientious about it. Puts me to shame.' He patted his belly.

'And your neighbours on the other side? What do you make of them?'

224

'The Laus? Never had any trouble. Keep to themselves. There's some on the street with old-fashioned views, you know the sort.' The policeman's face remained impassive. 'But I'd eat my hat if there was anything dodgy going on there.'

'Is there anything you can think of that I ought to know?'

'No. Nothing comes to mind. Only, can I ask . . .? I mean, all these questions about the neighbours, and this is all pretty bad and a shock for everyone and I've got this daughter, she's only twelve and prone to . . . well, I worry about her. And I'm looking after a boy who's asking questions about souls. The longer this drags on, the more I wonder if the kids are going to be OK. If we all are. What I want to know is, if you can say, do you think this was a one-off?'

'You mean is the killer likely to strike again?'

'Bloody hell, sounds ominous when you say it like that. But, yes, is he?'

'Here's the thing, Mr Lanahan. Usually in these types of cases, we'd be looking at the victim's family or ethnic community, because to be killed like this, in this way, it's no accident. Someone had a reason. Except Mr Marietti had no family in the country at the time of his death. And he had no connections with the Italian community in Canberra.' The detective took a hankie from his pocket and wiped his nose. 'We know he did odd jobs on the street. We think he fancied himself a bit of a ladies' man. Other than that, we don't really know what he did with his time, how he filled his days. The picture we're getting is that Mr Marietti had no connections in this country other than those he formed right here on Warrah Place.'

'So, what you're telling me is . . .?'

'What I'm telling you is, don't be so quick to trust everything you think you know about someone. And also, that any information you have to give us, anything at all, would be very welcome.'

★

Tammy slipped back into bed and tucked her knees up to her chest. On the other side of her desk, Colin lay motionless but for the steady rise and fall of his chest, his breathing uncomplicated.

The policeman clearly had it in for Joe. Poor, innocent Joe.

And what about poor, dead Antonio? Bits of him found in a bin, as if he were nothing more than rubbish. She felt humiliated on his behalf. It felt like an immense pressure, like she was being squashed under something heavy and couldn't move or breathe. It was the same feeling she'd had at school so many times last year.

Things had been OK for a while. No major incidents. There was a pattern: Tammy was let in, then pushed out. In, out, in, out, shaken all about. When she was allowed in, Tammy hung around Narelle and Simone and other girls too, just on the outskirts, and no one told her to leave. At the same time, Tammy was aware that notes were passed but not to her, that there were inside jokes she was on the outside of, that, at best, she was tolerated. Someone with dignity might have chosen to leave, but Tammy did not.

Then came a day heading towards Easter when all the trees had turned yellow, orange and red, and hot laughter lingered visibly in cold air. The aluminium benches in the playground had gone from too hot to sit on to too cold to sit on in a snap of overnight frost.

It was before the first bell. The fallen leaves were crisp, not yet trampled and slippery. The girls kicked them into the air as they walked and talked. Tammy felt light and free. She laughed because the others did and not because she'd heard what was said.

Simone stopped walking. So did the others.

'I'd like to hear from Tammy what she found funny,' said Simone.

Tammy's mouth dried up. She had nothing to say for herself.

'I find it very interesting that someone who's supposed to be so brainy can be such a space cadet socially. Like, not just a bit, but a real thicko in that department. Don't *you* think that's interesting, Tammy?' Simone continued, her head cocked to one side.

Narelle was the first to break the silence with laughter and at first Tammy was grateful. But then Narelle said, 'She's so thick she can't even come up with an answer.'

Tammy's desk had two drawers that hung underneath like an udder. On the surface facing Tammy's bed was a row of round sticker remains. The stubborn residue had refused to come off and now they faced Tammy as she slept every night. The stickers, an ad for TattsLotto, had come with the newspaper, and Tammy had liked their bright colours. She stuck the banner, *Thank Your Lucky Balls*, above the shiny lottery balls. Tammy's mum clucked her tongue when she saw it and said, 'I wish you'd asked first because that's not something appropriate for your bedroom.' She said *balls* was another word for men's testicles. After that, Tammy wasn't keen on having a row of testicles watching her sleep, so she tried to scrape them off. Every so often, she had another go at getting the last of the sticky stuff off, and that's what she was doing now.

Tammy looked over to the other bed to see if Colin was still sleeping and saw his wide eyes watching her.

'I need help with a plan,' said Tammy. It was true. She needed all the help she could get. If she could pull this off, no one would ever call her a thicko again. And she could save Joe, clear his name, at the same time.

'Oh, good. I like plans,' said Colin. 'Is it going to be fun?'

'It might be.' Or it might not be. But things were already bad, so it had to be better than doing nothing. 'Looks like I'm stuck with you, so you'll have to be in on it too. We'll be a team.'

Tammy found herself hoping he would agree. She realised now that getting used to him hanging around, that not being lonely anymore, that liking having someone to be attached to – even if it was only Colin – had crept up on her without her permission.

Colin didn't say anything. He might have been holding his breath. The only bit of him Tammy could see, his head on the pillow, looked like it was detached from the rest of him.

'You know how we've been watching the neighbours and recording our observations in the ant journal? Well, it has a purpose to it. A serious one.' She paused to check she had his attention. 'I'm trying to find out what happened to Antonio. I'm really good at finding things out, spying and that.' She didn't want to skite, but it was true.

It took a long time for Colin to answer. 'I can't help,' he whispered. 'I'm only eight.'

'That's a limitation, true. But you see, I've already set my mind to it, already started, so you might as well join in.' Tammy's cheery tone contradicted the feeling that was rising inside her: that she wanted Colin to do this with her, that she'd got used to him and didn't want to be on her own anymore, that time was running out and she needed help, that she didn't know what she'd do if he said no. 'Please, Colin.'

Again, Colin stayed quiet for a long time, thinking unreadable thoughts.

'I don't want to,' said Colin. 'But I want to be a team. Can we do a different plan?'

'No. I need you to help with this one,' said Tammy – no more bluster or cajoling. 'It's my only hope.'

'Will it make you feel better?' he asked. 'Will it stop you crying in the night-time?'

'I think it will.'

'Yes, OK then.'

'Yes?'

'Yes,' said Colin, more firmly this time. 'Does this mean we don't have to do the ants anymore?'

But Tammy had stopped listening. She was too busy imagining Simone's face when she found out that Tammy had not only spent her summer slap-bang in the middle of a murder investigation but had solved it too.

If you think that ants don't communicate because they don't use words, you'd be dead wrong. Their glands produce an enormous range of chemical compounds to send messages. Instead of noses, they receive messages through sensors on their antennae. They can send and receive all sorts of messages: about an attack being on the way, about where to find food, about who's in and who's out of the colony, about what their job is, etc. What they don't do is tell lies or purposefully withhold information from other ants in their colony. They don't leave each other trying to guess what the heck is going on.

27

Fourteen Days After The Murder

Saturday, 20 January 1979

Tammy woke up the next morning when the sky was light but the sun had not yet shown its face. She felt energised, ready to get up and get on. The best way to get the police off Joe's back was to show them where to look instead. For that, she needed evidence, something more solid than she already had on Ursula and Sheree. Would it be worth recruiting Debbie to the team? Tammy was in two minds. On the one hand, a team of her and Colin wasn't much. On the other, it was imperative that Tammy remain in charge. Maybe Debbie would think she could be in charge because she was older. And maybe she'd chuck a wobbly about spying on her auntie Ursula. *Best leave it for now*, thought Tammy.

And it was Saturday. That meant Dad's famous breakfast fry-up. Sometimes the smell of bacon would come to her in her dreams. When her mum did the bacon, the rind was like a rubber band. You could put your jaw out trying to get through it. But her dad turned the rind so crispy it crackled under your teeth and dissolved on your tongue. And the eggs. Her mum's eggs still had bits of stringy gelatinous gloop on top, but her dad pushed the eggs right to the edge of too far, until the bottom had turned brown and lacy, and the yolk had a bit of a wobble but wasn't about to run all over your plate.

When Colin and Tammy got up, though, there was no Saturday-morning smell coming from the kitchen. There was no telly on.

There was only a note.

> Had to pop into the office. Sorry.
> Don't do anything I wouldn't do. Haha.
> See ya later, crocodile. Haha.
> Dad
> P.S. When you've had brekky, go to Joe and Zlata's until I get back.
> P.P.S. Seriously, don't muck about. Go straight there.

So, no Saturday fry-up. And no Fruit Loops left. Or milk. Tammy and Colin ate dry Weet-Bix spread with margarine and Vegemite. Colin thought it was fabulous.

Tammy let Colin choose their clothes again. It probably wasn't wise to indulge him, but the truth was she didn't mind anymore. He chose matching sundresses in rainbow stripes with thin shoulder straps. They were loose and floaty; perfect for letting the air in, although Tammy's was getting tight under the arms. The colours on Colin's had faded to pastels by the suns of previous summers.

They hadn't got two steps outside before Colin tripped over and took the skin off his knee, old scab and all. It was bad. Colin cupped his hands over it and still blood dribbled down his leg. He peeked through his fingers and breathed fast.

'Come on, then,' said Tammy.

She led him into the bathroom and ran the tap in the bathtub over his knee while Colin tried to keep his shoes dry. He hitched his dress up and tucked the hem into his pants with one hand. He took his other hand away from his knee when she told him to. He held still when she told him to. He held onto her shoulder when she told him to so he wouldn't fall over again.

Tammy wasn't sure if she was doing it right. But Suzi, sitting like a sphynx and watching Tammy's every move, hadn't intervened yet.

Colin pressed his lips tightly together when Tammy dabbed his knee with a towel, and squeezed his eyes shut when she got out the Mercurochrome. His body shook with the effort to hold his leg and his face still.

'You're allowed to cry, you know,' said Tammy, painting his knee lurid red to stop the germs getting in.

'But I want you to see that I can be brave.'

'Being brave is overrated. Getting even is better.' Tammy sniffed the Mercurochrome and looked at the label on the bottle. Was merbromin poisonous?

'How do I get even with the back step?' said Colin. 'Anyway, the crying feeling has gone now. Thank you.'

On top of the compost bin, Tammy reached down for Colin's hand to help him up. He kept hold of her hand but also kept his feet planted. Suzi sprang onto the fence and waited patiently.

'Am I meant to write things down too now?' he said.

'What?'

'Only I don't have any paper. And my writing's not neat. Or quick.'

'What?'

'What about questions? Should we decide on questions first?'

'What?'

'For our spy mission.'

'Oh,' said Tammy. 'No. None of that. Just keep your eyes and ears open. But not in an obvious way.'

'Right,' said Colin. 'Should I wear a hat?'

'What?' They were still holding hands and Tammy shook hers free. 'They'll give us nothing if they know we want it.'

'Tammy?'

'Yeah?'

'Why would they tell us anything anyway? We're just kids.'

'The perfect disguise,' said Tammy. She reached again for his hand, which he'd kept dangling in the air.

The pergola outside Joe and Zlata's back door dripped with grapevines and bougainvillea. It always made Tammy feel like she was stepping through an enchanted portal. It was just an ordinary kitchen inside, though. There was a fly zapper on the wall, the sort you'd find in a fish-'n'-chip shop. It gave off a bluish light and a hum, each buzz and spark announcing another death.

'At last!' cried Joe with raised arms. He always made Tammy feel like he'd been longing for her to turn up, but today, his enthusiasm was at about 47 per cent of its usual intensity.

Joe ushered them in and then leant against the kitchen bench. He wore Hard Yakka shorts and socks. His big toe poked through one of the socks. By the back door sat his boots, creased at the ankles, laces splayed, one on its side like roadkill. Joe's fingers drummed on the bench.

Leslie from over the road sat at the table, his big hands holding a small cup of coffee, an expression of happy expectation on his face. More often than not, Leslie could be found at Joe and Zlata's at mealtimes.

'What's that you're putting in?' he asked Zlata.

Zlata was in her usual spot in front of the stove. Large chunks of tomatoes sizzled and steamed in a hot pan. Three plates with thick slices of Zlata's bread waited on the bench.

'Vinegar. Brings out the sweetness,' she said.

234

'Vinegar,' said Leslie. 'Who'd a thunk it? You're a marvel, Zlata.'

Tammy could tell that Zlata was smiling just from the shape of her back.

'You two want some?' said Zlata.

'We've already eaten,' said Tammy, because cooked tomatoes were gross, even Zlata's.

'Full as a goog,' said Colin.

Joe was there but not there. He stared out of the window, looking troubled.

Zlata piled the tomatoes onto the bread and put a plate in front of Leslie. She touched Joe's shoulder to bring him back to himself.

'So much better without the bread toasted,' said Leslie. 'Who'd a thunk it?'

Leslie had lots of little sayings like *who'd a thunk it?* and *it's better to be late than dead on time* and *steady as she goes* and *much of a muchness*. They all added up to make him someone who was reliable.

Zlata snapped her fingers under Joe's nose and he, too, sat and ate.

'I have some spare time today,' Leslie said to Joe. 'How about we do a search for your tools? I bet we could find them if we really put our minds to it.'

Joe shrugged helplessly. 'No use. I looked. I went back to working bee that night, with torch, and looked and looked. And no tools. And now I have big extra problem.' He sighed and rubbed his eyes. 'I went on my own and I told this to police. But no one saw me, so maybe no one believe me.' His next breath shook.

Zlata put a hand on his arm, reminded him with her eyes that Tammy and Colin were present, and gave a slight shake of her head. 'Enough,' she said, when actually it wasn't nearly enough.

235

Tammy wanted to know precisely what time Joe went back to the working bee. It might help her work out what time Antonio had left. And she wanted to know exactly where he had looked for his tools. It might help her work out where they were.

'Jeez. What's that smell?' Cecil was at the door, letting himself in and making Joe jump a mile.

Zlata's face looked like her tomatoes had turned rotten.

Cecil went straight for Leslie. 'A quiet word in your ear, if you don't mind.' He nodded at the door.

Leslie looked regretfully at his half-full plate, wiped vinegary juice from his chin, scraped his chair back and followed Cecil outside.

When he came back in, Leslie was subdued, his face tight. He looked like he'd swallowed a fly. He took a big gulp of coffee.

Now, *this* was interesting. What on earth had been said? Leslie worked with Antonio, so maybe he knew something Cecil wanted to know or vice versa.

Joe caught Tammy's eye and shook his head. 'We mind own beeswax,' he said.

'We, that is, Tammy and me have a particular interest in other people's beeswax,' said Colin, waggling his eyebrows at Tammy.

Tammy sent him a death glare.

Joe looked from one to the other and the look he settled on Tammy wasn't so much one of warning as of fear.

Leslie clapped his hands and rubbed them together as if closing one mood and opening another. 'You two at a loose end today?' he asked Tammy and Colin.

'Kinda,' said Tammy, hedging her bets until she knew what was on offer.

'Pop over if you want,' he said. 'Peggy would like the company.'

Tammy was sure Peggy would like nothing of the sort. But Peggy was a gossip. She might know something worth finding out. Also, Peggy and Leslie had a pool and it was another stinking-hot day.

'We'll be over in a bit,' said Tammy.

'That was abysmal,' said Tammy. 'What was that business about beeswax?'

They had climbed the fence back into Tammy's back yard and Tammy had called a strategy meeting by the barbecue. Suzi attended too.

'I'm going to dump you if you can't keep a secret,' said Tammy.

'But I didn't say anything about Antonio.' Colin wasn't contrite and simpering as Tammy had expected. He stood up straight, defiant. 'I'm pretty good with secrets, actually, if you want to know.'

'Go get your swimmers on and meet me back here,' said Tammy.

While Tammy and Colin were crossing over the island, a crowd of people turned the corner into Warrah Place and stood in front of the Italian House, gazing up at it as if they were at an art gallery or museum. Tammy recognised some of the people from houses on Carnegie Street. Within moments, Sheree launched herself from her house and into her front yard.

'Hey!' she called. 'Yeah, you. I'm talking to all of youse. Why don't you bring a deckchair and packed lunch and make a day of it?' She put her fists on her hips, staring down the intruders. 'Go on, piss off with the lot of you.'

Tammy and Colin sat side by side on a hard couch in the rumpus room with their knees together and their swimmers on under their dresses.

'Then she said the bit about the packed lunch,' said Colin, giggling. 'It was so funny.'

'So you said.' Peggy regarded them from behind an ironing board, warily eyeing Colin's traffic-light-red knee. 'Good on her for getting rid of them. I can't stand this being a spectacle for others to gawp at.' She ironed with one hand and smoked with the other, occasionally flicking ash into an ashtray on a shelf behind her without looking. 'Stand up,' she said to Colin.

He did.

'Turn around.'

He did.

'Who put you in that?' Peggy wafted her cigarette at Colin's dress.

'I did,' he said.

'Hmpf.' She turned back to her ironing and Colin sat down. 'You'd do better in a bias cut.'

'Good to know, Peggy, thanks,' said Colin. He then whispered to Tammy, 'Do you know what that is? Have we got one?'

'How have you been, Peggy?' said Tammy, ignoring Colin. She noticed that Peggy hadn't bothered to tell her what would suit her.

'Practically evaporating.' She looked it too. There wouldn't be much left of Peggy if you took away the make-up and hair. 'You?'

'Oh, same,' said Tammy. She rubbed her neck, pulled at the strap of her swimmers and looked wistfully outside to the pool.

Peggy grunted.

Being near Peggy was exhausting even if you were sitting down. She was always on the move; small, jerky, stop-start movements. No pause before the next, like a wind-up toy that never wound down. Her whole body on the go, shifting weight here, there, all over the place. Even her eyes didn't rest on one place for long. In between drags on her smoke, her fingers scuttled through the laundry she was ironing like a spider, flashing bright-pink nails.

238

The telly was on. Colin sang along to the Care for Kids ad, head and knees bouncing, dress swishing.

Tammy and Peggy met each other's eyes in a moment of shared amusement that felt weird.

Tammy shoved Colin to shut him up. She tried again.

'It's so hard to cool off, you know, without a pool.'

'Plenty of space in your back yard for a pool,' said Peggy.

'Which is exactly what I've been saying for literally *years*,' said Tammy. 'But still, no pool.'

'Such a hardship.'

'You've no idea.'Tammy meant it. Peggy could go for a swim whenever she wanted to.

'Don't you have any parents to look after you?' asked Peggy, looking at Colin.

'My mum's sick,' said Colin, apprehensively.

'So I hear. Bit irregular to be this bad, though. Sure she's not bunging it on to get some peace and quiet? Or for some other reason?' Colin looked at his lap and Tammy wanted to tell him to ignore Peggy, that she was just an old hag. 'Was she this crook when you were on the way?'

'I don't remember,' said Colin.

Peggy laughed; a sound that was a cross between scraping something along corrugated iron and a tractor engine starting up. 'Fair enough,' she said. 'What about you, missy?'

'Dad's at work,'Tammy said.

Peggy waited.

'And Mum's at a prayer retreat.'

Peggy stood the iron up and it hissed. 'Personally, I think introspection and rumination are indulgent,' she said. 'You can tell your mum I said that. I also think she'd do well to get a grip. She's not the only one with troubles.You can tell her I said that too. She should stick to hosting dinner parties. We could all do with another one of those.'

Leslie came in with a pot of tea, so Tammy had another go at tugging on the strap of her swimmers. Colin caught on and flapped his dress up to show his swimmers underneath.

'You two going for a swim?' said Leslie.

'That is, as yet, undecided,' said Tammy.

Colin squirmed beside her, and she pressed down hard on his foot with hers.

'Well, just say the word if you fancy it,' said Leslie.

Tammy and Colin exchanged hopeless looks.

'What's with you two?' said Peggy, pouring herself a cup of black tea. 'Why won't you just say you want a swim?'

'It's the rules,' blurted Colin. 'Helen said. We're only allowed to swim if we're invited and we're not to go asking or even hinting at wanting to swim because that amounts to the same thing and God can always see our motives right down to their murky depths and nothing can be hidden, so He would know, and we would know He knows, so there's no use trying to get away with anything. That's the rule, right, Tammy?'

Leslie burst out laughing. Peggy didn't. She fixed Tammy with a look that made Tammy feel like her skin was on inside out, like it wasn't just God who could see down to her murky depths.

'Consider yourselves invited to swim whenever you want,' said Leslie and he went out again.

Colin leapt to his feet and started dancing.

But, 'Oh, no,' said Peggy. 'I don't think so. No swim today. Maybe another day, but only if you ask first. I won't have a bar of Helen's rules. Or God's, for that matter.'

It was enough to make you want to holler your head off – the meanness for no good reason. Tammy could do it right now: stand up and scream and scream and scream until all the screaming was used up and there was none left.

'You might not know this yet,' said Tammy, congratulating

240

herself for staying still and keeping her voice even, 'but I'm friends with Debbie now. And she told me that Antonio said that someone on Warrah Place was mutton dressed as lamb, but I'm not sure what that means or who he meant. Do you have any ideas about that, Peggy?'

Another look from Peggy that felt like being sliced open. 'I don't think you should concern yourself with anything to do with Antonio,' said Peggy.

'Why? Do you know something?' said Tammy.

'Do *you*?' said Peggy. 'Maybe your new friend Debbie has told you things?'

'What would you know about Debbie?'

'What do *you* know about Debbie?' said Peggy. 'Maybe she's told you why Antonio was about to flee the country before he died?'

'He *what*?' said Tammy. 'Are you making that up?'

'They found his passport at the plaza when they found the . . . you know.'

Tammy turned to Colin, but he was absorbed in the telly, oblivious. Some spy he made. 'That doesn't make sense,' said Tammy. She knew exactly where Antonio's passport was, and it wasn't the plaza. 'You've got it wrong.'

'It's what I heard. On the grapevine.'

'I don't believe you,' said Tammy. Was Peggy telling lies just to send Tammy off-track?

'Look, I heard it directly from the detective's mouth,' said Peggy. 'I overheard him and Lydia talking about it outside Lydia's house. You're not the only one who's good at eavesdropping.'

Tammy's mind raced, tripping over dead ends, dipping into everything she already knew. There could only be one explanation. Sheree must have gone in – it was already clear she had no problem making herself at home at Naomi's – and taken

241

the passport. Then what? Had she given it to someone else? Or had she taken it, along with Antonio's body parts, to the plaza herself?

Peggy was staring at Tammy with an intensity that gave her a jolt. How long had Tammy been sitting there in shock with her mouth agape?

'I don't know what you think you're up to,' said Peggy, 'but keep out of it. This is no business for kids, especially kids with high opinions of themselves and beaks that are too sticky for their own good.'

'I'd like to go to the toilet now,' said Tammy, and Peggy released her from her glare.

The bathroom had Kermit-green carpet, and a chandelier, even though it was a tiny room. There was an ashtray full of butts on the edge of the bath.

The medicine cabinet was full, but there was nothing that grabbed Tammy's attention, nothing that looked promising.

She ducked down the hall and poked her head into another room. This was more like it. No bed. Just clothes. Over-stuffed clothes rails lined two walls. Tammy's wardrobes were nothing compared to this. Colin would go berserk if he was let loose in here. On another wall, dresses were displayed like pieces of art. Tammy had to grudgingly admit it was kind of cool. Against the last wall, next to the window, was a dressing table; a dressing table that really went to town, that turned make-up and jewellery and hair into a full-time job.

Tammy knew what she was looking for and found it quickly: Peggy's coral lipstick. Tammy took the lid off and wound it up. Not much left. Its shape had turned concave with a sharp peak at the end, moulded by Peggy's lips. There was something creepy about it.

She put the lid back on and slid it down the front of her swimmers.

Who did Peggy think she was, telling Tammy her beak was too sticky!

The lipstick should have been enough to make Tammy feel better, but it wasn't. Not when you added on the bit about high opinions and that business with the pool.

There was a long spike holding lots of rings. At the top was one Tammy had seen many times. It was an enormous opal ring that swamped Peggy's hand and carved through the air, flashing colours as Peggy smoked. Tammy took it from the spike. It felt cold and heavy in her hand. It didn't take long to find a thick woollen coat hanging on a rail. Deep dark brown. It would be ages before it was cold enough to wear coats again. Tammy dropped the ring into a pocket.

The sound of a cackle, loud and close, made Tammy jump out of her skin. It was the same as Peggy's tractor-engine laugh, but higher pitched.

'Stick 'em up,' said the voice. And then: 'Uh-oh, razzamatazz.'

Tammy peered cautiously from the room. On the other side of the hall, a door was ajar. It was a bedroom, floral and flouncy. Lots of fabric, cushions on the bed. Heavily ruffled curtains. Beside the bed, on a stand, was a cage, and in that cage was a budgie, watching Tammy.

'Hot potato,' said the bird, nodding its head up and down vigorously, its whole body in on the action. 'Up, up and away.'

Tammy flattened herself against the hall wall. She didn't like being spied on, not even by a bird.

Tammy returned to the rumpus room, stepping inside and then out again when she heard Leslie say, 'I'm worried about Joe.' She hadn't been seen. 'Cecil's been talking to the police about him. And then Cec has the gall to tell me to stay away from Joe unless I want to end up in hot water too, and if I'm not going to do that, to watch out for inconsistencies in Joe's story. To ask him questions and whatnot and try to catch him in a lie.

Joe's worried because he doesn't have an alibi for that night.'

Leslie and Peggy had their backs to Tammy. Beyond them was Colin, engrossed in *Rocky and Bullwinkle*. If anyone turned around, Tammy could easily pretend she was in the middle of walking back in rather than hovering in the doorway.

'As much as I loathe Cecil, he might be on to something,' said Peggy. 'Maybe you're blinded by your soft spot for Joe. After all, he's already been in prison.'

'Where did you hear that?' asked Leslie, his voice full of surprise.

'You, you great oaf.'

'I said prisoner-of-war camp.'

'Now you're splitting hairs.'

'And I shouldn't even have said that,' said Leslie. 'I don't think Joe wants everyone knowing.'

'I'm hardly everyone,' said Peggy. 'You have to admit, there's a chance he could be involved. Has he ever accounted for being out in the hills that morning, when he identified the foot?'

'Now you're sounding like Cecil.'

Tammy caught the scathing look that Peggy sent Leslie's way.

'I wish Richard was here,' said Peggy. 'The boy says he won't be back for another week.' She nodded at Colin. 'I wonder if there's a way of contacting him.'

Tammy had heard enough. If anyone was going to get the benefit of Richard's thoughts, it would be her, through Colin. She swept into the room breezily. Leslie picked up Peggy's tea-cup and the teapot and headed for the kitchen.

'Come on, let's go,' Tammy said to Colin.

They were almost out the door when Peggy sprang out from behind the ironing board and grabbed Tammy's arm, twisting and pulling. It hurt. The lipstick tube stuck to Tammy's skin over her thudding heart.

'Listen to me,' said Peggy. Tammy had never been this close to

Peggy before and she didn't like it. The stink of her breath made a lie of her perfume. Her make-up was caked and flaky. Deep shadows under her eyes showed through. Peggy peered into Tammy's eyes, and Tammy watched Peggy's mouth. 'For God's sake, girl, don't think you can handle things when you can't. This isn't a game. It's dangerous.'

'Righto,' said Tammy. Peggy's grip loosened and Tammy freed her arm. 'Keep your hair on.'

Peggy's gaze moved past Tammy to the back yard where Suzi was prowling. 'And keep that mangy cat away from here. It's a menace to the birds.'

Tammy wished she'd hidden an earring, just one, instead of the ring. That would be more infuriating, to have only one of a pair and not the other.

'What else did they say while I was out of the room?' Tammy asked Colin as she stomped across the island.

'I don't know. I wasn't listening.'

'Pathetic!' Tammy gave an exasperated huff. 'Tell me about Sheree. Why was she in your house that day I was there with Mum?'

'I don't know. Cos she's friends with Mum. Well, she was. Then she wasn't. Now she might be. I don't know.'

'Useless! What did you say about your dad to Peggy?' Tammy demanded, while Colin wilted under her anger.

'Nothing.' Colin looked close to tears. 'I kept my mouth shut about my dad.' He struggled to keep up with her. 'Tammy, do we really have to do this? I don't think I'm a very good spy.'

'You can say that again,' said Tammy, striding ahead of him, wishing she was with Debbie instead, the only person who made her feel that not everything was hopeless.

28

Three Weeks Before The Murder

Tuesday, 19 December 1978
2.48 a.m.

Dear Antonio,
I can't sleep. How can you sleep? Every bit of me is awake and fired up and my brain is zigzagging in every direction at once at supersonic speed. So I thought I'd write down some thoughts while you're sleeping. HOW can you be sleeping?

I find it easier to express myself on paper. I always have. But especially since Edgar (the ex/ teacher/affliction) and all that shit, I've grown another layer of protection around me when I'm with others, and that can keep people at a distance, which is mostly a good thing because most people suck, but there might also be the odd occasion when someone good comes along and you want to let them in A BIT.

I can't believe you're sleeping in my bed, approximately 52 (but who's counting? – ha!) hours after we first met and spent that magical night at the lookout. You look so young and innocent right now. I can't believe I ever fell for a man like Edgar. Your eyelashes stagger me. I would DIE for them.

I haven't decided yet if I'll give this to you.

Don't you think it's funny that our first time having sex was on an ordinary Monday night? No drug-induced pash. No grog. Don't you think Mondays are the least sexy day of the week? It makes us sound so fucking wholesome, like we're already a doddery old couple. It was great, though. Did you think it was great? Don't answer that – it makes me sound needy and I'm not. Do you mind that I made the first move? I've had enough of society telling women they should hang about waiting for a bloke to make a move.

I never thought that I'd get with someone who already knew about Edgar and what happened. I always thought if I met someone I liked (and I'm not saying that's you yet, so don't go getting a big head), I'd have to find a way to tell them or live with not telling them after getting with them. It's nice not to have that pressure of trying to decide when or if I should tell you.

We could just have a bit of fun and see how it goes. Take it cool and casual. I could go for that if that's how you want to play it. I guess I'll find out soon enough if you're the type to root and run. Or are you the type who will say what you want and express how you feel about things? If you're shy about it, that's one thing and it will be FRUSTRATING, but I will tolerate it. But if you're withholding or dishonest or playing games, then you can forget it because I'll be hotfooting it out of here. I've learnt the hard way (AS YOU KNOW) that respect for myself has to come first and it's my right to demand respect from others. I will not debase myself for anyone, not even someone with the sexiest eyes and top lip I've ever seen.

I'm going to have to wake you up soon to sneak you out before Ursula and Lydia get up. All I can say is thank fuck they gave me the rumpus room. It's not ideal because, boy I'd like to make some NOISE with you (wink wink). It'll be better when your family leave and we can use your house. I don't know why you're not going with them to Italy – you can tell me all about it later – but I'm glad you're not.

There is SO MUCH more to say but fuck it, the torch is conking out.

Debbie

Wednesday, 20 December 1978
5.14 p.m.

Dear Antonio,
I have had the absolute BEST day with you. I can't believe you've never been to Vinnie's before. I am the op shop queen and I am going to blow your mind with the fun we can have. Do you reckon you'd let me do some make-up on you too or are you a bit funny (REPRESSED) about that?

I will never forget your mum's face when she saw you, sniffing at the Afghan and checking it for fleas. And the way she turned her nose up at the Boney M dacks! I thought I was going to DIE from laughter. I still can't keep a straight face. Personally,

I think sequins suit you. Has your mum recovered yet? She looked like she was going to have a coronary.

Anyway, now that I'm home, I've got to thinking that I can't remember the last time I've laughed so much. It would have to be WAY before Edgar and all that shit, and I know I've said thank you for understanding but I don't think you fully realise how much it has meant to me to be able to spill my guts to someone who doesn't judge me or treat me like a dirty slut. It's like a dark cloud has evaporated and for the first time in a long time I can see good things. I didn't even realise I was so fucking ANGRY all the fucking time until it lifted. So thank you (again) for bringing back laughter (oh God, that sounds so corny). I never expected this to happen. I never expected YOU to happen. (How's that for a double dose of the corn-factor?)

That's well and truly enough soppy stuff or you'll be running for the hills like nobody's business. (Seriously, thanks though.)

I totally see why you want to keep us a secret from your mum. She is SCAAAR-YYY. I'm so glad they're all pissing off to Italy for Christmas. Can't wait to have your whole house to ourselves. Sex in your car sounded like a great idea and, let's face it, it's better than nothing, but a crick in my neck and a bruise on my arse are not overly romantic haha.

Maybe one day it could be you and me going to Italy. You could show me around. (It would have to fit around uni though.)

OK, so I can accept you're not one for putting things in writing. That's OK. You've got other skills (wink wink). Besides, I write enough for the both of us haha. BUT – you never know, you might take to it if you give it a go (hint hint). Keep checking your letterbox, OK? Because I have a feeling that I'm going to keep expressing myself to you like this. I have a freedom in writing that I don't otherwise feel, and it will help you better understand the REAL me. When we're together in person I still feel like I'm keeping my protective shell in place to a certain extent and I know you know why I've had to develop a tough exterior, but it will take time for me to dismantle it fully.

    Debbie

    xxxxxxxxxxxxxxxxxxxxx(to the power of infinity)

Friday, 22 December 1978
11.44 p.m.

Dear Antonio,
Correct me if I'm wrong, but there were some weird vibes coming off you today and I got the sense you were freaking out big time under the surface, even though you were trying to hide it. You should know by now that I have learnt the hard way to be perceptive and I'll always pick up on an undercurrent. There's just no point trying to hide anything from me. I don't say that to scare you. It's simply a matter of fact.

    You think I'm coming on too strong, don't you? Because I'm revealing something of my true self to you? Well, here's the thing: you might like to think about what it says about you if you're intimidated by truth. And another thing: it's not really about you at all. Maybe you could get your head out of your arse and see it's actually about me and that I am choosing to share something of significance with you and you could choose to treat that with respect.

Anyway, where are you? I've been knocking on your door every half-hour for the past three hours, feeling like a complete dropkick. I kind of thought, since it's Friday night, and since you've got the house to yourself now, we might get together, but no worries, no big deal.

Debbie

Saturday, 23 December 1978
10.32 a.m.

Dear Antonio,
Just back from your place and why is it that every time I see you, I have to start writing about it immediately I come home?

Yes, OF COURSE I believe you. It's just that it's so easy for my buttons to get pushed and for my brain to go spiralling until I can't tell what's real and what's not anymore. That's not your fault.
It's my responsibility to manage that. If you say there's nothing going on and you're not freaking out about my letters, then that's that and there's nothing left to say about it.

Debbie

P.S. Having said all that, you still seemed kinda out of it this morning. You never actually said where you were last night.

Sunday, 24 December 1978
4.45 p.m.

Dear Antonio,
I don't know why I got flustered just now when I saw you at your letterbox. I'm used to dropping off my letters unseen, like I'm on a covert ninja mission. By the way, I always check my letterbox too, just in case (hint hint).

Anyway, I feel like such a fuckwit. I don't know why I wrapped the pamphlets up in Christmas paper because they're really NOT a pressie. Feminist manifestos are a much more urgent and vital thing than some sort of frivolous gift. Anyway, oh God, the look on your face. And it's only now I'm home that it occurs to me that you thought I got you a present (well, DERRRR, it was wrapped) and you might have felt weird because that's not what we do, or because you haven't got me anything, which is 100% FINE. Deadset.

Anyway, spare a thought for me getting bored out of my brain and hot and sweaty and a numb bum on a hard church pew when I'd much rather be getting hot and sweaty with you.

Debbie

Tuesday, 26 December 1978
8.13 a.m.

Dear Antonio,
Who could ever have thought that the BEST Christmas night I would ever have would be sitting in a cold bath getting off my face with you??

252

I just love the way we've fallen into being together, like how one season blends into and then becomes the next and you can't pinpoint the exact moment it changes over. That's a roundabout way of saying I think it's ace that we don't have to define what we are or speak it because we can just BE it. We can be governed by nature and the TRUTH of what we are creating, while we eschew patriarchal paradigms about sex and permanence and always having to fit every fucking thing into reductive fucking boxes. I think what I am saying is that there is a BEAUTY, a sort of LIBERATION, in not defining what we are, and I find that so refreshing.

For so long, my aim, my fantasy, my mission, has been a feminist utopia with no men. I always thought if I had the choice, the option, the POWER to do away with all men, I'd do it in a heartbeat. But I think now, you might be the one exception I'd let stay. Don't go getting a big head about it though.

Also, I'll have you know, my entire body is covered with hickeys, thanks to you, which would make for an awkward convo with Auntie Ursula if she wasn't so distracted by hiding her true self and noticed. Thanks for agreeing not to tell anyone about her and Lydia. It's really important that you don't. Anyway, prepare to be got back on the hickey front haha.

Debbie

xxxxxxetc

Wednesday, 27 December 1978
11.34 a.m.

Dear Antonio,
Where are you? Your car's in the carport but no answer? It's just as well I'm not the paranoid type haha.

God, it's so hot, I feel like I'm going to DIE.

Anyway, I was thinking, if Manifesto of the 343 is too heavy-going for you, how about starting with Redstockings Manifesto? It's also very short so couldn't be classed as taxing to read, and although it's a bit old now (nearly ten years!), it is still salient and could serve as a springboard for further read-ing and discussion about women as an oppressed class.

Either way, let me know.

Debbie

P.S. I assume you're going to the street party tonight???

Thursday, 28 December 1978
1.25 p.m.

Dear Antonio,
What a hoot! That street party was suburban living to the MAX. Not my scene but interesting to watch from an anthropological stance.

I get that you don't want to go public with us. I respect that. And I don't need anyone's approval. Fuck 'em. Fuck 'em all. The only thing that matters is what happens in private, and we both know the truth of that. But don't think I didn't see you watching me like a hawk when I was talking to Richard and his wife. It was CUTE but there's no need to be jealous. Conventionally good-looking blokes in the way he is have never been my type. They always turn out to be arrogant in a lazy and boring way. Not worth the bother. You're much more my cup of tea – good-looking but interesting-looking too.

When will I see you next?
Debbie

P.S. I just found your little pencil in my bed. I love it. The way you've carved it is so dainty and pretty. I love that you have an artistic side. Did you leave it on purpose? Either way, I'm holding it hostage until you come back to my bed.

Friday, 29 December 1978
9.48 p.m.

Dear Antonio,
How about going back to the lookout for New Year's? You know, revisiting where things really started for us? Or would you rather something more private (wink wink)? You choose.

You know, it feels strange not seeing you since the street party. There are just SO MANY THINGS I want to tell you about – every little thing, actually. I like the way you listen. I like the way your head tilts down and you look at your hands or my hands, like that will help you concentrate better than if you were looking at my face, and I like how that makes me feel safe to say more stuff to you. Like today, it was such a small thing that happened, but it meant something big. I was in the newsagent's and there was a bloke standing in line in front of me, and after he paid, he turned around and we made eye contact. It wasn't weird or creepy eye contact, that's not what this is about. What it's about is that when he looked at me, I felt real. Like I exist. For so long, I've felt like I'm a shadow of myself, going through the motions of living, but not being present, not participating. Anyway, I wonder if it will last, this feeling of being a whole person again.

Debbie

Sunday, 31 December 1978
3.36 p.m.

Where are you?

I miss you. That feels kind of nice, to miss some-one. I don't mind it. But do you think that means my determination to stand on my own two feet as an independent woman is bullshit? I worry about that sometimes, although I wouldn't admit it to anyone except you.

Anyway, where the fuck are you?

7.47 p.m.

It's just as well for you that I'm cool with it. Imagine if I was clingy and dependent and not content with my own company and intellect. Imagine if I relied on you having proper input into this relationship/friendship/whatever you want to call it or NOT call it. That would really suck for me, but it would be worse for you cos you'd be in DEEP SHIT then haha.

Monday, 1 January 1979
11.02 a.m.

Seriously, is there someone else?

Friday, 5 January 1979
3.53 p.m.

D—
   Tonight, my house?
   —A

29

Sixteen Days After The Murder

Monday, 22 January 1979

'More noise,' said Guangyu, and Ursula pressed harder on the accelerator.

'Good,' said Guangyu. 'Now less noise.'

Ursula released both the accelerator and the clutch, and the car stalled again.

'I'm such a dunce,' said Ursula. 'Why can't my brain tell my feet to do different things?'

'Doesn't matter,' said Guangyu. 'Again, please.'

They were on a dirt track on the other side of the hills in Guangyu's car. It was a fortnight since Guangyu had given Ursula a lift home, and their fourth driving lesson. It was a stupid idea. Illegal. Ursula didn't have her learner licence yet. It was also a great idea. Guangyu couldn't remember when she'd last had this much fun. She didn't mind being out in her sweatbox car in the afternoon sun. She didn't mind the crunching of gears, the revving and readying for the nothing much that came next, the lurching and leaping, the riding of the clutch on the few occasions they'd actually got going. She had mixed feelings about the lack of progress they'd made.

On the one hand, lack of success did not sit well with Guangyu. On the other, these afternoons with Ursula, abominable driving aside, had been blissfully rage-free. For these moments, the irritation that plagued her was like a coat she'd shrugged off and discarded. She still hadn't decided what to do, if anything, about seeing Richard in the hills the morning that Antonio went missing. Now, weeks later, she wondered if she could be certain that it was Richard she saw in that tricky pre-dawn light. Completely certain? Yes, she knew what she saw. But during these blessed afternoons with Ursula, Guangyu allowed herself the luxury of not thinking about it.

Guangyu loved watching Ursula's earnest endeavours. Guangyu wished Jennifer would let her watch her like that; wouldn't be embarrassed and self-conscious and secretive about her efforts, about what mattered to her.

Ursula gripped the steering wheel like she was throttling it. They stalled again.

'Hadn't we better give it up as a bad job?' said Ursula.

'Never,' said Guangyu. 'I refuse. That would make me a failed teacher.'

Ursula, with eyes gleaming, patted the dashboard. 'Come on, my beauty,' she said. 'Don't let me down. Guangyu's ego is relying on us.' She grinned at Guangyu. 'Does she have a name?'

'Who?'

'Your car.'

What was this nonsense?

'We'll have to think of one,' said Ursula, fingers gently tapping the steering wheel.

The goal was a tall, lone gum and its shade, a benevolent presence that remained just out of reach. Ursula checked her mirrors.

This time, Guangyu put her hand on Ursula's left leg and

pressed down. 'More noise,' she said, then, lessening the pressure on Ursula's leg, 'less noise.'

'Just right noise.' Guangyu removed her hand and Ursula eased off the clutch. 'Now.'

They inched forward at infinitesimal speed and kept going in first gear until they made it to the tree.

Guangyu cheered, both hands in the air.

Ursula did too.

'Brake!' yelled Guangyu.

They bunny-hopped to a stop.

Ursula stroked the dashboard and cooed. 'Well done,' she said. 'And well done, Guangyu. Your ego is intact.'

'Let's not get ahead of ourselves.'

But Ursula's laughter was infectious and Guangyu couldn't help giving in to feeling carefree. They both hung their elbows out of the open windows. If only there was a breeze. They were suffocating on still air.

'Hildy,' said Ursula.

'What?'

'That's what we'll call her. Your car. After Hildegard von Bingen.'

'Who?'

'Hildegard von Bingen, the twelfth-century abbess. You haven't heard of her? She was everything a woman wasn't meant to be.' Ursula took her sunglasses off. Guangyu enjoyed seeing the fire in Ursula's eyes. 'A visionary and mystic. And medic. She composed music and wrote books and plays and poetry. She wrote about everything: religion and art and science and politics and philosophy and, let's see, what else? Medicine and herbs. She didn't give a hoot what anyone thought. That's the thing. She just did what she wanted, followed where her abilities led her.' Ursula blushed. 'She's something of a hero of mine.'

Guangyu wanted to ask more about this abbess who sounded

too incredible to be true; more about what Ursula would do if she followed where her abilities led her.

But Ursula, with glee, lay both hands on the dashboard and said, 'I christen you Hildecar von Holden. Hildy for short.' She made the sign of the cross.

'You're crackers,' said Guangyu.

'Do you know,' Ursula started, then paused. Her mood had sobered. It was like that with Ursula. Her emotional temperature could flip like turning a switch. 'You're going to think me foolish and it's embarrassing to say and I wasn't going to say in case you misunderstood but I also feel that I want to say . . .'

Guangyu waited. She was getting used to the prelude to Ursula saying something that was important to her.

'I keep saying your name in my head. Over and over. When I walk, I say a syllable with every step. I do it before I'm even aware of it.' As she spoke, she sneaked glances at Guangyu. But now, she looked at Guangyu steadily; if she felt the urge to look away, she didn't give in to it. It made her more vulnerable, her emotions and hesitancy as she chose her words more visible. Strange how such a simple act could cement a friendship. 'It's like an infatuation – oh, goodness, you're going to want to run a mile – but a friendship infatuation. Is that possible? When I say your name my heart rejoices and I give thanks to God for you. Every day I give thanks for you.' She looked intently at her hands on the steering wheel, a far-away smile on her face. Silence stretched, but Guangyu felt no need to fill it. She knew Ursula well enough to know there was more to come. There was. 'Is it wrong to discuss a friendship out in the open, I wonder? Should it just exist on its own without commentary?'

Guangyu was no great aficionado at making friends, and she found Ursula strange, very strange indeed sometimes, but she never felt she had to guess at what Ursula was thinking. Was this an unexpected benefit of a cross–cultural friendship? If you didn't know the rules of the other person's culture, could you make up your own rules as you went along?

'I used to think that not having friends didn't matter,' Ursula went on. 'And I used to think that someone knowing my secret would give them power over me, power to hurt me. I didn't understand that it could have a different kind of power, the power to bring closeness.'

'For me too,' said Guangyu. One day soon she would tell Ursula what a difference it made to her to be held dear, cherished. 'It's nice to have a friend.'

'I think I've embarrassed you,' said Ursula. 'You look flustered. I'm sorry.'

'You haven't. I have the menopause. It's horrible. I hate it. I hate every part of it.'

'Golly,' said Ursula. 'Something to look forward to.' She took off her tennis visor and fanned Guangyu with it.

'Stop flapping,' said Guangyu. 'It's too hot.'

Ursula stopped. She held onto the visor in her lap, fiddling with the elastic. 'Anyway, what I wanted to say is that I like your name. Such a pretty name.'

'It's not.'

'What?'

'My name. It's not pretty. In China it is tradition to give girls floral, soft, feminine names. My mother broke tradition to give me a masculine-sounding name.'

Guangyu watched a skink emerge from a burrow near the trunk of the tree. It sat on the ground, its short legs splayed, its blue tongue flicking, searching the air for the scent of prey.

'In China, it's also expected that a wife will give her husband a son. It's her duty. I made up a story in my mind about my mother feeling that she had failed. I thought my name was my mother's compensation for not having a boy, or revenge on me for not being a boy, even though that made no sense as she was an

262

affectionate mother in all other respects. Then I learnt the truth.'
Guangyu paused, feeling that she was disturbing the rest of things
she'd kept tucked away in the back alleys of her mind for a long
time. 'But you don't want to hear about such things,' she said.

'Oh, no you don't,' said Ursula. 'I do want to hear such things.
I want to hear everything.'

Guangyu decided on a way in. 'I have a particular memory
from when we were running away from the Japanese. All of us,
the whole village, had to leave our homes. I was eight.' Guangyu
had vague recollections of a big grey sky, and generalised sensa-
tions: the itch of unwashed clothes; weariness; cold feet; hunger;
the acrid smell of burning. She knew now that villages, towns
and whole cities were burnt. Some (but not enough) years later,
Guangyu watched war films and documentaries and realised
that the whirring insect noises of planes, deepening to a rumble,
and then the dive and splash and burst of falling bombs, were
sounds that weren't in her memory so much as lodged deep in
her marrow. 'I was whining on and on and on to my mother.
I suppose I was hungry and uncomfortable. And tired. I was
saying over and over that it wasn't fair. And my mother – she
stopped. The cart and the other villagers went on and she and
I stopped.' Guangyu remembered the taste of the dust that was
stirred up by a passing military Jeep. She remembered that her
mother's hair, usually immaculate and tight, was coming loose
from its bun. She remembered that her mother's voice, usually
as smooth as glaze on porcelain, was rough. 'My mother brought
her face up close to mine and she wasn't smiling and that's how I
knew she was deadly serious. And she said, *I know it's not fair. It's
never been fair. It will never be fair.* Then she told me that she had
done her best to equip me by giving me my name, that I carried
something afforded to men in my name, and the rest was up to
me. I didn't understand it. I was too young to know what she
meant. But after that, I felt better about my name.'

'I don't understand it,' said Ursula. 'What was she trying to give you? Strength? Courage?'

'No, I don't think so. My mother was — *is* — a formidable woman. She carries with her the weight of many lifetimes in one. She has strength and courage in abundance. I think what she meant to give me was something of the ease of a man. The way a man might travel through life with more ease than a woman.'

'The ease,' said Ursula. 'I like the sound of that. I wish someone would give me some of that.' She looked at Guangyu, square on, as was her way. 'Have you ever used it? Her gift to you?'

The question surprised Guangyu, and so did her answer: 'I've never thought about it. I've only ever thought about the giving of it, by her. Not the using of it, by me.'

'I could use a bit of your mother's strength and courage right now,' said Ursula, 'because I have a confession to make.' The anxiety in her voice made Guangyu worried for her friend. 'And you won't be happy about it. The policeman sent me into such a tizz, I lost my head. I'm afraid I put my foot in it.'

Guangyu stood outside Naomi's front door for a long time; stalled, doing nothing. Ursula's words, *I lied to the police about you*, ran laps in her head. She wasn't angry with Ursula. Guangyu knew that having people in your life could make things messy and uncontained. Ursula was worth it, even if Guangyu was now in a tight spot, even if she had to step out of character and act. Maybe it was just what she needed: something to dispense with indecision, to force her hand. If she was going to get ahead of Ursula's lie about where she was when Antonio was killed, she needed to know more about Richard and what he was doing in the hills that morning. Then she would decide if she had enough to tell the police.

Next to the front door was a plant pot of something that

needed deadheading. Behind it, in the small dark space between the pot and the brick wall, were letters. Not just junk mail, although there was plenty of that, but official-looking envelopes. It was as though someone had made the decision to discard them on the way from the letterbox to the front door, and had faltered at the last. Should Guangyu pick them up? It was an ideal habitat for redback spiders.

Guangyu left the letters where they were and knocked on the door with the ease of a man.

Naomi led her into the kitchen, offered her a cup of tea after a pause, during which Guangyu could feel Naomi wishing she would go away. Naomi proceeded to make the tea, appallingly.

Naomi wore a clean dress, but her face was drawn. She moved without her usual grace and airiness and was not taking care of her appearance as she used to. Her hand repeatedly and fleetingly rested on her belly. Guangyu cast her mind back to being pregnant with Jennifer, the thrill of it, but also what it took from you to grow another body inside your own.

'Bag in or out?' said Naomi. She had already sloshed in milk.

'Doesn't matter,' said Guangyu, because by this point it didn't.

A horrible stink came from a bowl of mouldy and deflated apricots sitting in a pool of their own sticky juice. Ants, drunk on sugar, had drowned in their feast. Naomi noticed Guangyu staring at it and whisked it away, dumping it, wooden bowl and all, in the bin. *What an extraordinary thing to do*, thought Guangyu.

Naomi got a biscuit tin out of a cupboard, opening it as she offered it to Guangyu, then said, 'Sorry,' when she saw it was empty. She put down the tin and folded her arms.

They were two wolves in a cage, circling; watchful and wary; waiting for the other to make the first move.

Guangyu felt overcome with exhaustion. She was tired of the games people played, tired of the empty spaces left by unspoken

265

words. She felt a band of heat where her skirt sat on her waist. She'd wanted to dress nicely for Ursula, as if it would make any difference. Her shoes pinched her toes.

'Nineteen is very young to die,' she said, not knowing where to start.

Naomi turned her back on Guangyu and busied herself with wiping her hands on a tea-towel. She folded it carefully and hung it over the oven-door handle. When she turned back to Guangyu, her face was perfectly composed.

'What were you doing when you were nineteen?' said Guangyu, trying a more indirect way in.

'Gosh, that's such a long time ago. I'm twenty-nine now. At nineteen, I was not long married, learning how to be a wife. Completely out of my depth.' She gave a tinkling laugh that, to Guangyu, felt forced, and wiped up the drop left by the teaspoon on the bench. 'It all turned out good, though.'

It was so hard to tell with Naomi, thought Guangyu, what was an outright lie and what was her just trying to create a certain impression or go along with social niceties.

'What were you doing? At nineteen?' Naomi blew on her tea, took a sip. They were still standing on opposite sides of the breakfast bar. She hadn't offered Guangyu a seat.

'At nineteen?' said Guangyu, taking her time. Best not to think too hard about the words. 'I was running away from war in China, towards squalor in Hong Kong. Trying to make a new start from nothing.'

'You win, then,' said Naomi, her face sour, her body stiff. She loosened and apologised almost immediately. 'God, that was an awful thing to say. I'm sorry. I'm not usually a bitch. I could never have been as brave as you've been. Or coped with what you have.'

'Neither could I until I did.'

The sun was getting low in the sky. Long rectangles of light spread across the floor and onto the dining table. Guangyu's eye travelled the path of the light to the back yard where she spotted Tammy and Colin. Tammy was looking through a gap in the fence to Sheree's house, her pen poised over a book.

'What are they doing?' she asked Naomi.

Naomi followed Guangyu's gaze. 'Oh. I wonder when they got here,' she said. 'I think they've been playing some game of make-believe. Wouldn't it be nice to be a kid again and pretend to be someone else?' It was a rare instance of Guangyu feeling that Naomi had let her guard down.

Colin didn't look all that enamoured with the game, thought Gaungyu. He sat with his back to the fence, the dress he was wearing pooled about his knees, tracing patterns in the dirt with his finger. Guangyu wondered if the dresses were part of the make-believe game.

'Look, I don't want to be rude, but why have you come here?' said Naomi.

Guangyu contemplated backing off, making her exit. But she'd got nowhere.

'Your husband, does he hit you?' It was clumsy, far blunter than Guangyu meant to be, but she needed some way of getting the measure of their relationship. It had occurred to her that Naomi might be frightened of Richard. That could explain her caginess and the feeling Guangyu had of not knowing what was true. Perhaps it wasn't safe for Naomi to tell the truth. Perhaps Richard had found out about her and Antonio and threatened her.

'Crikey,' said Naomi. 'You don't beat about the bush, do you?' She laughed and then straightened her face. 'No. Never.'

'He has other means.' It wasn't a question.

Naomi shifted her weight restlessly. 'That's not—' she began. 'I really don't—' she began again. 'Look. I don't have the time or energy for this. Maybe you don't know that I haven't been well. Richard's not a wife beater. How could you ever think

267

that? He's a man who knows what's right. Anyone will tell you that.' She pushed her hair back from her face. 'Are you going to drink your tea?'

Guangyu didn't answer.

'You do an awful lot of watching what goes on, don't you?' said Naomi. 'I don't know what you think you know, but you've got the wrong end of the stick about Richard.'

Guangyu still didn't answer, because the more Naomi talked, the more Guangyu was sure that Richard had something to do with Antonio's murder. Thinking about Herman's photograph and Naomi's affair, she wasn't entirely convinced Naomi wasn't also involved. A lovers' tiff gone wrong, perhaps? There were too many possibilities. If she went to the police now, though, would she end up landing herself, or Ursula – for giving Guangyu a false alibi – in hot water?

'I think you should go now,' said Naomi. 'There's nothing more to say.'

Guangyu stayed where she was and took a reluctant sip of tea.

'Look, Richard is a man of principle,' Naomi went on. 'He knows what he wants and what he stands for. And he knows what he won't stand for. He won't stand for you making up lies about him, for starters.'

'And if he doesn't get what he wants?' said Guangyu. 'If he won't stand?'

The question was left hanging, each woman's thoughts left to follow their own path. Guangyu breathed her way through a hot flush, hating the thought that Naomi would think her affected by their conversation. She watched the slight figure of Colin, staring at the ground, his bowed head drooping from a spindle of a neck. Such a small head to be so weighed down, she thought. She could weep for that boy.

'You're still young,' said Guangyu in a softer tone. 'Twenty-nine is nothing. You have many doors open to you.'

'How old are you?'

It was a fair question. They were long done with pleasantries. 'Forty-eight,' she said. 'Old.'

'Not quite old enough for you to mother me, though.'

'I'm not here to mother you,' said Guangyu. 'I'm here to warn you.'

'Warn me?'

The words that came to Guangyu hovered, within reach: *Warn you that I'm considering telling the police about your husband . . . that I saw him . . . that I've seen a photo of you and Antonio . . . that I'm choosing my words . . .*

'To tell you not to forget that you have options. For you and your boy and your baby.'

They looked at each other, neither looking away, until it became uncomfortable, and still, they looked at each other, until it moved beyond being uncomfortable and was something else, something that lay behind resistance, something full of unspoken words that only their eyes acknowledged. There would be time yet to speak them.

'Next time I come,' said Guangyu, cracking a smile, 'I will show you how I make tea. I am a good teacher.'

30

Four Months Before The Murder

September 1978

During September, 'You're the One That I Want' by Olivia Newton-John and John Travolta dominated the charts. The Rolling Stones released 'Beast of Burden' and Blondie had another album out, the second of the year. Pope John Paul died just thirty-three days after being installed. The USSR and the US conducted nuclear tests. An earthquake in Iran killed 25,000 people. Floods swept across India. Israel and Egypt signed a peace accord at Camp David. Rail workers and teachers went on strike. And the uranium mining dispute between Aboriginal leaders and the government rumbled on. All of it passed Naomi by. She had no space in her head for anything except Antonio.

With Richard, she'd always felt grateful for his attention, his desire. With Antonio, she gave in to her own. The depth and range of what she felt, what she wanted, was astonishing. Antonio had freed her. Naomi knew full well she was done for. There was no coming back from this.

With Richard away until October, the month was theirs. The house ticked along well enough without any of the maintenance jobs getting done. They stole the hours that Colin was at school to bask in each other. Soon, that wasn't enough. They began to rely on Sheree looking after Colin during the evenings and some nights. When she started asking questions, they had to let her into their secret. Naomi assured Antonio that Sheree wouldn't tell anyone. *No one likes her anyway,* she said. *I'm the only friend she's got.* Antonio knocked through a few panels of the fence so Colin could move between the two houses away from the prying eyes of Warrah Place. Naomi knew that Colin had need of a mother; she wasn't stupid. But Naomi had need to be more than a mother, to not be a mother sometimes. It wasn't unreasonable. And Sheree didn't mind.

Antonio's dad returned from Rome and Naomi worried that she'd have to share Antonio with him.

'He only notices me if I annoy him,' said Antonio. 'It's best if I stay out of his way.'

In the end, it made little difference. Giorgio worked long hours and was rarely home.

Naomi and Antonio were in Antonio's bedroom on a gloomy wet Tuesday, listening to opera on his record player. Naomi didn't understand why the arias moved her, but Antonio not only understood it, but seemed to expect it. There was something worldly wise about him, a melancholia that he showed in private but never in public.

'What was that?' asked Naomi as the final notes faded.

'Puccini. "O Mio Babbino Caro",' said Antonio, now returned to the room and to Naomi. While it played, Antonio's eyes had turned vacant. He was elsewhere, somewhere inaccessible to Naomi.

'How do you know this music?'

Antonio gave a half-shrug. 'I've always loved it. It's the only thing that makes me feel someone out there understands me.' He smiled sadly. 'And then the music stops.'

Naomi wanted him to feel that way when he was with her. She didn't want music to give him something she couldn't. *Imagine being jealous of a song*, she thought.

Antonio turned his face to nuzzle into her neck. 'But now I have you,' he said, and her heart skyrocketed.

When it was time to collect Colin from school, Naomi picked up a green booklet from Antonio's shelf. 'What's this?'

'Just my passport,' he said.

'What's it doing out?' She was unable to hide the concern from her voice. Was he leaving? Without telling her?

'Nothing,' he said, taking it from her. 'My mum just wanted some details. She's threatening to buy me a ticket. She wants me to go to Rome for Christmas.'

'Why haven't you told me?'

'Because I'm not going.' Antonio tossed the passport behind him and reached for Naomi, pulling her back to his bed. 'As if I could leave now.'

Naomi patted the space behind Antonio until her hand landed on the passport. 'I think I'll keep hold of this, just in case,' she said.

'Be my guest.' He laughed. 'Take it. Unless we run away together, I have no need for it.'

Naomi believed him completely. But she still took the passport with her when she went home that day.

Antonio's mum and sister came back to Canberra a week later. Why couldn't they make up their minds about where they wanted to be? Naomi wished they'd stayed away. It meant she had to be more careful about not being seen. The secrecy was taxing and Naomi resented it. It wasn't fair. A refrain kept passing through Naomi's mind: *It's not meant to be this way.* Why should they have to hide something that felt so right?

Naomi despatched Colin to Sheree's one Saturday morning

and waited for Antonio. Every minute he wasn't there was a waste.

'What kept you?' she asked when he finally turned up.

'I was waylaid by Tammy.' He rolled his eyes.

'What did she want?'

'Just a chat.'

'You shouldn't encourage her,' said Naomi, still annoyed. 'You know she has a crush on you.'

Antonio winced. 'I told her I was twenty-four, but it doesn't seem to have helped.' Then he got that overblown innocent look on his face that wasn't innocent at all, that Naomi loved so much. 'What else can I do? It's not my fault if I'm irresistible.'

'It is your fault if you're a flirt,' said Naomi, laughing. Her frosty mood was quickly thawing. 'You can't tell me you don't love it.'

Antonio became thoughtful. 'Honestly? A bit. But mostly I don't understand it. And I don't know what is the right thing to say.' He puffed out his cheeks, making up his mind about something. 'Look, I'll tell you this even though it will make you go off me—'

'Impossible.'

He smiled. 'I was a scrawny kid. And short. My friends developed first, and the girls liked them best. I just tagged along. And then I had a late growth spurt and then we moved to Australia and . . .'

'And now you're a hunk all the girls are crazy for.'

'There's only one girl I care about.' He pulled her to him. 'Remember what an idiot I was when I met you? Trying to be suave and sophisticated and mysterious. Oh, it's too embarrassing. What a cretin!' He looked at her shyly from lowered eyes. 'I was so intimidated by you and your beauty and how I felt about you. I was in way over my head. I'm still scared I'll mess things up.'

Naomi laughed. 'And I thought you hated me! I couldn't work out what was wrong with me.' After a while, she added, 'Is there something else bothering you?' He was subdued, not quite himself.

'Nothing that matters,' he said. 'I don't want to spoil our time together.'

'No, come on.' What if he was tiring of her? What if he'd met someone his own age, someone he didn't have to sneak around with? 'Tell me.'

'It's just that I had a fight with my parents.'

Relief flooded through Naomi. 'What about?'

'Uni. My lack of ambition. Wasting my time. I didn't want to tell you because maybe you'll agree with them. Or you'll think I'm too young for you because I have parents on my back and you don't.'

Naomi took his hand in hers. 'Was it bad?'

Antonio turned his face away from her. 'They want me to be an adult and make decisions, but whatever I decide isn't good enough for them. No matter what I do, it will never be good enough.'

Naomi turned his face back to her and wiped away a tear. 'Don't be embarrassed. Not in front of me. I like that you can talk to me like this. Besides, if you really want to know what it's like to have a parent breathing down your neck, you should meet my mum.'

'Bad?'

'She's a fucking nightmare.'

Antonio smiled. 'I haven't heard you swear before.'

'That's because I'm not allowed. I mean, I don't usually. It's not a habit I got into.'

'Not allowed?'

'Richard prefers nicely spoken women.' She'd broken their tacit agreement not to talk about Richard and she wanted to distance herself from it, but a shock realisation stunned her. She snorted with laughter.

'What?' said Antonio. 'What's so funny?'

'It's only just hit me,' she said. 'I was so desperate to get away from my mum because she controlled and restricted every little bit of my life that I jumped straight into a marriage with a man who . . . I guess I overlooked the strict side of him because I was just so glad someone wanted to look after me.'

Antonio looked at her like he was trying to work out what it all meant.

'Oh God, we're the same, you and me,' said Naomi. 'No wonder I . . .' Something stopped her from saying, *I love you*. Instead, she said, 'Do you think it's possible to change your life?'

'Sure.'

'Not just change your life, but change what your life *could* be.'

Antonio looked at her quizzically.

'My mum always said' – here, Naomi contorted her face into her mother's sneer and her voice into a throaty growl – '*A woman must play the hand she is dealt.*' She returned to her normal voice. 'Do you think you can not just make different choices, but change what choices are available to you?'

Antonio took his time, giving her question serious consideration, before saying, 'I think a woman like you can do whatever she wants to.'

'Well, I know *that's* not true.' Naomi laughed to hide her disappointment. Richard and 'married' were cards she held in her hand and she couldn't see any way of changing that.

'Our age difference doesn't bother you?' said Antonio, and, for the first time, she wondered if it bothered him.

'I don't see it. I . . .' Again, Naomi had very nearly said, *I love you*. Should she? What if he didn't say it back?

'How can it be that you make me feel like I'm flying and

275

drowning at the same time?' said Antonio 'Oddio, help me.' He cupped her face in his hands. 'I love you.'

'I love you too,' she said, and then, like a dam had burst, 'I love you. I love you. I love you.'

Towards the end of September, Naomi noticed all at once that spring had arrived. The sun was brighter now, and carried a new warmth that was intermittently cancelled out by a southerly wind. Golden wattles were in full bloom. Willie wagtail parents noisily defended their nests and male kookaburras made a racket calling for a mate.

On a warm day, Antonio was grumbling about being stuck inside, never able to go anywhere together, so they risked a walk to the milk bar on Carnegie Street. Naomi didn't dare ask him if his foul mood was because October was almost upon them, and with it, Richard's return.

It started to rain half-heartedly, not quite enough to bother with an umbrella. Naomi wished they'd brought one because sharing an umbrella was romantic and she'd like to add it to the stash of memories she'd collected to mull over when they were apart. She wanted to amass enough memories so she could say to herself: *See. This is real. We have history.*

Antonio bought cigarettes. Naomi sucked on a Chupa Chups and swung on a bike rail outside like a schoolgirl, kicking away the nagging worry, the sense of time running out. Antonio was having trouble with the plastic film covering the packet. He stood over the bin outside the shop and tore at it with his teeth. Naomi clapped when, at last, he got rid of it, fearing at the last minute that he would find it sarcastic. As Antonio turned his back to the wind to light a smoke, a carload of lads in a red Monaro slowed to a crawl beside the kerb.

'Oi. Dago,' called one from the backseat, elbow hanging out, leering at Naomi, egged on by his mates' sniggering. Naomi knew what was coming next. 'Do her, mate. We all have. Fair give it to her.' They took off, leaving behind the sound of laughter and revving.

Antonio frowned, not at the departing car, but at Naomi. 'You know these men? Each one of them, you have known?'

Naomi laughed nervously. She couldn't help herself. 'Don't be stupid. Of course not. No. They're just a bunch of hoons.' Why couldn't she stop laughing?

'This pleases you?' said Antonio, and Naomi once more felt under his scrutiny, his judgement, just as she had on the day they met. 'Attention from these . . . these hoons? It makes you feel . . . what? Happy? Desirable? You like that they say such things to me?'

Naomi's laughter died at once. 'No. God, no.' She was by his side, linking her arm through his, holding his hand and folding his fingers over hers. She started counting her breaths. 'Take me home, Antonio. Let's go home where it's just us and no one else matters.'

Antonio dropped her hand and shook her off him. He nodded ahead.

On the path, coming towards them, was Helen. What had she seen?

Naomi feigned surprise. 'Oh, goodness, hello there. I thought it was you. How lovely to see you. We've just come to get some . . . things. For Antonio. For his work at our house.' Too much? She should tone it down. What if Helen wanted to see what they'd bought?

'Isn't it exciting?' said Helen without even a *hello*. 'You must be beside yourself.' She didn't acknowledge Antonio.

Naomi searched for Helen's meaning and drew a blank.

'*Richard,* you silly duffer.' She swatted Naomi's arm with her hand. 'Less than a week to go. I bet you're counting down the sleeps.'

'Of course. Yep. Can't wait.' She tried to inject enthusiasm into her voice, but even to her own ears, she sounded flat and fake. It was too reckless to venture out. It wasn't fair, but they'd have to be more careful.

'Excuse me,' said Antonio. 'I've got work to do.'

Later, Antonio leant against the white headboard in Naomi's bedroom. He lit a cigarette with a match. 'Have you seen my Zippo?' he said with irritation, shaking the match. 'I haven't seen it all week. I want it back.'

In a few days, Richard would complain about the smell of cigarettes in the house, and Naomi would say that Sheree had taken up smoking and kept coming over and lighting up, and Richard would say, *Well, ask her not to*, and Naomi would say, *Yeah, OK, I'll do that*, and Richard would laugh and say, *No, you won't, you're hopeless at putting your foot down*. He might tap her on the nose.

Antonio's foot lay near her leg, his birthmark more like a shadow in the late-afternoon light. 'What's going to happen to us?' she asked him, hoping he had a magical answer she hadn't thought of. She pulled the covers over his foot.

'You think it's ugly?' he said, shaking his foot free of the covers. 'I've always been self-conscious about it.'

'Not ugly, no, but its shape – an hourglass – it always makes me think our time is running out.'

Antonio laid his cigarette in the ashtray and took Naomi's face in both his hands, steering it to rest cheek to cheek with his own. He bent his knee, bringing his foot closer. 'Look again. Now what do you see?'

Naomi took her time, enjoying the feel of his face against hers, the smell of him, his nearness.

'Infinity.'

31

Seven Months Before The Murder

Saturday, 20 May 1978

Helen had a chipped tooth. It was her own stupid fault. Her teeth were weak and she should know better than to use them to crack an almond shell. Her tongue kept seeking it out and worrying at it.

Duncan came into the kitchen and watched her.

'You look like a camel,' he said.

She gave him the hairy eyeball.

'You know, the way they moosh up their mouths.'

'Piss off.'

'A sexy, biddable camel.' He tried to nuzzle up to her, but Helen ducked under his arm and out of his embrace.

'Kinda busy here,' she said.

'You should have gone to the dentist if it's bothering you,' he said.

'Didn't have time.'

'How about a shoulder rub?'

'No, thanks.' Honestly, if she could just be left to get on.

'How about a drink?'

'Got one.' She nodded to her sherry in a teacup.

Duncan raised his eyebrows.

'For the tooth,' she said.

'I'll have a beer then.'

'Better not. I'm not sure you bought enough,' said Helen. It was Sunday and the bottle shop was shut. 'What if the men start with beer and then don't move on to something else?'

They were having a dinner party that night and Duncan had been tasked with getting in the drinks. Something decent in bottles, none of the cheap plonk in flagons. Beer. Spirits. Mixers. Port for after the food. Helen hoped they'd make a night of it. It was a belated welcome of sorts for the new couple who'd moved in over the road a month ago. Richard and Naomi. They had a little boy, just the one. Helen didn't know the story of why they only had one child.

It had been Helen's thirty-ninth birthday a fortnight ago, and in her mind, the birthday and the dinner party were linked. She'd never draw attention to herself by saying so, but she wanted it to feel like a celebration. She wanted it to feel like anything other than her thirties slipping through her fingers without another baby.

Helen had made herself a new dress in a Liberty print. It had a smocked bodice, puffed sleeves and a peplum hem. She'd been hankering after a Liberty print for years. The dress was a triumph. She loved it.

It was too late now, but Helen wished she'd thought to sew new curtains for the lounge room. The chintz was lovely, but it would have been nice to have something new; a bold apple green perhaps, something fresh-looking.

Duncan reached for the pile of grapes Helen had painstakingly peeled. She slapped his hand.

'Not those. Have one of those if you must.' She nodded to the unpeeled grapes.

'You're peeling them?' he said. 'What are they for?'

'Garnish.'

'Fancy.'

Helen didn't have time for a running commentary. 'Could you check the chairs are tucked in straight around the table?' she said.

'Hells-bells,' he said.

She spooned cream into a piping bag.

'Hells-bells,' he said again and waited until she'd put down the bag.

'What?'

'If you need me tonight, just give me a nod. I know it's that time and you'll be thinking about it.'

'Too late for that.'

'When?'

'This morning.'

'Oh, Hells.' By now, they could talk about her period starting without saying the word. 'I'm sorry. We'll have another go next month, yeah?'

Of course they'd have another go. It wasn't up for question. They'd keep having another go until she got another baby.

Duncan looked like he wanted to hug her again, but he'd missed his moment. Helen had taken the big bowl of chocolate mousse out of the fridge. She carried it to the bench, poured herself another sherry and got to work on the piping.

Maureen and Cecil were the first to arrive. Peggy and Leslie were hot on their heels, creating a jam at the front door. Peggy wore a clingy purple paisley dress. It was gorgeous. She was elaborately backcombed and heavily accessorised, her jewellery enormous on her small frame.

Cecil patted Helen on the shoulder by way of greeting. With Peggy, though, he ducked under her canopy of hair to plant a kiss on her cheek, ominously close to her mouth. 'Nice perfume,

Pegs.' He sniffed at her. 'Pungent.' He patted his pockets. 'Maur, duck back home, would you, and get my ciggies so I don't have to bum off Peg all night?'

Maureen pulled on the cardigan she had just taken off and backed out the door.

Richard and Naomi were late – not by a lot, but still, there was no apology when they turned up just after Maureen had returned. They were ruddy-cheeked and had an air about them that made Helen certain they'd just had sex; not perfunctory, business-as-usual, baby-making sex, but raunchy, spur-of-the-moment, can't-help-yourself, got-to-have-it-or-you'll-implode sex. She imagined Naomi afterwards, dressing hastily, drawing on her eyeliner in one go, then a slick of lipstick, running a brush though her hair because that's all her swishy bob needed, still giggling while Richard pawed at her, suggesting there might be time for round two if they were quick about it. His hair was damp from the shower.

Naomi wore a halter-neck top and capri pants. Capris might not be the height of fashion anymore, but on Naomi, they were perfect. But that top. Jeez, that top. It was a marbled organza in shades of green and gold that moved across Naomi's skin like sunlight over water. It tied behind her neck in a big bow that trailed down her back.

It was so divine, it made Helen want to weep. Her own dress was beginning to chafe under the arms where the smocking was pulled too tight and had puckered. The zip was rubbing a spot raw on her back and Helen kept reaching behind her to fiddle with it.

Helen felt tugged in two directions: a simultaneous desire to revere Naomi's beauty and to mar it. Were Naomi a picture, Helen wouldn't know whether to frame her or take to her with a pair of scissors. The shame was a double whammy: first, the fact of her, Helen, coming up short, always coming up short, as evidenced by the fact of Naomi, and second, that it mattered so much to her.

'Drinks!' said Duncan, interrupting Helen staring at the curve of Naomi's shoulder in the nick of time before it got weird and everyone noticed.

'Now you're talking,' said Cecil.

Helen brightened her face and her voice. 'Who'll join me in a brandy and dry?' she said in a cheery sing-song voice.

'Brandy, no dry, for me,' said Peggy.

'Atta girl,' said Cecil. 'Drink like you mean it.'

'No one for beer, then?' said Duncan.

The first course went without a hitch. Ham Royale. Conversation flowed, laughter rose and Duncan kept the Moselle coming.

Maureen helped Helen clear the plates and gave them a quick wash so Helen could dish up the main. Apricot chicken. Baked potatoes with sour cream and chives. Hot broccoli macaroni salad with soy sauce for a touch of the exotic. Helen was satisfied. She'd written out copies of the recipes by hand in advance in case anyone asked for them.

'It's going so well,' said Maureen. 'You're doing a splendid job.'

It really was going well. Helen felt like a fully-fledged, accomplished grown-up. She suspected this sort of thing came easy to most women, that they picked it up like osmosis from their mums. She was proud of herself for pulling it off.

'Richard's been telling me all about life in the navy,' said Helen. 'Lord, he's a dish.'

Maureen giggled like a girl. 'I wouldn't know what to say to him. Duncan's being awfully nice down my end of the table. I suspect you put me there so he'd look after me.'

Helen hadn't; she simply hadn't known where else to put Maureen.

Peals of laughter rang out from the dining room.

'Come on,' said Helen. 'For Peggy and Naomi.' She pointed to two plates. 'I'll do the chaps.'

'Tell us about this diet from Israel,' said Peggy once Helen was back in her seat.

Duncan looked sheepish, not sure if he should have mentioned it or not.

Helen might have minded had she not been in high spirits and well on her way to being drunk.

'It's the Israeli army diet. Maybe you know about it,' she said to Richard, 'you being a military man and all.' He shook his head. 'Anyway, it goes for eight days, four lots of two days, and for each of the two days you eat just one thing. Apples. Then cheese. Then chicken. Then salad. I did it last month.'

'How do you eat all of that every day?' said Peggy, who was pushing food around on her plate but hadn't yet put any of it in her mouth.

'No,' said Helen. 'It's two days of just apples, then two days of just cheese—'

'How much cheese?' said Peggy.

'I don't know,' said Helen, who had read about the diet in a magazine in the doctor's waiting room and had to fill in the gaps that she couldn't remember. 'As much as you want, I think.' Over those two days, Helen had eaten enough cheese to sink a ship.

'You'd need plenty of booze to keep you going, right, Hells?' said Cecil. 'Speaking of . . .' He tapped his empty goblet and Duncan sprang into action. 'Actually, got any red, Dunc? Join me, Helen – a gutsy red'll put hairs on your chest.'

'There's no alcohol allowed on the diet,' said Helen. 'Only black tea or coffee. I'll have whatever's going, Duncan.'

'God, how sad,' said Naomi. 'I mean, great if it works for you, Helen, but I'd never be able to stick to it. I've got no willpower whatsoever.'

Well, not all of us can look good in capris without even trying, thought Helen. Out loud she said, 'You just put your mind to it, that's all.' Helen had lasted four days on the diet. She hadn't yet psyched herself up for another go.

'I think it's admirable,' said Maureen. 'You have such enormous self-discipline. All these different diets. I don't know how you do it.'

Duncan caught Helen's eye and gave an encouraging nod on his way around the table, pouring more wine. Helen didn't mind, not really, that no one had mentioned her birthday.

Leslie was quiet and ate his food. His big hands looked clumsy holding cutlery rather than a spade or rake. He finished his food, then surreptitiously swapped his plate for Peggy's and tucked in again. He blushed when he saw Helen watching him.

'It's a beautiful spread, Helen,' he said.

'Top grub,' said Cecil, breaking off and raising his glass to her; the others followed suit.

Helen felt a glow of contentment. Then she looked at everyone's plates. Apart from Leslie's first plate in front of Peggy, Helen alone had polished off her food. Wolfing down her food was a habit she performed unthinkingly, one she'd learnt young with two older brothers ready to pounce on her plate.

Having eaten all her food, Helen had nothing to do with her hands except drink her wine. During dessert, talk turned to Sheree at Number One.

'Just popped another sprog,' said Cecil, 'and already, there's a new fella sniffing around. Reckon you should keep Dunc on a short leash, love, or she'll be having him next,' he said to Helen. His laugh was more like a shriek, the grog turning him raucous.

Helen noted that Cecil didn't give the same advice to Naomi.

'Duncan knows better than to make a fool of himself,' said Helen.

Cecil stood up, swaying, his goblet held aloft, and declared it a wonderful time to be alive.

'Sit down, you great lump,' said Peggy, but she was laughing like everyone else.

'What I don't get,' Helen said loudly, more loudly than she intended, 'is how she only has to look at a man sideways and she's pregnant. How is that fair?' She looked at the smears of chocolate mousse left in her bowl. She regretted eating it; was beginning to feel sick. She rubbed her chest with her knuckles.

Helen was a sloppy, maudlin drunk. She knew this about herself. She should shut up now.

'Is it too much to ask?' she said. 'Because I don't think it's too much to ask. For another baby.'

'Come on, love, cheer up,' said Cecil. 'You're worth a dozen of her. Some people don't deserve kids.' He was right. He was so goddamn right. 'You've got one, though. That's not nothing. More than some, eh Birdie?' He looked at Maureen. 'Nope, never happened for us. Made our peace with it years ago. Something not quite right down there.' He nodded at Maureen's lap. Maureen had the expression of a cracked teapot. 'Must be. Nothing wrong with my bad boys. Probably just as well. Maur's got her work cut out looking after me. That's enough. Not one of life's natural copers, eh Maur?'

'It's just not fair,' said Helen again. They weren't meant to be talking about Maureen now. It was Helen's turn.

'Why don't you come to our church with us?' said Maureen. It wasn't the first time she'd suggested it. 'You might find it a comfort. I do.'

'I don't want comfort,' said Helen. 'I want a fucking baby.'

She didn't care that everyone stared at her. She just wanted someone to put things right.

'A civilised society is known by its Christian faith, you know,' said Cecil. 'Sets us apart from the rest.'

'What a crock of shit,' said Peggy. 'I'm perfectly civilised without pretending to believe in magic.'

'I've been thinking I might give Buddhism a go,' said Naomi.

'Really?' said Helen despite herself, despite the conversation veering off-track again.

Helen hadn't tried Buddhism yet. Maybe it could be the basis of a friendship between her and Naomi. Maybe they could start popping in on each other, for a cuppa and a chat, or just for the heck of it. Maybe they'd both end up pregnant at the same time. Maybe—

'She doesn't mean it,' said Richard.

Naomi pressed her lips together.

'Can't she say for herself what she means?' said Peggy.

Richard leant forwards and surveyed Peggy for a moment before he relaxed back into his chair and said, 'Of course.' He cupped the back of Naomi's neck in his hand. 'But we're Christians. We go to church.'

'Do you?' said Helen. She hadn't known that. Maybe she'd give church a go after all.

'What about you two?' Cecil said to Peggy and Leslie. 'No kids? Reckon your engine's a bit of a goer, Pegs, let's give it a rev. Calm down, just jokes. No offence, Les.'

Richard started to gather the dessert bowls. 'I'll give you a hand with these, Helen.'

How long had everyone been sitting with dirty bowls in front of them? Helen sprang up to get the rest.

The kitchen was a state. Helen didn't want Richard to see it but felt a thrill at him being there, like he'd crossed a threshold into a private space. Every surface was covered. The sink was full. Richard didn't seem to know where to put the bowls or himself. Helen took the bowls from him. She considered the floor, before putting them in the fridge.

Richard folded his arms. 'Helen, I'm very sorry for the pain

287

you're feeling. It's not the same as it is for a woman, but in my own way, I, too, know something of the disappointment that comes after hoping for a baby.'

That floored Helen. It tapped into something deeper that she hadn't allowed to surface in the dining room. She had shown the anger but concealed the pain. Only Richard had seen the pain. She sobbed before she could help it, and once she'd started, it was impossible to stop. He didn't try to stop her and that touched her more deeply than anything had in a very long time.

'Oh, God,' she said, covering her face. 'I can't go back in there like this.'

'Let's step outside for a moment. Some fresh air will help.'

There was a chill in the air. They stood on the back deck facing away from the house. It was a clear night. The stars were out. Richard put his hands in his pockets.

Helen patted under her eyes with her fingers. She didn't want to look puffy.

'Oh, man,' she said. 'I think I've got something in my eye. Oh, it stings.'

'Hold still.' Richard held her shoulders. 'I can't really see in this light. Keep blinking.'

His face was right there. It was now or never, and Helen couldn't bear the thought of never. She leant forwards and pressed her lips to Richard's. Her eye still stung but she could go blind for all she cared about it now.

How long did it take for Richard to react? Afterwards, Helen would wonder again and again if he had lingered.

As he pulled away, Helen, still leaning into him, lost her balance and stumbled. Richard held onto her to prevent her falling, and together they careened into the rowan tree whose branches overhung the deck and spread into the Laus' back yard, before finding sure ground again.

'Let's chalk this one up to the drink and the emotion,' said

Richard, letting go of her. He was so kind. So gentle. 'I haven't forgotten you're a married woman. And I'm a married man.' He was so principled. 'Ready?' He nodded to the door. His hands were back in his pockets. 'Come on, it's cold. Let's get you back inside.'

They returned to the table to a conversation about nicknames.

'That's so cute he calls you Birdie,' Naomi was saying to Maureen.

'Is it?' said Maureen. 'It's short for bird brain.'

Naomi spluttered as she laughed. She was drunk, the stupid cow. 'Do all couples have nicknames, do you think?' Helen saw Naomi and Richard exchange a private look. 'What's yours, Duncan? How about Funky Dunc? That'll do. I'm going to call you Funky Dunc.' Was she flirting with him?

'I'll take it,' said Duncan. 'I can't for the life of me think of anything to rhyme with Naomi, sorry.'

'No one said they had to rhyme,' said Helen waspishly.

Cecil raised his goblet for another toast, to God knew what; Helen had stopped paying attention. She couldn't bear the thought of Richard and Naomi having cutesy nicknames for each other. She felt decidedly squiffy and wished everyone would go home.

Cecil got to his feet yet again – was he about to do *another* toast? – flung his arm out theatrically and walloped Maureen in the mouth.

'Oops, didn't see you there,' he said.

Helen laughed. She didn't mean to; it was an involuntary reaction; the absurdity of it, the look on Maureen's face as her head snapped back.

'Jesus,' said Peggy.

Maureen smiled shakily. There was blood on her teeth. 'No harm,' she said.

'I'll find some ice,' said Duncan.

289

'No need,' said Maureen. She pushed her chair back. 'I think maybe I'll make a move. No need for everyone else to go.'

Cecil looked at his watch. 'Quite right. Time to go. Say your goodbyes, Maur.'

As if Cecil were a ringleader or conductor, everyone decided to leave.

Someone turned the big light on so Peggy could find her matches. The table looked like a crime scene.

Richard and Naomi were the last to leave because Naomi suddenly needed to go to the toilet and, apparently, couldn't wait until she had crossed the road to her own house.

Helen watched them leave from the open front door. Her head was starting to split already. It was the crying as much as the drinking.

Peggy's cigarette flashed red with each drag. She and Leslie were at their front door as Richard and Naomi set off down the driveway, Naomi's shoulder tucked under Richard's arm. He kissed the top of her head and his voice carried on the still air.

'Christ, tell me we never have to do that again. Those people. I can't stand them.'

Those people? He must mean the others. Certainly not Helen, not after the connection they'd had. Well, Helen couldn't stand those people either. All the same, she'd like to see Richard's list of *those people*, ranked. She'd like to know what position she occupied on that list.

Duncan came and stood behind Helen. He rested his chin on her shoulder. It was heavy and uncomfortable. He wrapped his arms around her waist.

'I completely forgot to bring the port out,' he said. 'I'm sorry. Do you mind?'

'Why didn't you tell anyone it was my birthday?' said Helen.

'Because it's not,' he said, taken aback.

'But it was.'

290

'Jeez, Hells, why didn't you say you wanted them to know?'

'Because it shouldn't be for me to say.'

Possibly due to drink or distraction, Helen had forgotten about her chipped tooth. It now made itself known again, along with her shredded inner cheek. How could something so tiny do so much damage?

She extricated herself from Duncan's coarse embrace and ran her fingers back and forth over her smocked bodice to self-soothe.

Carpenter ants have a topsy-turvy name because carpenters build things with wood and carpenter ants destroy wood. They build their nests inside wood, chewing along the grain to make passages and galleries. If you have an infestation of carpenter ants in the structure of your house, you're unlikely to know about it until it's too late and the damage has been done.

32

Seventeen Days After The Murder

Tuesday, 23 January 1979

Tammy was outside on the deck, mopishly stripping berries from the rowan tree. Naomi had appeared that morning, up and dressed and coming back to life again, to take Colin on an outing to the bank. That's how she'd said it, like it was a treat: *Colin can't play today. We're going on an outing to the bank.* It was hardly the Royal Canberra Show. And it wasn't like Tammy and Colin didn't have important things to do.

But the real problem was that Tammy was missing the little twerp. It was so unfair to foist Colin on her and wait until she'd got used to him and wanted him there and then take him away. It was obvious to anyone with eyes that Colin didn't want to go, but no one took any notice of what he wanted either.

The sound of laughter came from over the fence, so Tammy went to look into the Laus' back yard. She could hear Mrs Lau's voice coming from inside and she realised two things at once. First, it was a one-way conversation. She must be on the phone. Secondly, Mrs Lau sounded different. Usually, her voice was brusque; she was spare with words, formal. Now, her voice was soft, with ups and downs, generous and carrying a smile.

She was talking to a friend, someone she liked.

'Tomorrow, then, same time as usual . . . I'm running out of excuses . . . I told Herman I was going to the library last time . . . [laughter] . . . Of course I want to . . . I think so too . . . I could never be angry with you . . . Yes, all right . . . and not a word to Lydia if you can bear it, it's not legal until . . . yes . . . [laughter] . . . Bye, then . . . bye, Ursula.'

Tammy sprang away from the fence. She *knew* it! Ursula was up to something shady (*not legal!*) and now Tammy knew that Mrs Lau was in on it. This was just as incriminating as the theft of Antonio's pencil and the lie to cover it up. Ursula was even keeping secrets from Lydia – was that because Lydia was her sister or was it because Lydia was a police officer?

Tammy was halfway down her driveway before she stopped. She needed a plan. She doubled back and went to her bedroom to consult her notes and pace until she could be sure it was time for Ursula to be at work.

'Your hair,' said Tammy when Debbie opened the door.

'Yep,' said Debbie, who then turned and led the way to her bedroom.

Debbie's long hair was gone, cut into a short pageboy style. It had changed direction, swerving in and under instead of flicking out. It wasn't the haircut itself so much that bothered Tammy, more that Debbie hadn't discussed it with her first. Tammy would absolutely have consulted Debbie about such an important decision. Tammy, with or without Colin, had been back at Debbie's as much as she could get away with.

'You here on your own?' Tammy asked Debbie's back.

'Dunno. Maybe. Probably.' Debbie was in a foul mood. 'I'm not up for anything except vegging out. You can stay if you want. Or go. I don't care.'

Every time Tammy steered the conversation towards Ursula,

Debbie steered it away again. It looked like Tammy wouldn't even get to start today. 'What's up *your* bum?' she said to Debbie's retreating back.

Debbie didn't answer. She bobbed down the stairs to the rumpus room and disappeared.

Actually, Tammy thought, here was an opportunity she hadn't had before. She went through the kitchen and headed down the hallway she'd never set foot in before.

The door to a bedroom was open. Eureka! They were definitely Ursula's clothes on the bed. Skirt and blouse. A bra, face up, with cups that held their shape and which Tammy wanted to look at but not touch. Stockings that looked like saggy skin.

There were two bedside tables. Both seemed to be in use. Strange. Both had a lamp. One had a glass of water on it, the other a mug. On the table closest to Tammy was a book called *The Thorn Birds*. It had a dead tree on the cover and looked boring.

Tammy had seen an episode of *Columbo* last year where clues were left inside the pages of books. She put her journal on the bed and picked up *The Thorn Birds*. She flicked through it and shook it upside down. Nothing. It didn't matter because the other bedside table had a stack of books. She walked around the bed to get to it. On the top was a book called *A Fringe of Leaves*. There were two blurry figures on the cover, which was weird. Tammy was about to start rifling through the pages but was distracted by the rest of the clutter on the table. A glasses case, hand cream, a hanky, a watch, a bottle of Oil of Ulan. A little dish of knick-knacks, among which was – amazingly – Ursula's cross lying on a coil of chain.

Tammy put the book down and picked up the cross, threading the chain through her fingers. She remembered how badly she'd wanted to steal it at the Bible study, thinking that she'd never get the chance.

A shower started running in the en suite behind a closed door. Of course! The clothes on the bed made sense now. Why hadn't she made sure that Ursula and Lydia weren't home? Big mistake! Tammy took one creeping step to get the flying fudge out of there when she heard the front door open and the clatter of keys on a bench. She was hemmed in, no way out, nowhere to hide. Footsteps approached.

Tammy sank onto her hands and knees, and crawled into a corner next to a chair laden with clothes, breathing in carpet dust. On the other side of her, the net curtain hung limply, like a lazy ghost. The cross dug into the palm of her hand. The corner was cloistered in shadow and Tammy was almost concealed by the chair. Only her head poked out. She might just get away with it if she could keep quiet enough. She sucked in a big breath like she was going underwater.

Lydia walked in at the same moment Ursula emerged from the en-suite. Ursula was entirely naked but for steamed-up glasses.

Lydia laughed like it was the most normal thing in the world to look at her sister without any clothes on.

Ursula smiled dryly, perfectly at ease, and said, 'Sprung. You've caught me forgetting my specs again.'

'You'd forget your head if it wasn't screwed on,' said Lydia.

Ursula tossed her glasses onto the pile of clothes on the bed and turned back to the en-suite. But Lydia caught hold of her hand and swung Ursula back towards her, kicking the door to the hall closed with her foot. It was like a dance move.

Lydia stood behind Ursula. They both faced Tammy's corner. Tammy gawped at Ursula, and then she watched Lydia absorbed in watching Ursula. Lydia's arm wrapped around Ursula's waist and her hand came to gently hold Ursula's breast. The other hand rested on Ursula's hip where her fingers made soft indentations in Ursula's flesh. She pressed her lips to Ursula's neck and kept them there. It was excruciatingly tender.

Ursula leant her head back, tilting her cheek into Lydia, and closed her eyes. The expression of pleasure and peacefulness on her face was at odds with everything Tammy thought she knew about Ursula.

It was the gradual awareness of the stillness of Lydia that alerted Tammy. She broke away from looking at Ursula and saw that Lydia was frowning at Tammy's journal on the bed. Tammy felt wobbly and instinctively grabbed at the clothes on the chair to keep her balance. The clothes slithered onto the floor and Lydia's eyes snapped to Tammy's.

Ursula screamed when she saw Tammy. Overtaken by panic, Tammy screamed too. Ursula clutched at the clothes on the bed and held them up to cover herself.

The movement released Tammy. She grabbed her journal and fled, barrelling into Debbie in the hall.

'What's all this screaming?' said Debbie, but then she saw Lydia's face appear in the doorway and Ursula in the background. 'Ah, shit.'

Debbie held tightly onto Tammy's shoulders.

'But they're sisters!' said Tammy in a voice that came out as a whine, before Debbie could say anything further. 'Sisters can't . . . It's not . . .' She didn't know what she wanted to say but she felt the need to lodge a protest against what she'd just seen.

'Oh, Tammy,' said Debbie, not without pity. 'Of course they're not sisters.'

Tammy wrenched herself free and ran through the kitchen, banging her hip on a chair as she went. Debbie followed.

Tammy yanked on the door, desperate to be free.

'You mustn't tell anyone,' said Debbie. 'Tammy, listen to me. Say you won't.'

The door wouldn't budge. The harder Tammy pulled on the handle, the firmer it stayed shut. Tears blurred her vision.

Then, a moment of clarity. It was the screen door. She pushed rather than pulled, the door opened, and she was off down the driveway with Debbie calling after her, 'You *really* mustn't tell. Say you won't.'

Tammy's thoughts were racing at a million kilometres an hour in every direction, all of them blind alleys.

She rounded the corner at the bottom of the driveway and, just when she needed to be alone to try to make sense of what she had seen, found herself slap-bang in the middle of a gathering. Her mum. Nosy parkers Peggy and Cecil. Sheree and her kids. Suzi. And two policemen, the same two who were there that first day on the island, one of them the one who came and spoke to her dad.

Tammy tried to swerve around them and nearly tripped over one of the kids. She tried to keep going but Suzi got in her way.

'Whoa, Tammy,' said her mum. 'You all right?' She put an arm around her, which might look from the outside like a nice thing to do.

Tammy was furious at the intrusion, at being waylaid, at Peggy for always plonking herself into things, at the uselessness of the police, at the way everyone was looking at her too closely.

Then she noticed what one of the policemen was holding. An axe, old but meticulously cared for. A pick, the stripe of red on its handle faded and flaking. A spade, a favourite because it was weighted just right for balance and leverage. A chainsaw. She recognised them immediately.

'What are you doing with those?' Tammy said.

'They're just asking some questions about these tools found over in the creek bed—' said Tammy's mum.

'They're not yours,' said Tammy. 'You can't have them. They're Joe's. Give them back.' She was shouting now.

She lunged at the tools, freeing them from the hands of the surprised policeman. The axe, spade and chainsaw clattered to

298

the ground, and Sheree dragged her smallest kid behind her. Tammy clutched the pick to her chest.

'Joe's?' said the other policeman, the one who had come to her house and talked to her dad. 'Josip Pavlović at Number Eight?'

Everyone looked up at Joe and Zlata's house.

'Thank you, young lady,' said the policeman. 'That's the confirmation we're after. A significant step forward in the investigation. Not a complete picture yet. But identification of weapons is a big help. You should get a special treat for that.' He turned to Helen. 'What do you say, Mum – a special treat for your girl?'

Tammy lost all feeling in her limbs.

Her arms dropped and the pick fell to the ground along with her journal. She snatched up the journal and ran.

She ran towards home and didn't stop running even when her legs burned as she went up the driveway. She didn't stop running until she had flung herself face down onto her bed, and even then, her legs kept kicking and she screamed into her pillow. Only after she was still did Tammy realise that, despite the hurly-burly of discovering and being discovered, of that awful business with Joe's tools, she'd held onto Ursula's cross. The chain was choking her little finger. The cross itself had left a red indent on Tammy's palm, like she'd been branded. Tammy shook her hand free. She picked up *The Incredible World of Ant Kingdoms* from her desk and nestled the necklace in among its pages.

Bullet ants have a sting that is so painful, it feels like being shot. It can send a person insane, that's how bad the pain is. Some people are like bullet ants, except the trouble is, you can't tell which ones. They should be forced to wear a sign. But also, what if you are the bullet ant and you don't realise it?

33

Eighteen Days After The Murder

Wednesday, 24 January 1979

Tammy's dad would be leaving for work soon. There was no reason for the rest of them to be up so early, but the heat had driven them from their beds. Tammy, her mum and dad, and Colin were taking it in turns to have a go on the new hanging chair on the veranda. Colin went first, spinning in circles. The others sat on the steps waiting their turn, like teammates on the bench. Tammy's heart wasn't in it. At least Naomi had let her have Colin back. She was certain that, had he been with her, she wouldn't have gone into Ursula and Lydia's bedroom, and she wouldn't have opened her big blabby mouth about Joe's tools.

When the wailing started, they all stood up. It wasn't the sort of sound you could sit for. It was so loud that they couldn't tell what direction it came from. Tammy felt it travel up and down her spine and lodge in her chest.

Then they saw Zlata, her slumped form lurching forwards as if propelled by the sounds coming from inside her. The wailing: it sounded inhuman, more like a wounded animal. It intensified as she struggled up the Lanahans' driveway with her arms raised imploringly. Her apron was still on, dotted with floury fingerprints. Her hair clips, normally precisely positioned, were askew, unable to contain her unruly waves. She hop-shuffled along at speed, half dragging a leg that looked like it had forgotten how to work.

They ran to meet her. Tammy's dad reached her just as she collapsed in the middle of the driveway. He caught her under her arms and they both fell heavily onto the concrete.

'My Josip, my Josip, my Josip,' she sobbed, a mantra of sorrow. 'My Josip. My Josip, my Josip.'

Tammy's mum took hold of Zlata's arm and tried to pull her up. But it was no use. She was limp and slithered out of her grasp. So Tammy's mum got down next to her, right there on the driveway, and wrapped her arms around her. Tammy knelt down on one knee and then stood up and backed away to stand next to Colin. She didn't know what to do with herself. It was unbearable to watch but she couldn't turn away.

The three of them, Zlata and her mum and dad, looked like a deformed animal, their bodies blurred into one blotch, their legs jutting out at awkward angles.

'It will be OK,' said Tammy's mum. 'Whatever's happened, it will be OK.'

Why did grown-ups say things like that when they couldn't possibly know, and when sometimes things were definitely not OK?

'No,' said Zlata, and then, more forcefully, 'No. You don't understand.' She turned and grabbed Tammy's dad by the arm. She clung to him like he was a life raft. 'He can't be there. He *can't*. You have to get him for me. Get him from police. The police, they come and they take him away.' She stopped shaking, was deathly still. 'They shoot him.'

'Zlata,' said Tammy's dad. 'Listen to me. No one's going to shoot Joe.'

'No, no, in the war,' said Zlata. 'They shoot him. They shoot him in the back and drag him.' She clutched at her chest near her shoulder and Tammy thought about all the times she'd seen the round shiny scar on Joe's shoulder blade and its twin on his chest. 'They take him to a camp and they . . . they . . . they . . .' Whatever it was, she couldn't say it.

Zlata shook her head and shook off all traces of weakness. She squared her shoulders. She was now steeled, determined. And for the first time, Tammy saw in the unwavering intensity of her eyes, the flick of her nose, the elegance of her mouth as she spoke, the power of the woman that Zlata had once been. That she'd had to be. That she continued to be.

'Josip won't survive being prisoner. Not again.'

Tammy's dad got to his feet, and this time, Zlata let him and Tammy's mum help her up.

'Phone work for me, Helen,' said Tammy's dad. 'Say I've got a gippy tummy or something. Just make it believable so they don't think I'm shirking. Say I've got the plans ready to go. You got that? They're ready to go.'

He was bundling Zlata into the car as he spoke. Zlata wound down her window and passed her apron to Tammy's mum. She looked ahead impatiently, ready to undertake her mission.

Tammy wasn't sure exactly what had happened to Joe. But of one thing she was certain: it was definitely her fault.

That evening, it was just Tammy and her mum at home. Colin was at his house. Naomi had called for him earlier, saying there were jobs for him to help with at home. Tammy's dad hadn't made it into work. He'd been at the police station all day. He'd phoned at teatime to say he'd got Joe home but thought he'd better stay with Joe and Zlata, that it didn't feel right to leave them alone yet. Tammy offered to go over too – she wanted to see with her own eyes how much damage she'd done – but her dad said it was probably best to leave it for a bit.

Had this happened because Tammy wanted to involve herself with the Antonio business so she would be liked at school? Was this what her mum meant when she talked about God seeing into the murky depths of your motivations?

Tammy's mum said she felt a bit flat and would creamed corn on toast be OK for tea? They ate on their laps in front of *The Paul Hogan Show* and let waves of canned laughter wash over them. Neither joined in. Afterwards, Tammy's mum did the dishes and Tammy washed her hair. She hadn't brushed it for several days and the comb was having difficulty working its way through. She brought the comb back with her to the couch in the lounge room. Her mum was already there. It wasn't usual for either of them to seek the other out for company, but Tammy didn't want to be alone. Maybe her mum didn't either.

'Here,' said her mum, taking the comb from her.

There was no telling-off for not looking after her hair. Tammy gritted her teeth and didn't complain as the comb tugged on the tangles.

'Oh, it's nice to have a bit of a sit-down,' said Tammy's mum, as though they hadn't just been sitting down to eat their tea. She always said *a bit of a sit-down* like it was the best – the most – she could hope for. It had always felt depressing – limiting – to Tammy, but now she wondered if she could do with some limits; someone to say, *Just wait and have a bit of a sit-down*, before she did anything disastrous again.

Still, Tammy wondered if her mum had ever wanted more.

'Debbie thinks you should go to uni,' she said.

'Does she now? Ha!' Tammy's mum got to work on a stubborn knot. 'Don't be ridiculous. My sort doesn't go to uni.' She paused. '*You* can, though. You *will*.'

'How come my sort is different to your sort?'

'Because I've made bloody sure of it.' She gave Tammy's hair one last going-over and put the comb on Tammy's knee. 'You're not making a nuisance of yourself with Debbie, are you?'

Tammy wobbled her leg to make the comb see-saw. She wanted to see how far she could push it before it lost its balance. The problem was, she wouldn't know what the limit was until she pushed it too far.

'Are you all right?' asked her mum, without warning. 'In life, generally, I mean.'

Tammy stilled her leg and considered the question. 'I don't know.'

The words hung in the air between them.

'Are you?' said Tammy.

Moments passed and Tammy thought her mum wasn't going to answer. Then: 'I don't know either.'

Her mum leant back into the couch. She lifted the hem of her skirt up over her knees and gave it a few flaps to get some cool air moving. There was a release of tension in her body; a sagging, a sinking. Her knees lolled apart. Her hand resting on the couch beside her flopped outwards and touched Tammy's leg. Just a light graze of a touch. She turned her face towards Tammy and said, 'We're a fine pair.' And then she closed her eyes.

With her mum's eyes shut, Tammy had an opportunity to look at her closely, in a way that she hadn't since the first inkling of self-awareness, of self-consciousness, had arrived. Now, Tammy looked at the pucker of her mum's vaccination scar, a bullseye in the rounded muscle of her arm. It felt as familiar to Tammy as if the needle had pierced her own skin. That place had been her pillow and her comfort. She looked at the knobble of her mum's elbow; the shape of her cuticles with their little moons, perfectly matched to Tammy's; the sloping pads of her thumbs; the spreading, inert flesh of her thigh; the pale, cracked skin on her heel, fissures in a row, on show where one ankle crossed over the other. All of it, all of her, Tammy had once thought of as her own territory.

Tammy had a vague sense that secrets acted as currency for intimacy. She'd seen it over and over again from the outside: juicy morsels whispered to cement alliances, to draw a boundary that kept a friendship within it tight and insulated from those not in the know.

Tammy was in possession of a secret. It didn't occur to her to consider whether it still counted as currency if it wasn't your secret to tell. Misgivings lurked, but she swatted them away. She yearned for remembered cadences of her mum's voice, the texture of her name spoken in tenderness.

Tammy took a big breath and took the plunge.

'Mum,' she said, nudging her mum's leg repeatedly until her mum grunted. 'You know how Ursula and Lydia are sisters?'

'Hm.'

'Well, they're not.'

Tammy's mum opened one eye. 'Not what?'

'Sisters.'

Tammy's mum opened both eyes. 'What are you on about?'

Tammy had hit a roadblock. She didn't know what to say next; how to explain what she had seen.

'I don't want you making up stories,' said her mum. 'Or repeating nasty gossip.'

'I saw them myself,' said Tammy, and her mum's head lifted. Tammy's voice went small and she looked at her lap when she said, 'They had no clothes on.' It was close enough to being true; one of them had had no clothes on.

'Go on,' said her mum, her voice dangerously quiet, unnervingly focused.

'And I saw them kissing.'

That wasn't, strictly speaking, true either. But Tammy didn't know how else to tell the truth without revealing the devastating impact of the way Ursula and Lydia had fitted together, the love in every touch and look between them. She didn't want to tell her mum that she hadn't been able to erase from her mind the image of Lydia's hand on Ursula's breast and the other on Ursula's hip.

'Are you sure?'

'Also, Debbie said they weren't sisters.'

That clinched it.

'Goodness,' said her mum.

Tammy felt that they were both thinking private thoughts about what two women might do together in bed and she felt her face redden.

'Goodness,' said her mum again, but now she was talking to herself, not to Tammy. Tammy had become irrelevant. 'There's much to consider . . . The implications . . . What to do about it.'

And with that, Tammy felt an unravelling of the most tenuous thread. She felt a million times worse than she had before. She must never be trusted again, not even – especially not – by herself.

34

Nineteen Days After The Murder

Thursday, 25 January 1979

Ursula's mood was buoyant – a new development. Her body had loosened, and all the fears that normally pounded on her attention were one step removed. Jeopardy held at bay. She had space to breathe, room to move and inhabit this strange life that brought moments of wonder and abundance if only you opened your eyes to them. She'd spent the afternoon with Guangyu: driving, talking, being friends.

Thank you, Lord, for the blessing of Guangyu. May you fill her heart with joy.

Ursula had decided to go to Bible study at Helen's house after all. When Debbie had reassured Ursula and Lydia that there was no way Tammy would divulge what she had seen, it had been easy to believe her. Ursula wanted to believe her and the cost of not believing her – the return of panic and the loss of peace – was too high.

'I know she won't tell, deadset, because I told her not to,' Debbie said to an incredulous look from Lydia. 'Seriously, that kid would do anything I say. I could tell her to murder a puppy and she would.'

'Kill,' said Lydia. 'It's only murder if you kill a person, not an animal.'

'Interesting,' said Debbie. 'Makes it sound like people are worth more than animals, and I'm just not sure some people make the grade. Anyway. She won't tell.'

'You sound awfully smug about it,' said Ursula.

'I do, don't I?' said Debbie, laughing. 'I'm letting the power go to my head. It's a real trip.'

Ursula made her grandma's apricot kuchen and arranged slices neatly on a plate.

'Are there going to be any leftovers I can take to Sheree's?' said Debbie, nodding at the kuchen. 'Helen's paying me to babysit again, but Sheree's going to ditch Bible study and we're going to have a piss-up at her house. Don't tell Helen. I still want the money.'

The moment Ursula walked into Helen's lounge room, she knew. The good mood that she had carried with her from her home bolted out the door before it had closed behind her. Even though she was right on time, everyone else was already there, already seated, clearly summoned to arrive at an earlier time. It was like emerging from a curtain onto a stage and realising that you are the main act.

Ursula became hyper-aware of her clothes: the waistband of her skirt digging in; her shoes suddenly feeling tight over the bridges of her feet; her blouse a shroud, quivering with her breaths that came too loud and shallow, and her heart that beat too fast. Her watch felt heavy on her wrist. Her stomach turned to silt. The air was hot and stale and clogged her throat. She held onto the plate of kuchen too tightly, with both hands, for fear of dropping it.

Lord, you have called me by name. I am yours. Save me.

Pastor Martin gave her a watery smile that contained more

apprehension than warmth, as if he were scared of her.

Peggy and Maureen were frowning faces on the far side of the room, too far away to be her salvation, too diffuse a relationship to be sure of their sympathy. Oh, what she wouldn't give for Lydia's presence by her side.

The girl, Tammy, stood with her back to the wall, her arms stiff rods by her sides. One look at her shame-filled face was confirmation of what Ursula already knew.

The rest of the faces were a sea of spectators. Waiting for action, for drama, for blood to spill.

Except Helen. This was Helen's house, Helen's show, and she had saved a leading role for herself. Where Pastor Martin's smile was limp, Helen's curdled the air. Her open, humble posture was a deception, a part to be played. She took the plate from Ursula, her movements as smooth as syrup.

Save me, Lord. I beseech you, have mercy, save me.

Next, Helen took hold of Ursula's wrist. She might as well have handcuffed her.

'Don't be alarmed,' said Pastor Martin, looking alarmed. 'We've gathered together to pray for you.'

'We need to talk about you and Lydia,' said Helen.

'My sister, Lydia . . .' began Ursula, but she didn't know how to go on. She cleared her throat and tried again, floundering. 'My sister, Lydia, and I . . .'

'Stop it,' snapped Helen. 'We know. We know you're not sisters. Everyone at church knows.' She turned to Pastor Martin. 'See? I told you. She's still lying.'

'Say what?' said Peggy. 'Just what the hell's going on here? What are all you church people in on?' Her voice carried from the other side of the room.

Ursula understood at last why she'd always felt uneasy around Peggy. Peggy was someone who held nothing back and Ursula was someone who held everything back.

'The Bible teaches us to hate the sin but love the sinner,' said Helen, ignoring Peggy, and still holding Ursula's wrist. She began to stroke Ursula's hand. 'We speak with love, Ursula.'

Helen's touch was unbearable. Ursula snatched her hand back. She clutched her own elbows, tucking her body in tight, trying to protect herself from Helen's onslaught of loving the sinner. She shook her head from side to side and began to keen, at first unaware that the sound was coming from her, and then aware but unable to stop. It was a sound that dingos make in the dead of night. Did dingoes mourn? Did they wail their laments?

The Lord is my light and my salvation – whom shall I fear? The Lord is the stronghold of my life – of whom shall I be afraid?

There was a presence on either side of her. Would they hold her down? Force an exorcism on her? She'd heard of such things, of course. Would she submit if they did?

But it was Maureen on one side and Peggy on the other, each of them insubstantial physically – neither would be much chop in a fight – but their presence formed a shield around Ursula. It gave her time to remember who she was: a precious child of God. He had called her by name. She was loved; loved by God and loved by Lydia.

This she knew. But it still hurt to have her innermost feelings spread out on display for others to pick over as they pleased. Only Tammy's face was downcast.

Peggy had been speaking but Ursula hadn't been listening. Whatever she'd said had raised Helen's hackles. 'Peggy, it's my house and this is a Bible study,' Helen said in a strained voice. 'You're welcome to stay if you can respect that. It's Pastor Martin who's in charge here, not you.'

'Perhaps we should start with a reading?' said Pastor Martin. He was flustered; bumbling and graceless. What must he think of her? She knew what he must think. But he was a weak, flimsy,

311

insipid thing of a man. There was no safe harbour to be had with him.

'I really think we should start with Ursula telling the truth,' said Helen.

'Tammy,' said Maureen in a surprisingly clear voice, 'go fetch your dad. Quick smart.'

But Duncan had already appeared. He stood next to Tammy and, for the first time, Tammy's eyes met Ursula's and the feeling that Tammy passed over in that look was full. Duncan's gaze raked over the room and settled on Helen.

'It's time to go,' said Duncan, casting his voice out to the whole room. 'The club's over.'

'Leave it, Duncan,' said Helen. 'We're handling this.'

'Perhaps if we just—' began Pastor Martin.

'You,' said Duncan. 'Wind your head in.' It was clear he was seething and barely trying to conceal it. 'Get out. All of you. Get out of my house.' His voice rose and, as if in anticipation of another interjection from Helen, he said, 'You've crossed a line, Hells. This isn't right. It's not right.'

That's when Ursula remembered that she had legs. She backed up until she felt the front door behind her, turned, opened the door and fled.

35

Five minutes after Duncan had shut the door firmly behind the last person, Lydia stormed in without knocking, out of breath. Her eyes searched the lounge room while Tammy and her parents stood stock still, stunned.

'Where is she?'

Lydia was shouting. Fuming. No, not just fuming, she was exploding with fury. It was coming out of her eyes and her voice and her whole body was full of springs ready to let loose. Although Tammy should have expected as much, seeing the truth of what she had done, showing itself in plain sight on Lydia's face, sent her heart thundering and her stomach plummeting. It was inevitable and yet breathtaking when it came.

Tammy's dad was the first to unfreeze. 'Lydia, I – I'm sorry, she's not here.'

Lydia pushed past him and rounded on Tammy's mum. 'You dumb bitch.' Her voice had gone eerily quiet and that was somehow worse. '*What have you done?*'

Tammy's mum stood on the other side of the coffee table. Untouched plates of food looked incongruently jolly, Ursula's kuchen among them.

'Me? Well!' Tammy's mum was all huff and indignation on the

outside, but she looked nervously to Tammy's dad for back-up. He folded his arms and remained silent, watching. 'She knew. She knew what she's done is wrong. Even if you don't. Why else would she run away like that?'

'You think she's ashamed? Of what she is? Of us?' Lydia's voice snagged on the last.

'You must understand,' Tammy's mum appealed to Lydia, moving towards her. Where Ursula had shrunk from Helen, Lydia stood her ground. This time it was Tammy's mum who floundered, her outstretched arm dropping to her side. 'It was all motivated by love. Love and doing the right thing by our community. You must see that. We feel only love for—'

'You stupid fuck.' Lydia announced each word clearly. It seemed a real possibility that she would lash out and hit Tammy's mum. 'This has nothing to do with your *feelings*.'

'Please,' said Tammy's mum. 'Your language.' She jerked her head at Tammy.

Lydia stared at Tammy with a look that went straight through her.

'You know, Helen, I'd feel sorry for you if you weren't so dangerous. Your feelings, your motives – none of that matters. The only thing that matters is the damage you've done.' She sighed and ran her hand through her hair. 'What – you think you could change her? You think you have that power? What was this?' Her arms opened out to the room. Her eyes rested on the plates of cake and biscuits. 'You thought you could *shame* her into not being who she is? Because here's the truth: Ursula's not ashamed. She loves what we are.' The pitch of Lydia's voice dropped, and the image that Tammy recalled of Lydia's lips touching Ursula's neck was so vivid she felt her own lips pucker. 'She just loved your church more.'

Defeated and diminished, all bluster gone, Lydia turned to leave.

'It's the lying as much as anything,' said Tammy's mum. 'She deceived us. You both did. All this time, pretending to be something you're not.'

Lydia turned back and scoffed. 'Everyone pretends to be something they're not.' The look she gave Tammy's mum was scathing.

'But the lying.' Tammy's mum wouldn't let it go, wouldn't let Lydia go. 'You took us all for fools. Duncan, you agree, don't you? With everything going on – a *murder*, for flip's sake – we have to protect our community. If they're lying about this, who knows what else they're lying about?'

Yesterday, Tammy would have seen this as noteworthy, would have added it to her list of things that made Ursula suspicious. But not anymore. Not now.

'Helen, that's enough,' said Tammy's dad. 'I'll say more when it's just us.' Tammy knew he was referring to her more than Lydia. This putting his foot down was new, unsettling; she didn't know how she felt about it or where it might lead. 'But for now, shut up. I'm ashamed of you.' He moved closer to Lydia. They both faced Helen. Tammy was to the side, caught in the middle, wanting to move but stuck to the spot. Her dad's words, *I'm ashamed of you*, pierced her. She deserved them even if he hadn't intended them for her too.

That might have been the end of it if Tammy's mum hadn't said, 'I don't see why I'm the villain here when I'm not the one who lied. Besides, there's this blessed heat to contend with. It makes everyone fraught. People overreact.'

'Oh, God, what did you do to her?' said Lydia. She ran her hand through her hair several times. Tammy could see the hair pulling at her scalp. 'I'm going to say this even though I don't think it will get through to you, because you're arrogant and, by God, I'd like to take you down a peg or two.' Lydia breathed hard. 'Helen, we owe you *nothing*. Can you get that through your thick skull? Not the truth. Not an explanation. Nothing. What do you want from us? You want us to ask for your *permission*? Who the fuck do you think you are?'

The question was left hanging in the air, and Tammy felt it land on her too.

Tammy's dad went to the door with Lydia. 'Will you be OK?' he asked. 'Will Ursula?'

'I don't know,' said Lydia.

'I'm so sorry. Sorry I didn't put a stop to this sooner. Will you tell Ursula I'm sorry?'

'I will, when I see her. If I see her. She hasn't come home. I only know because Peggy and Maureen came to tell me.'

'Where would she go?'

'I don't know.' Lydia's voice faltered and it was more frightening to hear that than her anger. 'She can't drive. She'll be on foot.'

'I'll help look. We don't want her roaming about on her own. And, listen, if you need anything else at all, call on me,' said Tammy's dad. Their heads were close together. He opened the door.

Lydia looked back into the room one last time. Her eyes were blank. 'One day you're going to regret what you've done. And I hope the guilt of it eats you alive.'

The sound of the door closing rang loud and then empty silence filled the room. Tammy felt she mustn't move and disturb it. Her dad leant his forearm against the door, and his head against his arm.

'Duncan,' said Tammy's mum.

'Not now,' he said. 'I've had a gutful. I can't even bear to look at you.'

Then he was out the door too, off, away, gone.

It was no good. Tammy couldn't sleep. She lay in her bed contemplating a future where everyone knew how repellent she was. Everything she touched turned bad. She shoved her hands underneath her: she mustn't touch anything. She imagined her lips sewn shut; she mustn't speak. She imagined walls built around her thoughts; they mustn't be let out.

Lydia's voice cut through her misery: *I hope the guilt of it eats you alive.* And so it should.

Joe and Zlata. Ursula and Lydia. Who else might Tammy damage if she didn't feel the full weight of guilt for what she'd done? From now on, no matter what happened, no matter what she found out, she was going to back up and shut up. No more opening her gob. No more stuff-ups.

Tammy didn't want to fall asleep because she didn't want to wake in the morning and have the new day deceive her that things weren't all that bad. Daylight had a way of doing that. She needed to keep her guilt at full strength, keep it big and upfront, and hope that it would rein her in, keep her in check.

Next came Simone's voice: *I find it very interesting that someone who's supposed to be so brainy can be such a space cadet socially.*

Tammy had kicked her eiderdown onto the floor. Her legs were tangled in her sheet and her nightie was twisted around her. Softness brushed her arm: the curtain lifting, swelling with a breeze. Something softer yet caressed her face: the breeze itself. It swept down from the hills, through Tammy's window, and came knocking on her face. Did it seek out secrets and carry them on its breath? Tammy imagined the breeze travelling over her, through her, saturating all of Warrah Place, moving in and over the houses, seeping into the whole city. It made Tammy feel small. How absurd to think she could play any part in finding out what happened to Antonio.

Antonio's laugh tinkled on the breeze: *Run along, Tamara. Go play.*

Tammy was nothing more than an ant, kidding herself that

she had any kind of chance while scuttling around beneath the feet of giants.

The breeze brought Lydia's voice again, depositing it on Tammy over and over in waves: *Who the fuck do you think you are?*

Tammy looked over to Colin's bed, forgetting for a moment that he wasn't there. He was sleeping at his house again. It seemed Naomi was getting back to the land of the living. His bed was made, the eiderdown neat, his nightie lying across it like an out-of-action ghost. Would she get him back? She missed the simplicity of him. She missed how easy it was to be with someone who didn't have a clue about anything. She missed how he didn't hate her.

The breeze finally took pity on Tammy and brought her Debbie: *Yeah, maybe I can help with that.*

Debbie. Tammy needed to find Debbie, to be near her. Just to clap eyes on her would be enough. And Tammy knew where she was.

The road had retained the heat of the day, searing the soles of Tammy's feet, but she was already at the island, and if she went back now to get her sandals, she'd lose her nerve. She paused, though, and looked back to the Italian House. With all of its upstairs lights still on, it looked like a landing strip, showing Antonio the way home.

She must stop thinking about Antonio. He was gone. He was none of her business. She needed Debbie now; Debbie, who would help show Tammy a way forwards, not drag her back.

Sheree's back yard was still a toy graveyard. Moonlight picked out debris, much of it unmoved since Tammy had been there a few weeks ago. She hadn't forgotten about Antonio's shoes at Sheree's house. She didn't like the idea of Debbie getting too friendly with Sheree, but now she was in a quandary. She was determined to stick to her vow not to interfere anymore. On the other hand, was she a disloyal friend to Debbie if she didn't warn her off Sheree?

Just watching couldn't hurt.

Under the kitchen window was a bench, a few of its slats rotted and splintered, its red paint faded and peeling. Tammy perched on it, her toes finding the sturdy slats. The screen on the window was crawling with insects clamouring to get inside. Empty butterfly casings littered the window ledge. Tammy brushed them aside and pressed her nose to the screen.

The light inside was green. Someone had sticky-taped green cellophane over the light bulb. Their green-tinged skin made Debbie and Sheree look out of this world, alien, ghoulish. There was a fold-up table – the sort that was part of an outdoor set – a few chairs and a banana lounge. The place was a mess – kids' stuff everywhere. So much stuff and not a thing worth stealing. Antonio's shoes were gone.

They'd been at it a while. Debbie and Sheree were too drunk to keep their voices down. There was an energy, an excitement to them that made Tammy feel excited too. Sheree was standing, dancing – swaying more like – to country music from the tape player, taking swigs from a mug. Debbie sat on a chair with one leg looped over the side, putting together a roll-up smoke. She wore huge wooden earrings that pulled on her earlobes and swung like pendulums whenever she moved her head.

'How can you listen to this shit?' said Debbie, laughing. 'All this wailing and moaning about men. *Men don't treat me right. How can I keep my man? Someone's stealing my man, wah, wah, wah.* I mean, who gives a fuck?'

'Me,' said Sheree. 'I do. I'm on a mission to get me another man.' She shimmied around the table. 'And not a dole bludger this time, neither. I want a decent man with a decent job.'

'I don't,' said Debbie. 'I'm done. I've got uni instead.'

'I was going to go to uni.'

'You?'

'No need to look so shocked. Yeah, I had it all planned.'

'What happened?'

'Daryl Travers happened. Behind the footy shed. And nine months later, Samantha happened.'

'Doesn't it make you so angry, though, to miss out?' said Debbie, and Tammy thought, *Yes. That's exactly the right question.*

'Mate, I don't have enough energy to be angry. Mostly just trying to get by. Get through another day with the kids still alive.' She laughed. 'Do you know how many sugars I have in my tea now? Five. Five sugars. To keep me going until the next cup of tea or the next biscuit. I know I'm pretty shithouse at being a mum some of the time. Shit, maybe most of the time. But I'm giving it a fair go, I reckon.' She licked her finger and wiped at something on the table. 'I used to be a one-sugar girl.'

'But the injustice. Surely that must get to you.'

'Injustice is just a fancy way of saying things aren't fair and I already know that. Wallowing won't help.' The tape had run out. Sheree got up, turned it over to the other side and pressed play. She wasn't dancing anymore. Her mouth was fixed in a line. 'I'm not thick, you know? People think I'm thick because I'm poor and on my own.' She picked at something that had spilled and dried on her T-shirt. 'Except when it comes to blokes. When it comes to blokes, I'm thick as pig shit. It's like I've got one-track vision. Only ever see the deadshits.' She cracked a goofy smile, her teeth glowing green in the light.

'Look, I've been going to these meetings with the Women's Electoral Lobby,' said Debbie. 'You should come. You can bring the kids. They're good about that there. They put up with all sorts. The ideas they've got – it could really make a difference.'

'A difference like getting my kids fed and dressed? Like getting me off the dole? Like someone taking a turn holding the baby so I can take a shit on my own? I don't want to piss on your parade, but what I need is a bloke with a job. A decent bloke. That'll do me. And firm lips. I want a bloke with substantial lips.'

'Lips?' Debbie's laugh was a splutter. 'What are you on about?'

'Flimsy lips. Can't stand 'em. You know, when you're kissing and the lips just give way? Nah, you want a man with lips of substance. You can tell a lot about a man from his lips.'

Outside, Tammy pressed her lips to her arm. She made them firm and pressed harder, squashing them against her teeth.

'Need a wee.' It was Monique, standing at the edge of the table, hand in her pants.

Sheree dragged a potty from under the table with her foot, whipped down Monique's pants and put her on it. Debbie looked away. Tammy's toes started to cramp and she squeezed them with her fingers. When Monique was done, Sheree pulled her onto her lap. Monique held onto a fistful of Sheree's hair and fell asleep again.

Tammy rubbed her calves and moved her bum around. She didn't want to get pins and needles. Her head snapped back to the window when she heard Antonio's name.

'Do you ever think about what it was like for him? At the end, I mean,' said Sheree, stroking Monique's hair. 'I keep thinking about that.'

A slow, doleful song was playing.

'I'd rather not,' said Debbie. She lifted up bottles, shaking each one until she found one with something left in it.

'I wonder if there was a point when he knew he was done for. If he panicked and fought against it. Or if he accepted it. I used to think I wouldn't mind too much about dying. I don't believe anything comes after, so you'd never know you were gone.'

'God, this is a bit morbid.'

'It's different now I've got kids. Cos I'd have to think about them too. I don't think I could let go without fighting to the very end.'

'So you're saying only people with kids have something worth living for?' said Debbie. 'Thanks.'

'No, that's not what I mean. It's just that for me—'

'Look, can we drop it?'

The mood had changed. Sheree was glum. Debbie was pissed off. The breeze ruffled Tammy's nightie and the net curtain at the window, but inside, nothing moved except Sheree rocking back and forth with Monique still on her lap.

'Sorry,' said Debbie, her head bowed and her voice low. 'I find it hard to talk about because I was with him. I mean, we were a couple. Antonio and me. We'd been together for weeks.'

What? Tammy's legs jerked and slipped from under her. Her fingers and toes clawed to keep her from slipping off the bench entirely, but her shin had got a scrape. She barely felt it. Her stumble had made a clattering sound and her gasp of surprise had sounded loud in the night air. But it was OK; she hadn't been seen. Inside, Sheree's mouth gaped open just as Tammy's had. Tammy held onto the window ledge with both hands.

Debbie? Debbie and *Antonio?*

'Shit a brick,' said Sheree. 'Oh, mate. We're going to need more grog for this.' She put Monique down on the banana lounge and broke open a cardboard wine box. She squeezed the bag inside as she emptied it into Debbie's mug. 'You poor thing.' She shook her head. 'You poor sad sack.'

Tammy wanted to run but her legs wouldn't budge. She was sweating in the creases behind her knees and under her arms. Her skin was prickly all over. When ants are in distress they release smelly chemicals. Would the smell of Tammy's distress waft in through the window? Was there anyone left who would care?

Debbie ran both her hands up and down her short hair. 'I don't want your pity,' she said. 'I wish I hadn't told you.' She looked agitated. 'Let's go back to talking about you. Don't you want to do something with your life?'

'I am. I'm being a mum. That's plenty to be getting on with.'

'No, I mean *really* do something. For you. For your future. Right now, you're basically just a servant. And I can tell you, you really are thick if you think a man is the answer.'

'Hey. That's a bit—'

'And maybe you're a bit thick when it comes to kids too.'

'What?'

'You can get abortions now. It's your right. It's every woman's right. Just think of all the women over all the years who've wanted one and couldn't get one.' Debbie stopped abruptly. She pulled up the bra strap that was slipping off her shoulder and leant forwards with her elbows on her knees. 'All I'm saying is that things didn't have to be like this. You *could* have chosen to have abortions. That's all.'

'What you're saying is that I *should* have had abortions.' Sheree got up and stood in front of Monique, still sleeping on the banana lounge. She pressed stop on the tape player.

Debbie shrugged into the silence. 'Whatever.' She stood up too. 'I'm not having a go at you. It's just sad to see people with miserable lives when it could have been different.' She picked up her tin of tobacco and put her papers and matches into it. 'I'm going to make a move.'

Sheree's face was thunder. She put her hands on her hips, her body still shielding the sleeping Monique from Debbie's view. 'You ought to know that you were just his bit on the side,' she said. 'Antonio was two-timing you. Him and Naomi. It was a full-on affair. In love and everything. I've never seen anyone as head over heels as he was with Naomi. And her with him. They'd been rooting like rabbits for months.'

This time, when Tammy's feet shifted, they broke through the slats, the wood splintering. This time, there was no hiding the scream she released. And this time, two shocked faces came

323

to the window as Tammy scrambled on the ground, getting her limbs into some sort of working order, and then took off over the road.

'Shit.' Sheree's voice chased after her. 'Shit, shit, shit.'

36

One Month Before The Murder

December 1978

The first two weeks of October, while Richard was home on leave, were torture for Naomi. Antonio was so close, just across the road, but out of reach. Then Richard went back to work, coming home every weekend. Naomi and Antonio snatched as much time as they could during the week, but it was never the same as those heady September days. Richard was a presence even when he wasn't there. For Naomi, the realisation that Antonio was everything she wanted and needed, in all the ways that Richard wasn't, became even more stark.

Christmas approached. Antonio's family stayed in Canberra, delaying their trip to Rome until a few days before Christmas. Sheree was starting to get narky about having Colin so much of the time, and soon, Colin would be off school for the long summer holidays. January weather arrived early, drawing people from their houses, making it more difficult to keep their secret and making Naomi feel that time was toying with her, stealing from her the stasis of the perfect, private moment. She hated the Christmas decorations and songs in the shops. She hated the advent candles in church. She hated the school wind-down and the demands it made of her: the notices and reminders and glue and glitter craft activities and end-of-year performance and assembly. And every weekend, Richard commented again on her being pale and out of sorts, so she had to pretend harder that her heart wasn't yearning for someone else. The threat of discovery was expanding.

One week before Christmas, Antonio turned up with a black eye.

'Leave it, it's nothing,' he said when she started to make a fuss.

'It's not nothing.' Naomi couldn't bear the thought of him being hurt. 'Where? How?'

'Really. Don't concern yourself. Just some thugs down by the lake on Saturday night.'

'How could they? Tell me what happened.' Naomi held his face to her chest and stroked his hair. He wriggled away from her. He'd been getting irritable lately, which Naomi put down to him being jealous of the time she spent with Richard. But couldn't he see it was worse for her, having to lead a double life?

'There's no point telling you now. I don't need to talk about it anymore. Anyway, it was because I'm foreign. It's not something you'd understand.'

They went to bed anyway. Naomi made love to him like she was pedalling backwards while reaching forwards.

'Have you met the new girl yet? There's a niece, just moved in with Ursula and Lydia.' Naomi had vowed to herself not to mention Debbie to Antonio. She'd been thinking about her for days – about her newness, how close she was to Antonio in age, how free and unencumbered she was. 'I bet she already has the hots for you.' Oh, God, *why* would she say such a thing to him? 'Maybe you're already tired of me.' *Shut up, shut up, shut up.*

'I'm not tired of you.' Antonio shook a cigarette from its packet and Naomi put a hand on his arm to stop him from lighting it. 'Sorry, I forgot.' Even in this small thing – not smoking in the bedroom anymore – Richard had wormed his way between them. 'I'm just tired of all . . .' – he waved his unlit cigarette around – '. . . this.'

Antonio got out of bed and started getting dressed.

'Stop,' said Naomi. 'Stop getting dressed. We still have time. Talk to me about something interesting. Tell me what it will be like when we go to Italy together.'

Antonio faced her while he pulled his T-shirt on and positioned his pencil behind his ear. 'I'm tired of spending daytime inside. It makes me feel cooped up. Lazy. Useless.' His feet didn't move, but he might as well have already left the room, set off down the street, whistling as he went.

'But it suits us,' Naomi said. 'We have so little time as it is.' She shouldn't have to explain any of this.

'Don't you find it too much to handle?'

'Not if we're together. I can handle anything if we're together. I could take on the world.'

'That's dramatic.'

'Maybe. But it's also true.'

He leant over to kiss her. Naomi linked her arms behind his neck. Antonio was the first to break the kiss. He prised her arms apart. 'I love you,' he said. 'I do.' The look on his face was heartbreakingly sad.

Why wouldn't he ask her to leave Richard? He had to be the one to ask, to prove he wanted this as much as she did. Didn't he know that's what she was waiting for? Didn't he know that her answer would be an unhesitating, emphatic *yes*?

The next day, Antonio didn't return at all. After a day of watching the clock, Naomi went to get Colin from Sheree's house at teatime, promising yet again that one day soon she'd have Sheree's kids for the day.

'Still waiting for that,' said Sheree. 'Going to hold you to it.'

Naomi went home and held Colin tight. Her heart, turned waxen, had been remoulded to fit the shape of Antonio's hand. Sometimes Naomi feared that he held it more loosely than he might. It was a madness of sorts: the wanting of him.

Antonio turned up the following day, looking like she'd never seen him.

'What's *this*?' said Naomi, doing a full three-sixty around him.

He wore white spangly flares. A long Afghan vest. A silk scarf, fashionably draped. Feathers clipped into his hair.

'From the opportunity shop,' he said. He was smiling. He'd had a good time, without her.

'Op shop,' she said. 'No one calls it an opportunity shop.'

He didn't respond. He smelled of absence. She was desperate to ask where he'd been, but equally desperate not to know.

'You'll get fleas from second-hand clothes,' she said, prodding at the Afghan and wrinkling her nose. 'Or lice.'

Antonio laughed. 'That's exactly what my mum said.'

'You look ridiculous.'

'She said that too. You want to tell me to clean my room?'

He took a step back. His eyes lowered. Was he about to leave? He'd only just got there.

'Stay,' she said. She wound her arms around him and buried her face in his neck to hide her shame. 'Stay and fuck me.' She licked his ear. 'There. I bet your mum has never said that to you.'

Antonio gripped her shoulders and held her at arm's length. 'Naomi,' he said, distaste in his voice and on his face.

'Now it's you sounding like *my* mum,' she said, and he gave her a half-smile, like he was doling out rations. 'Stay,' said Naomi again.

Antonio stayed. Afterwards, Naomi couldn't rid herself of the feeling that he'd slept with her as a favour. He sat on the edge of the bed with his back to her as he dressed, like an act of dismissal.

Antonio didn't return the next day. Naomi was beside herself with worry.

The following day was Friday, three days before Christmas and the last day before Richard would be home for his leave. Antonio turned up in the evening. Naomi sent Colin through the fence to Sheree's in his pyjamas. He went wordlessly, but not before she caught a look of reproach from him that made her feel like he was the parent and she the child.

'It's impossible,' said Antonio. 'I can't stay away from you.'

He was contrite, desperate, unable to get enough of her. He made love to her like a drowning man, gasping for air. Her fingers dug into him and left marks on his back. Afterwards, Antonio cried.

When Richard got home, he steered Naomi to the couch and sat opposite her so he was on her level and didn't loom above her. He looked her in the eye and used his gentle voice to say he was worried about her. He'd been worried for some time now. She was distracted, moody, not eating properly. He told her that he'd had a meeting with the rear admiral. They would start building on a new site for the Defence Force Academy soon in Canberra. Nothing could happen immediately, but there would be opportunities there. Richard could get a job with office hours. He could be home with Naomi and Colin every evening. He could get Colin's breakfast on days when Naomi was tired. Naomi released a squeak from her throat that Richard seemed to take as excitement, or acquiescence at the very least. But first, Richard said, once Christmas and New Year's was over with, they should get her seen to by a doctor. That's how he said it: *Let's get you seen to.* He said he'd find someone to fix her nerves, that he'd book the appointment himself. Naomi nodded and promised she'd go to an appointment if he thought that was best. Anything to get him to stop looking at her like that.

The day after Boxing Day was the Warrah Place street party. Instigated by Cecil five years ago, it had become a fixed date in the calendar for residents. It would be Naomi and Richard's first time.

Cecil and Duncan parked their cars in the road, blocking off Carnegie Street from Warrah Place. Then everyone wheeled barbecues to the ends of their driveways and went back and forth, carting eskies, folding chairs, trestle tables and more food than anyone could possibly eat. They set up on the island, surrounded by barbecues that stayed on the street.

Maureen went around with a bottle of sunscreen, trying to foist it on everyone even though the shadows were long and the worst of the sting had gone from the sun. Sheree brought buckets of water for her kids to sit in and told them to pretend they were paddling pools. The Laus brought food for themselves, not to share, and they sat at the base of their driveway as they ate it. Richard commented that they hadn't got the hang of a street party but at least they were trying. Peggy, as far as Naomi could tell, had nothing more than brandy and cigarettes. Cecil brought an esky full of prawns and made a big show of explaining how to cook them. Naomi couldn't bear the smell of them. Joe brought trout he'd smoked himself and that turned her stomach as well.

Naomi overheard Tammy ask her mum if she should bring out the Christmas cake. *No, it's a nice one,* said Helen, *leave it at home.* She overheard Helen tell Maureen that Richard had been left to organise all of their food because Naomi hadn't lifted a finger herself.

Lydia was working. Ursula was a no-show. Debbie was there, looking young and fresh and glancing in Antonio's direction as much as, if not more than, Naomi was.

Antonio lay sprawled on a picnic rug, accepting stubbies of beer whenever offered, drinking them quickly. He pretended he was a lion and chased Sheree's kids, who squealed in delight. He pulled funny faces at Tammy, who tried not to laugh, poor girl. He ate food and stacked plates and smoked cigarettes with his delicate fingers and kept away from Richard as much as he could. Richard kept a proprietorial hand on Naomi's back. She was aware of him talking to Debbie, teasing her about Antonio. She was aware of him talking to Antonio, teasing him about Debbie.

Sheree took hold of her arm, detaching her from Richard. 'Mate,' she said, once they were out of earshot. 'I can't keep covering for you if you're going to be so obvious. You've got to stop looking at Antonio like a homesick puppy.'

Naomi gave herself a shake. 'Is it really that obvious?'

'Only to me, so far. No one else seems to have copped on. But watch it. Or get yourself out of here.'

That seemed to be her only option. Naomi told Richard she needed a lie-down and left, but not before taking one last look at Antonio with blazing eyes. She used all her energy to convey to him: *I'm yours. I'm yours. I'm forever and only yours.*

Her line of sight was broken by Debbie approaching Antonio with a hula hoop, saying, 'On your feet. This'll be a hoot. I'm going to teach you.'

Richard had to go back to work the day before New Year's Eve. Sheree asked Naomi and Antonio to her house for a New Year's Eve bash, just the three of them and the kids. Naomi felt they had to say yes. They all squeezed through the gap in the fence. But as the evening progressed, as Sheree got louder the drunker she got, as she played her country and western tapes over and

331

over again, Naomi became more and more desperate to be alone with Antonio. In front of Sheree, they held hands, cuddled, stole kisses and touched each other as often and as much as they could, like kids at a school social, sending Sheree's eyes rolling like a Ferris wheel. But it wasn't enough. They had so little time as it was. They couldn't afford to share it.

'Nuh-uh. No way,' said Sheree when they tried to make their excuses. 'Just one measly bloody night. You can't give me one night after everything I've done? Just until midnight. Then you can go and root each other's brains out.'

'Sorry,' said Naomi, backing out of the door, Antonio's hand in hers.

'There's helping out a mate,' said Sheree, 'and then there's taking the piss, Naomi.'

Sheree was really mad. Livid, even. But Naomi couldn't think about that now. She'd make it up to Sheree another time.

They were halfway to the fence when Antonio said, 'My shoes.'

'Leave them,' said Naomi, giggling. 'We can't go back in there now. She'd have our guts for garters.'

They made love like they were clinging to the remains of the year, like tomorrow didn't belong to them.

Antonio lit a cigarette and Naomi didn't stop him.

'I've got something to tell you,' Naomi said, reaching for a teacup for him to use as an ashtray. She rested her head between his shoulder and his chest, the place she thought of as hers. He fiddled idly with her hair. She opened her mouth three times to speak and chickened out each time. She closed her eyes. 'I'm pregnant.'

His hand in her hair stilled. He took three more slow drags, blowing out smoke each time in a narrow stream.

'Is this a trick?'

Naomi shook her head, no.

'Is it a trap?'

Naomi didn't have an answer for him. Would anyone believe that she had simply forgotten to take her pill? That when she'd been desperate to find reasons for him to stay with her, that when she felt him slipping away, she accidentally became pregnant? Naomi wasn't sure she'd believe it herself. Perhaps there was part of her – a part that knew what Naomi wanted before the rest of her did – that found a way to hold fast to Antonio and took it.

'Are you sure?'

'Yes.' There was no mistaking it. She'd felt exactly the same with Colin.

'Is it mine?'

'Yes.'

'Are you sure?'

'*Yes.*' She was insistent. It was inconceivable that the baby wasn't his. Because she wanted Antonio's baby and didn't want Richard's. It was the only thing that made sense.

Antonio slid his arm out from under her head. She clung to his arm like a toddler. She fixed her eyes on an imaginary spot in thin air and started counting her breath. In through her nose. Out through her mouth. One. Two. Three. Four.

'What are you doing?' said Antonio. 'You look weird.' He plucked her fingers from his arm.

'Wait,' she said.

'I said you were too much to handle.'

Naomi wanted to argue semantics with him. That wasn't what he'd said at all. He'd implied that this *thing* – this glorious, runaway thing, the situation they were in – was difficult. She wanted to hold him to what he'd originally said. He wasn't allowed to change it now.

'How could you let this happen?' He looked frantically for his smokes and found them under a pillow. 'You're a big girl, Naomi. I thought you knew what you were doing.'

333

'You can't go,' she said. He was buttoning his trousers now. 'We have to talk about it, about this thing that's happened to us, about what we're going to do.'

'We? Us? This is a thing that's happened to *you*. Because you weren't careful.'

Neighbourhood shouts rang out. Someone blew a trumpet. Car horns sounded. Midnight. A new year.

'Please, Antonio.' Naomi felt a calm seep through her. If she could just talk to him. Remind him of all that he'd said, all that had been shared between them, how they'd changed each other for the better. They'd find a way. They had to. 'Do you remember when you said I could do anything I want? Well, this is what I want. With you.'

'I've slept with someone else.' A grenade. He wouldn't even look at her as he shattered everything.

Before she could ask, he added, 'I did it because it was easy. And because this is hard. It's too hard.'

Antonio didn't take the time to put on his shirt. He picked it up and carried it out of the door, pausing only to throw her a glance over his shoulder. It was only one glance and over in an instant.

Smoke coiled from the cigarette he'd left in the teacup. Naomi felt sick.

Days passed and Antonio didn't return. Naomi forgot about eating, she forgot about washing, she forgot about Colin. The only thing on her mind was Antonio and she couldn't rid herself of wanting him. She wanted to bite off her tongue lest she ever speak his name again in a casual, unthinking moment. As if his name wasn't already woven through her body. She wanted to pluck out her eyes lest she catch sight of him. As if his image wasn't seared on her heart.

★

Richard returned unexpectedly the following Friday night. He planned to tell her that he came home for the church working bee on Saturday, but when he saw the state of the place, the state of Naomi, he came clean and said he'd been worried sick about her and it was just as well he'd trusted his gut. He made no comment about the dishes and dirty clothes piled high, about the food left out to spoil, about Naomi's matted hair. There was no judgement in his voice when he quietly asked if she knew where Colin was. She was furious with him for being so reasonable, for giving her nothing to rail against. She used to love that nothing could topple him off the moral high ground, supposedly because he took her there with him. Now, she hated him for it. She was hankering for a fight.

The next morning, after a night lying awake next to Richard sleeping soundly, Naomi knew what to do. She might not have hope anymore, but she could choose truth. The truth was bigger than her or Richard. It must come out.

Naomi got dressed. She put on shoes and lipstick. She had a job to do and would borrow confidence from wherever she could get it.

Colin was sitting on a cushion in front of the Saturday-morning cartoons. Naomi tousled his hair. He really was a dear little boy. She closed the door behind her, shutting him in the family room. Then she took Richard by the hand and led him into their bedroom.

'He-*llo*,' he said, putting his strong hands on her hips and kicking the door shut behind them. He had the power to crush her if he chose to.

'Sit down, Richard.' She pushed him towards the bed. 'I've got something to tell you.' They were the same words she'd said to Antonio. But this time, her voice was dull. No warmth, no import, no urgency. Sure, her marriage and family were on the line, but not her heart; not this time.

335

Sitting on the end of the bed, Richard was almost the same height as Naomi. He looked up at her and grinned. His eyes travelled to her belly and then to her eyes again and he took her silence as confirmation. 'I knew it!' He leapt forwards and swept her up in his arms and spun her around before setting her down gently. 'Did you know at Christmas? I bet you did, you sly old thing.' His eyes welled up when he said, 'I never gave up, you know? Even when all seemed lost, all those years of trying and nothing. I kept quiet because I knew it hurt you too. But I never gave up.'

'Sit back down,' she said. 'The baby isn't yours.'

His eyes went cold. His face turned to stone. Naomi could hear the faint tinny sound of Colin's cartoons in the background while she waited for Richard to speak. 'I think you need to tell me more than that,' he said blandly. 'About your affair.'

'Not an affair,' said Naomi. It was such a cheap, inadequate word. A word that had nothing to do with how she felt about Antonio. Affairs were what other people had. 'I'm in love.'

'Who?'

'Antonio.' The sound of his name, out there in the room instead of in her head, made her cry. She sank to the floor.

Richard watched her cry. 'Tell me what you want,' he said. 'What we can do to put things right again.' His tone was full of reason, only a slight flaring of his nostrils to indicate that anything might be amiss.

'You can't,' said Naomi. 'There's nothing that can be put right now because my heart is broken and will never be fixed. It's over.' In that moment, she forgot that Richard was her husband. He had the demeanour of a friend who might offer her comfort; of a parent who cared about their child.

Richard stood and took his shirt off.

'What are you doing?' said Naomi.

He took an old Billabong T-shirt out of a drawer and put

336

it on. It was blue, faded to grey, rolling waves across the chest. Naomi felt seasick looking at it. 'I'm going to the working bee.' His face and tone were wooden, vacant. 'And if he did want you? If it wasn't over? Would you go to him?'

'In a heartbeat.' There it was: a flicker of something, a twitch of his cheek that pulled at his nose. 'I'm sorry if that's hurtful. I don't mean it to be. I'm just stating a fact. It would be impossible for me not to go to him.'

'I see.'

This was a Richard that Naomi was familiar with. He had a way about him, a studied stillness that he deployed to good effect. He used it to make people feel he was on their side.

Now, though, as moments passed with nothing to fill them, Naomi picked up in Richard's taut features an undercurrent, like static electricity. What looked like calm was actually a cold, clamped-down fury. He stood above her, tall and straight, while she remained a puddle on the floor.

Naomi was beyond caring about whether he hurt her. What was there to hope for now? She watched Richard's face, the hidden calculations taking place in his mind, and waited.

He left without another word, without acknowledging Naomi or all that had been said. She would have to keep waiting.

37

Twenty Days After The Murder

Friday, 26 January 1979

The sky blushed pink as Debbie made her way across Warrah Place to Number Three. The sun was readying itself for another hard day's work. The Southern Cross was high in the sky and Debbie looked up at it, wondering if she was doing the right thing.

The idea had taken shape as soon as Debbie left Sheree's house, and she'd been stewing on it and not sleeping ever since. She regretted telling Sheree about her and Antonio. What did she hope to gain by what she was about to do? She didn't know. All she knew was that being invisible, inconsequential, a footnote in the great love story of Antonio and Naomi, was intolerable. Because that's what it was, wasn't it? A great love. Sheree had said so, or near enough. What if Debbie had got to him first? She certainly wouldn't have let Naomi get a look-in for a start.

Debbie decided to try the front door first, expecting she'd have to go round the back, maybe through a window. People had taken to locking their doors at night. *But not Naomi,* thought Debbie, as the front door opened easily. *That's interesting.*

Debbie took a moment to get her bearings. How well did

Antonio know his way around this house? Along the corridor, the first door was already open. Colin slept on a stripy sheet, his limbs loose and open. The next room was the bathroom. Dawn was already peering through the frosted glass window, its light making the yellow and white too cheery for Debbie's liking. And then, Debbie opened the door to Naomi's bedroom. She stood at the foot of the bed.

Naomi slept in the middle of the mattress, her hands, palms together, beneath her cheek on a pillow. A sheet draped over her, outlining the gentle curves of her shoulder and hip. Debbie had been thinking of her as the older woman, but the figure here was smaller than Debbie. She looked childlike, vulnerable. Her mouth was open and her breath caught slightly in her throat; the precursor to a snore. It made every intake of breath sound like a miniature gasp of surprise. Was the sound familiar to Antonio? Did he find it endearing? Did he have a preferred side of this bed? Did their bodies touch as they slept?

Debbie had found ways to remove herself from conversations when anyone mentioned Naomi's pregnancy. She'd purpose-fully not given it her attention, not wanting to be reminded of her own pregnancy and its end. Until now. Now, the pain she'd felt trampled through her body, fresh as the first time, and Debbie both accepted its onslaught and withstood it.

She decided it didn't matter whose baby Naomi carried. It made no difference to her. The damage was done regardless.

Naomi woke gradually and Debbie waited for her to become aware of her presence. Naomi's eyes widened and she jolted up-right. Her hands reached to either side of her. Was she looking for Antonio? For Richard?

Before Naomi could speak, Debbie said what she'd come here to say: 'He loved you. I thought you should know. Don't bother asking me how I know because I will never tell you. But you should know. Right up until the end, he loved you. Just you.'

It cost her to say it. And now she had to leave.

Debbie stopped in the doorway and, without turning back around to face Naomi, she said, 'He didn't deserve you, you know? It might not be much comfort to you now, but maybe one day it will. And if you want any more acts of goodwill from me, you can forget it. This is my limit.'

'Wait,' croaked Naomi. 'Don't go yet. I—'

Debbie shut the door, closing off Naomi and her baby, putting them away. There was nothing left to say.

On her way home, Debbie looked towards Antonio's house before she could stop herself, like it was muscle memory. She took her time, so she could feel the full force of his rejection and build another layer of hardened protection around her heart. Never again. The hairs on the back of her neck rose and her gaze broke away. Next door to Antonio's house, opposite Naomi's, Mrs Lau stood on her balcony, immobile, watching, giving Debbie the creeps.

38

Three Weeks After The Murder

Saturday, 27 January 1979

Before Naomi had made a start on her Saturday morning, Richard arrived home in a Kingswood station wagon.

'Where's your car?' she asked.

'Traded it in.'

She circled the car. 'Can we afford it?'

'Can we afford not to?'

Naomi looked up in alarm. 'But you said you'd cleaned the car. That it wasn't a problem.'

'Relax.' He slung his arm around her shoulder. 'It's just to be on the safe side, to cover all bases. We're home free, everything accounted for. Trust me.' He kissed her nose. 'Check out the front seat. Perfect for cuddling up.'

Naomi wasn't interested in the car, or in cuddling up. Debbie's words were still in her ears — *he loved you* — and Antonio's name in her mouth. The more she felt repelled by Richard's nearness, the more he insinuated himself into her line of vision, the more he talked, the more bonhomie he exuded. He decided they would take the car for a spin and go to the Cotter for the day. They were to be a happy family having fun together whether she liked it or not.

The Cotter was a reserve alongside the Murrumbidgee River, a great place for barbecues and walks. The scenery was stunning, especially in autumn when you felt enveloped in a riot of colour. The water, if you were brave enough to go in, was bracing, having made its way down from the Snowy Mountains. A trip to the Cotter always had a sense of occasion to it.

Colin sat quietly in the back, a small, lone figure on the huge bench seat, wearing shorts and a T-shirt that he'd grown out of. He'd had the wherewithal to change back into his own clothes before Richard had arrived. Naomi was glad. She hadn't yet decided what she thought about him wearing girls' clothes and she couldn't face Richard's inevitable questions about it.

Richard sang along to the radio and drummed his fingers on the steering wheel, unaware that his wedding ring was flickering glints of sunlight in Naomi's eyes.

'The Cotter's nicer in autumn,' said Naomi.

Richard glanced at her and spoke to Colin over his shoulder. 'Hey, Colin. Mum's got a sourpuss face on her. Let's cheer her up with a few rounds of "Ten Green Bottles".'

'He's too old for that,' said Naomi.

'You really are a grumble-bum today,' Richard said to her in the same cheery voice he'd used on Colin. 'We'll have a good time. You'll see.'

Had Richard always spoken to her like a child? Why had it taken Antonio to open her eyes to it? How had she not always seen that Richard was like this: authoritative, sometimes indulgent, but always in control?

Naomi's mind traced back over the day she'd told Richard about Antonio. What could she have done differently? What words should she have used? Should she have stayed silent? Remorse rode roughshod over her. It was too painful, knowing that she'd played her part in Antonio's death, made all the more painful by knowing, now, that he loved her. *He loved her.* She

342

closed her eyes and pretended that Antonio was still alive, that when the car stopped, Antonio would be there waiting for her and Richard would disappear. It would be as if Richard had never existed.

'That's better,' said Richard, and Naomi opened her eyes. He was grinning at her, like they were sharing a moment. 'I like seeing you smile. We should entertain more. Have dinner parties. So I can show off that gorgeous smile of yours.'

It was another hot day. It felt like there had been hot days for aeons, but today, there were also moderate winds, which meant a total fire ban. The barbecues at the Cotter were out of action. With no way of cooking their sausages, they ate plain bread spread with tomato sauce. 'We'll make do like the bushrangers had to when they couldn't build a fire and give away their location,' said Richard. 'It'll be an adventure.' The bread turned to clag in Naomi's mouth. Colin ate his without complaining.

The public toilets were filthy. Dead flies caught in cobwebs, others alive, fat and lazy. Dirt and sand brought in from the outside onto the floor and sinks. A smell, bad to begin with, intensified by the heat. It was a brief moment of solitude, enough for Naomi to catch her breath but not enough to be restorative. Her pregnancy was starting to show and in private moments like this, Naomi cupped her hands over her baby, imagining Antonio's fingers entwining with hers. She slipped off her shoes and put her bare feet on the cool concrete. She held her wrists under the cold tap and wetted the back of her neck. In the dirty mirror above the sink, she practised a look of vacant serenity, knowing that she must conceal her weakness. But, more importantly, she must conceal the hidden, fervent, initial stirrings of her strength.

Next to the playground equipment, the river was low. Emus had been drawn to the water to cool off. They sat in the shallows,

343

looking tired and wilted in their heavy feathery cloaks. Naomi sat on a bench in the shade while Richard led Colin to a high climbing frame.

'I think that's for the big kids,' said Naomi.

'He is a big kid,' said Richard. 'Like you were saying in the car.'

Dutifully, Colin began to climb, egged on by Richard. He paused and looked down nervously.

'Come on,' called Richard. 'There are girls your age who could get higher than that.'

Colin continued to climb.

'I want you to get to the platform at the top,' said Richard.

Colin was halfway to the platform. His ascent slowed. He placed his feet carefully, making sure before transferring his weight. His little knees shook, and Naomi felt his fear. But he didn't stop.

At the platform, Colin clung to the central pole. There was a rope to slide down.

'Good boy! I knew you could do it.' Richard looked pointedly at Naomi. 'Now, here's what I want you to do next. Grab hold of the knot in the rope and do a run off the edge. I want you to swing out as far as you can and I'll catch you.' Richard positioned himself between Colin and Naomi.

'I don't think he's going to want to,' muttered Naomi.

'I don't want to,' Colin said. He sounded close to tears.

'None of that,' said Richard. 'Come on, be a man.' He put a grunt into his voice. 'Trust me. I won't let you fall.' He held out his arms like a cradle. 'Show some grit, son.'

Colin didn't move. Wind blew his hair across his eyes.

'He doesn't want to,' said Naomi.

'Don't interfere,' said Richard.

'He's scared.'

'That's the point. I'm teaching him to overcome his fears.

It's important. I need to know he trusts me. I need to know *he* knows he can trust me.'

'Please don't make me.' Colin held on with one hand and wiped his nose and eyes with the other.

'Just do it,' said Richard. 'Nobody likes a whinger.'

His words stripped back the years until Naomi heard her mum's voice: *Nobody likes a whinger.* Same words. Same inflection.

Naomi shielded her eyes and looked up at Colin. She knew how it felt to be small and have those words spoken to you. She knew how they could shape a life. She knew what it was like to have no one else make it stop.

On the bench, next to Naomi, a Christmas beetle shuffled along a gum leaf. Naomi watched the iridescent caped compartments of its back, thinking you could get away with anything if you were that glorious. Merely sitting on a leaf constituted showing off. Meanwhile, Richard was still goading Colin, going on at him to *jump, boy, grow a pair and jump.* The Christmas beetle raised its wings, preparing for take-off. It launched itself into the air, riding the wind to find somewhere else to be spectacular.

Eventually, Colin turned around and went down the way he'd gone up.

On the way home, Richard said, 'The thing that disappoints me is that you didn't even try. Now you'll never know if you could have done it.' He glanced at Naomi, at the way she glared at him, and said through gritted teeth, 'That goes for you and your wedding vows too.'

When they got home, Peggy and Leslie were in their front yard with Cecil. They accosted Richard as soon as he got out of the car and Naomi wondered how long they'd been hanging about waiting to do just that.

'Very swish,' said Cecil, referring to the new car. 'Someone's doing all right.'

'Made sense to get something bigger,' said Richard. 'You know, with a growing family.' He looked proudly at Naomi, lingering, so everyone noticed.

Peggy said they'd been talking about Joe and his run-in with the police.

'You think you know a person,' said Cecil. 'Goes to show, you can't be too careful with foreigners, even the ones you think are all right. He always seemed so cheerful. Maybe that was a sign.'

Colin backed away and made for the Lanahans' house. Naomi let him go.

'You can mask a lot with a smile,' said Peggy. She coughed, like a reluctant engine failing to start.

'I think it's hard for us to really understand what war does to a man,' said Richard. 'Joe lived through the Italian occupation of Yugoslavia. Messy business. The Mariettis being here, well, it's got to have stirred up difficult memories.'

'I hadn't even considered that,' said Peggy.

'I'm pleased at least most of us are Aussies,' said Cecil. 'Proud to say I'm true blue, four generations and counting. My lot came from ship-building folk. Respectable industry. Wouldn't be surprised if some of you reprobates came from convict stock.' He nudged Peggy roughly and laughed.

'I suppose you'll be off telling falsehoods to the press about us again,' said Peggy, and Cecil looked unabashed.

Naomi glanced over the road. There was no press van out today. She hoped that was the end of them, that they'd given up and moved on to another story.

'Although,' Peggy went on, 'if you want to say things about Helen, I won't stop you.' Peggy's face tightened. 'I just want to know if we're in danger, if there's a chance Joe could turn on us.'

'I trust Joe,' said Leslie. 'And the police let him go. So I reckon he's more in the clear than anyone.'

Peggy didn't look convinced. 'What do you think?' she asked Richard.

'I think the police had reason to question him,' said Richard. 'But they wouldn't have been able to hold him without any evidence.'

'So he could still be a suspect, still be the killer, but they don't have enough to put him away. Is that what you're saying?' said Peggy.

Richard raised his eyebrows and shrugged.

'Didn't I say from the start we needed to keep an eye on Joe?' said Cecil.

'Hang on,' said Naomi. 'A man's life is at stake here.'

'All our lives are at stake,' said Cecil. 'That's the worry.'

Richard kept his lips tightly shut.

39

Twenty-Three Days After The Murder

Monday, 29 January 1979

Ursula had been at Guangyu's house for four nights, having arrived distraught from Thursday's Bible study. She recruited Jennifer to deliver her notes to Lydia under the cover of darkness, not venturing out of the house herself. Guangyu hushed Herman or Jia Li as soon as either of them looked like they were about to question how long Ursula would be there. She could stay as long as she liked, as far as Guangyu was concerned. Jennifer was surprisingly sanguine about it. 'I think it's nice you've got a friend,' she said. 'Gives you something to do other than hassle me.'

For the first night, the two women had sat side by side on the couch in the lounge room, eventually sleeping fitfully between bouts of crying (Ursula) and talking (mostly Ursula). By morning, Ursula's eyes were red and raw. Guangyu's felt scratchy with lack of sleep, her back sore and off-centre.

'I know you think I'm overreacting,' Ursula said. She'd cried so much, she'd become dehydrated and had a pounding headache.

Guangyu prevaricated, wanting to deny it, but, yes, it was true.

348

Guangyu could see that it was a big deal, Ursula getting lured into a trap at the Bible study, and all of it done so publicly. But did it have to be *such* a big deal?

'I can't help but wonder, since it's so important to you, if there is another church that might be more, I don't know, accommodating,' said Guangyu. 'It would still be the same God, wouldn't it?'

Guangyu watched Ursula's face while Ursula stared at the footstool in front of her as if it were the most interesting thing she'd ever seen.

'I'm sorry,' said Guangyu. 'I've offended you.'

'No, it's not that. I want to explain something, but I don't know where to start.' Guangyu loved how she could see Ursula's thoughts play out across her face, even if she didn't yet know what they were. She watched them settle. 'Us white Australians, we might like to think of this land as ours, but we weren't always here. We weren't here first. We've all come from somewhere else. And it might look like we're all the same, but we're not. We all have histories we carry with us – for the most part, invisible histories. And mine is all wrapped up with being a Lutheran.'

Ursula looked set to stop there, so Guangyu said, 'I need you to tell me more so I understand.'

'I've never tried to explain this before. Not even to myself.' She took a slow sip of water. 'The Lutherans who came here settled together and their faith bound them to each other even more than where they came from. We had it drummed into us as kids how blessed we are to have religious freedom and how grateful we must be to our forebears for everything they endured. It makes the ties strong, to each other and to the generations who came before us.' Ursula's hand kept feeling for the cross necklace that was absent from her throat. It was strange to see her without it.

Guangyu kept quiet. She knew that if she gave Ursula space

to think and talk, Ursula would feel her way into that space. She'd learnt this because it was what Ursula did for her.

'When I was young,' Ursula continued, 'we used to have these family picnics in the park and hundreds of people would turn up. I know who many of my second and third cousins are. I have two family history books with branches of the family tree spanning hundreds of pages.' Ursula rubbed her tired face, her fingers dragging at her eyes until they drooped.

'Go on.' Guangyu laid an encouraging hand on Ursula's knee.

'You see, for me, the church isn't just about faith. If it was, you would be right, I could go find another church. But being a Lutheran is my heritage, it's who I've always been, what I was born into. If I can't be a part of the church, it will mean my foundations have crumbled, that I've lost solid ground to stand on.'

As Ursula spoke, dawn broke. Night gave way to day in the way it always did, and Ursula was back where she started, still not knowing what to do.

During the days that followed, Guangyu thought about her own foundations. Maybe life didn't always have to be about moving forwards and moving away. Maybe it could also be about returning. For so long, she'd trained her gaze away from China. It would be nice to turn back, to feel proud of being Chinese again. She'd phone her mum. Plan a trip, perhaps.

On the Monday morning after the Bible study, Guangyu brought a cup of tea into the lounge room where Ursula was sleeping on the couch.

Ursula raised her bleary but smiling face. 'You spoil me,' she said, sitting up. 'I might never go home.'

'Suits me,' said Guangyu.

Ursula's face darkened, clouded by difficult thoughts. 'It's time, though. I've been putting it off because every direction

I look, there is pain. To lose Lydia or lose my church. But one thing is certain. I miss Lydia.' She stood up. For the first time in days, she had a look of resolve. She began to pace, her face and movements animated as she gained momentum. 'Whatever happens, I owe Lydia the right to be a part of it. Yes? That's right, isn't it?' Guangyu wasn't sure if she was asking Guangyu or herself. 'I've been stuck, trying to find a way without pain, without loss. But there isn't one. All I know now is that the greater loss is not being with Lydia. I can't bear not seeing her any longer.'

Guangyu felt helpless in the face of Ursula's dilemma. There was nothing she could add, no solution that would smooth the pathway ahead. She wished she could be of more use.

'Do you think Lydia will understand why I have been away? Will my notes be enough?' said Ursula. 'Will she forgive me?'

'She will,' said Guangyu. 'When you tell her you've been grieving.'

'Grieving?'

'Grieving the foundations. First you grieve. Then you build again.'

It sounded simple, said like that. But Guangyu had done neither. No grieving. No building new foundations. Instead, she had been straddling different cultures that didn't claim her, without her feet landing. It was time for her feet to find some ground.

There was a timid knock on the door. Guangyu might not have heard it had she not been in the lounge room. The knocking grew louder and more insistent as she shuffled to the door. It was Naomi, wearing a flimsy nightgown with an inside-out cardigan over the top.

Wordlessly, Guangyu stepped back and ushered Naomi inside. The moment the door closed behind her, Naomi launched into a speech that, initially at least, had the tenor of being rehearsed.

'After much consideration, and after Richard being home for the weekend, and after an event that occurred on Friday morning, an unexpected visit, which, surprisingly, I have to say, has served the purpose of clarifying the mind and strengthening the resolve – *my* mind and *my* resolve, I mean, I must talk with you, despite the risks that entails, and no, please don't interrupt me until I've said what I've come here to say. Where was I?' Naomi paused for breath and held up a stop-sign hand when Guangyu cleared her throat. 'No. Please. I must get through this before I chicken out. I believe there are things you know, or suspect, about my husband in relation to Antonio's death, things you insinuated when you came to see me. Yes?'

'Yes, but—' Guangyu looked over her shoulder as Naomi interrupted her.

'The thing is – I know you have . . . views, and I'm not interested in copping an earful, although I deserve it, that's true enough. So. The thing is, I've been scared all this time of saying things, of upsetting the apple cart, you know? I've almost piked lots of times on the way over here. I thought – stupidly, I see that now – that things could stay the same. Well, perhaps not the same exactly, because, well, *you know*, but I thought we could go on in a somewhat liveable way, patch over the things that went wrong and so forth. But now, I find that I am more frightened of saying nothing than I am of saying something. Are you following me?'

'Perhaps,' said Guangyu. 'To some extent. But—'

'That's why I'm here. I thought I was all alone in the world and then you came over. I'd been thinking everything's hopeless, and it could well still be hopeless, and, well, at first you scared me. But then you said I had options.'

She paused, which would have been an ideal time for Guangyu to get a word in, but Guangyu's head was spinning. She'd never heard Naomi talk so much or so fast before. Normally guarded and aloof, she'd now opened the floodgates, her words racing each other to get out.

'I need your help,' she continued. 'I don't know how to go about it – that's where you come in – but I do know that . . .' – she took a deep breath – '. . . I can no longer go on living with a murderer.'

A gasp came from the open doorway to the lounge room and Naomi was startled.

She shouldered her way past Guangyu to the lounge room. Guangyu followed and found Naomi and Ursula facing each other, both of them with their hands over their mouths and wild looks in their eyes.

'You might have said!' said Naomi to Guangyu. 'That she was here. Listening.'

'I did try,' said Guangyu.

'Under the circumstances, you might have tried harder.'

'Am I to understand', said Ursula with her hands still holding up her face, 'that you are referring to Richard being a murderer? And that it is Antonio he murdered?' Naomi was silent. *There it is,* thought Guangyu. Confirmation that her eyes and instincts were right. That she wasn't crazy. 'Oh, my dear good Lord,' said Ursula.

A small face appeared at the doorway. 'Not now, Ma,' said Guangyu, steering Jia Li out of the room. Once the door was shut, the air in the lounge room became taut. At any moment it might snap.

'What's she doing here?' said Naomi, pointing at Ursula. Her eyes travelled to the pillow and blanket on the couch, the cup of tea on the footstool.

'I came for sanctuary,' said Ursula. 'Not that there aren't other, more pressing matters at hand now.'

'What?' said Naomi.

'Ursula is here because she needed a friend after suffering cruelty,' said Guangyu.

A look of compassion from Guangyu and one of gratitude from Ursula passed between the two women.

Naomi looked at Ursula with curiosity and pity.

'For goodness' sake, both of you, don't be nice to me,' said Ursula. 'I'll fall apart if you're nice to me.'

For a while, each woman seemed lost in her own thoughts. Guangyu had a sense that things had reached a head, at last. But what she didn't know was what Naomi wanted from her.

'But why?' said Ursula. 'I don't understand. Why would Richard . . .?' She didn't seem to be able to say the words.

Guangyu saw Naomi's hands reach instinctively for her belly and saw that Ursula had noticed too. Realisation dawned on Ursula's face and in Guangyu's mind at the same time. Ursula blushed.

'All these secrets!' said Ursula. 'How can you people live like this?'

Guangyu raised her eyebrows at Ursula and Ursula acknowledged her meaning with a sigh and a nod.

'Yes, all right, fair enough,' she said.

Guangyu's apprehension had been growing like a steadily inflating balloon ever since Naomi had said, *That's where you come in.*

'I still don't know what you want from me,' she said to Naomi.

'I can't be implicated,' said Naomi, as if that were all there was to say.

Guangyu waited for more.

'Which is to say,' said Naomi, 'I can't be the one to go to the police.'

Guangyu's heart sank.

'I have to say I didn't know,' said Naomi. 'Or they'll make me an accessory. I've thought it through. It's the only way.'

Not for the first time, Guangyu wondered what involvement Naomi might have had in the murder. At the very least, she'd clearly known about it all along. 'The truth matters,' she said.

'Only relatively,' said Naomi.

'What?' said Guangyu.

'Truth matters relative to how much other things matter,' said Naomi. 'Colin matters most.'

A bit rich, thought Guangyu, given how little attention Naomi had been paying him of late. 'Convenient for you,' said Guangyu. She was getting irritated. Sweat rolled down the valley between her shoulder blades. She felt she was being manipulated, backed into a corner, and didn't know what she could do about it. Was there something she was missing? She looked more closely at Naomi and saw a face without artifice looking back at her. Her gaze was direct, lacking the avoidance that always made Guangyu think she was hiding something.

'There are different ways a parent can hurt a child,' said Naomi, her voice halting, her eyes downcast. 'I know that from both sides. I just hope it's not too late for Colin, to repair the damage.' Sadness came off her in waves.

'Every parent must feel like that from time to time,' said Ursula. 'I'm sure it's not nearly as bad as you think.' She put her arm around Naomi's shoulder, but Naomi would not lean into it.

'I don't want you to make me feel better,' said Naomi. 'I've been a terrible mum, that's the truth, and it's time I faced up to it. But I'm the mum Colin got, poor kid. He doesn't get to choose another one. No.' She gently held off Ursula's attempt to comfort her again, giving her a shaky smile at the same time. 'Please don't tell me it's all right. It's not, and I have to be grown up about it.'

'Why not face up to hiding the truth from the police, then?' said Guangyu.

'Because I need to make things all right for Colin. He needs me,' said Naomi. 'You've seen him. What do you think happens to little boys who like to wear dresses?'

355

'Not much at all, so far as I can see.' Guangyu wasn't ready yet to let go of her mistrust entirely. 'He's had no trouble. Helen has cared for him OK.'

'Naomi is right,' said Ursula. 'Having had my own run-in with Helen's brand of care, I wouldn't want her near the boy. If Naomi can love him as he is, he'll need her. Naomi can't be implicated.'

Guangyu wanted to call time-out. To confer with Ursula without Naomi. To get her thoughts in order. 'Let's have tea,' she said.

'No, thanks,' said Naomi.

Guangyu picked up a cushion, plumped it and put it down again, then picked up the blanket from the couch, folded it carefully and draped it over an arm. She felt like a visitor in her own home. There was no doubt that Naomi did indeed mean what she said. This was no great ploy. She shifted her weight uneasily. 'What do you suggest?' she asked Naomi.

'I'm thinking that you go to the police and tell them you saw something. I don't know what. Maybe you saw Richard in the hills. Or at the church or the creek. You say you didn't go to the police earlier because you don't speak English very well.' Guangyu gave her a withering look. 'Or you say you were too scared to go earlier. Scared of Richard or something or other.'

'I *did* see him in the hills,' said Guangyu to two shocked faces. 'That's how I guessed. And I didn't go to the police because I *was* scared.'

'You've been sitting on this the whole time?' said Naomi. 'But you just said that truth matters. Why didn't you tell the police?'

'Oh, come on,' said Ursula. 'Truth is never as straightforward as people think it is.'

Guangyu was surprised to discover that Ursula was good in a crisis, as long as the crisis belonged to someone else.

'I urge speed,' said Ursula. 'Every moment of delay makes

it worse. For you – both of you – but I also need to consider De— well, we could all do with this being over with.'

Naomi chewed on her thumbnail. She seemed uncertain, childlike. 'I don't know,' she said. 'I think, maybe, I need to see Richard again first. He'll be back in a few days. And then I can gauge how to go about things, *when* to go about things. I need to be prepared, make arrangements.' She picked at the nail with her fingers. 'Quite suddenly, I feel very scared. More scared than usual, I mean. I need time to make sure Colin is safe. I don't *think* Richard would harm Colin, but how can I know for certain? I would have said he was never capable of murder before he did what he did.' She turned anxiously to Guangyu. 'What do you think?'

'I think,' said Guangyu, keeping her attention fixed on Ursula, who gave a slight nod, 'that it has to be up to you, Naomi.' Another nod from Ursula, reluctant but definite. 'When we tell the police. Your choice. We can't put Colin in harm's way.'

'I'll have to stay here, then,' said Ursula. A pained look crossed her face. 'I can't go back to Lydia yet. I can't keep secrets from her. Even if I wanted to, I'd crack.'

It occurred to Guangyu that there was going to be a mountain of consequences to this path that they hadn't yet begun to contemplate. She had a sudden yearning to be with Jennifer, to scoop her up and take her far away from here.

'I should have come to you sooner,' Naomi said to Guangyu, then she turned to Ursula. 'I'm sorry you're in a difficult position with Lydia.'

'Yes. It's not great,' said Ursula. 'But I also know it can take time for the right thing to make itself known.'

Ursula reached for both of their hands. Guangyu took Naomi's because she felt she must, that it would be a glaring omission not to, and the three of them stood in an awkward triangle.

'We're agreed?' said Ursula.

'Agreed.' Naomi nodded. She gently squeezed Guangyu's hand.

'All right, then,' said Guangyu.

It stopped feeling awkward. They took their time, giving and receiving strength from each other, before letting go.

40

Twenty-Four Days After The Murder

Tuesday, 30 January 1979

Naomi sat in the waiting room, watching the clock. If the second hand made it around one more time and she hadn't been called, she'd leave. She counted along with it, and as it neared sixty, she clenched her teeth. One more go around, she decided.

'Naomi Kreeger?'

Dr Fraser stood in the doorway of her consulting room and looked up from the notes in her hand.

'Let's see,' she said, once they were both settled in chairs and the door was closed. Her finger traced over a previous entry in Naomi's notes. 'You'll be due another script for the contraceptive pill.' She stopped. 'Overdue, actually.' She looked up sharply.

'I'm pregnant,' said Naomi.

'Oh, dear. The pills failed?'

'I forgot to take them.'

Dr Fraser gave her a stern, appraising look, and Naomi felt her nerve slipping away.

'I'm afraid they can't do their job if you don't actually take them,' said Dr Fraser.

Naomi couldn't bring herself to look at Dr Fraser, certain

359

that she would be met with disapproval if she did. She stared hard at a diagram of the inner ear on the wall.

Naomi felt a hand on her shoulder and a gentle squeeze.

'Let's hop you up on the examination table and have a feel,' said Dr Fraser. 'Then we can talk about options.'

'That's not why I'm here,' said Naomi.

'No?'

Naomi reached into her handbag and pulled out a wedge of papers. 'I went to the bank to open an account of my own,' she said, 'and they gave me all these forms to fill in. But I can't make head or tail of it all. I've never done anything like this before.' She held the forms out towards Dr Fraser.

'That's not really ...' Dr Fraser began, and then stopped. Naomi watched a series of indecipherable thoughts travel across her face. Then her expression softened and she said, 'Sure. Let's have a look.'

'Also,' said Naomi. 'Can you talk me through how to apply for a job? Maybe not for right now,' she said, patting her belly. 'But one day. I want to know how.'

Rain getting into nests is bad news for ants. The entrances to a nest are often high up to mitigate the risk, but if it rains heavily, the passageways of a nest will get flooded and collapse. If all the ants are at home in the nest, they all drown in one go, caput. If the ants aren't at home, rain is still bad news. It washes away their trails and smelly chemicals, which help them find each other. Ants that can't find their mates get lost, and if they get lost, they die.

41

Twenty-Five Days After The Murder

Wednesday, 31 January 1979

Tammy found Colin crouched on the floor of her wardrobe, knobbly knees pointing up. He had changed back into the clothes he'd been wearing that first Sunday. Brown seersucker, draining the colour out of him. He looked younger.

'There you are,' said Tammy. 'Let's go.'

'Where?'

'Dunno.'

Colin didn't move an inch, didn't even look at Tammy.

Tammy knelt on the carpet in front of him. 'How about we go check on the ants? I left cordial ice blocks out for them.'

Colin shook his head, a touch too vigorously for Tammy's liking.

'Do you want to pick rowan berries and chuck them at each other?'

'No, thank you.'

'Your dad's coming home today, right?'

Colin was silent.

'Squidge up.' Tammy climbed into the wardrobe, closed the door behind her and immediately regretted it. The sliver of light where the doors met wasn't enough to convince her it was still daytime and still her bedroom outside. There wasn't enough air for them to share and Colin's little body pressed up against hers was like a hot-water bottle. Hemlines of hanging dresses tickled her face; restless, dancing ghost-babies.

Since Thursday night, Tammy had been absorbed by Debbie's betrayal. All those chats, all that being on the same wavelength, and not once had Debbie mentioned the small matter of her and Antonio doing sex with each other. Now, sitting next to Colin, Tammy thought about Naomi, also doing sex with Antonio. They only had each other, her and Colin. It was up to Tammy to protect him from the truth of what his mother was, of what she'd done.

Tammy had wasted so much time on other people's lies. She still didn't know what was going on with Ursula and Mrs Lau, why Ursula had Antonio's pencil, why Sheree had Antonio's shoes, how on earth his passport got to the plaza or why Antonio had lied about his age. She was fed up with all of it. From now on, they could make their own messes without her. The only person she had faith in was Colin.

'I'll play Fuzzy-Felt with you if you want,' said Tammy. 'Farmyard or seascape, you choose. Or we could turn the telly on and wait for *The Curiosity Show*. Or we could make lists of crimes and devise elaborate punishments to match.'

Tammy felt rather than saw Colin shake his head.

They sat in silence for a while longer and Tammy began to see the appeal of the wardrobe. She liked the feel of Colin's warm breath on her shoulder. If they were very, very quiet, could they stay there until school started and beyond? As long as she had Colin with her, she reckoned she could last a good while. But, no, someone would eventually find them, maybe even today, maybe soon. They could be mere minutes away from being found.

Tammy pushed the door open with her foot, climbed out and pulled Colin after her. 'I've got an idea,' she said. 'Come on.'

'But I don't want to see anyone,' said Colin. 'Except you.'

'You won't have to. We're going on a bushwalk. Just you and me. We're heading for the hills.'

'But we're not allowed.'

'Sticking to what you're allowed is no guarantee of staying out of trouble.'

Tammy sent Colin off to do a going-away wee while she made Vegemite sandwiches. He came back wearing a dress of bold pink, orange and green vertical stripes. Tammy recognised it from photos. It was a tent dress that Helen had worn as a mini-dress when pregnant with Tammy. On Colin, it just covered the toes of his sneakers. When he walked, his knees made it flounce out ahead of him. He looked like a kite. To stop the straps slipping off his shoulders, he'd tied them together behind his neck with a sky-blue satin sash he'd taken from another dress. The sash trailed down his back like a waterfall.

'What about maggies?' said Colin.

'It's not swooping season,' said Tammy. 'We'll be right.'

But Colin was still scared, so Tammy got an empty ice-cream tub out of the cupboard and put it on his head. 'Perfect,' she said, checking he could still see from under it. 'Here, give it back and I'll put some eyes on it.' Everyone knew magpies didn't swoop if they thought you were looking at them.

Colin disappeared again while Tammy drew two eyes, round and unblinking, with short eyelashes. He returned wearing the hat that Tammy's mum used for hanging up washing, which he'd pilfered from the laundry. It was an old fishing hat of Tammy's dad's, with a broad rim that Helen had embellished with appliquéd flowers and a raffia bow and a long white ribbon, which, on Colin, followed the path of the blue sash down his back.

'You can have that one.' Colin nodded at the ice-cream tub. 'I'll make do with this.'

The sound of a car accelerating up the driveway brought Tammy and Colin to the window overlooking Warrah Place. Sure enough, there was a grim-mouthed Helen at the wheel. As the car neared the carport and disappeared from view, another car drove into Warrah Place and looped around the cul-de-sac. Tammy felt Colin stiffen beside her. Richard reverse-parked into the driveway of Number Three and the back of Helen's head emerged from the carport of Number Six, gradually followed by the rest of her body as she went down the driveway, presumably to go and talk to Richard. Colin's hand slipped into Tammy's and they didn't stay to watch. Tammy grabbed the Glad-wrapped sandwiches and the ice-cream tub and they were off out the back door.

'Watch out for the oleanders,' said Tammy as they crossed the boundary from back yard to scrub. 'If you get a leaf in your eye, you can go blind. And watch your feet,' she added. 'We don't want you to come a cropper again.'

Colin lifted a fistful of his dress above his knees.

'If you breathe through your nose,' said Tammy, 'you can conserve energy.' She wasn't sure that was true, but it sounded scientific. And useful. She really wanted to be useful.

They gained some ground before looking back. Joe was a diminished figure in his back yard, facing away from the hills. His eyes hadn't smiled at Tammy since he'd been back from the police station, which she accepted because she didn't deserve his smiles. She hadn't brought herself to apologise to him because he might forgive her, and she didn't deserve that either.

The sky pressed down on them. They gained more ground. Tammy could hear the crunch of gravel beneath her sandals, the sway of tufts of dry grass, the swish of Colin's dress, her hair brushing against her ears and her laboured breathing. But no birds. Where were the birds?

When the roofs of Warrah Place were small enough to be laid out before them like stepping stones, Colin's hand began to loosen in Tammy's. They stopped to sit down and eat the sandwiches. The breeze had picked up pace but there was something not right. Looking down on the trees that marked out suburbia from scrub, Tammy realised that although the air was on the move, and the trees swayed in response, they didn't rustle and shimmer with birds flitting to and fro. The sky in the distance, above the city, was a seeping bruise.

Tammy pointed to a lone gum standing tall in the distance. 'We'll get to that tree,' she told Colin. 'And then we'll decide what's next.'

'OK,' said Colin, and the simplicity of it shot into Tammy's heart.

'Tammy,' said Colin, 'do you remember the other day when Debbie said there was no way she was going to get married and chain herself to another person, and when she said that anyone who changed their name when they got married had sh— poo for brains?'

'Mm.' Tammy didn't want to be thinking about Debbie right now because Tammy had lapped up everything Debbie had said and now everything was up in the air again. Tammy felt dizzy with knowing too much and not knowing anything at the same time.

'Do you think it makes me a bad feminist if I want to get married? I don't mean right now. I'd have to get older first. And would it make me an extra-bad feminist if I changed my name? Because I wouldn't mind being Colin Lanahan.'

Tammy pursed her lips and side-eyed Colin.

'Bear in mind that when I'm older I'll be taller and that would be a bonus. Also bear in mind that Australia is a big place and we could go somewhere else because we'd be grown-ups then, somewhere far away from here, and we'd go together so you wouldn't have to be lonely anymore.'

Tammy picked up her pace and let Colin trail behind.

'But if you wanted to have sexual intercourse, that would be a no from me because it's disgusting and makes people go stupid.'

Tammy stopped and looked at him. 'What would you know about it?'

'Enough. More than necessary, really. Did you bring a drink? I'm thirsty.'

Tammy hadn't thought of drinks. That was a big mistake.

They walked on, heads bent over, looking at where they were placing their feet, occasionally glancing up to keep the tree in their sights. The methodical one foot in front of the other was hypnotic and soothing. Tammy felt her worries recede; they belonged elsewhere now. They came across tyre tracks and followed them gratefully to the tree where they came to an abrupt end. They sat down, backs to the trunk, legs outstretched like spokes. A gecko skittered away from them as if affronted by their intrusion.

Colin took off his hat and fanned his face with it. Tammy took off the ice-cream tub. Her hair was wet with sweat and plastered to her face.

They were hot and sticky, but the sun had lost its ferocity. Now that they'd stopped, Tammy broadened her gaze. The dark clouds she had seen earlier were on the march, swallowing the light. They brought the wind, gusts cooling and goose-pimpling their skin. The air thrummed and fizzed. Colin reached for Tammy's hand again and she let him. The taller limbs of the tree listed and creaked. It felt like the sky had something very important to say and couldn't wait much longer. The clouds were now barrelling forwards, holding rank. Thunder gathered its forces before Tammy was ready for it. Was it God's voice

367

rolling around in a menacing grumble? With a boom that trav-elled through Tammy's head to her toes, the sky cracked open. Lightning flashed almost immediately and Tammy yanked Colin up and ran, dragging him behind her. She put the ice-cream tub on her head and held it on with her spare hand. More thunder came and rattled around inside it.

'We've got to get away from the tree!' she shouted.

They kept running and thunder took up the chase. Splinters of lightning had them changing direction, zigzagging through the gloom between flashes. Rocks in their path stubbed their toes and tripped them. Some rocks were smooth and flat; safe. Others bit at the soles of their feet.

The first fat drop of rain slapped the ground near Tammy's sandal, kicking up a circle of dirt. More followed, fat splodge after fat splodge, polka-dotting the ground, until they joined up in rivulets, staying on the surface and not sinking in. And then, all at once, an almighty deluge drenched Tammy and Colin in seconds.

Every direction looked the same: a sheet of grey; needles of rain. Tammy ducked her head, weaving as she walked, as though it were possible to dodge pelting raindrops. The drops hitting the ice-cream tub on her head drowned out all other noise except for the booming sky. Her only awareness of Colin was the slippery hand gripping her own, except for when lightning illuminated his wide eyes and hunched form. If he was talking, there was no chance of hearing him.

They ran, half stumbling, as Tammy's hope dwindled. It was pointless to go on. They huddled, squatting at first to avoid sitting in the sludge of dirt and water, then yielding to it when their legs ached. They shuffled backwards until they sat with their backs to a boulder. It was of no use, no protection, to them. Nothing could stop the onslaught of rain. They were desperately thirsty now, so Tammy took off the ice-cream tub to gather water. It was the last layer of separation between Tammy and the sky, leaving her completely in its thrall. Colin drank the first trickle of water, and the next and the next. Tammy waited, determined to protect him, even though she had never felt more like a kid herself, even though it was almost certain they would both die in the hills tonight.

Time passed; maybe a little, maybe a lot. Still, the rain came. Tammy decided it was time to move. This time, she gave herself a talking-to, made herself choose a direction – just one – pointed her face, squared her shoulders and shouted to Colin, 'This way. We keep going this way.' As if she had any clue. Her wet feet slipped around in her wet sandals as she walked and she held more tightly onto Colin's hand. Her legs were sore where her wet shorts rubbed. Water ran into her eyes and off her chin.

Colin didn't complain. A crack of lightning showed his hair flattened and dripping, his dress clinging to his body and tangling between his legs. Tammy slowed down to let him keep up. Their feet plodded and sloshed at a snail's pace, but as long as they kept going, there was a chance they might come to a road, maybe even a house. A distinction, a dividing line, formed between the inside and outside of Tammy's body. Outside, the world raged and roared and fractured. Inside, a calm descended. Tammy focused intently on her breath. She felt it travel through her body, threading her muscles and bones together, securing her skin in place so no part of her split off. She sent her breath out to weave through Colin as well.

Colin's hand left Tammy's, jolting her back into her body and its discomfort. He'd slipped over in the mud and landed flat on his bum. Tammy's breath unravelled. She was tired. She was hungry. She sat down next to Colin. Another rest wouldn't hurt. Now that they weren't moving, cold settled deep in Tammy's bones. It was impossible to believe it had ever been hot or ever would be again. Summer was just a meaningless word.

Eventually the rain eased to a pattering rather than bombarding. Tammy became aware that it was dark and also that Colin was crying.

'I'm so sorry for bringing you here,' said Tammy. She could hear her voice on the outside of her head now.

'It's not that,' said Colin. 'I lost your mum's hat. Do you think I'll get in trouble? Should I go back and look for it?'

'No way are we going back.' Tammy had no idea which direction they'd come from. 'You won't get in trouble. And if you do, I'll stick up for you. Anyway, if anyone's getting in trouble, it's me.'

'In that case, I'll stick up for you.'

The rain slowed and then stopped abruptly. It was so sudden that Tammy wondered if she had imagined it. The clouds rolled away, their job done, revealing a spectacular dome of stars. Night-time had arrived like a burglar stealing the light.

'What time do you think it is?' said Colin.

Tammy didn't know.

Colin snuggled in closer to Tammy. 'Can we stay here a bit longer?'

Tammy thought they should probably keep moving. There was a slight chance that she would accidentally choose the right direction. But her legs felt like blocks of concrete and her feet hurt so bad.

The scale of the sky made Tammy feel uprooted, weightless.

Tammy and Colin leant into each other and fell asleep.

Tammy woke to Colin stirring and stretching. She had no idea how long they'd slept. She had a crick in her neck and was thirstier than ever.

Something warm and soft brushed against Tammy and she jumped a mile. Colin collapsed in a fit of giggles.

It was Suzi. She wound herself in and around their bodies,

brushing against them, painting them with comfort. Suzi head-butted Tammy gently, and Tammy buried her face in Suzi's neck, pouring into her all the fear she had pushed away while being brave for Colin. Suzi took it all.

Then she moved off a few paces and waited. Tammy got up and tried to brush off her shorts, but they were caked in mud. 'The state of us!' she said and laughed.

But Colin wasn't laughing. He hadn't even got up. Tammy looked nervously at Suzi, who was now wandering further away; a shape disappearing into the darkness.

'It was scary but we're OK now,' said Tammy. 'Suzi will get us back.'

Colin still seemed reluctant to move. 'I wasn't scared of the storm.' At first Tammy thought he was showing off, but that wasn't at all like Colin. And then his voice lowered and he said, 'Even in the storm I felt safer here with you than I do down there.' He pointed in the direction Suzi had taken.

'You mean cos there was a murder?' Of course, he was scared. Murder was scary, and what was worse, Tammy had talked him into helping her spy on people. He must have thought he was going to end up face to face with a murderer. She should have been more careful with him.

Colin didn't say anything more, but he did get up and take Tammy's hand again. They set off, following Suzi.

'Talking of murder,' said Tammy, 'I could murder a hotdog.'

'Macaroni cheese,' said Colin. 'Like your mum does it.'

'Burger with the lot.'

'Even pineapple?'

'Pineapple, yes. Beetroot, no.'

'Beetroot, yuck,' said Colin.

'Blue Heaven milkshake,' said Tammy.

'Chocolate for me.'

'Are you hungry enough to eat tuna patties and peas?'

'Yuck but yes.'

'What about a soggy salad roll? Or tomato jelly? Or tapioca pudding? Or baked beans and ice cream but you've got to eat them together?'

But Colin had stopped answering.

'When we get home,' he said, 'will we still be looking for clues about Antonio?'

'No, no way, absolutely not,' said Tammy. She thought about the person who had thought it a good idea to rope Colin into helping her, that person who was so puffed up with her own importance that she didn't realise what a danger she was, and she was embarrassed. 'We're doing the opposite. We're going to avoid finding out anything that's none of our business. And if we accidentally find out anything, we're going to forget about it quick smart.'

'And not tell anyone else about it?'

Tammy motioned zipping her lips shut. 'Not a soul.'

'In that case,' said Colin, 'I've got something I need to tell you.'

Colin talked as they walked, handing over parcelled-up fragments of memory, pausing only for breaths, uninterrupted by Tammy. And as he talked and as they walked, dawn peeked over the horizon.

42

That Night

Saturday, 6 January 1979

'Divorce you?' Colin's dad said to Colin's mum. 'Don't be stupid. Why would I want to do that? I love you.' He didn't use his normal voice to say, *I love you.*

'I'm going back to the working bee to see if there's more packing-up to do,' said Colin's dad. 'I'll take Colin with me. Pull yourself together by the time we get back.' Colin's mum tried to say something, but Colin's dad wouldn't let her. 'Let's go, Colin,' he said. Colin didn't understand what was happening, but he knew enough to do what he was told.

The sun was going down. There was no one left at the church, only mess, and Colin's dad said it was Colin's job to pick up rubbish. There were lots of napkins. There was some butcher's paper under a rock. Colin flapped his arms to shoo maggies away from the empty bread bags. They opened their beaks and shouted at him.

Colin's dad had an axe and a pick in one hand and the handle

373

of a chainsaw in the other. Colin wanted to help with the tools, not the rubbish. There was a spade he could carry. His dad was looking towards the trees and Colin saw Antonio sitting down, facing the same way. He wanted to go and say hello. Maybe if his dad said hello to Antonio, everyone could be friends and his mum wouldn't cry anymore.

Colin's dad put a finger to his lips. 'Back to the car, pronto. Then stay put.'

From the passenger seat, Colin watched his dad hold the pick like a bat, saw him walk like he was strolling onto the MCG, ready to hit a six.

Colin couldn't see Antonio from the car. There was a pile of logs in the way. But he saw the swing of the pick and heard the sound – more of a crack than a thud, which was surprising. After the first swing, Colin stopped watching, but he couldn't turn off his ears, even with all the windows wound up.

In the footwell of the car, the carpet was scratchy. It smelled like feet and petrol. Tiny pebbles dug into the scab on Colin's knee. The seat near his face was hot, the vinyl old and cracking. Colin traced the stitches with his finger and counted how many until the bend. If he got the right number, his dad would come back. Fifty-six stitches. Make sure. Fifty-seven stitches. Wrong. Get it right. Fifty-six stitches. Again. Fifty-seven stitches. A decider, then. Fifty-four stitches. Colin rubbed his eyes.

He was Batman in his Batcave, waiting for the same Bat-time and the same Bat-channel, so he could spring into action and save the day.

He was the little red engine, his fists, elbows, knees and feet wheels on the tracks, chugging along to the sound of a chainsaw, blowing steam.

Colin could still taste sausage from the sausage sizzle. He liked the black crunchy bits that made the bread look dirty. Colin's dad said two were enough, but Colin was sneaky and had three.

Colin took a peek. His dad was digging with a spade like the working bee was still going instead of finishing ages ago and like something terrible hadn't happened in the meantime.

Colin woke up when the boot opened and then slammed shut. After a while it opened and shut again. And again. Then the back door opened and the car shook and smelled funny and the back door shut. Colin's dad got into the driver's seat. He looked funny and smelled funny and breathed hard like he'd been for a big run. He took off his gardening gloves. 'Sit up,' he said. 'And belt up.' Colin put his seatbelt on. It was dark outside.

Colin put himself to bed but couldn't sleep. His mum made siren sounds, like her own voice was strangling her. The sounds came from the kitchen, down the hallway, through the gap under Colin's bedroom door, under his quilt and under his sheet and under his pillow. They forced their way under Colin's hands and into his ears. They pulled him out of bed, onto his feet and out the door.

Down the hallway, Colin saw his mum on the floor and his dad standing over her. 'I'm going to have a shower and you're going to calm down,' said his dad. His hand was in her hair. 'It's done now,' said Colin's dad. 'Everything's going to be OK.' His eyes looked at Colin. His eyes told Colin not to even think of coming any closer.

Colin's mum sat on a couch in the lounge room. Colin snuck a peek at her from the doorway. There was a cup of tea next to her and Colin's dad on his knees in front of her. He held both of her hands in his. 'I took no pleasure in it,' said Colin's dad. 'My hand was forced, you have to see that. The opportunity was there to take.'

'Why did you have to be so vicious and cruel?' said Colin's mum. 'To cut him into pieces? It's . . . I can't bear it . . .' She leant forwards, just a tad, and did sicky-up into her lap, then folded the edge of her nightie over it. 'It's barbaric.' Colin's dad rubbed his mum's back, like she might do sicky-up again. 'I think you're overreacting,' he said. 'It was a purely practical decision, to send the police off in different directions.' Round and round in circles went his hand on her back.

'I can offer you this consolation,' said Colin's dad. 'He didn't suffer. Probably didn't feel a thing, he was that blotto. Pissed as a newt, reeked of beer. He didn't see me coming, wouldn't have had time to get scared. All right, it might not mean much to you now, but down the track, when you've got some perspective, you might find it a comfort.'

'We're a team, you, me and Colin,' said Colin's dad. 'You under-stand? We're in this together.' He put his hands on Colin's mum's shoulders and his face right in front of hers. 'You have to nod so I know you understand.'

Colin's mum stared and blinked and that was all she did for a long time. Until she said, 'Why him, though? Why not me?' Colin's dad looked confused. 'Because that wouldn't make sense,' he said. 'Why would I destroy something of mine?'

376

Colin's dad was in Colin's room. He smelled of soap. In the background, the washing machine whirred. 'Colin,' said his dad. 'Let me explain. A man's got to take a stand for what's his. You'll need to know this when you're older. You might as well learn it now. It's not always easy. And it's not always pretty. But being a man comes with responsibilities, Colin. A man has to protect his family, which means he has to eliminate any threat to his family. A man also knows when to keep his mouth shut. So not a word, right? For your mum's sake, Colin. To protect your mum and to keep the family together. Show me you understand.' Colin nodded. 'There's a good boy.' Colin didn't understand why his dad kept saying his name.

Doors opened and closed. Curtains were pulled tight together. Lights and taps went on and off and on and off. Footsteps. Whispers. Whimpers. Crying and crying and crying.

Colin woke up in a wet bed. At first the wee on his legs was warm. Then it got cold. Then it got stingy. He rolled his wet undies down his legs and screwed them up into a ball, then pushed them down to the bottom of his bed. From his top drawer, he took out his Road Runner pants and put them on. From his bottom drawer, he took out jumpers and trousers and piled them onto the wet patch on his bed, then pulled the quilt up and over the lot. He stood back and stared at the monster he had made.

Colin could hear his dad in the kitchen. The light was on in the bathroom. Colin went to have a look. 'Mum,' said Colin. 'It's all right, darling,' said the woman who looked a bit like Colin's mum.

43

Twenty-Six Days After The Murder

Thursday, 1 February 1979

When Colin had finished saying all he had to say, Tammy stopped walking.

'Are you having me on?' she asked.

'As if I could make all that up,' said Colin. 'And why would I want to?'

'Yeah, but—'

'Look at my face.'

Colin's face spoke as true as his words.

The storm had washed the air clean, making way for a glorious, sweeping sunrise. New light spread its reach far, cutting a clear path in and around and through. There was nowhere for the truth to hide.

Tammy started walking again. She forgot that her legs felt like dead weights. She forgot that she was thirsty. She forgot that she wanted to get home. She thought about all the time she had spent with Colin, all this time when he had known and she had not.

'Why didn't you say anything?' she said, glaring at him. 'Especially after I asked you to help me find things out.'

Colin made himself and his voice small. 'Because he said he'd know if I did.'

Tammy's anger evaporated. 'So why are you telling me now?'

'Because I can't hold it inside anymore.'

Tammy tried putting herself in Colin's shoes.

'Are you scared of him?'

'What do *you* think?' said Colin incredulously. Then he looked down. 'Mostly I'm scared of what he might do to Mum.'

Tammy reached for Colin's hand and he took hers gratefully. They walked together in silence, following Suzi, letting her lead them wherever she thought best.

'What are you thinking?' asked Colin after they'd walked for some time and there was still no sign of a house or a road. His voice was hoarse with thirst and all the talking he'd done.

'I'm thinking about what we should do.'

Tammy didn't know what to do. She was tired. Her thoughts were as sluggish as her legs.

'You said we wouldn't do anything. You said if we found something out, we'd forget about it. You said we wouldn't tell.'

'You want me to keep it secret?'

Colin looked at her with big eyes and nodded.

Tammy looked at his face, awash with trust and goodness, at the tracks his tears had made through the dirt on his cheeks, at the rain-soaked dress, limp and clinging to his scrawny body. She'd once thought him a waste of her time, a drain, a leech. Now, there was nothing she wouldn't do for Colin, her one true friend. She had made a vow to keep secrets safe and now she was being tested with the biggest secret of all.

The only thing left to do, the only thing she *could* do, was also the hardest: nothing.

44

Two figures – kids – were up ahead, weaving their way in and around the concrete bollards by the side of the road, like they were dizzy, drunk or playing a game. Lydia scanned the area. No adults. Lydia indicated and pulled in along a double yellow. They turned to her, two bedraggled rats looking extremely sorry for themselves. They recognised Lydia at the same time she recognised them. The small one, Colin, plopped down on the ground, whatever fumes of energy he'd been running on depleted. Tammy got busy trying to lift Colin up, hiding her face in his hair.

'What the blazes did you think you were doing?' said Lydia once she'd got them in the car. Their feet were a state. Tammy had a stream of dried blood on her leg. By the smell of them, at least one had had a toileting mishap.

'The storm got us,' said Colin.

Lydia gave them her flask of tea. 'Not the best,' said Colin, pulling a face, but he gulped down his share anyway.

'Suzi saved us,' said Tammy. It was the first thing she'd said. But she still avoided looking directly at Lydia.

'The cat?' said Lydia.

'Yes,' said Colin. 'But not just any cat. She led us all the way home.'

'She didn't lead you home, you doofus. You've ended up two suburbs away.'

Lydia drove, considering what she might say to Helen. She was in uniform and must be professional, must keep her contempt in check. But what kind of mother loses track of two children, all night and during a storm? As much as Lydia would have liked never to clap eyes on Helen again, there would be grim satisfaction in being the one who got to rub her nose in her own monumental cock-up.

It was getting on for seven-thirty. Where was Ursula now? Had she already begun to build a new life, putting the first pieces into place, away from Lydia? 'It was meant to last forever,' said Lydia aloud, because it was the phrase that kept going around and around in her head and she didn't know what to do with it anymore.

Seven nights. Ursula had been gone for seven nights and Lydia was going out of her mind. The only thing stopping her from reporting Ursula as a missing person were the notes on scraps of paper. The first, left in the letterbox on the night of the Bible study: *I'm safe. Talk soon.*

Then two days later: <u>Please</u> *don't worry.*

Then, two days after that: *Soon, I hope, but it's out of my hands. As soon as I can, I promise.*

Nothing since.

Tammy's eyes met Lydia's in the rear-view mirror, and held them until Colin whispered to her and drew her away. There was a flurry of whispers between the two kids.

'Are you going to tell me what's going on?' said Lydia.

'Nothing,' they both said quickly, together.

'Can't,' said Tammy, and Lydia had to strain to hear her. 'I mean, I can, but I won't. I promised I wouldn't. It's not my thing to tell.' Tammy's voice got quieter yet, but there was no mistaking the 'I'm sorry' that came next.

'Sorry you won't tell or sorry you told about me and Ursula?' said Lydia, wishing she wasn't driving so she didn't have to keep glancing at the road.

'Both,' said Tammy, and then after a pause: 'Has she come home?'

Now Lydia was glad of having the road to look at. 'Nope.'

'Will she?'

'Don't know.'

'I'm really sorry.'

'Are you, then.'

The inside of the car had steamed up with damp clothes and loaded breaths. Lydia wiped the windscreen with her shirt cuff pulled over her wrist. They wound their way through the streets, the nature reserve on one side and suburbia on the other. Canberrans were starting their day in a new reality: the heat broken; trees and roofs whipped by rain and wind; the air now carrying a cooling breeze and new beginnings. The birds were fulsome of voice, relentlessly cheerful. Lydia wanted it all undone. She would never complain about the heat again, if only she could have Ursula back.

Lydia held her breath as they turned into Warrah Place, scanning for Ursula in every direction.

Leslie was outside his house, loading equipment into his ute. He gave Lydia a cheery wave. His hand froze when he saw the two wan faces in the backseat.

Next door to Leslie's, Richard was dragging a fallen tree limb off his driveway, a casualty of the storm. When had he got home? Lydia supposed someone had got him up to speed on the goings-on at the Bible study, now that her business and Ursula's was anyone's for the taking.

Lydia parked in front of Number Six and saw Helen opening her front door to look at the police car. So, Helen's humiliation was to be a public affair. Good.

Lydia slammed her car door when she got out. It drew the attention of Richard, who frowned, but it wasn't his reaction Lydia was after. Helen peered down her driveway. She, too, frowned and then her eyes and whole face widened with shock when she saw the kids in the backseat. The kids made no attempt to get out of the car. They sat close and huddled, heads together.

Helen's shock didn't dissipate. Instead, it deepened and accelerated as she made her way down the driveway. She began to scream, her arms outstretched, like she'd been robbed of sight.

The noise summoned others from their homes. First, Duncan emerged, wearing a short-sleeved dressing gown belted at the waist and a pair of thongs. Peggy came out too, pushing past Leslie to get a better look. Sheree came running, head whipping around looking for the source of the screaming. She slowed to a walk when she saw the police car and Lydia in uniform. Next came Cecil in long, heavy strides, buttoning his shirt on the way, and Maureen, slower, trailing after him.

Duncan coaxed the kids from the car and held them both close. Given how mortified Duncan and Helen looked when Lydia explained that the kids had been out all night, lost and in the storm, it was clear they'd had no idea the kids were missing at all.

'Didn't you . . .?' said Duncan.

'Didn't *you*?' said Helen. 'All was quiet, so I thought you'd put them to bed.'

'But didn't you give them their tea?'

'I've been *upset*!' Helen's voice was a screech. 'Ever since the . . .' – she cast her eyes about and lowered her voice – '. . . Bible study. I thought you might have stepped in, under the circumstances, when I've been low.'

Duncan turned his back on Helen. 'I'm afraid we haven't exactly been on top of things,' he said to Lydia.

'What's gone on here?' said Richard, arriving to hear Duncan's last comment and taking hold of Colin's hand. Tammy kept hold of Colin's other hand.

Lydia explained. 'Don't think they meant to do a runner,' she said. 'More misadventure than deliberate, I think.'

Duncan, looking thoroughly ashamed, said, 'I'm so sorry, mate. I know this isn't what you had in mind when you said he could stay over.'

Richard stared at his son for a long time, and Lydia imagined that she, too, would stare at Ursula for a long time, if she returned.

'No harm done in the end,' said Richard. 'Let's go, son.' But Tammy wasn't releasing Colin and Richard couldn't keep pulling on his arm without turning it into a tug of war and making a scene.

Joe and Zlata joined Peggy and Leslie, Maureen and Cecil, and Sheree on the island, drawn by the commotion, no doubt. They must all be thinking there was a breakthrough in the murder investigation. They were close enough for Lydia to hear them talking about the storm and the broken heat, like a debrief was needed. Debbie also emerged, bleary-eyed, hair mussed up, with a blanket draped around her shoulders. She didn't join the others but sat alone at the base of their driveway. Lydia searched Debbie's face for news of Ursula and Debbie shook her head; *nothing, no news, sorry.*

When Lydia turned around again, she saw that Guangyu Lau had come to the island. She hadn't joined the others and she wasn't interested in looking at the ruckus over the kids. She stood alone and stared intently at Richard and Naomi's house. Lydia followed her gaze but saw nothing. Still, Guangyu watched.

Movement caught Lydia's attention, over by the big tree out the front of the Laus' house and — oh! It was enough to make Lydia want to bow down in thanks before a Lord she didn't believe in. Ursula. Ursula hiding behind the tree, peering out, watching Mrs Lau watch that house. Then, Ursula's head turned. Ursula and Lydia locked eyes. Ursula cupped her hands around her mouth and called out loud to Lydia, ignoring everyone else, 'Guangyu is telling the truth.'

Lydia didn't pay much attention to the words because her heart had left her body. She was just about to follow it when another police car swung into Warrah Place and stopped in the middle of the road beside Lydia. An ashen-faced Pastor Martin sat in the backseat.

Detective Sergeant Mark Leagrove got out of the car and began to speak, and all Lydia wanted to do was tell him to go jump because the only thing that mattered now was getting to Ursula.

But Lydia was in uniform and that meant something too. Mark was talking about last night's rain as if she had any interest in discussing the weather. Then she caught the words *remains of the deceased*, so she turned away from Ursula, just for a moment, and said, 'Come again?'

The heavy rain had washed away patches of landscaping in the church grounds, revealing the missing remains of Antonio Marietti. The discovery had been made by the pastor this morning, who had been in a bit of a state ever since.

'Couldn't leave him there on his own,' said Mark, nodding at the pastor, who was now out of the car and sitting in the gutter with his head between his knees. 'I get the distinct impression this lot have been giving us the runaround.' He scanned the gathering of neighbours. 'Time to get some straight answers.' He adjusted his cap. 'And to think, that path was due to be concreted over today. As it was, stones had been laid over the body to redirect the path, so we missed it in our searches. If it hadn't rained, we could've been going round in circles ad infinitum.' He nodded at the kids and the sorry faces of their parents. 'What's going on?'

'I'm going to leave you to it,' said Richard. 'Come on, Colin, we need to check on Mum.' He tugged hard on Colin's hand, and this time, Tammy, as well as keeping a firm grip on Colin's other hand, pushed Richard.

'You can't have him,' she said. Tammy turned pleading eyes towards Lydia and Lydia recalled Tammy in the car, saying there was something not hers to tell. None of it was coherent yet, but instinct told Lydia to keep an eye on these kids.

Things happened quickly after that, all at once and in all directions. Guangyu Lau's gaze had not wavered and Lydia followed it to where Naomi was now standing in her doorway. A silent communication, a nod from one to the other, passed from Naomi to Guangyu to Ursula, then back again in reverse.

Guangyu tugged on Lydia's sleeve and drew her aside. She spoke in a low, urgent voice.

And as she spoke, she pointed at Richard.

45

Naomi saw Peggy's jaw slacken. She heard a series of gasps. Richard was facing away from her, giving her a moment's reprieve from what she knew was to come. She saw his shoulders set firm. She would recognise the setting of those shoulders anywhere.

'That's quite the accusation,' the policeman, Mark, said to Guangyu Lau, his own shoulders set back, his mouth set to dubious.

'Hold on and listen,' said Lydia. 'She's telling the truth.'

Guangyu's insistent murmurings, directed towards Lydia, increased in pace and pitch. Naomi still couldn't hear the words, but there was no mistaking her meaning. Heads turned, agape, to Richard.

'What a crock of shit.' Cecil's voice rang out clear.

Richard dropped Colin's hand. He took a step backwards, and another, and the next had him butting up against Ursula who had positioned herself behind him like a rock, her arms folded, her face grim.

This was it. The beginning of the end.

Naomi remembered what Debbie had told her: *Right up until the end, he loved you. Just you.*

The words carried her forwards, lifted her chin and levelled her gaze.

Every day without Antonio had been an uphill climb. Now, she looked around her and saw the distance travelled. The view was breathtaking. There was no going back.

It might not be much comfort to you now, but maybe one day it will, Debbie had said. It was better than comfort, knowing that Antonio loved her; it was the reason for everything she was about to do.

Naomi stumbled forwards. The trembling in her legs was both real and for show. She cried out, a strangled, choking sound, and wondered if Antonio had made a noise as Richard killed him. She felt her own blood draining away.

Sheree rushed towards her and Naomi sagged into her arms.

Time stilled and Naomi became hyperaware of her audience. She saw Ursula stand beside Lydia and touch her elbow. She saw Peggy failing to notice the ash falling from her forgotten cigarette. She saw Cecil with hands on his hips, saying, 'Oh, come off it. No way. Are we just meant to take *her* word for it?' She saw Guangyu bristle. She saw Sheree, arms around her like a vice, asking for someone, anyone, for Pete's sake, to go fetch Naomi some sweet tea. She saw the eldest of Sheree's kids coming towards them and Sheree release Naomi and rush off to scoop her up. She saw Joe and Zlata, frightened, pale, holding hands. She saw Pastor Martin sitting in the gutter. She saw Helen, gormless, confused, once again not knowing which way was up. She saw Colin hiding behind Tammy. She saw Maureen, inconspicuous, forgotten. She saw Debbie pat Tammy's cat who had settled beside her, then tuck up her knees and lean forward, waiting for what would happen next, enjoying the show.

And then she saw Richard, calculating, deciding her next step like he always did, except this time, not realising he was getting ahead of himself.

'Look, listen here,' he said to Mark.

'I'm sure you mean well,' he said to Guangyu. 'But really . . .

'This is ridiculous,' he said to everyone.

'My wife here' – he was appealing to Mark again, man to man – 'she can account for my whereabouts that night.'

He gave Naomi an almost imperceptible nod. He waited. And as he waited, Naomi watched his expression of satisfaction, of trust in his calculation, turn to uncertainty.

'Go on, tell them,' he said. 'Tell them all.'

Naomi, silent, waited. He became incredulous, his eyes pleading with hers. Still, she remained silent.

'Nomes?' His voice was childlike, while his face looked aged. Frightened like this, he had never been more frightening.

Naomi gathered all the courage she had. She looked up into Richard's eyes boring down into hers. He embraced her, grasping the back of her head, fingers digging in. 'Get it together,' he whispered. 'Now.'

She was as limp as a paper doll in his arms and he gave her a shake. Everyone backed off to give them space.

'Everything I did, I did for you. I did *because* of you. From start to finish, the whole thing is your fault.' Barely contained anger came off Richard in waves. It made arrows of his words, delivered straight into her ear so no one else could hear.

Naomi allowed herself a momentary triumphant smile with her face against him, before she placed both hands on his chest and pushed with all her might.

'It must be true,' Naomi said to Lydia and Mark. Her voice was low but her words were sure. She felt the certainty that comes only after a decision is made, an action taken. 'I can see that now. Richard was gone that night. And in the early hours of the morning. I wouldn't have known if I hadn't been kept awake with morning sickness. He told me not to say. I should have but I was scared of him. If she says she saw him' – here, she pointed

389

towards Guangyu – 'I couldn't say that she didn't.'

And with that, Naomi played the card she'd dealt herself.

Richard was struck like a flint. A torrent of unleashed fury came at her, and he sprang from the ground, lunging, his roar filling Warrah Place. For a moment, it seemed that his hands would reach her throat. Naomi leapt back, propelled by instinct.

Mark drew his gun and shouted, 'On your knees!'

There was a scream, probably from Maureen, and the scream cut through, making Richard stop. He panted heavily and Naomi had no idea what he would do next. Anything was possible. He was not the man she knew.

Richard glowered at Naomi, his rage still burning. Disdain made a gargoyle of his handsome face.

'On your knees,' repeated Mark. A note of desperation had crept into his voice.

But Richard kept standing. Naomi was out of reach but not by much. She didn't move. Their focus narrowed to fix on each other, each trying to anticipate the other's next move.

Helen dashed forwards and stood in front of Naomi, her arms spread wide. 'She's pregnant,' she said to Richard. 'For goodness' sake, she's *pregnant*.'

'On. Your. Knees,' said Mark again, circling closer to Richard, his gun held with both hands, pointing at Richard's chest.

At last, the shutters came down on Richard's face and he got to his knees. He put his hands on his head. 'All right,' he said.

'You slimy bastard!' shouted Duncan. 'We trusted you. We all trusted you.'

An unintelligible cry came from Peggy. She ran at Richard, ignoring the policeman, his calls for her to stop, his gun. 'Murderer. You filthy lying bastard mongrel murderer. You—'

She was cut off by Leslie's big arms encircling her, holding her back. He cooed to her gently as if to a baby. 'All right, now. I've got you.'

Mark held the gun with one hand and took handcuffs from his belt with the other. He held them out to Lydia and said, 'Want to do the honours?'

'Love to,' said Lydia.

Everyone watched the back of Richard's head through the rear window of the police car as it left Warrah Place.

Maureen opened a folding chair for Naomi to sit on and pressed a cup of tea into her hands, and Naomi was grateful for both. Her tastebuds zinged with the sweetness of the tea.

Cecil folded his arms high on his chest. 'Nuh-uh,' he said. 'I don't buy it.' No one paid him any attention. His words fell into empty space.

Maureen had brought a second folding chair. She held it awkwardly, not knowing what to do with it. Cecil grabbed it from her, shook it open and sat down.

Debbie hadn't moved from her spot on the driveway and nor had the cat beside her.

Sheree put her arm around Colin. 'OK with you if I take him home and get him cleaned up and fed?' she said to Duncan rather than Naomi. 'Looks like he's been through the wringer.'

Duncan nodded. Everyone looked like they'd been through the wringer.

As Sheree drew Colin close to her, Tammy lunged and bit Sheree's arm.

'Ow!' said Sheree, springing back. 'You little—'

Naomi felt an urge to laugh.

'Tammy!' said Helen.

'I'm sorry,' said Tammy. 'I don't know why I did that. I didn't mean to. It's just,' she pulled Colin closer to her, 'you can't have him. No one can.'

'Colin's coming home with me,' said Naomi. Then she directly addressed Tammy. 'I've got him now.'

The rain had softened the ground in places. One side of Cecil's chair gradually subsided, giving Cecil a creeping tilt until, with a crack, it broke. With a grunt, he landed heavily. No one rushed to help him at first, and when Maureen did, he swatted her away.

The fall had released Naomi from being the focus of everyone's attention.

Well, how about that, Mum? she thought.

Naomi had done the impossible. She had changed her hand. And in playing her trump card, her betrayal was complete. She held the mug of tea up to her face to hide her smile.

Looking up, her eyes met Debbie's and Debbie looked at her unwaveringly, her gaze reaching inside Naomi. Debbie didn't flinch at what she found there. Her half-smile was one of grudging admiration, as if she were surprised that Naomi had managed to pull it off. She touched two fingers to her head: a salute.

The purpose of an ant is to keep its colony alive. They have an instinct for survival of the group, and they have many sophisticated mechanisms to help them achieve this. This makes them seem clever and altruistic (that means they care about each other). But here's the thing. They don't have emotions. Not in the ways that count. They act on instinct instead of putting thought into making decisions. I used to think this was cool because they could be let off the hook if they stuffed up.

Ants live in a society of winners and losers and the aim is to make sure you're on the winning side. Only the colony matters. Individual ants can lose track of the bigger picture and end up following the ant in front of them even if that ant is leading them to their death. Ants don't grieve. They don't love. They don't get their feelings hurt or feel guilty about their mistakes or want revenge or have someone that is special to them.

What kind of life is that, where no one matters to you and you matter to no one? Everyone needs someone they matter to and who matters to them. You have to have both.

In conclusion, who'd want to be an ant? Not me.

46

Two Months After The Murder

Friday, 2 March 1979

Debbie and Tammy sat on the veranda of Ursula and Lydia's house, their chairs shuffled back against the wall to escape the worst of the wind. It had been a blowy but fine day. No hint of rain. Fire danger: very high to extreme, on account of the wind rather than heat. The high temperatures of those stifling January days were behind them.

Four weeks of high school and uni down. They'd met up last Friday too. It was becoming a habit. Debbie wasn't sure she wanted that. But Tammy was OK. She'd talked her mum into getting her a proper haircut and it wasn't half bad. She finally had the flick she wanted. It made her look older.

Debbie rolled smokes from her tin of tobacco and lined them up like sardines in a spare tin. She still preferred rolling them to smoking them. Tammy had a bottle of Coke, her Friday treat. If they craned their necks, they could watch men going back and forth between Colin's house and the removal van outside the front. Occasionally Naomi and Colin came out with things to put in their car. Colin looked fabulous in a gold lamé cape that Debbie had found for him in an op shop. The wind whipped it around his body as he moved, making him look like a magician or a matador in miniature.

'Maybe we should help,' said Tammy.

'Maybe,' said Debbie. Neither of them moved. Debbie considered Tammy more carefully. Her face looked taut. 'You going to be OK? Without him?' She nodded towards Colin's house.

'Course,' said Tammy. 'I don't know. Maybe.'

Tammy took a swig of Coke and Debbie tried to light a smoke, but the wind kept taking her flame. Tammy cupped her hands to help.

'Everyone says Richard's going to jail for a long time,' said Tammy. 'What do you reckon?'

'Sounds about right.'

'I hope he gets haunted by Antonio and by what he did. I hope he never gets any peace from it.'

Opposite them, the stout figure of Zlata in her apron appeared, carrying a basket and keeping her eyes on her feet. The basket was laden with fruit and veggies and other things wrapped in paper. Bunches of grapes trailed over the side. A plastic bag, swollen with wind, cartwheeled through the air, chasing Zlata down Warrah Place. It got snagged in the upper branches of the tree out the front of the Laus', where it flapped and crackled, trying to free itself. Zlata laid the basket down at the bottom of the Laus' driveway like she was laying a wreath, then went home, again not lifting her eyes, seemingly unaware that – or maybe because – she was being watched. Mrs Lau had amazed everyone, but Zlata had a special reason to be grateful: with Richard arrested, Joe was off the hook.

As Zlata disappeared, Peggy emerged. She carried a budgie in a cage, obviously unaware that she had an audience. She carried the cage around the front garden, lifting it up to flowers and foliage, all the while murmuring to the bird in loving tones.

'I don't believe it,' whispered Debbie. 'She's taking her bird for a walk.'

For a while, Peggy and her bird watched the boxes being loaded into the van next door. Then she disappeared around the side of the house, maybe to continue their outing in the back yard.

'People are strange,' said Tammy.

'You said it,' said Debbie. Then she grinned at Tammy. 'Except for you and me.'

'Except for you and me,' Tammy repeated. She grinned too. 'We're ace.'

Debbie nudged elbows with Tammy. 'Too bloody right we are.'

A strong gust of wind rattled nearby trees and swept leaves and dirt across the veranda. It blew ash from Debbie's cigarette onto her arm.

'How're things with your mum?' said Debbie.

Tammy shrugged one shoulder.

'She'll come good,' said Debbie.

'How do you know?'

'Because she has to. Because women have deep reserves of resilience. Because sometimes you have to dismantle yourself before you can start to rebuild.'

'I told her you said there was a botany course at uni. She looked at me like I'd gone round the twist.'

'If she's into plants and trees and shit like you said she is, then she should do it. I've got some info I can give her.'

Tammy tapped a nervous finger against her Coke bottle and Debbie struggled with her cigarette in the wind.

'I dunno,' said Tammy.

'Dunno about the course?'

'Dunno if Mum and Dad are going to make it.'

They sat in silence.

'How are things in there? With those two?' Tammy jerked her head at the house behind them.

'Dunno,' said Debbie. 'Different.'

Who knew if Ursula and Lydia were going to make it? There was more separation between them now, each their own person, less enmeshed. Maybe they'd be all the stronger for it. Or maybe they'd drift too far apart. Either way, Debbie wouldn't be around to see it. She was going to look for a new place to live. A share house, or perhaps a place of her own. She'd have to get a job to pay rent. That'd be OK; it might even be fun. Not everything had to revolve around uni.

As if reading her mind, Tammy said, 'How's uni been this week?'

'It's good, yeah,' said Debbie. 'I just thought it'd be more ...' She trailed off. More what? 'It's early days yet. Maybe it'll pick up.' That was the problem with having hopes and expectations. Nothing could live up to them. 'Hey, what about that Simone girl? Simone *Bummer*?'

'Bummer, haha, good one,' said Tammy. 'I might use that. Actually, I forgot to worry about her, you know, with everything else going on. Now it feels too late.'

'Too late?'

'To worry.' Tammy sat up, suddenly animated. 'There is this, though. Get this. I heard some of the others talking in the toilets. They said Simone spat the dummy because all the other girls grew boobs over the summer except her.' She spluttered with laughter.

Debbie looked pointedly at Tammy's flat chest.

'Yeah but,' said Tammy, 'I don't care. That's the beauty of it. I mean, seriously, what use are boobs to me?'

They watched Duncan's car swing into Warrah Place, and Duncan in the driver's seat with a weekend look on his face. As soon as he saw Tammy, his smile broadened and his face lit up and he waved his biggest goofy wave. Tammy drank the last dregs of her Coke and got up. 'See ya, see ya, wouldn't want to be ya,' she sang, and skipped off down the driveway, swishing her hair as she went.

As she crossed the island, the wind barrelled down between the houses on either side of Warrah Place, lifting Tammy's hair straight up. She raised both her arms as well: in surrender to the wind? In defiance? In joy? She ran halfway up her driveway, stopped to scratch her cat under the chin, and then took the railway sleeper steps the rest of the way up, two at a time.

An unfamiliar hatchback car pulled up in front of the Italian House. The driver banged a 'For Sale' sign into the ground with a mallet. Then he swept the worst of the dirt from the driveway, frequently pausing to cough and hide his face as the wind carried it into his throat and eyes. He snapped off bits of dead foliage and tossed it behind a bush. Lastly, he removed the contents of the letterbox, tossing it through the car window onto the passenger seat.

It was this, the lifting of the letterbox lid, with its stiff and squeaky hinge, that sent Debbie's thoughts down a path she usually kept closed off.

47

That Day

On the morning of the working bee, all Debbie wanted was to keep lazing in bed with Antonio. The church thing meant nothing to them – they could easily dodge it. It had been ages since things had felt 100-per-cent cool between them. He'd been keeping a mysterious distance from her and it wasn't charming anymore. It was pissing her off, and that took her to a dark place. If he thought it made him enigmatic, if he thought it would keep her hooked, he had another thing coming. Except she *was* hooked, dammit.

Antonio came in from the kitchen with two cups of coffee, hers milky, just how she liked it, and his black. She'd tried his once and screwed up her face. It tasted medicinal, like Altona Drops.

Debbie sipped her coffee and watched Antonio move around the room, naked, his lithe body catching the early-morning light from the window, picking up clothes from the floor and tossing them down again. She stretched her own naked body, elongating it on the bed, showing it off, knowing she looked good, knowing the angles that excited him.

Debbie didn't want to leave until the mood had lightened, until she was sure that all was well between them. She was like a gambler, wanting to have just one more go to win it all back. Cutting her losses would mean facing too many things that were too painful.

'Drink,' said Antonio. He downed his coffee in two.

Debbie reached for a pair of his undies on the floor and flicked them at him playfully, drawing them back to do it again.

He grabbed hold of them and yanked hard, pulling her across the bed in an ungainly sprawl. 'I don't have time for silliness.'

'You're being a jerk,' she said. It had gone past the point where she should have had a stern word with herself about having some fucking dignity.

'Perhaps.' He tossed her clothes onto the bed.

Debbie pulled them on. 'You can be cruel, you know.'

'It's not my intention,' he said. 'I'm sorry.'

Dressed now, he faced her and their eyes connected, and yes, he really was sorry. It was all over his face. He didn't have it in him to hurt her.

'There you are,' said Debbie. 'That's better.'

He drew her into a hug and she relaxed into him. It was unreal how safe she felt whenever he wrapped his arms around her. She'd begun to depend on it.

'I'm sorry,' he said again. 'I'm distracted. A lot on my mind. But you shouldn't worry.' He pressed a kiss onto her hair. 'You are so strong. I want you to always know how much I admire you. A tough cookie, yes?'

'Yes,' she said.

'It will be OK,' he said. 'Whatever happens, it will be OK.'

On the short walk from his house to hers, a nagging doubt interrupted her contentment. Was *I admire you* something you said to someone you had the hots for? Someone you were falling for?

And when he said it would be OK, did he mean that they,

together, as a couple, would be OK? Or did he mean that she, singular, without him, would be OK?

The working bee was in full swing. Debbie hated herself for constantly seeking out Antonio. She hated him for not giving her a second glance. If she could just get him on his own.

Duncan Lanahan gave her a wide smile when he skewered a sausage on the barbie, making fat spurt out of it, and wrapped it in bread. 'Get your laughing gear round that,' he said. 'Careful, it's hot.'

Debbie coated it in sauce and took it down a path of turned, dry sods, to Antonio. He'd been wielding a chainsaw and was coated with wood dust and chips.

'Good,' he said, taking the sausage. 'I wanted to see you.'

Debbie's heart soared. Was that all it took? Shame on her.

'Here.' He took a wad of paper from his back pocket. 'Your letters.' Stupidly, stunned, she took them from him. 'You were right. There is someone else. There always was. I wish I could have been more honest with you, but I couldn't tell you about her. Out of respect to her and her situation.' Antonio bit into the sausage and bread, being careful with the sauce. Even in this, he was delicate, mannered. He chewed, swallowed. Debbie waited. 'I love her. It's not just an ordinary love. It's more love than I thought possible. I can't ignore that, even if I wanted to. And I don't want to anymore.' He had the nerve to show his happiness. It spread across his face, trampling over any remorse he was feigning. 'I'm going to make things right with her. It's best that you know the truth.' He thought he was doing her a favour. The slimy scumbag actually thought he was doing her a favour. 'I hope there are no hard feelings.'

Maybe not in the details, but in essence, it was Edgar all over again.

Debbie turned and walked away.

★

The working bee was winding up. People were hot, sticky, sun-burnt. They trickled away in dribs and drabs. Debbie had come back with beer from the bottle-o attached to the servo down the road, and the first inklings of a plan.

Antonio was still working, lifting logs and arranging them neatly in a row. Whose good books was he trying to get into? She didn't want to know. She didn't want to know anything about him anymore. She preferred to think of him as something put behind her, irrelevant.

Debbie used her letters to cushion the two long necks in the paper bag to stop them clanking together. She was sitting under the pines; a good vantage point for viewing Antonio, the barbecue area and the car park. She waited, occasionally slapping at her ankles when insects ventured too close.

The last car left the car park: Duncan with his shit-for-brains wife and strange space-case kid. The wife – Helen, Debbie thought her name was – waved to Antonio like she was flagging down a passing ship. 'See ya later!' she called.

Antonio put another log into place, stretched his back, rolled his shoulders and wiped his hands down the front of his jeans.

Barbecue tools lay on the ground, anchoring a pile of butcher's paper and plastic bags. Debbie picked them up – tongs, spatula, a skewer with a sharp edge, all long-handled – and put a rock on the paper. Antonio saw her and Debbie smiled at him. She discarded the tongs and spatula and tucked the skewer under her arm.

'Truce,' she said, meeting him by the logs and holding the paper bag aloft. 'I come in peace.'

Antonio put a lightweight, zip-up jacket on over his black T-shirt and left it undone. He jostled his shoulders to get it sitting straight, and looked at Debbie sideways from a cocked head, sceptically, with forbearance. It made Debbie's blood boil.

402

Even so, Debbie still found him infuriatingly sexy. It was a curse that had to be broken.

'How about we toast the end of things?' she said. 'To show you I can be a good sport about it.'

Twilight brought out auburn flecks in Antonio's hair that Debbie had never noticed before. She stood with her back to the setting sun and Antonio stood in her long shadow, squinting at her. Condensation dripped down the brown glass of the two long necks. They still had a slight chill from the fridge. She took a bottle opener – also bought from the bottle-o; she was good with details – from her back pocket and took the top off each bottle. 'Here, hold these,' she said, holding them both out. 'Don't spill. It's all we've got.'

As soon as Antonio had a bottle in each hand, Debbie swiftly pushed the skewer into his chest. She knew what she was doing, having researched options for dealing with Edgar. She never got her revenge on Edgar, and there was grim satisfaction now in knowing her research hadn't gone to waste, that sometimes life had you wait a little longer than you thought would be necessary to right wrongs.

First, the layers of skin: epidermis, dermis, superficial fascia. No interference there. The thing about the heart is that it's not as far over to the left as you might think. But you don't want to go straight for the centre because the sternum will block you. Pectoralis major. Then slide between two ribs. Intercostal muscles. A hard push with both hands through the pericardium, and then, at last, into the heart. It was only fair, since he had broken hers.

Antonio held onto the bottles at first, obeying her simple instruction not to spill. The look on his face was puzzlement. Was it the surprise? The pain? The steady look in her eyes as her gaze held his? Then he dropped the bottles and dropped to his knees. Too late, he tried to clutch at the skewer, but Debbie had already removed it. His breath came in gasps. His arms fell to his sides, palms facing up. He sank further onto the ground, his legs stacked to one side, his back propped up against the log pile. His face aged years in a matter of moments.

Debbie took a few steps back and watched. Blood blossomed on Antonio's black T-shirt, barely noticeable unless you were looking for it. Beer emptied from the bottles, frothing and forming streams in the dirt. By the time the streams from the two bottles had pooled together, Antonio had lost consciousness. The sun had disappeared, taking its shadows with it, leaving only left-over light. Debbie straightened Antonio's legs out in front of him to keep his position stable. She pulled his jacket together over his T-shirt and zipped it up.

While washing the skewer at the outside tap by the church hall, Debbie heard car tyres crunching the gravel. She jolted and nicked her palm with the sharp edge. It stung. She tossed the skewer towards the barbecue area and made for the trees with her bag of letters. From there, she saw that tall, good-looking navy bloke, Richard, and his kid get out of their car in the car park. She didn't hang around any longer but made her way through the trees and onto a footpath that led her down the road and to a bus stop, where she waited, applying pressure to the cut on her hand.

48

Two Months After The Murder

Friday, 2 March 1979

Helen had been waking each morning next to the cot in the spare room. She'd cleared out everything else and the cot would be the last thing to go. She'd even cleared out the clothes from Tammy's wardrobe and let Colin have his pick. At first, the impetus had been to make enough space for her to sleep in the spare room, away from Duncan, but once she'd started, she couldn't stop, driven by the inevitability. She expected to feel miserable, and she did. But she also felt a sense of completion, of a door closing, of not having to endure that piercing hope all the time.

'What do you want for tea tonight?' she asked Duncan over breakfast.

'Don't mind,' he said. He was shovelling toast into his mouth like nobody's business.

'I'm ready to drive you to work, whenever you're ready.'

'I've sorted out a lift, thanks.'

'I could go to a bit of effort,' said Helen. 'Over tea. I've got the time.'

'Sure.'

'So, what do you feel like?'

'Whatever, Helen. You choose. I don't care.'

He never called her Hells-bells anymore. He never talked to her at all if he could help it. Duncan had withdrawn something from Helen; she could feel the loss of it. And she could feel Tammy aligning with Duncan. It wasn't surprising; they were a natural fit, and Helen the odd one out. Looking back now, she could see that they had moved away from her in increments, and then, all at once. The pain of it picked away at her relentlessly.

It was the same outside the house. Helen had given up on going to church. It didn't do anything for her anymore. Ever since the Bible study, the last that Helen would ever host, Peggy had shunned her. Maureen, once her friend, had retreated into her shell, available to no one. Sheree, having heard what had happened, glared at her with open hostility. Ursula scurried away as fast as she could if she ever caught sight of Helen. Strangely, it was Lydia who had softened towards her somewhat, at least to the extent of nodding a curt greeting. Maybe she felt that she had said her piece and let her anger out. Helen was constantly bracing herself for another outpouring. She wondered if it might be preferable to the silent treatment. She had tried so hard to avoid people thinking less of her, had poured so much effort into her attempts to be liked. And to what avail?

The thought had her grabbing the car keys. Duncan had just got home from work and she wanted to avoid more helpings of his cold shoulder. There was once a time when Friday nights felt full of promise. Now they felt like the beginning of an endurance test.

Helen drove 20 kilometres east to Queanbeyan and followed the river to the outskirts of town. She could have found her way there with her eyes closed. She pulled up along the side of the track, adjacent to the back yard. The house looked smaller, more tired and dilapidated than she remembered it. There were patches of corrosion on the roof where it overhung and Helen had a hankering for an uncomplicated childhood when she lay in bed and listened to rain drumming on corrugated iron, when understanding what she lacked was still way off in the distance.

The fence needed repairs. The posts were lopsided, rotting through in places. There was no outdoor furniture, only a lonely Hills Hoist with sagging lines. There was no planting. The ground was dotted with rabbit holes and clusters of droppings. Her eldest brother, Scott, was the only one who did any work around the house, made things close to nice. He must have been put away again.

Helen was about to leave, not knowing why she had come in the first place, what she'd hoped for, when the back door scraped open and her mum came outside carrying a washing basket on her hip. She wore a housedress that came to her knees, a cardigan over the top, pulled together by a single button under her breasts. She bent at the hips to pick clothes out of the basket, never fully straightening as she raised her arms to peg them to the line. Helen felt a pang of nostalgia when she saw the shape of her mum's legs, as familiar as her own, followed quickly by revulsion when she envisioned her future extending before her.

Helen fumbled for her seatbelt, started the car and drove away, using only her peripheral vision to see the road until she was well clear of the house.

When she got home, and as she got out of the car, Debbie appeared and handed her a brochure. One might think Debbie had been watching and waiting for her.

'What's this?' Helen asked.

'Just in case you're interested,' said Debbie. 'A uni course in botany.'

'Why?' Helen meant: why would anyone think she was interested in uni; why would uni be interested in her; why would Debbie do anything for her?

Her eyes must have conveyed something of the last.

'I've always been interested in the person everyone hates.' Debbie's gaze was intense and intrusive, like she was helping herself to Helen's pain and humiliation. 'It was shitty what you did. But I assume you had your reasons.'

One Year Later

Debbie had answered an ad pinned to a noticeboard at uni for a share house and moved out of Ursula and Lydia's house. She was a bad housemate. She stole money from the kitty for the food shop and hoarded bananas in her room that were meant to be for the whole house. She hogged the bathroom and the hot water and was slapdash with the dishes and cleaning, if she bothered at all, when it was her turn.

She got a job in a club serving drinks to the punters playing the poker machines. She regularly pocketed a portion of their change, reasoning that if they were too dumb to notice, they didn't deserve it.

She grew her underarm hair, and decided to get a tattoo but couldn't settle on what to get or where to put it.

She attended Women's Electoral Lobby meetings and got a name for herself for being gobby. The other women either loved her or hated her; no in between. It bothered her intermittently that she hadn't formed any female friendships that stuck.

She went to protests and lost her voice, and once spat in the face of a policeman and dared him to arrest her.

She went to gigs and danced barefoot until she couldn't feel her toes.

She chain-smoked rollies and clove cigarettes, and one chest infection ran into the next.

She didn't write much anymore. She was waiting until she had something worth saying. Her uni marks were all over the place. She only attended the seminars of lecturers she liked. She only completed the assignments with premises she agreed with. She failed three subjects and was told she had to make up extra credits or lose her place, which made her angry.

She got into a relationship with a bloke in a band. He called himself Rasputin, or Razza for short, and had blond dreadlocks. His real name, as Debbie found out by looking through his wallet, was Gavin. Razza didn't drink or smoke cigarettes or pot or do any other drugs. He said sex was the only drug he needed, and he wanted it all the time. Debbie found the sex disappointingly average, and when she'd had enough of him, she broke up with him by sleeping with a Liberal Party-voting economics student who always tucked his shirts in, even T-shirts. He told Debbie he found her refreshing, so she left him for dust too. Since then, there had been one-night stands. Nothing that lasted.

If she thought of Antonio, it was as of an experience she'd once had. Just one part of a piecemeal, patchwork life. It was Richard she thought about. Everyone else annoyed her, but with Richard she felt only unity. She felt certain that he was as attuned to her as she was to him, even if he didn't understand what it was. She often felt she knew what he was doing, how he was feeling, what he was thinking moment by moment. An invisible thread bound them to each other, and Debbie came to think of him as an extension of herself. She wondered if he enjoyed the taste of an orange as she ate it. She squeezed the flesh against her teeth to release the juice so he could savour it. She scratched an itch for his relief as much as her own.

Debbie never felt sorry for Richard. He was hardly innocent.

He got what he deserved and he got what Debbie deserved too. She was grateful, but not sorry. And did Debbie get what she deserved? She hadn't yet met anyone worthy of being the judge of that.

At work one night, Debbie let her temper run away with her. It wasn't one thing in particular, just a growing feeling of injustices adding up, discontentment swelling, agitation without an outlet, until she put a bar stool through one of the pokies. She was sacked on the spot, of course; no first warning, nothing like that.

Soon afterwards, Debbie ran out of chances with her house-mates and they kicked her out. She packed a bag and went back to Warrah Place for the first time in over a year. She'd ask if she could stay with Ursula and Lydia again, just until something else came up.

She stashed her bag behind a bush outside the Italian House. It would be too humiliating to turn up with it. She'd wait and test the waters first. She looked up at Antonio's house. She had remembered it bright and gleaming in the summer sun. Now, it looked drab in the muted autumnal light, but it still stood tall at the base of the street like a sentinel. There was still a For Sale sign in front of it.

There was no sign in front of Richard's house, and no sign of life. The yard had an air of neglect about it. It was uninviting, as if the house had turned its back on the street. Debbie couldn't feel Richard's presence as she'd hoped she might.

From the bottom of the street, Ursula and Lydia's house looked the same as it had before: disappointingly homely; boring; suburban. As she took her first step towards it, Tammy came barrelling down the Laus' driveway.

'Hey!' Tammy's face lit up. She was wearing her school uniform, her bag slung over one shoulder.

Tammy was different in a way that was hard for Debbie

411

to put her finger on. She had grown into her face; it moved naturally through her expressions. And she had grown into her body; she inhabited it unself-consciously. It was fluid rather than stilted and restrained in its movements, like she was no longer travelling through life with the brakes on.

There was an awkward moment when they didn't seem to know if they should hug or not. They didn't. Tammy laughed.

'Tell me everything,' said Debbie. 'Catch me up.'

'I don't know where to start.'

'Start with why you were in there.' Debbie nodded to the Laus' house.

'Oh, I go there every afternoon. I ride my bike home from school with Jennifer and I wait there 'til Dad gets home from work.'

'Really?'

'Yeah, she really likes me now.' Tammy beamed with undiluted pleasure. 'You wouldn't think it, but we've got a lot in common. We're both really good at Human Cannonball on the Atari, and we're making circuits together. It's cool.' She shrugged. Her tone was matter-of-fact, not seeking Debbie's approval, just saying it how it was.

'Circuits?'

'You know, electronics.'

'So I guess you don't need me anymore,' said Debbie, hating that she sounded like a pathetic meathead.

'Nah, I'm all right,' said Tammy. And then the worst thing happened: Tammy looked at her with pity. 'But you could hang out with us if you want. I bet Jennifer wouldn't mind.'

Debbie looked away and spotted Peggy, at a window in her house, watching them. Debbie pointed her out to Tammy and they both laughed and looked openly while Peggy scurried away.

'What's the story with her now?' asked Debbie.

'Still spitting chips that she never guessed about Richard.'

Debbie was about to ask about Richard, if there was any news of him, but there was a knot in her throat that wouldn't let the words past. She didn't want anything to spoil the idea of Richard that she carried with her.

'How come you have to wait 'til your dad gets home? Where's your mum?'

Tammy rolled her eyes. 'God, you've been gone ages, haven't you? Mum's gone too. Well, only sort of gone. She's at uni and she lives in a dorm, but sometimes she comes home and sleeps in the spare room, supposedly to keep things *normal* for me. I think Dad feels sorry for her. They're really polite to each other in front of me. It's horrible.'

'God, I'm sorry,' said Debbie.

'Are you?'

Debbie laughed. 'Not really. Shit happens, right? Maybe it's for the best.'

'Maybe. Actually, Mum takes me out quite a lot, just me and her, and it's nice. It's like, the busier she gets, the more she takes her time with me. Weird. But good.'

Debbie took a deep breath and swallowed the knot of fear. She couldn't resist after all. 'Ever hear anything about them?' She indicated Richard's house with a jerk of her head.

'Yeah, Colin writes to me all the time,' said Tammy, brightening again. 'You're going to love this. Colin and Naomi moved to the coast and they live in a caravan park and Naomi has a surfie boyfriend. Colin's learning to surf and he's grown his hair long and he feeds the kangaroos and I think he's gone feral. Here, look at this.' Tammy fished around in her bag and pulled out a photograph from between some papers.

It was Colin, looking windswept on the beach, carefree and happier than Debbie had ever seen him. But it was the baby girl in his arms that knocked the breath out of Debbie. A shock of

413

dark hair with a soft wave at the front. Those eyelashes. She was Antonio all over.

Debbie thrust the photo back at Tammy. 'Cute,' she said.

'Come on,' said Tammy. 'I'll go with you. I have to go and get Guangyu from your place anyway.'

'What?'

'Jennifer's mum. Jennifer wants her to come home and make tea and I said I'd go get her. She's always up at yours with Ursula and Lydia. Hey, are you moving back?'

'I've got to go,' said Debbie, looking back over her shoulder, already taking a step backwards.

'Aren't you going to see them first? Ursula and Lydia?'

'Not today. I've got too much going on.'

'Weirdo,' said Tammy. She started to walk away, backwards, increasing the space between them. 'You'll come back, though, right?' she called.

'Sure,' said Debbie.

She waited for Tammy to be out of sight before retrieving her bag.

Was this what she deserved – her comeuppance? Being alone, never finding calm or a place where she fitted? Well, it was no great shakes. She wouldn't settle for being anyone's afterthought. She would be her own main person. That was the best way. The world was laid out before her as a series of possibilities and there was no one to hold her back or get in her way. She saw it clearly now: it was hope for something that no longer existed that brought her back to Warrah Place. It was sentimentality, and sentimentality was weakness and Debbie knew better than to give it sustenance. It wouldn't happen again. She'd find somewhere else to stay. And if that didn't work out, she'd find somewhere else. It was all part of the fun, to keep on moving, not knowing what was around the corner, and the next corner and the next.

Acknowledgements

Thank you to Nelle Andrew, my agent, champion and confidante. What an incredible woman to team up with! Thank you for always telling it to me straight and for the creative freedom that affords me. Spending time with you is always a joy. And thank you to Alexandra Cliff, Charlotte Bowerman and Rachel Mills. I love the agency you have built together and feel so proud to be a tiny part of it.

Thank you to Francesca Main, my editor at Phoenix Books, Orion. Was there ever a person and editor so lovely? Your insight, sensitivity and clarity are boundless. Thank you for creating the space and conditions to play with words. I've had so much fun. Under your careful, astute and deft guidance, this book has transformed into something so much better than it was.

Thank you to Vanessa Radnidge, my editor at Hachette Australia, for your enthusiasm and welcome, and for creating the perfect home for my Australian book.

Thank you to the wider teams at Orion UK and Hachette Australia for your clever and creative minds, hard work and safe hands.

Thank you to Lyn Ellis, my dear friend and first reader, for all the conversations that go straight to the heart of what matters. I love you.

Thank you to my writing pals, Ian Russell-Hsieh, Clare Milling, Mouna Mounaya, Theresa Ildefonso, Sallie Clement, Audrey Healy, Babatdor Dkhar, Angela Martin and Gayle Roberts for the solidarity, humour and company on this wild ride.

Thank you to Andrew Wille for your generosity of spirit, time and attention.

Thank you to Sarah Pfitzner, Sarah Allen and Karen Barton. Even before you read this book, you believed in it simply because you believed in me. What a gift!

Thank you to all the authors whose books have inspired and taught me.

Thank you to Dad and Re, for everything. I'm so lucky and grateful to be in a family with you.

And most of all, thank you to Will, Ayden and Freddie, along with my love, in abundance, always.

About The Author

Kate Kemp is an Australian writer living in the UK. She trained as an occupational therapist and then as a systemic psychotherapist, and has worked with families and individuals in mental health services in both Australia and the UK. In 2021, she won the *Stylist* Prize for Feminist Fiction and the Yeovil Literary Prize. *The Grapevine* is her first novel.

Credits

Kate Kemp and Phoenix would like to thank everyone at Orion who worked on the publication of *The Grapevine* in the UK:

Editorial
Francesca Main
Lucinda McNeile
Alice Graham

Copyeditor
Holly Kyte

Proofreader
Clare Hubbard

Audio
Paul Stark
Louise Richardson

Contracts
Dan Herron
Ellie Bowker
Oliver Chacón

Design
Nick Shah
Jessica Hart
Charlotte Abrams-Simpson
Helen Ewing

Editorial Management
Charlie Panayiotou
Jane Hughes
Bartley Shaw

Finance
Jasdip Nandra
Nick Gibson
Sue Baker

Production
Hannah Cox

Marketing
Louis Patel

Publicity
Sarah Lundy
Emily Cary-Elwes

Sales
David Murphy
Esther Waters
Victoria Laws
Frances Doyle
Georgina Cutler
Karin Burnik

Operations
Group Sales Operations team

Rights
Rebecca Folland
Tara Hiatt
Marie Henckel